say yes to the nemesis

AN ENEMIES TO LOVERS HOCKEY ROM COM

WILDFLOWER LANE

VIVIAN WOOD

author's copyright

To all the nerdy, sarcastic hearts that are afraid that no one will love you for who you are... this book was written for *you*.

I'd also like to thank my ride or die women: Patricia, Priscilla, Lizzi, and Danielle. This book would have never happened if not for you.

Extra, extra love to my editor Theresa and my proofreader Christine. Thanks for putting up with my shit. Wrangling author brain ain't easy!

THE TIN SHED Pub is busy when I step inside. I wave at Bennett, the owner who's busy behind the bar, and head straight to the back. Stuffing myself into one of the cramped booths, I wince as I bang my kneecap on the bottom of the table.

I'm a pro hockey player. Most of my life is spent ducking, trying to fit in too-small spaces, and sitting with my knees touching the row in front of me. I have the option of a table at the front of the restaurant... but that comes with visibility. Right now, I'd rather be at an uncomfortable table at my favorite bar than be the center of attention.

That's almost always the case.

A waiter swings by to take my order. I ask him for my usual, a pale ale and a basket of French fries. Hockey is over for the season. This is my version of cutting loose. He hurries off and I spread out as much as I can on my side of the booth.

This place gets me. No expectations, no cameras, no one asking me to smile pretty for the sponsors. Just beer, finger foods, and the loud burble of customers talking, mixed with plates clanking.

I'm savoring what might be my last moment of peace for the next two months when Jay Rustin slides into the seat across from me like he owns the place. On numerous occasions, Jay has tried to buy into the bar. Bennett always says no; he likes us enough to be good friends and neighbors but doesn't ever want to give up even a little part of the oasis he's built for himself.

Jay is an Instagram influencer with a huge following. So huge that he has a staff of twelve people, has his own extremely successful line of camping gear, and takes almost as many fan selfies as I do. I don't know if that speaks more for how little the city of Atlanta cares about professional hockey players or for Jay's insane charisma and charm.

"Well, well," Jay says, flagging down the waiter with two fingers. "America's most lovable man-whore is drowning his sorrows before letting a bunch of Instagram models fight over him on national television."

I don't even look up from my beer. "They'll be lucky if I remember their names by the end of the first cocktail party. Hell, I don't even remember yours half the time."

"Good thing I come with a distinctive scent profile and a legally binding friendship pact. You're my best friend for life." Jay slides a fresh beer across the table toward me. "Plus, I'm way prettier than most of your usual conquests."

"Debatable." I clink my bottle against his. "To making terrible life decisions."

"To getting paid obscene amounts of money for making terrible life decisions," Jay says. He cocks a brow, making me laugh, and we both drink to his joke.

Well, sort of joke. Half a joke, half reality.

"I can't believe I'm actually doing this show. I need my

head examined. Too many concussions. That's the only explanation. Well, that and the fact that the show shoots here so I don't have to uproot my life too much in order to film it."

The familiar burn of alcohol hits my throat. I let myself sink deeper into the booth. Tomorrow filming starts. Tomorrow I start pretending that finding love on a reality show is anything more than an elaborate business transaction wrapped in rose petals and hot tub steam.

"About the show..." He says it like he's about to ask for something, but I can't guess what it could be. "You know that Calla and I are doing a cooking show on the same network?"

I bob my head. "Yeah. You two were discussing show titles the last time we were here."

"Right. Well, as part of my contract, I hooked Wren up with an executive producing gig with the network."

Wren is Jay's little sister. She's eight years younger than us, a complete nerd, and a sweetheart. Well, she's shy and sweet to everyone else. With me, she's a mouthy little nightmare.

I furrow my brow. The thought of potentially working in the same building as Wren is irritating, but that's not really Jay's problem. I shrug. "Okay. That's good, I guess."

Jay tilts his head. "Wren just texted me this morning and let me know that she got assigned to work on *The Last Kiss*."

I feel like he just punched me in the solar plexus. My breath whooshes out.

Wren working on my show? Watching everything I do? Judging? Making that fucking face she has when she finds something too dumb for her superior intellect? Mumbling a constant string of sarcastic comments I can't quite make out?

It sounds hellish.

"There are a ton of shows the network produces. Why does she have to work on mine?" It sounds whiny even to me, but I can't help it.

"I knew you would say that." Jay rubs the back of his neck and fidgets. "Here's the thing. This is Wren's first job with a boss that isn't her big brother. She's really nervous about it. You should see the research she's compiled on it. So many sticky notes. Such a huge binder."

I picture Wren as she often looked in college. Sitting at Jay's kitchen table with books spread before her. Copper hair piled in a messy bun on her head. A wrinkle between her brows as she scribbled something on a sticky note. I once looked at one of her classics textbooks and was hard-pressed to find a section that wasn't highlighted, under-lined, or covered by a sticky note.

Yeah, that does sound like exactly how she would approach anything new and scary. Research is her strong suit.

"Let me guess." I spread my hands wide. "You want me to go easy on her."

He chuckles. "Look, I know that you and Wren can't stand each other. But do me a solid as your best friend of many, many years. Not to mention I'm your next-door neighbor..."

"You're laying it on pretty thick, Jay." I roll my eyes.

"Do me a solid. Don't make a big deal out of Wren being on the show. Please don't tell her I asked you, but look out for her. She keeps swearing that she's saving money to move out of my house." He puts his hand over his heart, admitting, "I can't help but think of all the ways she could be mistreated. She's my baby sister, Ryan. Wouldn't you want me to look out for Ellie if the roles were reversed?"

He knows just where to slip the knife in between my ribs to make me roll over and die. I close my eyes, thinking of my little sister. I would do anything to protect her. The question is, can I transfer some of that protective, loving feeling to Wren, a girl who openly hates me?

"Fine." I sigh and open my eyes again. "You got me when you mentioned Ellie."

"I figured." He grins. "Thanks, Ryan. Wren will be appreciative. Besides, she won't be in the way. They'll probably stick her in the back with a clipboard or something."

"She'll manage to be her usual self. Combative and snobby."

"I won't argue with that." He leans back with that shit-eating grin he's perfected over the past eight years of friendship. "Now that you agreed to my demands, let's change the subject. Remind me how you ended up on this dating reality show? Because last time we talked, you were bitching about your endorsement deals. Now apparently, you're signing up to have your dating life turned into prime-time entertainment. What gives?"

I run a hand through my hair, already dreading this conversation. "I didn't volunteer for this circus. My business manager landed me this late-minute deal after I spent three months complaining about how my sponsorship portfolio looks like a garage sale."

"Ah yes, the eternal struggle of being a hockey player in a city that thinks icing is something you put on cupcakes."

"I'm one of the highest-paid guys on the team and still somehow invisible," I say. My frustration bleeds through. "I get recognized more in the damn TSA line than I do at the grocery store. Atlanta's not exactly a hockey town."

Jay takes a long pull from his beer. "So your solution was to whore yourself out on reality TV?"

"My solution was to let my manager handle my career while I focus on not getting my teeth knocked out during the season." I shrug. "This show isn't about love, Jay. It's about brand growth and national exposure. With hot tubs and champagne and whatever other bullshit they think makes good television."

"But you're kinda hoping for a hot girl with half a brain cell to rub against you in said hot tub?"

The question hits closer to home than I want to admit. I stare at the condensation ring my bottle's left on the scarred wood table, tracing the edge with my finger. "Yeah. I mean, sure. I wouldn't mind meeting someone who doesn't feel like she's auditioning for something every time she opens her mouth. Someone who surprises me."

What I really want? Someone who doesn't feel like she's selling something. Someone who doesn't look at me like a prize to be won or a trophy to be displayed. God, I don't even know what that would feel like anymore.

Jay's grin widens. "Look at you getting all soft and romantic. I predict that you're gonna cry on week two."

I grin and shrug. There isn't much that Jay doesn't know about me. Ever since we were assigned as roommates in college, we've been through thick and thin. He knows all my secrets.

Well, most of them, anyway.

"I'm not ruling it out," I say, mostly in jest. Kind of. I do want to meet the future Mrs. Haart eventually. I'm just not sure reality TV is the place I'll find her.

We sit in comfortable silence for a moment, the kind that only comes from years of friendship and shared bad decisions. The Tin Shed Pub hums around us. Neither of us speaks. We have that rare connection where we don't need to fill every second with conversation.

I don't even have that with Ellie, my beloved little sister. While I'm filming, nights off are going to be hard to come by. I'm going to miss hanging out with Jay as often as I do. He might not be on the hockey team, but we do live next door to each other and hang out all the time.

A movement across the bar catches my eye. I see a blonde woman waving at me from a high-top table near the windows. She's got that look. The kind of smile that says she remembers more about our night together than I do. I wave back because I'm not a complete asshole, then lean toward Jay.

"Is that... tequila girl?"

Jay follows my gaze and snorts. "That's Claire. She's a middle school teacher."

I screw up my face. "That doesn't help."

"She's one of Calla's friends. You met her here? She made you French toast the next morning."

Calla is his bubbly raven-haired wife. That does help; I have a vague memory of Calla introducing me to a blonde. But when I pulled my usual shit and never called the number my hookup left for me, Calla scolded me. Something about not breaking teachers' hearts.

My bad. It was just one night...

"Right." I take another sip of beer. "Tequila. I kind of remember now."

"Jesus Christ, Ryan." Jay shakes his head. "You know, for a guy who's about to go on a show specifically designed to help you fall in love, you sure have a shitty track record with actual human connection."

"I connect just fine. We had a good time. We spent the night at her place. She made excellent French toast."

"You didn't even remember her name."

I point at her. "I remembered the French toast."

Jay stares at me for a long moment. I can practically see him gearing up for one of his lectures. Being friends for so many years means I know all his tells. The way he's drumming his fingers against the table means he's about to get philosophical.

Shoot me.

"You know what your problem is?" he says finally.

"I can't wait for you to tell me."

"Your problem is that you treat dating like a drive-through. Quick, efficient, no lingering afterward to see if you actually liked the experience."

I laugh, but there's no real humor in it. "At least I don't pretend it's more than it is. I'm honest about what I want and what I can give. People say 'love' when they mean 'you'll regret this later.'"

"You're like a Waffle House," Jay muses. I notice he is just straight up ignoring my cynicism. "Open all night, zero emotional ambiance, but somehow people keep coming back."

"But the food's good, right? You've never personally been stabbed there."

"Depends on your definition of good. Safe, too." He pauses. "Speaking of safe, at least I sleep easy knowing there's one woman in the world you'll never corrupt."

I raise an eyebrow. "Just one? I'm losing my touch."

After a long pause, he says, "I know I probably don't need to say this, but keep your dick in your pants when it comes to my baby sister. I don't need you messing with Wren's head. She's not one of the girls you usually hook up with."

My eyebrows rise and I feel heat creep up my neck. The idea of me and Wren together is heinous.

"Come on. You know I'd never—"

"No, I don't. You're reckless when you're bored. So I'll say it again. Don't touch her."

"Jesus, man." I squint at him. "Wren hates me. So I'm pretty sure you're safe there."

"Thank God," Jay says. His voice takes on that protective big brother tone that always makes me want to mess with him. "I never want to have to worry about you trying to sleep with her."

The mention of Wren sends an automatic spike of irritation through my system. She's a pretty little redhead with a serious attitude problem when it comes to me. "She would rather marry a ferret."

"And you'd probably still flirt with the ferret."

"Only if it had good French toast-making skills." I lean back in my seat, already feeling the familiar pattern of our Wren-related banter settling into place. "Besides, your sister made it pretty clear what she thinks of me last Christmas."

"Oh, you mean when she called you an emotionally bankrupt caveman?"

"She also told me she'd rather wax her own bikini line with duct tape than be caught dead flirting with me."

"Jesus!" Jay sputters, spitting out foam and beer. "Don't talk about Wren's bikini line. And she's not wrong. You do have the emotional depth of a puddle."

"A very attractive puddle." I flex my biceps. "A puddle that gets a lot of women."

His lips twitch. "With good puck handling skills."

"And excellent taste in beer."

We're both grinning now, falling back into the easy

rhythm that's carried us through college. Through the NHL draft, my hockey career, and Jay's Instagram influencer business blowing up. This is what I'm going to miss most about the next two months. This kind of normal. No scripts, no cameras, no producers asking me to dig deeper into my feelings for the sake of good television.

I have the impression that asking "What feelings?" will not exactly get me a gold star from the producers.

A familiar voice cuts through my thoughts like a white-hot knife through butter. "Are you talking about me?"

I look up and there she is. Wren Rustin, in all her schlubby glory. Oversized cardigan that probably belongs to someone twice her size, jeans that could fit another person in there with her, and those thick-rimmed glasses that make her look like she's cosplaying a librarian. But even buried under all that fabric, there's no hiding the fact that she's pretty. Flame-red hair that falls in waves around her face and those ridiculous green eyes that are currently narrowing at me with suspicion.

And fuck me, but I can't help thinking about Lake Lanier. Our annual group trip where she shows up in some tiny bikini that makes it impossible to look anywhere else. Not that I should be thinking about that. Not that I want to be thinking about that. But the brain wants what the brain wants, and apparently my brain wants to remember exactly what Wren Rustin looks like in a swimsuit.

It shouldn't matter that she's pretty. That she grew up and got sharp-tongued and sharp-eyed. That she hates me. But it does. And I hate that.

"Wren," Jay says, sliding over to make room for her in the booth. "Perfect timing."

"Is it?" She settles next to her brother, her eyes still fixed on me. "Because Ryan looks like he just swallowed something unpleasant."

"That's just my natural reaction to your presence," I say. I have no defense other than that poking the dragon is apparently hardwired into my DNA.

Scratch that. I'm a giant teddy bear to everyone else. But with Wren, messing with her is just too much fun.

Her lips curve upward. "How sweet. You have all the charm of a pit viper."

"And you're still exactly as tall as I remember," I shoot back. "What are you, five two? Five three on a good day?"

"Five four, thank you very much. And you're still exactly as observant as ever. Really putting that college education to good use."

"Cut it out." Jay snorts. "You know, it's weird. Wren's shy around literally everyone except you."

I'm not sure how to feel about that, so I volley back a joke.

"That's because her hatred overcomes her natural personality defects," I say.

"My natural personality defects?" Wren's eyebrows shoot up. "That's rich coming from someone whose personality is basically 'hockey stick with legs.'"

"At least I have a personality. You spend most of your time hiding behind books and computers."

"I prefer the term 'selectively social.' Not all of us can survive on pure ego and protein powder."

Jay looks between us like he's watching a tennis match. "This is actually kind of entertaining."

"Glad we can provide you with quality programming," I say. Then I turn back to Wren. "So, your brother tells me you're going to be working on my show."

Something flickers across her face. "It's not your show.

You're just the guy they're paying to look pretty and say scripted things."

"Right. Well, maybe the producers will give you the really important job of fetching my bagels and being my personal assistant. You know, something that matches your skill set."

Her face goes pale, and for a second, I think I've actually crossed a line. "I'm going to try to stay as far away from you as possible, actually."

"Good. That works for both of us."

Jay motions to Wren to let him out. She gets up and he stands up, tossing a twenty on the table. Wren sits down across from me again, eyeing me with uncertainty. We're not usually alone together. Is that what she is thinking?

I'm certainly not forcing her to be here. The door is right there.

Jay says, "Okay, children, I'm going to leave you two to your mutual destruction. Early morning tomorrow." He looks at me seriously. "Take care of her, Ryan."

Great. Just what I need. Jay's little sister reporting back to her big brother every time I get within ten feet of a bikini. Or a cocktail. Or literally anything that could be construed as inappropriate behavior.

"I'm pretty sure she'll tase me if I get out of line."

"She owns a taser," Wren confirms cheerfully. "And knows how to use it."

"Atta girl." Jay leaves, shaking his head.

Wren and I stare at each other across the table. The tension is thick enough to cut with a knife. Then something in her expression shifts, goes softer, almost vulnerable.

"Can I ask you something?"

"I don't know. Does this question count as asking me something?" I quip.

"You're terrible." She narrows her eyes, biting her lower lip. She is clearly annoyed and trying to battle through it. Shit, she must really want something from me.

Drawn in like a magnet, I lean forward with a grin. "Shoot, kid."

I expect her to react to me calling her a nickname, but she doesn't. Her eyes pin me in place. She looks... worried?

"You're not going to blow up my spot, are you?" she asks quietly. "On the show, I mean. Tell them we know each other?"

The question catches me off guard. There's something almost fragile in her voice and it makes my chest tighten in a way I don't like. Does she think I'm a monster?

"No. I wouldn't do that. We won't even have to interact. You'll be behind the scenes; I'll be in front of the cameras. Different worlds."

A smile flickers across her face, quick and genuine. For a split second she looks almost grateful. Then the moment passes and she's back to her usual self. She sits back against the booth.

"Good. Because the last thing I need is America thinking I'm associated with someone whose biggest accomplishment is putting a piece of rubber in a net."

"It's called a puck, genius. And it's harder than it looks."

"I'm sure it is. Almost as hard as remembering the names of the last five women you slept with."

I give her a cocky grin. "You know, jealousy is a good look on you. Goes with your eyes."

"Jealous!" Wren's jaw drops and she scoots out of the booth. "You're the last man I would ever be jealous of, Ryan Haart."

"You're turning green."

"Yeah, right." She scoffs. "Have a nice night. And don't forget, from this moment on, we're strangers."

Wren walks away without waiting for a response, weaving between tables toward the exit. I'm left alone with my beer and the weight of tomorrow's departure. I watch Claire finish her drink and leave with her friends. That bridge has definitely been burned. I catch the waiter's eye for one more round and try not to think about the next two months.

Somewhere in Atlanta, twelve women are probably packing their bags, preparing to compete for my attention. At her bedroom in Jay's house, Wren Rustin is probably doing the same thing. She'll be armed with her clipboard and her attitude and her complete conviction that I'm exactly the kind of man who'll eventually disappoint everyone.

She's going to be behind the camera. I'll barely see her. And even if I do... so what? It's Wren. I've seen her a thousand times. This won't be any different.

It won't.

But as I sit here, staring at the empty booth where she just sat, I can't shake the feeling that something shifted tonight. The way she looked at me when she asked me not to blow her cover. The way her voice went soft and uncertain. The way she said we'd be strangers from now on, like it actually mattered.

I take a long drink and let the beer work its magic, smoothing the sharp edges of my anxiety into something manageable. As long as she stays behind the camera, I'm safe. As long as I focus on the job (be charming, be available, be the kind of man America wants to fall in love with), everything will work out fine.

And if one of those ten bachelorettes turns out to be

something real? Someone who surprises me, who doesn't feel like she's performing every moment we're together?

Maybe this won't be the dumbest thing I've ever done.

The bar settles around me, familiar and forgiving, and I raise my bottle in a silent toast to whatever comes next. To brand growth and national exposure. To hot tubs and fantasy suites and the kind of love that looks good on camera.

To surviving two months in close proximity to Wren Rustin without either of us committing homicide.

I drain the last of my beer and head for the door, ready to face whatever fresh hell I've signed up for.

Tomorrow, everything changes. Somewhere in the back of my mind, I can't shake the feeling that Wren being there is going to complicate things in ways I haven't even thought of yet.

I CAN DO THIS. I'm a grown-up.

Those two phrases are a mantra I repeat to myself as I walk into the TV studio. I can do this. *This* being walking into my first full day as an executive producer at *The Last Kiss*, the longtime dating reality TV show. I'm not sure how much reality actually goes into the events of the show. As I walk down a long hallway, I see photos of seasons past.

There's a bachelor down on one knee before a bachelorette on a horse. A bachelorette in the crowd during a parade, flashing her breasts at a bachelor on a parade float. Four bachelorettes at the famous rose ceremony, all waiting hopefully while the bachelor they are competing to win holds a rose out, teasing them. As I continue to walk by photos of women being dunked in water and running away from geese, my thought is that if any of it is real, the contestants are complete fools.

And yet, I'm still nervous about starting my job. This is the first time I'm working outside of my brother's company. It feels like a big step for me, a kid who has been coddled by her overbearing big brother for too long.

And now, my main goal is to succeed on my own merit. No help from Jay. No influence from the hunky bachelor-to-be, either. Ryan is technically doing me a favor by letting me stay on the show.

All I want is to be anonymous. Not Ryan's pet project. Not Jay's nepotism hire. Just Wren, the PA who does her job and everyone respects.

This was supposed to be my reset. My chance to be something more than Jay Rustin's little sister. If I blow this? I might as well go back to folding T-shirts for his merch line.

I step into the production office and pull up short. The showrunner and executive producer Elena is mid-speech, passionately lecturing the show's director, Marcus White, and a young-looking Japanese woman. Elena pauses, her expressive hands spread wide and cuts her eyes over to me.

"You're late," she says. Her accent wrapped around the words, thick with the warmth of her native Spanish. Intonations rose where they didn't in English, giving everything she said a kind of melodic urgency. "Come in, Wren."

She gestures to me with a perfectly-manicured hand. I gulp and step into the office, which holds a large conference table stacked with photos of beautiful women. This season's bachelorettes, I presume. There are usually ten or twelve women selected for this show and one bachelor they all compete for. The man is generally a minor celebrity; from my research, past bachelors have been child actors, a failed politician, one of the Baldwins, and one-hit wonders.

Of course, the cherry on top of this flaming sundae? The bachelor is Ryan Haart. My brother's best friend. The guy who once said I looked like a burnt Q-tip in a bridesmaid dress. That guy. And now I'm going to spend the next two months watching him make out with Instagram models on camera.

"I'm so sorry. I was told to be here..."

"Sit!" Elena orders. She points to a chair beside the young woman. "We were just talking about people not living up to our expectations."

My eyes widen as I slink to my seat. Is she talking about me? Elena's the one who told me to be here at eleven!

The girl next to me gives me a sympathetic look. She sits up and offers me her hand. "Hana. I'm an assistant producer."

"Wren. Same," I say. "Nice to meet you."

"If you're done, ladies," Elena huffs. "I asked you two to be here because we had a bachelorette drop out at the very last moment. You two will be handling the bachelorettes, so I thought you should be included in the decision-making."

Marcus smiles at me and then pushes a headshot across the table. "This is the bachelorette who just backed out. She was a contortionist for Cirque du Soleil. And she had her master's in education."

I look down at the headshot and see a blonde with a magnetic smile. "Ah. Too bad."

"She worked for us. She was supposed to be our inside man," Elena says, frowning. "We already had a plan in place that she would make it to the very end. Then our bachelor could pick who he really wants to be with. Now we're back at the beginning."

Marcus taps a headshot with one thick finger. "I still say Shannon would be a good replacement."

"Shannon? No way." Hana wrinkles her nose. "She's a real estate agent. I'm so sick of real estate agents. There were five last season."

Elena sighs. "Who, then?"

"None of these are really good candidates. They're all boring. We need someone smart to be our mole."

"Are we calling her a man on the inside or a mole?" Marcus strokes his chin.

Elena's gaze flicks to me. "And you? What do you think?"

"Me?"

Her eyes narrow. "Yes."

I clear my throat. "Well. You want someone smart. You want someone who stands out..." I rush to explain. "I watched the last three seasons in preparation for today. What became apparent to me was that the winning contestants were sort of your average yoga-loving, astrology-believing, Cosmo-drinking women. But the runners-up... that's what you're looking for, isn't it?" Elena nods. "Well, the runners-up were kooky. They all had big personalities and an easily identifiable schtick. Remember the woman who loved alligators? Or the one who was a rodeo champion? They had something easy to reference."

Marcus strokes his chin again.

"Could we get somebody we already know is smart and have them fake it till they make it?"

"Definitely," Hana agrees.

Elena crosses her arms. She looks unconvinced. "Do you have any idea how hard it is to find another perfect specimen? Melanie was perfect. Perfect hair. Perfect teeth. Perfect *tetas*. She was a power yoga instructor in her spare time. Have you ever tried to touch your heels to the back of your head? Because Melanie could. She was the whole package."

I wonder what Elena would say about me right now. My long copper-colored hair is a frizzy mess. My comically large glasses are smudged. My oversized T-shirt looks like something a toddler would swim in.

I've never been hip or magnetic like Jay. He's the guy with the perfect Instagram life. I'm the girl in the background, hiding behind a camera.

Basically, I'm none of the things that made Melanie perfect. What does that leave for the rest of us? Not much.

"You have pretty eyes, carina." Elena reaches out and smooths back my hair. "So green! You should wear your hair up more, let those eyes do some of the talking for you."

I'm entranced by her touch. Gulping, I nod. Then Elena gives me a once-over. I can almost see the gears in her head turning.

I get a bad feeling in the pit of my stomach.

"What about a ringer?" Elena wonders aloud. "If we used someone from the crew, we could control the storyline."

Marcus's eyes light up. "That would be a lot cheaper than hiring someone new. We could script the drama. Make it more believable."

I scrunch my face. "Sure..."

"What about you?" she asks. She tilts her head.

My stomach does a somersault. My very first thought is *no*. Absolutely not. This is the worst idea in the history of bad ideas.

"I—I'm not really camera material," I squeak out. Elena doesn't blink. I try again, louder. "This isn't exactly in my job description."

Plus, Ryan is the bachelor. I'd be... competing for his affections? Ugh, gag me with a spoon. I'm supposed to flirt with him? The same guy who told me last night that we're strangers?

Elena tilts her head. She's still staring at me. "You

wouldn't have to 'win' the show. The bachelor would just be instructed to keep you on until the end. We need drama."

"I don't think that's a good idea," I blurt out. "Like, at all."

Ryan aside, I do not have the sparkly personality necessary to be on a show like this. I would die under the spotlight. I didn't even want my senior yearbook photo retaken when I had the flu. I've spent my entire life ducking the spotlight. What the hell makes them think I belong in front of a camera now?

"Would you do it if I asked nicely?" She pauses. She considers her next words. "We need you to fill in for Melanie. We'll glam you up. Make sure you get close to the end. We're not asking for you to actually fall in love with our bachelor. What do you think?"

Me, captured on film while I try to pretend not to hate Ryan? I can't think of a bigger nightmare.

"I'm really more comfortable behind the scenes." My voice is shaky. "I'm a shy girl. Uncomfortable on camera. I don't even like having my picture taken."

Elena isn't listening. Or maybe she's ignoring me. Her lips purse. She's studying me like a puzzle she's determined to solve.

"Your brother, he is very successful, no? Very... visible. Always in the spotlight with his influencer business." Elena's tone is casual, but there's something calculating in her eyes. "You must be tired of being in his shadow all the time."

My cheeks flush. How does she know about that? How does she know exactly where to hit me where it hurts?

"Would you like a hundred thousand dollars? I could arrange that to be your bonus if you played along. Plus, a promotion. You would be helping me out, Wren. I would consider it a personal favor."

A personal favor and a hundred grand? My mind races. The promotion would mean job security. My first venture outside of working for Jay would be a success. I have to work twice as hard to prove I'm not just a nepotism hire.

But this? Elena's horrible idea would sure do the trick. God, I really want that.

I make a face. "I'm not even the type of girl usually featured on these shows. They're poised and polished. I'm... something else."

"We could fix that for you." Marcus sizes me up. "A haircut, a new wardrobe. Maybe we'd whiten your teeth so they pop on camera..."

My hand flies up to my mouth. "What's wrong with my teeth?"

"Nothing," Elena says, patting my arm. "When you're on camera, darling, things have to be bigger and brighter. That's all."

"Oh." I scrunch my face up.

"Don't do that with your face. You will give yourself wrinkles." Elena grabs my hand. "Listen to me, carina. You are the perfect ringer. You are the right age, the right height, the right..." Her eyes travel to my waist and snag on my bulky clothing. "Well, I can't see what kind of body you have. But it doesn't matter. Say yes, and I could be writing you the biggest check you could imagine."

I picture a yassified version of myself: elegant, radiant, dolled up in Audrey Hepburn's pearls and that little black dress she wears in *Breakfast at Tiffany's.* In my head, I'm accepting a giant foam check from Elena like I just saved the world. I giggle.

I have to admit, the money is pretty damn tantalizing.

It's enough to make Ryan seem... less repulsive. I'm trapped. They know it.

But more than the money, it's the thought that's been nagging at me since I walked in here. Jay always said I couldn't handle pressure. Couldn't handle risk. Couldn't be the face of anything important. I'm not doing this for Elena. Or even for the money.

I'm doing this to prove everyone wrong. Especially him.

I picture myself six months from now, still invisible, still being introduced as "Jay's little sister." Still folding merchandise and staying safely in the background where no one can judge me or find me lacking.

"I..." My heart pounds so hard I can hear it in my ears. "Okay." My voice is barely a whisper, but it's out there. I can't take it back.

"*Excelente.*" Elena's tone is firm. "This will do wonders for your career."

"You think so?" I flush. "I want to be like you."

The moment it's out of my mouth, I cringe. God, how embarrassing. I want to be like you? Ugh, pathetic. I sound like a kid talking to her favorite teacher.

She wraps her arm around my waist and winks at me. "Smart girls like us, we have to stick together, *si?* We know how to make things happen."

There's something almost maternal in her touch, but also predatory. Like she's claiming me.

"Let's get you over to the makeup department. Give you a glow-up, you know?"

Elena pushes me out the door. I swallow, wondering just what I have signed myself up for.

One thing is certain: I know a certain six-foot-five hockey player that will not be thrilled to find out this latest news.

Ryan is going to be pissed.

Actually, scratch that. Ryan's going to be more than pissed. He's going to be absolutely furious. And somehow, the thought of his shocked face when he realizes what I've done makes this whole insane plan almost worth it.

Almost.

God, what have I gotten myself into?

three

WREN

ONE TIME, when I was in sixth grade, I was a bridesmaid at my cousin Jenna's wedding. The girls in the wedding party sat in big chairs while an extremely hip man carefully did our hair and our makeup. At twelve, I was deeply excited to wear a fancy dress and a little bit of colored lip gloss. I ended up getting food poisoning and vomiting on myself during the reception, but that's beside the point.

That's the only experience I can really compare being Cinderella'd to. Except I didn't ask to be Cinderella this time. I didn't ask for the fairy godmother or the glitter. I just wanted a job. A purpose. Not a mirror filled with someone I barely recognize.

Elena sits me down in a big, comfortable chair facing a mirror. There's a massive spread of cosmetics laid out in front of me, glittering under the lights like treasure.

A gorgeous, perfectly made-up blonde woman pokes her head into the room. "Hey, do you need something?" she asks.

Elena smiles and pats my arm encouragingly. "This is

Wren. She's going to be one of the contestants on this season of *The Last Kiss*. Wren, this is Jennifer."

"Oh! We'll be spending lots of time together, then." Jennifer gives me a wide, warm smile. "You look nervous, hon."

"I don't think I have what it takes to be a bachelorette on the show," I admit, already feeling the nerves twist in my stomach. My laugh comes out too loud, too sharp. "I mean, look at me. And don't even get me started on the fact that I get sweaty and awkward on camera."

Elena and Jennifer exchange a look. Jennifer shrugs. "I'm sure we can handle the first one, at least."

"What kind of makeover are we talking about here?" I start to say I just want something minimal—maybe a haircut and a little blush—but Elena cuts in.

"Push yourself, Wren. Go outside your comfort zone. Do you want to go full glam? Or maybe something cute and perky? We could play up your youth to make you stand out. Most of the other bachelorettes are in their late twenties and early thirties."

I frown. "I don't know, Elena. I was thinking we'd just change my top and throw on a little lipstick, maybe."

Elena gives me a long, assessing look. "Carina, you have the chance to do whatever you want here. I think you should try something completely new. It doesn't have to be your identity after the show wraps in two months, but who knows? You might like it."

My eye twitches. I press my fingers to the spot, trying to rub away my irritation.

Jennifer approaches with a thick binder full of clothing and hairstyles. The style name is printed on each glossy sheet and surrounded by cut and pasted models wearing clothes that match the aesthetic. Princess. Glam. Cottagecore. Androgynous. Bohemian. Goth.

This binder is a little like an old school version of Pinterest. Each style is more impressive than the last. They're all bold, dramatic, and attention-grabbing. So, the antithesis of my wallflower style.

"These styles are nice, but they're very dramatic. I can't imagine myself in any of these."

All I wanted was to get through this gig quietly. A little lipstick. A sensible ponytail. Something safe. Something invisible. I didn't want to be seen. That was the whole point of how I dress. Now they want to turn me into a headline waiting to happen. A new girl in a borrowed face.

I turn the page to peer at Sporty and Retro. Yeah, there's no way anyone is getting me into a 1950s style A-line dress.

"These are just for inspiration," Jennifer says. She's flitting around me, laying out hair spray, a couple of expensive bras, and a set of fake eyelashes on the table in front of me. "Just look through them all first before you reject the entire project."

I don't even wear bras like these. I don't let anyone see me undressed, period. The idea of being a sexualized version of myself makes me want to crawl under the vanity and disappear.

So I'm a project now? I sink low in my chair and keep my eyes down so Jennifer won't see how much I hate this entire process.

"Oh. Sure. I mean, yeah. I trust you. Totally." I force a smile that feels too wide. "Please transform me into a human Bratz doll. God."

After a few minutes flipping through it, I point to a look that feels just on the edge of ridiculous. It's bratty and punk, but still kind of sexy. Pink and black dominate the color palette. There's something in it that appeals to me.

"Maybe this one?" I say, voice unsure.

Jennifer blinks, then grins. "Oh. I didn't expect you to pick that, but I think it'll look amazing on you. How do you feel about changing your hair color?"

I shrug. "I guess... we can talk about it?" It comes out sounding more like a question than I'd like.

Elena folds her hands and looks pleased. "I'll be back later to see what you two come up with."

* * *

Three hours later, the transformation is complete.

I step out of the dressing room and glance down at my damp palms. I want to wipe them off, but I'm wearing a borrowed dress, so I just squeeze my hands into tight fists.

Jennifer rushes over, eyes raking over me with satisfaction. "Wait until you see yourself in the mirror."

She leads me over to a three-way mirror, and when I look up, I stop breathing.

The woman staring back at me is fierce. Sexy, even. What kind of magical makeup and mystical bra tape did she use on me to get me looking this good?

I'm rocking a custom baby doll dress made from gauzy blue material. The hem hits just below my crotch. My legs look long and lean in white tights. A black silk tie highlights my narrow waist. It matches with the patent leather high-heeled Mary Janes and black silk choker around my neck.

Holy shit. Wearing this outfit, I'm a babe. I have no idea where the attractive woman peering back at me came from.

She's hot. Whoever she is. I'm not sure she's me. But if I

take this off... what happens then? Do I disappear again? What if this is the only version of me people care about?

Jay would probably have a coronary if he saw me in this. He's always been the overprotective big brother type, and this outfit? Yeah. This would push every single one of his panic buttons.

I'm glad to say, Jennifer decided my fiery copper tresses were too beautiful to dye. Instead, she left my hair long, bluntly cut, and styled in a way that makes me seem rebellious. I'm wearing heavy eyeliner and bold red lipstick. My cheeks are brushed with a light pink blush that somehow makes me look younger and more alluring all at once.

I don't even know what to say.

"Well?" Jennifer asks, eyes shining. "What do you think? Isn't it amazing? You look incredible."

I stare at myself for a beat too long. "I feel like I'm going to walk out of this room and immediately flash my butt at a stranger."

She laughs. "You're gonna be fine. Honestly, I think you picked the perfect look. You might just win the whole competition based on this style alone."

My cheeks, already pink from blush, turn bright red.

I back away from the mirror and shake my head. "I'm not trying to win based on looks. I just want to compete, like Elena said... and hopefully get voted off early."

Jennifer winks.

I start to head back into the dressing room, but she stops me.

"Where are you going?"

"I'm going to change," I say, motioning to the tiny dress. "I'm not walking out of here in this."

"Why not?" she asks.

"I'm part of the crew. I don't want everyone judging

me... and walking around dressed like this? People will definitely notice."

Jennifer taps a perfectly painted nail against her lips. "I get it. You want to keep this under wraps while you're working. But I've spent all afternoon getting you gussied up. You can't let the makeover go to waste already."

I gesture to the dress. "I can't leave like this."

She holds up a finger. "Hang on."

She darts into the wardrobe room and comes back with a coat. It's a dark trench that hits just at my knees.

"Here. Put this on. That way you can leave without anyone knowing what kind of magic is going on underneath. Later, you can go out and look hot. Trust me."

She shoves the coat into my arms. I put it on—mostly to appease her.

But she's right. As soon as I button it up and belt it, I look like a perfectly modest, respectable young woman. No one would guess what's underneath.

Jennifer nods approvingly. "I'll go get Elena."

"Let's both go." Cinching the coat tightly at my waist, I follow her. "I'm ready to get out of here and go back to my real life. It's much less exciting and sparkly, but it's where I'm comfortable."

"You never know. You might get used to your new look." She smiles as we head toward the production office.

I hear a deep male voice down the hallway. "Hey, y'all are paying me to be here. I'll do whatever and go wherever you need me to."

No. Hearing that voice in my workplace feels as though someone suddenly splashed me with a bucketful of ice water. It can't be.

My steps slow as Jennifer and I walk around the corner. And there he is. Six foot five, broad shoulders, dark hair, and that stupid haughty look he always has on his fucking face. The kind of blue eyes that make you believe in clichés. His abs have abs.

Ryan is here. And he's... shirtless. He's wearing tight black jeans and black boots. His shoulders and chest gleam, his abs ripple, his arms flex. As we move closer, I can see the freckles that cover his body from head to toe standing out on his shoulders.

And then he turns. Ryan fucking Haart. Shirtless. Muscled. Smirking. And looking right at me. I want to die. I want to disappear. I want him to say something awful so I can be angry instead of whatever the hell this feeling is.

I stifle my automatic reaction.

Jennifer moves forward, gently waving to Elena. When Elena shifts her attention, Ryan looks over his shoulder. Then he does a double take. His eyes widen and his nostrils flare.

We stare at each other for what feels like an hour but is probably only ten seconds. Jennifer looks between us, squinting.

"You two know each other?"

I widen my eyes at him. Don't say anything... don't say anything...

But of course, he does.

Ryan rolls his eyes. "She's my best friend's little sister."

My face heats. "And he's a jerk."

"Sorry to blow up your spot, but she asked. Did you expect me to lie, Chirp?"

Oh. My. God. I could kill him right now. I grate out, "Don't call me that."

"Wow! You two have some amazing chemistry." Jennifer gives us a grin. To Elena, she says, "Maybe you could play up the history on the show."

A look of puzzlement flashes across Ryan's handsome features. I can't say I blame him. I'm super lost right now.

"Ooh." Elena smiles, tossing her dark mane over her shoulder. "You know, Jennifer, I think you might be right. Wren is going to be an excellent bachelorette."

"Wait. She's a part of the cast now?" Ryan asks, jerking his thumb in my direction. "Chirp, I thought you were working as someone's assistant or something."

I couldn't glare at him any harder if I tried. *I'll murder him, Agamemnon-style. I will Clytemnestra his ass in the bathtub and he'll never see it coming.*

Ryan fucking Haart. He starts to put his shirt back on and all his muscles flex. My heart does that stupid flutter thing it's been doing since I was twelve.

He's also fucking awful to me. Literally the meanest, most immature guy I've ever met.

"Do not call me that." I cross my arms. "And yes, I just agreed to be a bachelorette."

"Do they know we don't exactly like each other?" His gaze bores into me. "I don't think they're looking for the kind of fireworks we would put off."

This is a nightmare. A full-on, pantsless-in-public, teeth-falling-out dream. Except I'm awake, and he's standing there shirtless and smug and real.

Please don't make me be nice to Ryan. But also, please still give me a chance at that big fat bonus.

"If you two can't work together…" Elena starts.

I turn my eyes to Ryan, ready to plead. He studies me for a beat and then shrugs. Casually, like it's not really his business either way.

"It won't be a problem," Ryan says, waving her concern away. He smiles at her, his expression tightening. "We can work together just fine. Right? We don't have to actually fall in love or anything."

He shoots me a withering look. I might hate Ryan, but I jump to agree with him.

"Absolutely. We're both adults. We can playact."

Fake it. Smile. Pretend he hasn't been the star of every secret daydream and every worst moment since I was a teenager.

"If you think so." Elena purses her lips for a second. Then her phone vibrates. She sighs and checks it, then tsks. "Jennifer, the rep from Alice + Olivia is here with several rolling racks of clothing. Can you sign for it? I have to go return this call."

"Of course!" Jennifer says. She gives me a wink. "I'll see you later, Wren."

The two women hurry off, Jennifer's heels clicking all the way down the hall. My gaze slides to Ryan. He purses his lips, shoves his hands in the pockets of his jeans, and sizes me up.

A part of me, in the back of my head, says *Yeah, of course Ryan is the bachelor you're supposed to lust after. You didn't think getting a hundred grand was going to be easy, did you?*

Eventually, I break the silence, leaning against the wall. I'm careful to put a couple feet between us. Just to be safe. "So..."

If I stand too close, I'll remember too much. How he used to ruffle my hair and call me *kid*. How I once stole one of his T-shirts and slept in it for a month. How we once ruined a fancy New Year's Eve party by fighting so loudly that we missed the countdown—I shattered a champagne flute, he yelled over the rest of the restaurant, and now we're both banned from Atlanta's finest five-star restaurant.

Ryan smirks, which makes me faintly nauseated. "I'm surprised to see that you even made it to work. I just assumed you'd be too busy being your usual charming self. You know, starting fights with priests, glaring at anyone who breathes, and giving panic attacks to puppies."

My brows lower and I glare at him. "And you're so charming?"

He laughs, which makes me want to punch him right in his pretty face. "You know what?" I put my hands on my hips and slant a look up and down his body. "I can't decide whether you are more delusional or cocky."

It's easier to insult him than admit how badly I want him to look at me with something besides disdain. Easier to pretend I hate him than admit I've never really stopped wanting him.

He flashes me a smile. God, how great it would probably feel to slap him. My fingers itch with the desire to cause him bodily harm.

"It's only cocky if I can't back up what I'm selling."

I can't deny what everyone in Atlanta already knows about Ryan Haart's reputation, so I change the subject. Crossing my arms, I roll my eyes and groan. "Just because you have a big ego doesn't mean you aren't the worst human being on the planet."

Ryan folds his arms across his chest and smirks. "You're never going to win *The Last Kiss*. You realize that, right?"

"Like I would even want to. What would my prize be at the end of the labyrinth? Not exactly Ariadne."

Ryan blinks. "I don't even know what that means. No one does."

"The Minotaur? You know, half man, half bull, lived in this elaborate, confusing structure called the labyrinth. Theseus volunteered to..."

"Jesus, Chirp." He cuts me off again. "Are you kidding with that story? Get to the point already."

"Fine." I glare at him. "The point is that you're an idiot. The dumbest jock of all the morons."

"You're cooked." He studies me for a moment. I can't read his expression. "Good luck, Wren. You're going to need it."

I turn to stomp down the hallway, but Ryan stops me with a question. "Hey, Wren. Remember that time we played truth or dare in your basement?"

I freeze. How could I forget? It was the night I thought my heart would explode from sheer joy. Then shatter from crushing disappointment. All at Ryan's hands.

"I remember." My voice is tight. "What about it?"

He pauses. For a moment I think he's going to apologize. Instead, he says, "I dared you to kiss me. You chickened out back then. You realize that you're going to have to do a lot more than kiss me while the world watches?"

"In your dreams, jerkoff." I wince. I swear, it sounded cooler in my head. As I walk away, he calls after me.

"Bye, Chirp. I'll be seeing you real soon."

Raising my middle finger, I stalk away. My heart pounds in my ears.

Making this TV show is going to be a disaster.

As I'm opening the door to the parking lot, Elena catches up with me.

"Carina!"

I stop and wait for her, like a dutiful golden retriever. My work crush on the older producer is almost embarrassing. She holds the door open and I step out.

"Don't worry about Ryan." Elena sounds so calm. "He'll play along."

I bolt toward the street, desperate to escape. "Why

didn't you tell him I'm just filling in? That I'm still part of the crew?"

Elena smiles. It's the kind of smile that holds secrets. "First of all, darling, you're not a part of the crew anymore. You're part of the cast now. But you'll be my mole, my double agent. I'll let you view the footage and brainstorm with you in private. We can craft your image accordingly." She waves a hand in the air. "Think of it as acting."

Part of me cheers. Finally, I'm visible! The rest of me? Terrified. Because being seen means being judged. And I've spent my whole life avoiding both.

I'm speechless. This woman is a genius. A manipulative, brilliant genius. Or a psycho. I'm not sure which.

"Trust me, Wren." Her tone is confident. "This will be good for you."

"Thanks," I mumble. She squeezes my shoulder and then turns away, back toward the building.

I'm not ready. I was supposed to be behind the camera, blending into the background, not becoming some kind of on-screen drama magnet. But now it's too late. The train has left the station with me chained to the tracks.

The walk to catch the subway is a blur. I'm wounded, or maybe just numb.

I pull my coat tighter, wishing I could disappear into the subway walls. The idea of people watching me, like, really watching me, makes my stomach churn. I've spent my whole life avoiding the spotlight.

Now they want to aim a floodlight straight at my face.

As I slide into my seat on the train, I just sit and stare into space. My brain practically overheats trying to process everything that has happened today.

Ryan is my tormentor. My almost bully. He's also the guy I've never gotten over.

He was the first boy I ever thought about kissing. And now, somehow, I'm supposed to fake a romance with him on national television. I can barely look at him without flushing. How in the hell am I supposed to pretend to fall in love?

Thanks to Ryan being best friends with my brother, he's been a fixture in my life since I was twelve years old. Jay brought him into our lives, and I never got a say. He's everywhere. At holiday gatherings. In our group chats. Even now, when I finally try to build something on my own, he's here. Again.

Ryan picks on me relentlessly. I've always suspected it's because he knows how I feel. But if that's true, his reaction to my secret yearning is inappropriate. Not to mention cruel.

Now, Elena is dangling some serious cash in front of me and telling me to play along.

The thing is, I thought taking this job would be a fresh start. I'd do it all on my own, work my way up the ladder. Stretch my wings and try to fly solo.

Now I'm not so sure. Ryan is the rotten apple in my brand-new barrel. If I'm not careful, he's going to turn this opportunity to mealy, wormy mush.

Maybe I was never meant to leave the shadows. Maybe the universe is trying to tell me that I'm not cut out for this. That I'll never be one of the shiny girls who belongs in the spotlight.

One thing is certain. I'm in way over my head. But worse than that... I think part of me wants Ryan to look at me. Just once. And mean it.

Filming starts tomorrow. I have less than twenty-four hours to figure out how to pretend I don't care about him while competing for his fake affections on national television.

RYAN

WHEN I WALK into the Tin Shed Pub, I'm already in a shitty mood. I couldn't sleep last night after running into Wren at *The Last Kiss* production offices. Something about the way she looked at me before she left. Like I was already a disappointment. Like she'd written me off before I even opened my mouth.

I hate that she gets under my skin. That she looks at me like I'm exactly what she expected... nothing special. I don't know why that bothers me, but it does.

It's easier to tell myself she's just Jay's annoying little sister. That she's always been there, wide-eyed and irritating, full of herself, stuck-up as hell, and annoying as all fuck.

It's easier to remember her that way. Easier to justify keeping her at arm's length. The truth is, if I let myself think of her as anything but a pest, I'll lose every bit of control I've got left.

It's been a long day, and the bitter topper on my cake? Finding out I have to work with Wren.

I don't want to work with her. Hell, I don't even want to talk to her.

Working with her means seeing her. Really seeing her. And being seen in return. That's the part that makes my skin crawl. She sees things I don't want anyone to see.

She's younger, bratty, and worst of all, way too used to getting her own way. But she's not a kid anymore, is she? And that's the problem. She walks in with those big eyes and sharp tongue, and I feel... unsteady. I don't like that. I have zero interest in being talked down to by someone who used to follow me around like a puppy and now thinks she's the shit because she grew up and learned how to use eyeliner.

But *The Last Kiss* is paying me three hundred thousand dollars to be their bachelor this season. That kind of money means safety. It means never having to tell Ellie there's no dinner. I haven't had to do that for years, but it doesn't matter. I still wake up racked with guilt, fresh from a nightmare that nothing ever changed.

It means I can breathe at least for a little while. And that kind of money? I don't say no to it.

I've saved every penny I've ever earned from hockey and endorsements. You don't grow up the way I did and shake it off just because you signed a couple endorsement deals. You grow up hoarding paychecks and checking account balances like your life depends on it. Because once, mine did.

I refuse to go broke again. Ever. That kind of fear sticks with you. Trying to keep the teachers at your sister's school in the dark about your parents vanishing. Being a kid and watching the lights get cut off, seeing your little sister cry when there's no food in the fridge. It rewires your brain.

Makes you hold on tight to anything that smells like security.

I scan the pub and spot my friends at a large round table near the front.

I walk over, clap Bennett on the back, and drop into the empty seat beside him. Jay and Gabe are already here, beers in hand. At the bar, I spot Reese in black jeans and a leather jacket, completely ignoring some guy trying to talk to her. That tracks.

Jay shifts so he's sitting right next to me. He gives me a once-over, then frowns. "What happened to you? You look terrible."

I let out a sigh. "I'm fine."

A waitress drops off several pitchers of beer, and I take a long pull from my pint glass.

Bennett smirks. "Thirsty?"

I set the glass down and push it away. "Just needed a drink. It's been that kind of day."

The front door swings open again, the bell clanging above it.

Jay's wife, Calla, steps inside. Her jet-black hair is damp from the rain, and she shakes off a few drops as she enters. Behind her is her sister, Cora, who looks like a slightly sharper, more intimidating version of Calla. Same hair, same golden-tan skin, same smile.

They're laughing about something as they walk in, and Jay instantly stands. His entire face changes when he sees Calla. He looks at her like she hung the damn moon. Like she's some kind of myth made into flesh.

She heads straight for him, arms open.

He wraps her up and kisses her like he hasn't seen her in weeks. "I missed you," he growls against her mouth.

I roll my eyes.

It's not that I begrudge him the relationship. Calla's great for him. She's warm and funny and grounded. It's just... a lot sometimes.

The bell rings again, and I notice Cora has paused, waiting for someone.

Then I see a flash of copper-red hair and know exactly who it is.

Wren.

Of course, it's Wren.

She's still wearing that ridiculous dark trench coat. Her makeup is heavy. Cat-eye liner, bright red lipstick. It's all the more infuriating because it works on her. Like... really works. *Damn.*

I have the same thought I had earlier this afternoon: I didn't know Wren got dressed up.

But apparently, she does.

And worse, she looks good.

Her face is all soft curves and sharp contrasts. A heart-shaped face framed by long copper waves, an upturned nose, pouty mouth, and those wide, expressive eyes.

She does the same little shake Calla did, brushing off rain, and then she looks right at me.

Her mouth parts slightly, and she bites her lower lip.

God help me.

Cora pulls her forward, guiding her to the table. Jay is rearranging chairs, and when all is said and done, there's one open seat left.

The one right next to mine.

Wren circles around Calla and Cora, then drops into the seat beside me.

Of course, she does.

I give Wren a once-over, then turn to Bennett. He's the owner of the establishment we're sitting in.

"How's the bar business these days?" I ask.

He nods and sips his beer. "It's good. Things are booming, actually. I'm gonna have to hire more staff now. Wren was my go-to for part-time help around here, but I guess all good things must come to an end."

I resist the urge to glance at her. "Yeah, I guess so. But I'm sure you'll find somebody great."

Bennett jerks his chin toward Reese, who's weaving her way between tables toward us.

"I think Reese has a friend who's going to interview for the position," he says.

I look over at Reese as she slides into the seat across from me. Reese and I dated briefly. It was five and a half years ago, but I'm still a little sensitive about the topic.

She once told me I was hot but brainless, right after I got into my fifth bar fight that month. That was about ten minutes before she dumped me and told me we should just be friends.

She made the right call. That doesn't mean I'm not still a little touchy about it.

I push the memory aside and tell Bennett, "I think you'll find someone solid. Most of your employees have been here for years. Odds are definitely in your favor."

Gabe launches into a conversation with Bennett about a board game they both play. My brain checks out immediately. Board games are not my thing.

I'm all action, always ready to move. Make me sit still and strategize? I dry out like a dead battery.

The waitress brings over a bunch of appetizers: French fries, chicken wings, quesadillas. I grab a whole quesadilla and a pile of fries, stacking them on a plate.

Wren leans over me to grab a fry straight from the basket. She smirks.

I glance down at my plate, trying to figure out what, exactly, she finds so amusing.

"Can I help you with something?" I ask.

She shrugs a shoulder, casual and careless, then tilts her head to look at me. "You don't have to guard your food, you know."

I glance down and realize I've got my hands bracketing the plate like I'm about to fight someone off. Defensive much? I roll my eyes.

"You don't have to be such a nerd," I shoot back, "but here we are."

She sucks her teeth, clearly amused. "You know, just because you get by on being hot and dumb doesn't mean the rest of us can. Some of us actually have to work for a living."

I smirk. "Still pretending sarcasm is a personality, I see."

I stuff a few fries in my mouth and chew, letting the burn sit for a second.

I know she's got a degree in classics from Agnes Glenn College. Cute little liberal arts school just up the road.

But I've got a poli-sci degree from Emory, which is, let's be honest, far better known.

"At least people have heard of where I went to school," I retort.

She narrows her eyes. "Agnes Glenn is a women's college. Emory's a giant university. The two don't exactly compete in the same arenas. But if it helps, you still look like every frat boy who peaked senior year."

I arch a brow. "And you look like someone playing dress-up in their mom's coats."

Wren rolls her eyes and stands, fingers slipping into the belt of her trench coat. Then she opens it.

My eyes widen.

She's wearing a dress. No, she's wearing a pink crop top and a fitted black leather skirt. The thing barely covers her ass.

She's paired that with white tights. Black heels. And this dainty little black choker around her neck. It's like she wants people to stare at her.

She's still Wren. Same stubborn jaw. Same impossible eyes. But the way she walks now... it's like she's finally realized everyone's watching. And she doesn't hate it.

Wren tosses her copper hair over her shoulder in a fiery wave and shoots me a glare.

"I'm going to the bar," she declares.

I watch her walk away, my jaw tightening. What's going on? Wren's always so meek and shy. With everybody except me, she's a quiet type with her nose forever in a book.

One guy lets his eyes follow her ass as she passes. Another nudges his buddy and grins, both of them leering at her. Actually, scratch that. Every single guy in the pub is staring at her, and she's doing absolutely nothing to stop them.

I glance at Jay. He hasn't even noticed she left the table. He's listening to Calla tell a story, completely absorbed, stroking her arm like the lovesick puppy he is.

I was hoping he'd notice. That he'd step in, say something, tell her to throw a jacket back on. But nope.

Looks like I'll have to take control of the situation.

I usually don't follow Wren to the bar.

But then again, she usually isn't dressed like this.

Actually, now that I think about it, I've never seen her

wear a dress. Never seen her show off her legs like this. Not since I was in college, going on lake trips with the rest of the crew. She would tag along and wear a bikini that I made sure to never, ever study. This is very different from those days, because she's filled out since then, grown into her body.

This?

This is new.

And it's going to be a problem.

I turn around and stare a hole into Wren's curtain of hair.

She ignores me at first, accepting a glass of cider from the bartender. But when I don't move, she sighs and finally turns toward me.

"What, you gonna stand there all night?"

I fold my arms across my chest. "I'll stand wherever I need to if it keeps you from making a terrible mistake. Those guys weren't interested in hearing about Greek mythology, Wren. They were only checking you out because of that outrageous outfit."

Her eyes drop to her dress, and she feigns surprise. "What, this old thing? Golly, mister, thank you for saving me from those horrible men."

The sarcasm isn't lost on me. A muscle ticks in my jaw.

I swear, ninety-five percent of the time when I'm looking at Wren, I'm glaring at her so hard that she'd be incinerated if I had superpowers.

"Wren, you can't just dress like that and hang out here. You look like some fucked-up *Alice in Wonderland* sex doll. I can't in good conscience..."

She cuts me off. "You're not my big brother. You're just some dumb jock who peaked in college and has been chasing that high ever since."

Her words don't shake me.

I may just be a poli-sci major, but I graduated with a three point eight from a hard school. I'm not dumb, no matter how often Wren insists otherwise.

I hold out her coat. "Put this on."

She gives me a flat look and rolls her eyes.

"I'm fine, Ryan. Seriously. Let it go. This isn't..."

"You can't just be dressed like that. You know men can see you, right?"

Wren pins me with a stare. "Whatever, Ryan. If you think you're not gonna dream about me in this dress later, you've got another thing coming. I look good."

She's right, of course. There's about zero chance I won't jerk off to the image of her in that dress later. But that's not the damn point.

"Whatever, Chirp." I lift my chin. "Dream on."

Two younger guys walk up to us, and at first, I assume they're here to sweet-talk her. I give them the meanest look I can manage.

One of them is clutching a jersey. He takes a step back, eyes wide.

"Oh, sorry, man. I just... you're Ryan Haart, aren't you?"

I press my tongue against the inside of my cheek. Shit.

These guys aren't leering at Jay's little sister. They're just hockey fans.

"This really isn't the best time," I hedge. "Can we do this later?"

The second guy, shorter and stockier, tries to wedge himself between me and Wren, basically pushing her out of the way to get to the bar. She stumbles back, frowning.

"Hey, watch it," she snaps.

The guy doesn't even look at her. He just thrusts a hat and a pen at me. "Sign this for me," he demands.

Oh, hell no.

Nobody shoves my friends around to get to me.

I growl, "Were you raised in a fucking barn? You just shoved my friend out of the way. That's disrespectful as hell."

The two guys exchange awkward looks.

"Sorry, man," the first one mutters. "We didn't mean to interrupt..."

"We just wanted to say we're really big fans," the second one adds.

"I appreciate you watching my games," I say, still blocking them. "But right now, I'm talking to her."

Both of them reflexively glance at Wren. The stockier guy seems to put two and two together.

"Oh, sorry, man. Didn't mean to intrude on your date."

Wren lets out a disgusted sound. My eye twitches.

I corral both guys and move them back a few steps. "Have a good night."

Wren sips her cider and watches them as they go, muttering to each other.

"Sorry about that. You know how fans are," I say.

She gives me a slight nod. "You were saying?"

I don't even remember what I was saying, but I do still want her to put the fucking coat on.

I check my watch. It's almost seven thirty. I promised Ellie I'd swing by her place to help Jake move some furniture. They're still getting settled, and the place is a maze of boxes.

"I have to leave in a couple minutes to go help my sister with something. I think you should put this coat on, finish that cider, and let me drop you at home."

"I can get home just fine." She pauses. Her face reddens slightly.

I hold the coat out again, staring at her. "I'm definitely not letting you walk anywhere in that outfit. You'll cause a riot."

"You're so dramatic," she groans. "I just got here!"

"We have to be on set early tomorrow." I have no idea where that comes from, but it at least sounds plausible. Really, I just need to get the girl away from those hockey bros at the bar. And anyone with eyes. "It's time to get some rest. Beauty sleep, I think they call it."

"Fine." Wren bunches her mouth up and narrows her gaze at me. "I'll go. I'll only walk with you if it'll make you stop bugging me about my dress, though."

"Good."

She takes the coat from me and slips it on, but she doesn't bother belting the front.

I'm not thrilled about it, but at least the chances of someone getting a full view of her ass have dropped significantly.

She takes another sip of her drink, then turns to me. "Lead the way."

I head toward the door, pulling my phone from my pocket. I'll text Jay to let him know I got Wren home safe.

A tiny part of me feels like an excited golden fucking retriever knowing that I'll see her tomorrow. Even if I tell myself I'm here for the money. For the exposure. For the brand deals. Now I'm here for something else as well.

As we step outside, I catch her tugging at the hem of her dress when she thinks I'm not looking. Her confident mask slips for just a second, and I see something vulnerable underneath.

If I stop talking, he'll see it, I imagine her thinking. *See that I'm not really this confident. See the way my knees are shaking.*

But then she catches me watching and immediately straightens up, chin lifted in defiance.

"What?" she asks.

"Nothing," I say, looking away.

But it's not nothing. It's the realization that Wren Rustin might be even more complicated than I thought.

Great. As if this whole situation wasn't messy enough already.

RYAN

"OKAY, right. Ryan, can you just skate around and maybe hit a couple pucks into the net?" Rich asks.

"Yeah, sure," I say.

I grab my practice stick and a few pucks from the PA standing on the side of the rink.

It's just B-roll, I remind myself. Smile. Be charming. Don't think about the girl who used to flinch when I said her name and now looks at me like she's daring me to flinch instead.

"We're just establishing you as a person in these shots," Rich continues. "What you like, what you don't, what kind of woman you're looking for... all that jazz."

He gestures toward the ice. "We've got a bunch of B-roll of your town, your friends and family talking about you, but now we need your story straight from the source. Hans here is going to follow you out while you skate and score a bunch of goals. That cool?"

"Yeah. Whatever you want."

I push away from the sidewall and skate into the center, dropping the pucks and controlling them with my stick.

I'm a defenseman for the Atlanta Ice Storms, so I don't even know if slapping pucks into the net is a good representation of what I actually do. But Rich is pretty insistent on people needing to see pucks in goals.

Rich wades out onto the ice behind the cameraman. Neither of them moves like they're comfortable out here. This is their first time shooting on location at a hockey rink. This show isn't about hockey players in general.

I slap the puck toward the net. It hits the back of the goal cleanly. I skate around the cameraman and Rich in a wide circle.

"So, Ryan," Rich calls, "go ahead and explain why you're on *The Last Kiss* this year. What are you looking for in a relationship? Your goals romantically, etcetera."

I knit my brows as I skate. The ice is smooth, perfect, like it is just before a game.

How the hell do I even begin to answer that?

"I'm on *The Last Kiss* because I want to find my soulmate."

Okay. That's a little bit of a lie.

I barely keep a straight face. If I really believed in soulmates, I wouldn't be here. I'm here for one reason: money. Security. Making damn sure I never end up back in that shitty apartment with no power and nothing in the fridge.

But nobody's really asked me that outright.

The lines come easy. They're not mine, but I've said worse things with a smile. I'm not looking for love. I'm looking for survival. And a little less silence in my apartment.

I suck in a breath. "I would like to meet my soulmate. I've dated a lot, and so far, I haven't found the one I'm meant to be with forever. But I think I have a real shot here."

At what, though? Fame? Faking it? Getting clipped into some girl's dream montage before we ever even have a real conversation?

Stopping near the pile of pucks, I grab another and move it down the ice toward the goal.

I know I need to recite the lines Rich has been drilling into me. He's not just a showrunner, he's a coach, my coach, in a way. Helping me craft the perfect answers.

It feels phony saying most of it out loud, but that's what I'm getting paid for. These lines aren't mine. They're scripted. Manufactured. A real relationship? That's a hell of a lot messier. I know, because I've never actually had one that didn't crash and burn.

I shoot the puck into the net and turn, lifting my hands in the air like I just won the Cup.

"Yes!" I exclaim.

Rich grins. "You're looking good out there, Ryan. Can you talk a little about your expectations? How do you feel about meeting the bachelorettes? Nervous?"

I skate in another wide circle.

"I'm excited," I say. "You know, I have a little bit of a reputation as a ladies' man. But that's the old Ryan. I want to settle down. Hopefully, one of the women I'm going to meet today makes me want to get down on one knee."

It's a half truth. I'm not excited about the spotlight or the contestants or the weekly eliminations. But there's one thing I can't stop thinking about. Or one person, perhaps. And that's very much not a part of the script.

If Wren sees this, she'll roll her eyes. Call it a performance. Maybe it is. But I'm not lying about everything.

"Tell us a little about your family, Ryan."

My jaw tightens. I skate back to the pile of pucks, separating one and controlling it with my stick as I loop the rink.

"Well... Ellie's my little sister."

I flip the puck upward and catch it on the blade, then dribble it a few times. It's pure showboating. I know that. But I can't help myself.

"Ellie's my whole world. We're extremely close. I'm lucky to have her in my life."

Rich tilts his head. "And your parents?"

"My parents aren't really in my life," I say flatly. "That's not something I want to get into."

"Well, who raised you, then?"

"My Aunt Diane did a lot of the heavy lifting. We're lucky we had her." I glance toward the camera. "And he's not technically family, but I owe a lot of my hockey skills, and honestly, my temper control, to Coach T. He's been with me since I was a kid. Still comes to almost all of my games."

"No mom and dad, though, huh?" Rich asks.

I feel my expression pinch.

"I think I turned out okay. What do you think?"

I turn away from the camera and skate hard toward the goal, firing a shot that bounces off the post and into the net.

"Well..." Rich starts, but a low buzzing sound cuts him off.

He pulls a walkie-talkie from his back pocket, speaks into it, and then nods.

"Okay. We're going to start bringing the girls in now."

"What, here?" I ask, gesturing to the ice. "You got a bunch of girls who can skate or something?"

Living in Atlanta, I know most of these women probably didn't grow up ice skating. Roller skating, maybe. But ice? That's niche.

As I finish speaking, several crew members rush out carrying a wide strip of carpet. They roll it across the ice from one opening to the other.

I arch a brow. "I guess not."

Rich carefully makes his way over to me, hand out for my stick. I pass it to him.

"A lot of the girls can't skate, so we're making do," he says. "We're only shooting down here for about twenty minutes, just long enough to get all the girls out on the ice, on the carpet, and introduce them. You'll hang out at one end and greet each of them individually."

I squint. "How many are we talking?"

"Twelve to start," he says.

Thirteen women are about to step into this rink and pretend they're here for love. One of them isn't pretending. One of them already knows me too well. And she might be the biggest threat in the room.

He points to the far end of the carpet. "If you can hang out over there, that would be immensely helpful."

I'm standing at center ice in a tailored suit and skates because, apparently, that's part of the bit. The whole "I'm a famous hockey player" thing that the producers feel will make me bachelor material. Rich insisted it would look great on camera. One by one, the bachelorettes step onto the carpet with practiced smiles and camera-ready waves, each introduction more surreal than the last.

Annabeth is first. She's a pediatric nurse with ice-blonde hair and a voice like spun sugar. She flashes a megawatt smile, says she's "ready to give her heart a checkup," and hugs me like we've known each other for years. JacqLyn follows, a pageant coach in towering stilettos and a rhinestone-studded dress. She says something flirty about "competing for the biggest prize of all." I honestly can't tell if she means love or the spin-off brand deals.

Nikki makes her entrance in knee-high boots and a dress I'm pretty sure breaks a few broadcast codes. She's a social media strategist, all confidence and red lipstick, and her handshake feels like a dare. Brooke is a flight attendant who winks as she adjusts her silk scarf and says something about "first-class chemistry." Heidi, a sleek corporate lawyer with a smirk that says she's already judging me, just nods once and moves along.

Letitia works in luxury real estate and struts like she's selling the rink itself. Divya is an ER resident who looks like she hasn't slept in three days but still manages to radiate poise. Trinity, a yoga instructor and part-time astrologer, greets me with a deep breath and a promise that "our signs are aligned." Whitney, an event planner, gives me a clip-board once she's done introducing herself, as if I'm already on her to-do list.

Mei is a social media influencer like Jay; she snaps several selfies and tells her fans how amazing this experience is. I'm not really needed or wanted in that interaction. Daisy, a kindergarten teacher, is sweet enough to give me a toothache and clutches a handmade card with glitter on it. And finally, there's Raven, last on the lineup, a bartender with a tattoo sleeve and the kind of stare that makes you forget your own name. "I can't believe I'm talking to the Ryan Haart." She smirks and says, "Bet I'm not what you were expecting." She's not wrong.

There it is again. The full name. The image. Ryan the brand, not the man. I've had women fall for that version of me before. And every time, they look disappointed when the real me shows up.

When Rich tells me to wrap it up, I look around and whisper, "Isn't someone missing?"

"You'll meet the surprise contestant upstairs in the lounge," he says. "Now, I need you to announce to everyone that we are going to move upstairs to the high rollers' box. Make the announcement dramatic!"

"Welcome, everyone," I call out. "I can't wait to meet y'all. If you will follow me up to the owner's box, we can have a drink and talk a bit."

Marcus calls *cut*. Rich holds out a hand. "We'll need you to wait, Ryan. There are a few lines we'll have you say into the camera. That'll give us some wiggle room in the editing bay."

"O-kay..." I watch the women as they leave the ice, their attention more on hustling toward the stairs than on me. How silly of me to think that I'd be the star of the show.

I'm starting to think that I don't know a damn thing about being on reality television.

six

RYAN

I TAKE a calming breath and look around the owner's suite, which has been decked out in lavish style: velvet furniture, a swanky bar, and clusters of contestants sitting and waiting for me. It's a little daunting.

Rich is about to say something, but before he can get a word out, the bachelorettes begin to rise.

The first wave of girls to come talk to me are Daisy and Raven.

Daisy flips her long blonde hair over her shoulder as she approaches, a devilish smile on her face. I have to admit, I like her attitude toward this whole dating on TV game.

"Hey, Ryan," she says. "I just thought I'd come over and try to spend some time with you. Let you know that I am sweet, sassy, and down for anything."

I force myself to look at her rather than letting my eyes trail to the cameraman watching us with rapt attention.

"Thanks, Daisy. Where did you say you were from again?"

She moves closer, cradling a glass of champagne in one

hand and giving me the most winning smile I've probably ever seen.

"I'm from a little place called Nashville, Tennessee. Maybe you've heard of it?"

"Oh, I love Nashville. So much history and music."

"Are you into country music?" she asks, fluttering her eyelashes. "I'm a country singer, well, not professionally, but that's my aspiration. I spend a lot of time writing songs and arranging music. I'm actually a kindergarten teacher. That's just until I meet my husband, though. I plan to stay at home with our kids and keep a perfect home."

She winks. My mouth goes dry. Does she think that I'm looking for a housewife? Because that is not my bag. Off camera, Rich gestures to me to respond.

"Right..." I say. "Well, it's nice to meet you."

Raven saunters over, wearing a long black silk dress, looking every bit the goth girl. "What are you two kids chatting about?"

Daisy immediately rolls her eyes. "Just getting to know each other. It's a private conversation."

I squint. Daisy's reaction to Raven joining us rubs me the wrong way.

"Hey, there's plenty of room for everyone here," I say. "Let's all just relax."

Raven slips her arm through mine, smiling.

"I was a little starstruck downstairs," she says. "I can't believe Ryan Haart, superstar hockey player for the Atlanta Ice Storms, is actually here. I'm completely freaking out. I've been to a lot of games over the past few years... mostly because I've had a terrible crush on you."

I keep the PR smile on my face, but my interest in Raven drops fast. I don't like girls who are into Ryan the hockey god.

"I'm just a person," I say with a smile. "Same as anybody else. But I'm glad you enjoyed the games."

Raven seems to realize she said something wrong. Her lips part like she's about to explain herself, but before she can, the lighting in the room shifts.

I check my watch. When are the producers going to bring in Wren?

The lights dim. A spotlight shines on the door to the hall.

The host clears his throat. "Ryan, we've saved one special bachelorette for you. Someone you already know. Do you have any idea who might be behind this door?"

I've got the script in my head. Smile. Wink. Pretend like I don't already know who's about to walk through that door. But even with all the prep, my pulse jumps when I hear the footsteps. Because I know. And I'm not ready.

My palms go sweaty. My jaw tightens.

What if I lose control on national TV? Not just of my temper, but of how I feel?

I look at him, keeping my face neutral. Of course, I know what he's going to say, but I have to pretend it's a surprise. Cameras are trained on me from three different angles.

"No idea," I say. "I thought all my bachelorettes were already here."

The host grins and points to the door. "Let's have the reveal."

The door opens, and a petite, slender girl steps through in a short white dress and fishnet stockings.

I hear several girls gasp or murmur.

Wren tosses her long coppery hair with a defiant flick.

She's wearing a ton of makeup. The eyeliner and

mascara look dramatic and heavy, totally out of place on her normally bare but beautiful face.

She cocks her hip and announces herself.

"Hello, everyone. I'm Wren. Ryan and I go way back. I fully expect to beat out the competition for Ryan's last rose."

She's wearing confidence like armor. The dress is short, the makeup is bold, but it's the glint in her eye that floors me. I've never seen her like this, and it hits me like a slap. I should've seen it coming.

My jaw drops. I can't help it.

Wren glances at me, and for just a split second, I see the nervousness in her eyes before she tosses her hair again.

"Ryan," the host says. "Any reaction?"

I want to say something clever. Something easy. But all I can think is—this just got real. And I have no fucking clue how I'm supposed to protect her, or myself, when the cameras roll.

I scrunch up my face.

Rich and I talked about playing up my feelings for the camera. I've been carefully coached.

But it's hard to hide the fact that Wren being here as a contestant? Not the twist I wanted.

The host is still waiting for my answer. Thirteen women are staring at me like I just grew a second head. I have about three seconds to figure out what the hell I'm supposed to say.

"I'm very intrigued. I want to get to know Wren, just like all of the bachelorettes. I'm... um... a lucky bachelor."

The girls break into applause, which makes the back of my neck heat with embarrassment. I force a smile and look around.

Marcus calls cut and instantly, the set is flooded with

PAs, gaffers, grips, and boom mic operators. The contestants move toward their assigned production assistants, accepting bottles of water and fanning themselves from the heat generated by the lights that were set up.

A man with a clipboard shouts, "That's a wrap on the arena! Let's get the cast down to the vans for transport. We have a whole second setup back at the house set."

Those words mean almost nothing to me, but I go to where I'm pointed. This is my new life, my reality for the foreseeable future. I should get used to it.

* * *

We've moved to the set, our first scene shot at the house. The dining room is straight out of a fairy tale. Candles. Rose petals. A string quartet tucked in the corner. A camera crew lurking just out of frame, pretending not to be there.

I swirl the wine in my glass while Trinity talks about her faith.

My first date was a one-on-one dinner, and I chose Trinity, because she seems safe. She is wearing a giant gold cross necklace and a modest-enough dress, so I figured she's a girl who might be the saving-it-until-marriage type.

Trinity's been on a roll since the appetizers. She's told me about her dream of a big family and her plans to start a ministry. Is that the same as a church? I don't know and I don't dare ask. She says it all with conviction. I respect that.

What I don't love is how she assumes we're a perfect match. Like being attractive is all it takes.

"We're both driven," she says, reaching across the table. "People have told me we'd make gorgeous babies."

"You have such a magnetic aura," she continues,

blinking like she's in a shampoo commercial. "Are you an Aries?"

I stare at her. "No."

She giggles like I told a joke. I didn't.

It's like she's reading from a Pinterest board labeled "Marriage Goals." I don't even know her middle name. But sure. Let's build a fantasy life together based on jawlines and astrological compatibility.

I smile politely and squeeze her hand. Inside, I'm gritting my teeth.

Gorgeous babies. Right.

I glance at the nearest camera, the red light blinking steadily. It's angled low, probably trying to catch my smile. I give them one.

She thinks this is fate. I think we're two strangers having a heavily-produced dinner.

She thinks I'm the guy who eats up this kind of attention. The cocky player who'll take her bait and flash a smirk. I'm not. Not anymore.

At least, I don't want to be. That's the old Ryan Haart.

When the entrées arrive, she shifts the conversation to what she wants in a husband. A traditional leader. Someone who makes the decisions. A man who "knows who he is."

I want someone who'll stand beside me. On the ice, in the fire, wherever we end up.

She says it with pride. I nod along, but my stomach tenses.

I can be decisive. That's not the issue. But I don't see marriage as a hierarchy. I don't want to be anyone's king. I want a partner.

I sip my water and glance again toward the crew. One of

the producers is watching us like it's a soap opera. This whole thing is weird. Nothing about this is normal.

I feel like a prop in a romance movie where someone forgot to write a soul for my character. I'm sitting across from a woman who's already planning our wedding hashtags. All I can think about is how badly I want to be somewhere else.

Out of the corner of my eye, I catch Wren standing off to the side, arms crossed, watching this circus unfold. No fake giggle. No tossed hair. Just a raised eyebrow and a mouth that's twitching like she's trying not to laugh. I'd rather spend ten hours with her silence than ten minutes of this.

I clear my throat and return my attention to Trinity. "Have you ever been to a drag show?"

She sputters. Actually sputters. Her eyes widen. "A... drag show?"

It's a test. A quiet one. A toe over the line of who I really am. And her reaction, a tight smile, fingers gripping the cross, says more than anything she doesn't say out loud.

"Yeah," I say. "Some of my close friends are gay. A few perform. We go to shows sometimes. They're fun."

Trinity blinks hard, then gives me a smile that doesn't reach her eyes. "That's... nice. Uh, no. Can't say I've ever been."

Her voice is higher now. Her fingers toy with the cross around her neck. She shifts in her seat like she's trying not to squirm.

I glance toward the boom mic hovering above us, wondering if they're loving this.

I don't press. She's trying to be polite, but it's obvious. She doesn't get it. Maybe doesn't want to.

We move on to dessert, but the mood has changed. She

keeps talking, but her words don't land. We've both gone stiff. The cameras are still rolling, but it feels like we're just killing time.

After a long silence, she says, "I had a really nice time tonight."

She smiles, hesitant now. "Would you kiss me?"

I pause. It's not that she's not pretty. She is. But I already know this isn't going anywhere. She has a moral code that doesn't jive with mine.

"I'd rather not," I admit.

Her lips stay puckered for a beat too long. Her eyes flicker with disappointment before she covers it.

It's not her fault. She came here hoping to fall in love with a handsome hockey player. To win. And all I can give her is a camera-ready peck and an apology I can't say out loud.

"Thanks, Ryan," she says. "I look forward to spending some more time with you."

Like hell. I nod. "Thanks for tonight."

As I stand, I glance once more at the camera crew. One guy gives me a thumbs-up, like I just nailed a scene. I want to tell him this isn't a scene. It's real for her. It's completely fake for me.

It wasn't a disaster. She was polite about our obvious differences. But it wasn't a connection, either.

And in a few hours, I'll be back under the lights, handing out roses.

She walks away thinking this is a win. That I'll keep her around. In the long run, we have different priorities. And let's face it. I'm not worried about Trinity.

If this is what the next few weeks look like, I'm going to need stronger coffee. Or better lies. Because if they think

I'm going to fall for someone like Trinity, they haven't been paying attention.

Rich appears at my elbow with that fake producer smile. "Great date, Ryan. We need to talk about tomorrow's group date. There's been a change of plans."

BY NOON THE NEXT DAY, I'm the opposite of cool. I'm tense, anxious, and halfway unglued. I stare at myself in the three-way mirror of the wardrobe room and have a minor freak-out. Or major, depending on how good your self-esteem is normally.

God. Am I really going through with this? I think about how I've been assigned to fawn over Ryan and my neck heats.

This can only go badly.

"Are you sure this isn't too much skin?" I call to Jennifer, staring at my reflection in the mirror. I'm wearing a full-length tulle skirt, a black crop top that says PRINCESS across the chest, spike heels, and the ever-present black choker.

My hair is fuller and shinier than it's ever been. My skin glows. I look... not like me, but like a version of me from a parallel universe where I got enough sleep and had a personal stylist.

I should feel like an impostor. I should feel like a fraud. But instead, I kind of like it. The heels make me feel taller.

The skirt hugs my hips just right. There's something bold in my reflection I've never seen before. I don't fully recognize Mirror Wren, but she looks like someone who gets what she wants.

I'm not used to this much skin. Or sparkle. Or attention. My usual look is "invisible intern," not "backup singer at a royal wedding." Right now, I look like I'm either about to strut down a runway or start a riot. I don't even know which.

Jennifer stands behind me, clucking her tongue.

"It's perfect. I know you can't see it, but you're really pulling it off. I'm not ever going to lie to you about that. You have a banging body."

My cheeks heat. "Thanks. You too, obviously. I mean, look at you." I gesture at her little blue dress.

She chuckles. "At least someone appreciates it. Now, come here."

She crooks a finger at me and leads me back into the crowded dressing area where the other bachelorettes are milling around. Jennifer steers me to an unoccupied vanity, grabs a little pot of silvery highlighter, and brushes it along my cheekbones and the tip of my nose. I wrinkle my nose, but she just grins.

"You look perfect," she declares. "Really gorgeous. I'm sure you have nothing to worry about tonight."

The word gorgeous doesn't fit me. It's like a borrowed dress. Pretty, but not mine. Not meant to stay.

It's only week one out of eight. At the rose ceremony at the end of each week, Ryan will line up the bachelorettes and eliminate one or more of us. Supposedly, he has a lot of say over who stays and goes. And I already want to crawl into a prop closet and stay there until filming wraps.

A snort escapes me. "The bachelor hates me. Like, literally. I'll probably make the cut, but it doesn't mean anything. Trust me."

Ryan definitely wants me gone. It's only by Elena's magic "I'm the head producer of this show" juice that I'm even here, much less that I'll make it through the eliminations round.

I'm not just nervous. I'm spiraling. It's not about the show. It's about standing up there, waiting to be chosen. Or not. It's every school dance I never got asked to all over again.

I try to tell myself that I have nothing to be worried about, but that specific exposed nerve is being trod upon over and over again.

"Hey." Jennifer squeezes my arm. "It'll be okay. Even if you're kicked off the show, you'll get your promotion sooner. Isn't that what you're here for?"

"Whoa." I blink. "Jennifer, you are a gem. Thanks for reframing the situation like that."

"That's what I'm here for." She opens her arms and I give her a tiny hug.

I laugh. "That's not your job at all, but I really appreciate it."

Someone calls her name and she pats me once more before hurrying off. I glance around the dressing area, taking in the other contestants for the first time as a group.

Whitney's already laughing like she's on a first-name basis with the crew. Annabeth's adjusting her mic for the third time while JacqLyn poses like it's a high-glam photo shoot. And me? I'm just trying to remember how to breathe.

A girl named Divya narrows her eyes when she catches me looking, like she's already decided I'm competition. Joke's on her. I don't even want the prize.

I glance sideways at the contestant next to me. A girl named Brooke.

Brooke has toned arms, sleek dark hair, and the kind of confidence that comes from years of winning things. She catches me looking and raises an eyebrow.

"What?"

"Nothing," I say quickly. "You just look... fierce, that's all."

Her mouth curves into something that might be a smile. "Thanks. I'm Brooke, by the way."

I nod. She doesn't know it, but she was one of the earliest picks for the season, so I've already dug through her bachelorette file. Not that I say any of that. My status as a PA is still under wraps.

"I'm Wren," I offer.

She smirks. "Yeah, no kidding. After your entrance earlier, I think everyone knows who you are. Honestly, you're probably number one on the hit list of most of the girls here. Because of the history you and Ryan have."

I drop my gaze. I spent the morning with Elena, going over how to present myself as confident and self-assured, someone with history and chemistry with Ryan. If only the others knew the real story. That I've never even kissed him.

Meanwhile, some of these girls probably have entire relationship resumes. Mine is a blank sheet of paper. If they knew that, I'd be a joke.

Elena's advice was to let people draw their own conclusions. Let them think what they want. The truth is so much more pathetic than their assumptions.

A PA steps into the doorway. "Ladies, five minutes to air. Please make your way down to the patio set."

Brooke stands and smiles at me. "Good luck tonight. Though I don't think you'll need it."

I don't need luck. I need armor. Because when he looks at me, I'm never sure if he wants to mock me or kill me.

I smile back. "You too, Brooke." I follow her into the hallway.

The patio set looks like the courtyard of a Mediterranean mansion: stone walls, a pool, string lights, and rose petals everywhere. White silk is draped between pillars. It's romantic in that stagey, TV kind of way.

Lights. Cameras. Red wine breath and tight smiles. This isn't a date. It's a firing squad in formalwear.

All the bachelorettes are guided to their places. Hana, the goth producer who's in charge of me, waves me over.

"Hey Wren. Funny seeing you here."

"Where do you want me?"

She points to the far right, front row. "Right here."

I take a deep breath and head to the spot. Around me, the other contestants settle into place. Divya's talking about a five-year plan with anyone who'll listen. Letitia's modeling her champagne flute like a lifestyle influencer. I've never felt smaller or faker.

"Don't worry," Hana whispers. "It would be ridiculous to let you get cut this early."

"Right," I murmur. "Because *The Last Kiss* definitely controls Ryan."

She grins. "I saw your scene earlier. There's definitely chemistry."

"Places!" Marcus shouts. "I don't want to lose the light."

"Break a leg," Hana says before disappearing.

I stand there, willing my face into something neutral. My feet hurt. My stomach is in knots. I keep thinking about the bare inches of skin between my skirt and top, how unlike me this outfit is.

Everyone else looks like they belong on a magazine

cover. I look like someone broke into their sister's closet and prayed the cameras wouldn't zoom in.

Then Ryan walks in. The world shifts. Not because he's hot, though God help me, he is. But because suddenly, this whole ridiculous show feels like it might actually hurt.

He swaggers into the center of the circle and smiles.

"Wow, it's beautiful out here," he says.

Several girls titter like he's hilarious. I don't roll my eyes, but it's close.

I hang back as the other women cluster together. They all seem to know how to pose, how to laugh, how to sparkle. I tug on my skirt and silently count my breaths.

Ryan brushes lint off his fitted suit. He looks good. Tall, broad-shouldered, the jacket cinched perfectly at the waist. I hate that I notice.

He spots me and his eyes linger. His brows rise slightly. Then comes the smirk.

God, I hate him so much.

He's drinking me in like he can't help it, and I suddenly regret every decision that brought me here. I miss my over-sized T-shirts. I miss being invisible. I miss not caring what Ryan Haart thinks when he looks at me.

Okay, I'm lying to myself. I've always cared what he thought.

The host steps up. "Welcome back to *The Last Kiss*. Ryan is about to make his selections. Ryan, how are you feeling?"

"Good," he says. "Excited. Blown away by the beauty and brains here. It's honestly intimidating."

"Are you ready to let one of these women go?"

He nods. "I've talked to a lot of the girls. I'm making my decision based on the vibes I felt."

My stomach sinks. If he's going off vibes, I'm toast.

This is it. I'm the girl who joined late, who doesn't flirt

loud enough or dress sexy enough. I'm the freak with a classics degree and a three-book-a-week habit. Of course, I'm not the right choice.

The host hands Ryan the tray of roses.

He starts with the obvious choices. Brooke. Letitia. Annabeth. Heidi. JacqLyn. Then a bunch of others: Divya, Whitney, Mei, Raven, Daisy.

It comes down to three of us without roses: Nikki, Trinity, and me.

Even though I'm relatively sure that I'm safe, owing to the fact that I'm here because Elena wants me to be, I still find myself getting nervous. The fact is, I don't really know Elena that well. She says I'm not getting kicked off, but is that what will happen?

Ryan steps toward Trinity. "We had an interesting conversation, but I'm not sure our visions for the future align. Are our values really on the same page?"

Trinity flushes. "Of course, there will be differences. But maybe we could find common ground."

He gives her a tight smile, then moves on.

"Nikki, you're gorgeous and fun, but I didn't feel that spark. You know what I mean?"

"I do," she admits, though her smile looks forced. "But sometimes sparks take time to catch fire."

He nods. Then he turns to me.

"Well, well. It's down to you, Wren. What do you think should happen here?"

I try not to grimace. I'm not going to beg for a date on national TV. I am, however, going to use the lines that Hana slipped to me earlier. I lift my chin and try to flutter my eyelashes.

"I don't know, Ryan. I thought we had good chemistry. There's history here. I think it's worth exploring. Don't you?"

His smirk spreads. My stomach tightens.

He hands me one of the two remaining roses. "I'll be sure to take you up on that."

I don't let myself smile. I don't let myself breathe. This doesn't mean anything. It can't. He's playing a role, same as me. Still, I tuck the rose close to my chest like it might shatter if I don't protect it.

Then he turns back to Nikki and gives her the last rose. Trinity's out.

Whatever happened during their time together must've been rough. Her smile doesn't reach her eyes as she walks away, and just like that, we're down to eleven.

The cameras cut. I exhale hard and make a beeline for the guy with the champagne tray.

I have never needed a drink more in my entire life.

I made it through the first rose ceremony. One down. Seven to go.

I can fake this. I have to. Even if someone's already watching too closely. Even if Divya keeps shooting me looks like she's trying to solve a puzzle. Even if Ryan's smirk felt like a white-hot dagger when he handed me that rose.

WREN

AFTER THE SHOWDOWN in the rose garden, I can't wait to be alone. I'm definitely an introvert, and I've officially used up all my conversation talking points for the day. I just want to stare at the wall and sort through my thoughts in peace. My throat's tight, my hands won't stop shaking, and my skin feels too tight for my bones.

I need quiet. I need *out*.

The whole night feels like emotional whiplash. I've gone from zero to heartbreak to hope in less than an hour, and now I just want to shut my brain off.

Ryan disappears off set, and I trail behind the other contestants as we're herded away from the rose garden and into the house. It's weird. Everyone is smiling like they're in a toothpaste commercial while also trying to look very sexy climbing the stairs.

I'm just trying not to trip in the heels Jennifer picked out for me as I head upstairs toward the bedroom I share with several other bachelorettes.

The bedroom doors have tags with our names. I'm

staying in the third bedroom with Heidi, Raven, and Divya. Heidi opens the door and leads the way. The bedroom is gorgeous—white bedding, blush accents, very Instagram-ready. Two sets of bunk beds make me nervous, but the vibe is pretty. A little too cheerful, maybe.

Heidi is on the top bunk on the right, I'm on the bottom. On the left side of the room, Divya is on the top bunk and Raven is on the bottom.

Heidi gives me a sly look. "Hey, we made it through night one. That's something to be proud of."

I laugh while she claims a bureau and vanity on our side of the room. "Honestly, I'm just glad I didn't combust during the final rose ceremony. I've never been on TV before."

"Neither have I." She grins. "I guess we both did pretty well."

I glance at Divya and Raven, silently moving around across the room, unpacking and straightening. Divya saw me falter tonight. She'll use it. Maybe not today. But it's coming.

I see that Raven has pulled out a book titled *Spiritual Divination* and tossed it on her bunk. She shimmies out of her dress and hangs it up, then changes into dark jammies. Divya pulls on a satin teddy and carefully applies gold under-eye patches.

It's quiet in the room as we all change. Heidi takes off her makeup with a disposable cleaning cloth. Seeing the girls in their natural state is a bit startling. There are no cameras, so there's no reason for Divya to needle me or Heidi to be flirtatious.

Raven arches a brow at me. "Do you want me to do your tarot?"

"No." I sit down on my bunk and shake my head. "I'm

completely wiped out by the elimination ceremony. I feel like all that aggressive energy flowing around stole my vigor."

"I get that. The rose ceremony was weird." Raven sighs. "It's nice that we can be friendly, at least for now. Maybe we'll make some new friends."

"That a nice change of pace. Usually girls on these shows are like, 'I'm not here to make friends, I'm here to *win.*' Which is gross."

As we settle in, Raven stretches out on her bed. "I just want to see if falling in love on reality TV actually works. That and the free wine. That's really why I'm here."

"That's very honest of you," Heidi says, chuckling.

Raven shrugs. "I'm an honest bitch."

Divya looks up. "Well, I'm here to be seen. What else is there to do after med school?"

"I don't know. Save lives?" Raven suggests.

"Ugh. Boring," Divya shoots back, grabbing her toiletry bag like it's sacred. "I'm changing and starting my self-care routine."

"This feels like summer camp," Heidi says.

I've never been good at summer camp. Or sleepovers. Or any place where I have to pretend I belong. I'm great at school and structure. I'm not great at competing for love in front of a camera.

I pull on pink silk shorts and a white camisole. "Yeah. If summer camp had cameras, heels, and one guy dating twelve women."

Heidi winks but says nothing.

After unpacking, I pull out a Greek mythology book and drop it on my bed. My phone, given to me by the show and which has no internet capability, buzzes. I check it and immediately wish I hadn't.

A text from Ryan:

> Outside patio. Five minutes. Don't make me come find you, Rustin.

My heart stutters. Ryan. Demanding as always. Even here. Where we can get caught. Cameras are everywhere. Doesn't he care?

If anyone sees me sneaking off to meet him, the narrative will write itself. I'll go from weird invisible girl to desperate villain in one episode flat.

I should ignore it. I should delete it. But my fingers hover over the screen like they're waiting for permission to want something impossible.

Unfortunately, my body tenses with excitement anyway. It's muscle memory at this point. Hear from Ryan? Heart races. Brain short-circuits. Soul quietly begs for dignity. I hate that my body doesn't listen.

When I look up, Raven is smirking. "What? Did your evil overlord text you or something?"

"No," I lie. My ears warm.

"You're blushing," Heidi says gently.

"It's warm in here."

"Only your ears are red," Raven adds.

"God. Don't worry about it. I'm going to wash my face."

Grabbing a hoodie and my toiletry bag, I slip out quickly. I stash my bag in the nearest open bathroom and hurry downstairs. The house is quiet, dimly lit.

I open the sliding door to the rose garden.

Ryan's standing by a column, looking at his phone. He's out of his suit now, wearing a tank top and gray sweatpants. His body is big and solid, like always. I can see every line of his arms and back.

He's lounging like a great cat, all slow confidence and

dangerous smiles. It's criminal how good he looks in sweatpants. I want to hate him. I do hate him. Just not enough.

As much as I despise it, I feel a jolt low in my belly. I clench my jaw.

This is not what I need right now.

The second I see him, I feel everything at once—relief, dread, that fluttery warning in my gut. Like stepping into shade and realizing you still might burn.

I step out and glance at the camera angled toward him. Ryan looks up, sees me, and turns. I press a finger to my lips, point to the camera, and slip around the corner to one of the blind spots.

He follows, his presence prickling across my skin.

He crosses his arms, cocky and relaxed. Like he owns the place. Unfortunately, he kind of does.

"Wow," I say. "Summoning me like a villain. Very on-brand."

He drags his eyes down my bare legs. A shiver runs through me.

"You showed up," he says. "Must've missed me."

"Maybe I was worried you'd do something dramatic. Like bang on my windows and scream my name."

He grins. "Don't tempt me, Chirp."

I scowl. "I hate that nickname."

"Yep. I know. But you can deal. You snuck out to see me. You're on a show where I'm the prize, so as far as I'm concerned, you do what I say."

I should lie. I should deny it. But the truth is clinging to my skin like humidity. I hate that he knows I'll come when he calls. I hate that he might be the only person who sees me this clearly.

Everyone else makes me shrink. With Ryan, I snap back.

I don't know why. Maybe it's because he's never let me be invisible. And I'm scared of how much I like that.

"Yeah, that's always worked well. Expectations and me? Besties."

"Well, you're still here. I could've eliminated you."

I cross my arms. He keeps looking at my chest, and my body—traitorous and evil—reacts. I swear, my nipples tighten under the thin fabric of my cami.

"I don't know what I'm supposed to do with you, Ryan. I thought you'd cut me immediately."

"Where's the fun in that? Now I get to watch you squirm on national TV."

"Glad my suffering is so entertaining."

"Oh, it's more than entertaining. It's the highlight of my day."

"You're really leaning into the whole bachelor villain thing, huh?"

He shrugs. "Only because you make it so easy. You're the perfect storm. Sarcastic, hostile, and still blushing like I'm your first crush."

"I'm not blushing."

He taps my earlobe. "Looks like a blush to me."

"I hate you."

"Yeah, yeah. So you keep saying. But here you are."

I heave a sigh. "I'm not one of your groupies. I'm not even dating material, okay?"

Because I'm not. I'm awkward and too smart and not hot in the way people want. No one has ever picked me. Not really. So why would he?

"Oh yeah? So you're just waiting for some dream boyfriend to appear out of thin air?"

"I'm waiting for the right person. Someone who respects me. My first boyfriend. My first... everything. And unless you're volunteering to be a respectful soulmate—which you're not—I suggest you back off."

My voice cracks on the word. I wish it didn't. But there's a part of me that meant it. That wants it. That wants him to be different, even when I know better.

He tilts his head. "I'm not the right person."

"Good. Because you're not even in the running. If you were the last man on earth, the human race would die out before I slept with you."

"You say that a lot. But you keep showing up when I text." He smirks at me.

Yeah. Because I'm an idiot. And because some small, masochistic part of me likes pretending I'm important to you, even if it's just for five minutes in the dark.

"Because you're manipulative. And I don't trust you not to blow up my time here by dredging up our past. Whatever this... thing is."

"There's a difference between hating me and fantasizing about me."

"You're inescapable. That's not the same as fantasizing."

"Sure. Keep telling yourself that."

"There are plenty of women here who want your attention. Just let me exist until the producers send me home. That's it."

He cocks his head.

"You do realize we will probably have to kiss at some point?"

My face flames. "What? No we won't."

"Yes, we will. This is a dating show. That's what people do when they're trying to figure out if they're compatible." He squints at me. "Maybe you've never done that."

"I'm not talking to you about this," I grit out.

"What's a matter, Chirp? Never kissed anyone before?"

"I've kissed people. Jesus. What is this, middle school?"

"I'm not sure that you have."

"I have," I growl. "You sure are interested for someone that absolutely shouldn't touch me lest you risk Jay killing you."

His smile slides through me like a superheated knife.

"Relax, Wren. You're Jay's little sister. You're innocent. Off-limits."

"Off-limits," I repeat.

He shrugs. "Yeah. And I've got self-control."

"Could've fooled me."

"Believe it or not, I'm doing you a favor."

"Oh, now you're protecting me?"

His smile slips. His voice softens. "You're too good for this."

It's the softest he's ever spoken to me. And I hate that it hits harder than any insult ever could.

"You mean too good for you."

He shrugs again. "Same thing."

"Eventually, I'll find someone I don't want to strangle every time they talk."

"What does that mean?"

"You know what? Don't answer that. You're exhausting."

"And yet," he says, "here you are."

I glance around. We've been talking too long.

"Yeah, I should go."

"Sure. Run back to your room. Try not to dream about me, Chirp."

I fix him with a glare. "You're not even a real person. You're just nice teeth and a smirk."

He laughs. "You love me."

I turn away, my cheeks flaming bright red. He says I'm too good for this. But he's the one who keeps pulling me in. And I'm the one who keeps letting him.

I don't say thank you. I don't say anything. I just breathe him in and pretend, for one selfish second, that this could be real.

nine

MY PHONE BUZZES in my pocket and I pull it out to discover a text from my little sister.

So? How's the show?

I grit my teeth and text back.

Horrible. This whole thing feels like a circus.

You're the ringmaster, dude. Own it.

Dude? You're not supposed to call your brother dude. You sound like Aunt Diane.

I love Aunt Diane. She gives you that face when you're being dumb.

I huff out a laugh and slouch deeper into the booth.

All three of us have that face. I've seen it in the mirror. It's haunting.

Maybe that's why your dates keep bailing.

No one's bailed yet. I did let one of the girls go because she was too conservative for me. I asked if she would go to a drag show with me and she nearly puked. Which would have been pretty funny if I wasn't supposedly interviewing women to be my wife.

God. How did you not melt into the floor from secondhand embarrassment?

I avoided eye contact by looking at a spot on the carpet the entire time.

Inspiring stuff.

This is my villain origin story, isn't it.

Oh, for sure. You're halfway to a brooding monologue already.

Chuckling, I drag myself to breakfast with my executive producer slash coach, Rich. He's patient as always, gently needling me about my feelings so far. I shovel a healthy granola parfait into my face and try to answer his questions.

"So, what do you think about Heidi?" he asks.

I nod. "She's really pretty. Professional and polished. I like that."

"And JacqLyn?"

"Also pretty with that girl-next-door flair, but she hasn't really opened up yet. She's mostly been watching everyone else."

Rich nods. "Yeah, it's early days right now. But what

about Wren? You already know her. Have you guys found your connection yet?"

I brush his question aside. "Look, between you and me, I know Wren has to be here, but she has no chance of winning. She's a brat. She's my best friend's little sister. There are a lot of ways that could go sideways. But I get why you all want to keep her around. She definitely keeps me on my toes."

I say it like it's a joke, like I don't lie awake wondering what she's thinking when she looks at me. But I do. I always have.

Rich smirks, then covers it with a sip of coffee. "Well, today should be interesting. I think if you picked Wren for your three-on-one date, it would shake things up. Let the other contestants know they've got real competition. Even if you don't think Wren is a serious contender."

I sigh. I hadn't been thinking about who I'd pick for today, but of course, the EPs want drama.

"I'll consider it," I say grudgingly.

"Good man." Rich pats me on the shoulder. "We're leaving in a few. Get ready."

My gut says don't pick her. But my eyes drift to her anyway, like they always do. She's become this gravity sink in my brain. Every thought bends toward her in a cosmic way.

"I'm ready," I mutter, finishing my parfait with a final gulp of coffee.

We pull up to a large conference center on the outskirts of town. I throw Rich a quizzical look.

"Are you sure we're at the right place?"

He grins. "Yep. I think you'll be impressed. The whole day's built around things we know you like."

"Okay," I say, uncertain.

Turns out, he's not totally wrong. Inside, they've cleared out the entire floor to create a winter wonderland scene. It's over-the-top. Fake snow drifts through the air, a full-sized ice rink dominates one corner. Fairy-tale style buildings have been set up like a tiny village. Trees are wrapped in lights. Benches sparkle with glitter. It's all very romantic. Very fake. I guess pageantry is the point.

Still, I can't help picturing Wren under those lights. Probably hating every second of it but shining all the same. God, I'm so screwed.

We arrive early, so I wander over to the themed coffee stand. They make me a damn good latte. I sip it while watching PAs dart around like sugared-up toddlers.

Rich returns with a cameraman in tow.

"Okay, Ryan," Rich says. "Let's talk about today. Just give us a little intro. Say you're excited about the three-on-one. Announce who you're picking. The rest of the girls will be seated over there by the food."

I rub my hands together and nod. I don't actually care about any of this, but it's paying me hundreds of thousands. That money's going straight into savings for the day I inevitably get hurt and can't play anymore.

I take a breath and smile at the camera.

"Hey, Ryan here. I'm really excited about today. *The Last Kiss* threw me this insane winter wonderland party. I'm honestly blown away. Today, I get to take three contestants on a private date and teach them how to ice skate.

"A lot of the girls didn't grow up skating, so this'll be a fun opportunity. I'm taking Wren, Mei, and JacqLyn. I know Wren pretty well, but we've never skated together. That should be interesting. Mei and JacqLyn are still kind of mysteries to me. I'm looking forward to getting to know them."

I glance at Rich. He mouths, *Play up Wren.*

I redirect. "Especially Wren. I've known her for years, but never really considered her as someone I could date. She's a risky choice because of her brother, but I'm willing to take the heat if she and I really click."

I clap my hands. "Let's go see what the girls are up to."

The camera pans as the big conference doors swing open. The girls file in, laughing and chattering.

I walk over. "What's up, ladies? Welcome to my winter wonderland. I wanted to grab some time with a small group today. Mei, JacqLyn, and Wren. The rest of you can hang out at the concession area. We'll meet up after our date. Sound good?"

Mei squeals. Wren scowls. JacqLyn grins.

The rest mutter as they're herded toward the food.

"Ladies, shall we?" I gesture toward the ice. "We're going skating."

Mei lets out a quiet shriek. "I don't know how to skate. You'll have to teach me."

JacqLyn slips her arm through mine. "Me either. You'll have to keep a close eye on me."

Wren trails behind us, pouting.

She didn't expect me to pick her. But she should've. Choosing her was the only play. First, the cameras love her. Rich said as much. Second, she makes the other women twitchy. Maybe, just maybe, it's partly for me.

I can't stop thinking about how she looked at me yesterday. Like I was both a threat and a joke. Dangerous, but impossible to ignore.

Mei and JacqLyn take up most of my attention while we lace up skates and talk about how cute the rink is. Mei takes at least six selfies and a video.

"My followers are going to freak when they see I'm learning to skate with the Ryan Haart," she says.

"Followers?"

She smiles. "Yeah, I'm an influencer. I was going to be a wedding influencer, but my wedding got canceled. So now I'm back in the saddle."

I blink. "Oh. That's... something."

"Always a plan," she chirps.

JacqLyn and Mei step onto the ice, wobbling. Wren drags her feet, glowering like I personally offended her.

"Come on, Rustin," I say, motioning to the rink. "Let's go."

"Ryan, are you really making me do this? I'm going to fall on my ass."

"Yep," I say. "You bet I am."

I skate over, grinning. "You good?"

"Don't touch me," she mutters.

Which, obviously, means I have to. I coast in a little closer, just to mess with her. She lets go of the wall and takes one awkward step. She immediately starts to tip forward. I catch her before she hits the ice, one arm slipping around her waist.

My arm wraps easily around her waist. Something primal flashes through me. Protect. Steady. Hold. I don't know where the hell that comes from, but it's loud as fuck.

Wren's hands land on my chest.

Her eyes go wide.

For a second, neither of us moves. Her fingers are curled against my shirt. I can feel the stutter of her breath. She's staring at me like she's not sure whether to punch me or kiss me.

It's a disaster. My brain short-circuits. She's right there, breath shallow, eyes wide. For a second, I forget we're on a date. I forget there are cameras. All I can think is, don't let go yet.

Then she shoves me back. "I will be so happy when this date is over."

I smirk. "You're fun when you're mad."

The rest of the skating is chaos in every direction. JacqLyn grabs both my hands and twirls in a full circle, laughing like this is the best moment of her life. Mei films a slow-motion reel of herself doing one very hesitant spin, then yells at me not to ruin the lighting. Wren clings to the wall like she's negotiating a hostage situation. Every time I skate past her, she glares like I personally invented ice just to ruin her day.

I live for it. The glares. The huffing. The fact that she's clearly thinking about me. It's better than silence. Better than being ignored. I'll take her anger over her absence any day.

After the rink, we head over to the cozy setup. Firepit, faux fur blankets, hot cocoa in glass mugs with little gold spoons. The producers really went all out. It's cheesy. Romantic. If you ignore the ten cameras lurking around the edges, it almost feels real.

JacqLyn grabs me first for solo time. We sit by the fire. She's got that easy, breezy charm down pat. Cracking jokes, making increasingly filthy innuendos. Somehow managing to flirt and roast me at the same time.

"You're not bad at this," she says, sipping her cocoa. "I figured you'd be boring."

"Some offense taken," I say. "But you're not wrong."

She winks. "Don't worry, Haart. You've got that broody ex-frat boy thing going for you. It's like catnip."

They're funny, they're flirty, they're perfect for TV. But I'm only half listening. Because Wren's sitting ten feet away, arms crossed like she's trying to hold herself together. I want to go to her. I do.

Mei's next. She slides in beside me, phone already out, her energy buzzing. "Okay, we've got to talk brand strategy," she says. "Are you going family-man Ryan or reformed bad boy?"

I blink. "Depends on the edit."

She points at me. "Good answer. Honestly, I think you're tracking complicated but lovable. Very season six energy."

"Season six?"

"The one where the guy fakes a breakdown but ends up married. Classic."

Mei trips me out. She's so busy looking at her own reflection that I'm not even sure she clocks me as a person. I'm just a prize to her, something she wins along the way on her journey to influencer fame. It's unsettling to say the least.

The producers have saved Wren for last. I feel oddly heavy as I head over to where she is perched. What is she thinking about as she stares off into the distance?

She sits stiffly on the edge of a bench near the firepit, arms crossed like she's trying to shield herself from more than just the cold. Her knees are pressed together, feet tucked to the side like she's ready to bolt at the first sign of danger. Or me.

I flop down next to her.

"You're welcome, by the way."

She doesn't look at me. "For what?"

"For giving the producers what they want."

She finally turns her head, glaring. "You picked me because it makes good TV. Congratulations. We're probably already in the preview trailer."

She's talking about my persona, the mask I wear. It's a role. The cocky hockey player. The safe bet. I lean into it because it's easier than letting anyone close enough to see what's under it.

It shouldn't sting. In my line of work, I've had worse shouted at me. But coming from her? It feels like she took a scalpel to my chest and smiled while doing it.

"You think I'd risk your brother's wrath just for ratings?" I lean in, lowering my voice. "If I wanted easy TV, I'd be making out with JacqLyn in a hot tub right now. But here I am."

Wren huffs, but doesn't say a word. I push it a little further because I can't help myself.

"You're the one who makes good TV," I say. "You glare like a girl with a vendetta."

"I have several," she replies coolly. "You're on the receiving end of most of them."

I nudge the edge of the blanket draped across the bench toward her. "You can't be that mad if you're still sitting here."

"I'm cold," she says.

I grin. "Then get under the blanket."

She gives me a look that says she'd rather walk into traffic. But I lift the corner anyway. After a beat of hesitation, she sighs and slides under it. We sit shoulder to shoulder, sharing heat, the tension thick between us.

I glance at her. "You know, for someone who didn't want to be on this date, you're really committing to the cozy aesthetic."

"I'm committed to not freezing to death. Don't read into it."

"Too late."

She huffs. Her breath fogs slightly in the cool air. Her

skin glows in the firelight. That ridiculous little choker around her neck makes me think things I should absolutely not be thinking.

I reach out and gently tip her chin toward me.

Her eyes go wide. "Ryan..."

But I'm already leaning in. I kiss her.

It's soft at first. Just a brush of lips. But the second she sighs into my mouth, I lose whatever fragile grip on sanity I had. I deepen the kiss. Her mouth opens under mine. I taste her. Sweet. A little uncertain. Completely addictive.

My hand slides to the back of her neck. Her fingers curl into the front of my sweater. I want to devour her. Take and take until she forgets to hate me.

I shouldn't be doing this. She's Jay's little sister. She's too young. Too off-limits. But none of that matters. Not with her in my arms, melting against me like she was made for this.

My body is fully, painfully aware of her. I'm glad the blanket is still draped across my lap. I shift slightly, trying to hide the evidence of just how much I want her. Because I do want her.

There's no doubting it because my cock awakens and salutes her. I admit it. I've wanted to kiss Wren like this for years. Wanted some kind of contact, even if I said the opposite.

Sometimes, I lie to myself. But right now, the way Wren's taste bursts over my tongue, the way she leans into the embrace and makes this very tiny noise... It's making me want to guzzle more of her rather than slaking my thirst.

If Wren didn't eventually put her hand on my chest and push me back, I'm not sure I would've stopped. She pulls away, breathless. Her lips are red and kiss-swollen, her eyes wide. "Are you kidding me?"

The look in her eyes is perplexation edged with fire. I want her to kiss me again. I want her to want me to...

"Ryan." Wren snaps her fingers in front of my face. "Say words. Let me know you're not having a stroke."

I blink. Then I look around.

Right. Cameras.

Fuck.

I glance up and spot not one, not two, but at least five cameras trained on us. All of them capturing every second of what just happened.

Wren follows my gaze. Her face flames. She stands abruptly.

"I need some air," she mutters, then turns and walks away, fast.

I don't stop her. I just sit there, heart pounding, chest tight, trying to calm myself down. I can't walk back to the others yet. Not like this. My cock is hard. I would be telling on myself if I got up now.

I grab my cell phone, pretending to check my texts. But I can't even make sense of the words in front of me. A minute later, when my body finally catches up with my brain, I stand and make my way back to the rest of the contestants.

No one says anything.

But they all saw.

Wren's off-limits. Too young. Too innocent. Too everything. So why does it already feel like this whole show is just a long, slow slide into disaster with her at the center?

I'm not supposed to want her. Not like this. But I do. If I'm not careful, I'll forget why I ever tried to stay away in the first place.

THE CAST and crew are headed to an off-site shoot at The Righteous Room, a bar that's not quite a hole-in-the-wall but definitely isn't upscale, either. It's wedged at the intersection of three major nightlife zones: the sleek rooftop bars of East Midtown, the divey music joints off Edgewood, and the raucous college bars on Peachtree. The result is a wild mix of regulars, tourists, and off-duty bartenders, all crammed into one chaotic space.

Ryan's been acting weird ever since the group date. I can't stop thinking about that moment. The kiss. The breath we shared. The static in the air.

Ugh, this is terrible.

I ride in an SUV with a bunch of the other contestants, most of whom are giggling and gossiping about the skating date. JacqLyn is in our car. Thankfully, she's soaking up the attention like a sponge. She's busy dishing about how amazing her mini date with Ryan was and how they are *so meant to be*. I do my best to stifle my reflexive eye roll.

I pull out my phone and text Elena.

Hey, do you have a plan for how long I'll be on the show? Just trying to be prepared. I don't want my brother to be surprised when the show airs.

She replies with a single thumbs-up emoji. Nothing else. Great. It's only the second week of filming and I'm already feeling trapped. Why did I ever agree to this, again?

By the time we pull up to The Righteous Room, I'm resigned to the fact that she's either ignoring me or negotiating something more important. Either way, my stomach's tight with nerves.

We changed clothes during the break, so now I'm stepping out of the SUV in a very short black silk skirt that barely covers my ass. It's paired with a distressed white crop top with a cartoon drawing of a pair of red lips with vampire fangs and the words LOVE BITES. I tell myself that the outfit is strategic. My armor for the upcoming battle.

My hair has been tousled into what the stylist called "casual bedroom energy." I feel like a half-dressed pop star wandering into someone else's dream.

I'm playing a part. The seductive wild card, the edgy pick. But underneath the makeup and sky-high stilettoes, I'm still the weird girl who sat alone in high school reading Greek mythology at lunch. I'm not sure anyone here would believe that.

Inside, the place is packed. Booths line the right side of the room, the bar stretches down the left. There's a glowing neon double jukebox at the back, already surrounded by tipsy locals. James Brown wails over the speakers. The crowd is so loud, they barely notice our arrival.

The second I walk in, everything goes quiet. People turn. Eyes land on me. I brace for someone to laugh.

But no one does.

They just stare. And for once, it's not because I've said something awkward or tripped over my own feet. It's because I look good. That thought sticks to my ribs, strange and sweet. I'm not invisible today. And it feels kind of amazing.

This place is a sensory overload nightmare. Too loud. Too bright. Too many eyes. But I'm not the same girl I was last year. I'm supposed to own this version of me. Supposed to.

The production crew ushers us into a sectioned-off row of booths where they've discreetly planted cameras. I slide into one of the booths and order a vodka cranberry and a basket of fries from a server who looks vaguely thrilled to be part of the chaos.

Heidi slides into the seat across from me and casually drops a tray of Jell-O shots on the table. "You seem like you need this," she says, pushing one toward me.

I grin and down the cherry-flavored monstrosity in one go. It burns all the way down. "That was... aggressively alcoholic," I choke.

Good. That's what I want. To feel something loud and fuzzy. To be bold and reckless and maybe even a little bit seen.

"You're welcome," she says sweetly.

A few minutes later, she asks, "Wanna hit the jukebox?"

"Yes. God, yes."

She hands me another Jell-O shot on the way, which I toss back even quicker than the first. We link arms and weave through the crowd.

I'm not here to play it safe. Safe got me overlooked. Safe got me stuck. So screw it. Let's go full chaos.

"What are you gonna play?" she asks.

"Something classic. Ariana Grande, maybe?"

Her brows rise. "I didn't expect that. I figured you'd go full emo."

"I might look like I listen to Screamo, but I'm in my Ariana era."

"You wear it well," she says with a wink.

We get in line behind three people. While we wait, Heidi confesses that she's also wearing clothes way sexier than usual, which makes me laugh. "Glad I'm not the only one who got a little push in the wardrobe department."

"You clean up good, though," she tells me.

I rest my head on her shoulder and sigh. "I didn't think I'd make friends here. Glad I was wrong."

"We're hanging out after this show ends," she promises. "No matter what happens. Though let's be real. Ryan's totally into you."

"Nope." I shake my head fast. "He's pretending. It's all for the show."

She gives me a look but doesn't argue. I want to tell her everything. That I'm a producer plant, that I'm not supposed to fall for him. But I don't. I just swallow it down and pretend I'm not dying inside.

We take turns picking songs at the jukebox, then drift over to the bar to watch the chaos unfold. The lighting is flattering, the drinks are flowing. For a moment, I forget I'm being filmed.

A guy appears next to me. Tall, flirty, and trying way too hard. But he's funny. I don't hate talking to him. He leans closer, his arm brushing mine. "You don't look like a barfly," he says.

I smile. "I can be full of surprises."

We chat easily. It feels safe. Detached.

Until I feel it.

A prickle on the back of my neck.

I turn and see Ryan watching me from the other end of the bar. His jaw's tight. His eyes laser focused. His hand lands on my shoulder. Warm, possessive, totally unwelcome.

"Didn't know you were making friends, Wren," he says.

I don't even flinch. Just flash a smile, all teeth. "Didn't know you cared."

The guy beside me stiffens. "Is there a problem?"

Ryan doesn't answer. Just glares until the guy mumbles an apology and disappears.

I whirl on him. "Are you serious?"

He shrugs. "This is my dating show. You're here to make me happy."

I blink. "That wasn't about me making bad decisions. That was about you not liking someone else talking to me."

"In your dreams, Chirp. I was rescuing you. Like always."

I turn back to the bar and try to order another shot.

"What was that?" the bartender shouts, cocking his head and putting his hand to his ear.

It is getting louder in here for sure. There are more people crowding into this tight space, making it difficult for someone like me, who's basically invisible, to be heard. I mumble something about needing a shot and the bartender squints at me.

"One more time!"

"Tequila!" I finally shout. I hold my fingers up. "Two shots!"

"Got it!"

He hustles off to get my order. I tug at my sleeve, already second-guessing myself. This bar is a nightmare for an introvert. When he returns with two shots, I take them both, one after the other.

Anything to make this feeling fade.

When I glance over, Ryan's already sauntered down to JacqLyn. She grabs his shirt, pulls him close, and presses a kiss to his mouth. It's deliberate. Slow. Camera ready.

I can't look away.

Of course, Ryan opens his eyes mid-kiss.

He's looking right at me.

I bolt. Out the back door. Into the alley. Into the cold.

I just need one minute to breathe.

But then...

"Are you always this dramatic?" I know that voice all too well.

I whip around. "Are you always this annoying?"

Ryan steps into the light, arms crossed, eyes hot. "Thought you had a line of women waiting to kiss you."

"I got bored." He shrugs. "Came to see what you were doing."

"Wow. High praise for JacqLyn's tongue."

He steps closer. "Didn't know you were so interested in my mouth, Chirp."

"I'm not," I lie.

He smirks. "Jealousy looks good on you."

"You're the worst."

"You keep saying that, but you're still here. Still dressing like that. Still showing up."

"It's a skirt," I snap. "Adults wear them."

His gaze drops. "You having fun yet?"

I look away. "Maybe a little."

Ryan leans in, palm flat against the wall beside my head. "What was that?"

"I said maybe."

"You know what your problem is?" His breath brushes my cheek.

"Oh please. Enlighten me."

"You like me," he whispers. "You hate it, but you like it. You liked the kiss."

"I did not..."

He cuts me off. "Say you wouldn't let me kiss you right now. No cameras. Just us."

I open my mouth. Nothing comes out.

He tips my chin up. "That's what I thought."

Ryan's hand finds my waist, cupping it and guiding my body. I lift my face. His mouth brushes mine. A whisper of heat. I shiver as he chuckles and then kisses me for real—his lips pressing against mine, his mouth opening, tongue seeking my own. I gasp. He catches the sound with his kiss. In that moment, everything else vanishes. His hands explore me, pulling me close, his body heat soaking through my skirt, his mouth devouring me like a starving beast.

I melt. Instantly. All my protests simply vanish.

I kiss him back like I've never kissed anyone before. In truth, I've never experienced a kiss like this. None of those clumsy, fumbling kisses exist anymore. He leans in further, pressing a knee between my legs. I can feel his arousal through his pants. His hand leaves the wall to brush my thigh as he continues exploring my mouth.

His tongue strokes mine tenderly, while his hand sneaks up my short skirt until his fingers are teasing the outside of my underwear. I'm already wet for him. He growls into my mouth, "You sweet little thing, always pretending to hate me."

His teeth graze my lower lip and I gasp, as if trying to trap him in my lungs.

"You don't hate me, though, do you?" he murmurs.

"That's not true," I whisper back against his lips. "I do hate you."

He laughs. "Then why are you so wet for me?"

My hands bury themselves in his shirt. I know I should stop, that I should push him away, but instead, I yank him closer.

"You think I'm the only one who enjoys this?" I murmur as my hand slips between our bodies and finds the erection hidden under his pants.

He's hard, big and long and thick. Just like I remember him. Fuck, I'm horny.

"Oh honey, I've been thinking about kissing you for a long time now," he murmurs. His mouth finds mine again, this time deeper and hungrier. I want it. I want him to devour me.

A scuffling noise breaks through the haze of lust.

Then a voice cuts through, sharp and furious.

"What the hell?"

Rich. Ryan's coach.

We spring apart like guilty teenagers caught making out under the bleachers. My heart drops into my stomach. Ryan's chest is still rising and falling hard. My lipstick is probably smeared halfway across my face. His clothes are rumpled. Mine too.

"Save it for the damn cameras," Rich barks. "Jesus, you think we're paying you to sneak off and hook up like horny high schoolers?"

My face burns. "We weren't... this wasn't... nothing happened. Rich, I swear."

Ryan wipes his mouth with the back of his hand. He doesn't say anything. Just stands there, looking equal parts dazed and pissed.

"It was just a conversation," he says finally, voice rough.

Rich glares at both of us like he wants to murder us and then salt the earth.

"You walked far enough away that your mic packs went out of range. There's no usable audio. You just wasted a gold moment."

My mouth opens, but I've got nothing. No defense. No way to spin this. I mumble, "I'm sorry."

Rich yanks the back door open and holds it like he's daring us not to walk through it.

Ryan glances at me, then licks his teeth and nods toward the door. His breath is still uneven, his hands clenched at his sides.

We don't say another word.

We just walk back inside like nothing ever happened.

But my lips are still tingling. My stomach's flipping over itself. I feel foolish. Like I just handed Ryan every piece of leverage he could ever want.

The worst part is how much I liked it.

What will I do when Ryan pulls away? Because he will. If I keep on this trajectory, he's going to devastate me.

WOW. Annabeth may have been portrayed as a cute girl next door, but when Ryan eliminated her last night, she punched a hole in the kitchen wall. I stare at it as I eat my yogurt and berries.

It's weird to me that anybody would be so upset over being kicked off, period, let alone being sent home so early into the contest. Who cares about winning? It's so unlikely that Ryan will actually pick any particular bachelorette.

And yet, here is evidence that Heidi *cared*.

I rush through getting dressed and getting my makeup done. I'm yawning the whole time even though I had coffee with breakfast. The elimination ceremony last night took *forever*. We were all up past 1 a.m. and now we're supposed to be perky and camera ready. *Great*.

Letitia's crystals, Brooke's endless juice cleanses, Mei's obnoxious filming every single second. All of them were gone after last night's ceremony.

Three less competitors... and yet, still I'm here.

We get in vans, bundled off on a day trip. I don't even have the energy to be worried right now. At least I get my grande latte with whipped cream to soothe me as we drive. The girls are all silent, staring out the windows as they caffeinate themselves.

When the vans pull up in front of a small brick building with a faded sign that reads Hope Kitchen and Pantry, I think we've taken a wrong turn. I was expecting the contestants to be carried to an obstacle course or a paintball arena, but no. There's no thrilling, heart-pounding ride to go on. Just a line of people waiting quietly outside and a folding table with someone taking down names.

I glance down at the hem of my dress, smoothing the fabric between my fingers. It's soft and expensive, the kind of thing I never imagined wearing.

These clothes feel like armor. Not fake or flashy. Just... strong. I don't feel like Jay's awkward little sister in a hoodie. I feel sharp. Feminine. Like maybe I belong here after all.

This isn't a date. It's not even a challenge. I was bracing for paintball bruises or a pop quiz in heels, not... sincerity. This might actually be worse.

We move forward, the other bachelorettes clamoring as we crowd inside. As we go, the director claps his hands together.

"Okay, everyone. Today we're going to do something a little different. There's gonna be no competition here. We're all going to work together to support a cause that means a lot to Ryan. Hunger relief."

"Everybody will prep and serve meals or help pack boxes for the pantry. There is no end goal and no reward for finishing quickly. It's important that we do our best work here. Right, Ryan?"

Apparently, Ryan has entered the building right behind

us because he speaks from just behind me, scaring me half to death.

"That's right. Thank you all for volunteering. Even though you weren't actually volunteers. Today we're going to do something that I do on a regular basis. So spread out and make sure you listen to the people that work here."

There are groans coming from several of the bachelorettes. Mei starts filming immediately. Raven looks around and elbows Heidi. JacqLyn finds a pantry employee and starts asking for a rundown of the positions that need to be filled. Me? I just stand here, trying to recalibrate.

This feels too sincere for a show that once held a "roses and rejections" dodgeball tournament.

A crew member comes up to me, offering an apron. I take it and put it over my head.

"Is this a real place?" I ask.

She just nods. "Yeah. It is. Ryan requested it specifically."

I blink. "He requested a food pantry? Why?"

A woman in an apron hears me and looks up from a clipboard. "He volunteers here twice a month. No cameras, no press. He just shows up and works."

Something thuds in my chest. He does this? For real? No spotlight, no Instagram reel? It doesn't track. It doesn't fit. Somehow, that makes it even harder to breathe.

I stare at her, wide-eyed. "Are we talking about the same Ryan?"

She points at him. Ryan, who's standing across the room, talking to a person who came in for assistance. Definitely a description of a needy patron, even if I don't want to say homeless.

This is the guy I've been crushing on from a safe

distance? The one I wrote off as cocky and selfish? Maybe I was wrong. Maybe I don't know him at all.

"That Ryan. Six-five. Dark hair. Handsome as hell? Yeah, that's the one. He's a regular volunteer here."

Ryan ties his apron around his waist and laughs with someone while he unpacks produce. He looks relaxed and comfortable. He gives every indication that this isn't a joke. It throws me. Hard.

It's not just the apron or the laugh. It's the way he blends in here. Like this isn't a gimmick for him. It's a habit. I've never seen him like this. I've never seen anyone like this.

Tying the apron around my waist, I put my head down and start assembling boxes for the food pantry. After I stack about fifty boxes in a towering pile against the wall, I back up into a hard surface.

"Watch out."

I jump out of my skin and look up. Of course, it's him. Ryan is right there, looking down at me with those blue eyes.

I try to play it off. "I didn't realize you did charity work," I say, sort of making conversation as I move away.

He gives me a knowing look. "You say that as if you think I can't be a decent human being."

He's right. I definitely did not imagine this was one of his off-ice activities, but there's no reason to admit that.

"I never said that," I lie.

He shrugs. "When I was a kid, my sister and I used to come to places like this. We didn't always have enough food or know where our next meal was coming from. So kitchens and pantries like this got us through a lot of really hard times."

His voice is calm, but his words land like a punch. He's

not telling me for drama or attention. There are no cameras watching.

Apparently, there's a wealth of things I don't know about my so-called best enemy.

I don't know what to say, so I just shrug awkwardly. "It's saintly that you give back," I finish lamely.

He gives me a funny look, like I've just said something off the wall. But before I can say anything else, a volunteer comes over and pulls us both into packing some of the boxes I just made with canned goods and produce. I'm paired with Ryan because of proximity, but he doesn't even prod me like I'm expecting him to. He's efficient and focused, stuffing cans into boxes without saying a word.

I expect his usual self. Flirty, joking, distracted. But he's just working. Quick hands. Quiet intensity. Like this actually matters to him.

"Wren."

I blink and cough into my elbow. "What? What now?"

He stares at me. "Are you going to finish putting apples in the boxes?"

"Yup. Yep. Doing that right now."

He isn't just economical with his own time. He expects everyone else to be, too. There's no screwing around here. The look on his face is slightly impatient, like I'm a wayward boat that he has to steer in the right direction yet again.

For a hot second, I long to be the one he notices. Like I matter. Like I'm part of the world he keeps for himself. But I don't get that look. I never have.

I pick up my pace and try to focus only on getting produce into boxes. He comes right behind me and fills in a few more pantry staples, then I tape the boxes closed.

I look at him expectantly. "What now?"

He glances at his watch and jerks his head toward the kitchen. "Come on. Let's go jump onto the line and help distribute hot meals for a while. We can tell the girls working there to come over here and make some more boxes."

I nod. "I'm following you."

He cuts in, telling a couple of the contestants to take over where we just were. JacqLyn sweetly welcomes him, offering to give him mashed potatoes to dole out.

I roll my eyes and put on a fresh pair of clear plastic kitchen gloves, then get to work with a slotted spoon full of green beans. JacqLyn is suddenly very into giving out the rolls at the end of the line and squeezes next to Ryan affectionately.

"I just love doing this," she says. "Thanks so much for setting this up. This is really important work."

She's not wrong, but she is flirting her ass off.

Ryan thanks her for being here and then diverts his attention back to the line of people getting Styrofoam containers full of hot food. JacqLyn is not deterred. She keeps brushing his arm, making silly jokes. Saying things like "I bet you're good with your hands."

I roll my eyes so hard it might qualify as a workout.

Ryan eyes me and leans over with a sneaky smile. "Careful. You're spooning with rage. You don't wanna break anyone's to-go box."

"Your ego is beyond." I grit my teeth. "Just focus on your mashed potatoes."

He leans closer, whispering in my ear. "You know, it occurs to me that you might think I'm doing this for the show. But I'm not."

I touch the back of his arm and peer up into his eyes.

"You don't have to convince me. I get it. This place matters to you. It's just... not what I expected. That's all."

His expression is carefully neutral. "Yeah, well. People don't expect much from me. They just want me to put on the act."

That makes me snort. "I've seen the act. The protein powder. The stupid smirk. The girl-of-the-week energy. It's exhausting."

He shoots me a look. "Hey, at least it's working for me."

"What's that supposed to mean?" I ask.

"I'm not sitting alone every weekend night. I'm definitely not a virgin. Unlike some people I know."

I drop my spoon with a clatter and practically swallow my tongue. "What did you just say?"

He elbows me in the ribs. "Jesus, Rustin. I was just joking."

I'm too busy blushing and staring at the green beans to answer.

"Wait," he says. "You're not actually a virgin, are you?"

My entire body locks up. I can feel the flush rising up my neck. I want to disappear into the piles of mashed potatoes more than I can say.

"S-shut up," I stammer.

"Oh my God. You are. Jesus."

I sneak a look at him. His eyes are as wide as if I've just grown a third head.

"Shut up," I whisper. "Seriously. Don't talk to me. There are people all around."

He raises his hands innocently but starts grinning like a hillbilly maniac.

"I didn't mean anything by it. I just didn't see that coming, either. I guess there are surprises for both of us."

A volunteer cuts in with a tray of green beans to freshen

my tray. I set mine back and roll, heading to the food pantry area before I can do something embarrassing like, for instance, cry. Or punch him. Or maybe both.

As I stalk out of the kitchen, I try not to think about how much I hate him. Or how much it hurt that he was amused.

He's not the villain I've made him out to be. Not entirely. If he's not the villain... then what am I? Just a girl who's been wrong this whole time?

RYAN

"SO WE HAVE the next few days off?" I ask Rich, who's currently jotting notes into his phone.

He doesn't look up. Just nods. "Yup. Two days off for everybody to mellow out. I suggest you go somewhere you won't be bothered by anyone. At least, that's what I'm gonna do. I book a hotel room, get some room service, and put the do-not-disturb sign on the door. It's heaven."

"Sounds lonely," I tell him.

That finally gets his attention. He looks up. "It's not. It's actually very relaxing. I get a massage and everything."

"All right. Well, if you don't need me..."

He waves a hand. "We're back on call Monday morning. I don't expect to hear from anyone until then."

I stand up in the production office and make my way out toward the house set. Rich's idea does appeal to me, but there's something more important right now.

Wren pops into my head. The way she looked at me after I kissed her the other night... That image is burned into my brain. This whole show is going to drive me insane.

I'll never stop remembering the way her lips curved up as she challenged me. *"You think I'm the only one who enjoys this?"*

I shudder. Wren avoided me all day yesterday. During the horseback riding excursion, she was radio silent. We had a group movie night in the common room and she sat behind a couch on the floor. When I called her name, she flinched.

What I did to deserve that? I don't know. Okay, yeah, I teased her about being a virgin. But I didn't know I was crossing a line. It was just a joke. I didn't mean to hit a nerve, but apparently I did.

It was a joke. A dumb, careless joke. I didn't know it would hit like that. I didn't know it would hollow her out from the inside. Now I can't stop replaying Wren's face as she walked away.

Maybe I could ignore it. Pretend I don't care. Let her stew in it.

That's what I've always done. Shut the door before someone else can slam it first. But she didn't even slam the door. She disappeared through it like I didn't matter. Like I didn't exist.

She wouldn't even look at me at the catered early dinner *The Last Kiss* hosted. I tried to talk to her. She set down a plate she'd been piling with salad and walked off the set.

Yikes.

Now she's stuck in my head in a way that's not even fun anymore. It's just distracting, I guess. I don't mind being the villain in her story, but not even appearing on the page? That's unacceptable.

I spend a few minutes scrolling on my phone before I hit

on exactly what I need. A local event on the other side of Atlanta. A little rinky-dink ice skating rink that pairs night-time skating with overhead projections of constellations. It just so happens that tonight is "Stargazer Night." Constellations and mythology and all that. I don't think she's into skating, but stars? Maybe.

I remember her rambling once about some Greek myth, eyes lit up like she was casting spells. I didn't listen closely back then. I wish now that I would have.

I hope this little excursion is enough to act as an apology for what I said to make it weird between us.

When I knock on the door to the room she's staying in, I find her alone. She's stacking some books beside a back-pack, so I assume she's packing to head home. When I interrupt her, Wren looks up, then flushes.

"What do you want?" she asks. Not angry this time. Just flat. Without tone. "Haven't you gotten your kicks out of tormenting me for the week?"

"What are you doing right now?" I ask instead of answering her question.

I glance around the room and purse my lips, thinking how it kind of sucks that the women are all bunking together like this.

"What am I doing?" she repeats. "Throwing some books into my bag so I can go home and not look at anyone."

"Is your apartment fixed then?"

Wren fixes me with a look. "No. Jay said they found mold, so the apartment has to be completely stripped and renovated. Good timing, I guess, since I have to be here for the next month and a half."

I tilt my head. "Well, rather than go home to your brother's house, I think you should throw on some jeans and sneakers. Dress like you used to."

Her eyes narrow. "Why? You gonna stop me from flirting with guys at bars again?"

God, she tries my patience. But this Wren, combative Wren, is better than the one who flinched when I said her name.

"You'll see."

She shakes her head and looks down. "This better not be a date, Haart. Are you dreaming? Because if not, we're in reality, and we are not going on a fucking date. Now get ready."

"Only one way to find out," I tease.

"Fuck off." Her face grows hot pink. She flicks her hand in a sweeping motion. "Out. So I can change."

God, she's so hot when she's mad. I can't help the smile the breaks across my face.

Ten minutes later, I'm waiting downstairs when she walks out carrying an overstuffed backpack, wearing jeans and a black-and-red Atlanta Ice Storms jersey.

My mouth goes dry.

That jersey... I lost that thing a few years ago. Washed it so many times it turned soft and faded. It disappeared. I mourned it. But I'm pretty sure I just found it.

My practice jersey.

She gives me a subtle smirk, then hides the jersey beneath her coat, buttoning it up.

With her hair down and her lips glossy, I forget how to swallow.

I can't even check out how low her jeans are riding on her hips because I refuse to let myself look.

"Is that my shirt?" I ask, narrowing my eyes as she gets closer.

Her lips twitch with dark amusement. "Maybe. You said jeans. Didn't say no team merch."

"You can't just wear that around," I argue. "Especially if this isn't a date or anything."

"I can wear whatever I want," she says, arching a brow. "Unless you feel like it's too precious."

I glare at her, grab her backpack, and frog-march her the couple hundred yards to the parking lot. I open the passenger door without a word, chuck her bag in the back seat, and slide into the driver's side.

"Is this what it's like when you glitch?" Wren asks, amused.

I don't even glance at her. My grip tightens on the steering wheel. "Don't start with me right now, little girl."

When we pull into the rink's half-empty parking lot, Wren doesn't say much. But I can see her trying to puzzle out what we're doing here.

The second we step inside, she makes a soft sound. Almost a gasp.

I have to agree. It's gasp worthy.

There are a million fairy lights strung around the rink's walls. But the main attraction is the projection. Smooth white silk panels hung from the ceiling, with constellations in pink, white, and purple drifting slowly overhead. They shimmer against the dark backdrop, mirrored faintly in the ice below. Soft, romantic music plays over the speakers. The whole place smells like popcorn and crisp air.

"This..." Wren trails off. "I don't hate this."

I nudge her with my elbow and wink. "Yeah, don't get emotional or anything."

"I'd have to have emotions to get emotional," Wren fires back.

It takes a minute for me to grab a pair of rental skates. Once I've got them, we lace up in silence.

I glance over. She's struggling to lace the first skate,

hands fumbling. I finish tying mine, then bend down in front of her and wave her hands away.

"What are you doing?" she asks, tone slightly offended.

"I don't want to be here for the rest of my life, Chirp," I tease. "Let me help you. I'm a pro, after all."

I grab her foot and angle her ankle, lacing her skate like it's second nature. She goes weirdly quiet. Her face turns pink.

I don't comment on it. But I feel it too. The electricity, flowing back and forth between us like a live wire.

We get onto the ice and she wobbles but somehow manages to stay upright. I have the urge to show off, skate lazy circles around her, but I repress it. Maybe later, when she's more comfortable. Then I can tease her again.

"So you picked this place?" she asks.

"What, you think I can't pick something you'd actually like?"

She pokes her cheek out with her tongue and shrugs. "No. I figured you heard about it from someone else."

"Ouch." I place a hand over my heart, pretending to be wounded. "That stings, Rustin. Just so you know, I set this up. I knew you'd like the stars. I think they're being projected from a live telescope in New Mexico or something."

She tilts her head up and stares at the projected sky, mouth dropping open. But because she's so tragically bad at skating, she immediately trips and almost eats it.

I catch her by the arms and steady her. Then I shift, skating backward so she can cling to my hands.

She looks embarrassed. Extremely so. But honestly, it's kind of awesome that she's even trying. She sucks, yeah. But most Georgia girls would've tapped out by now.

"This feels like a setup," Wren mutters.

I snort. "It's not. You're just awful at skating."

"Rude," she says, but she flashes me a quick grin.

We make slow loops around the rink, taking our time, watching the constellations shift above us. Every time she stumbles, I catch her. Our hands stay locked longer than they need to. Our faces hover too close.

God, this does feel like a date. I hate how easy it is to pretend. How natural it feels to hold her hands, to catch her when she stumbles, to want her to lean on me. It's too real. That's the problem.

It's not a date. I've been explicit about that. If she were another girl, any other girl, it would be.

But she's Jay's little sister. God knows, every time we so much as bicker in front of him, he loses his shit. I can't even imagine trying to tell him I was dating his baby sister.

It's not even worth imagining.

Somewhere around the third lap, Wren points up. "Do you see that one?"

She points at a cluster of stars. "That's Orion. The guy with the belt. Fun fact. He was super arrogant and said he could kill all the animals on earth. So the gods sent a giant scorpion to murder him."

I grin. "That's morbid."

Her eyes sparkle. "Greek myths are all chaos and consequences."

"You love them."

"Oh yeah." She lights up, launching into a story about Cassiopeia, who bragged too much and got thrown into the sky upside down. Then about her daughter Andromeda, who was so beautiful that her mother boasted she was more gorgeous than Poseidon's sea nymphs.

"So Andromeda got chained to a rock in the middle of the sea as a sacrifice to a sea monster named Cetus," she explains. "Then, somehow, the story turns into Perseus riding a flying horse and accidentally killing people with Medusa's head."

I can't interrupt her. Or maybe I don't want to. Her eyes are glowing, her face animated. Her words tumble out faster than her mouth can keep up.

I realize I've never seen her like this.

In all the years I've known her, I've been more interested in embarrassing her than actually paying attention to what lights her up.

The problem is, it's not just hot.

It's adorable.

Wren's talking about the stars, telling their stories. She forgets to be defensive. She forgets to glare.

She just... glows. I've spent years giving her hell, keeping her at arm's length, pretending she's nothing but a nuisance. But right now, I want to bottle this version of her. The one who forgets to hate me. The one who smiles like she's not afraid of being seen.

It's not much longer until she heaves a sigh and wrinkles her nose. "I think my legs are going to give out if we skate anymore."

"Well, we can't have that, can we?" I glance toward the benches. "Come on, let's sit down. I bet there's a booth where we can get some hot cocoa. What do you say?"

This part? The gentle part? It's new to me. I don't know what I'm doing, but something about Wren makes me want to try anyway.

She looks up at me like I'm the sun and she's the moon, quietly orbiting. "That sounds perfect."

I grab the cocoa while she takes off her skates. When I return, we sit together in the stands. As I settle next to her, she slides closer without hesitation, her eyes locked on the hot cocoa in my hands.

"For me?" she asks.

My lips tip up. "For you."

I hand it over. Our fingers brush. She doesn't even seem to notice that she's leaning against my shoulder as she sips. I don't move. I grip my own Styrofoam cup with both hands, afraid that if I shift, I'll ruin the moment.

"This is good," Wren murmurs, taking another sip. "I think I needed this. Maybe I had a little low blood sugar or something."

I smile and glance up at the drifting constellations. We sit like that for a long time. Silent, but close. I don't quite know what's happening here. This kind of quiet wouldn't be something I'd aim for on a normal date.

Not that this is a date.

But Wren makes the silence feel easy. Companionable. I don't have to impress her. I don't have to be funny or smooth or try at all. I can just be myself.

That's a strange sort of relief.

We stay quiet on the drive home, too. The good kind of quiet. Her head tilts toward the window. My hand flexes on the steering wheel like it wants to do something dumb.

What, I don't even know. Maybe touch her. Maybe something worse. My hormones are trying to get me killed.

I pull into the driveway beside my house. She unbuckles her seat belt but doesn't move to get out. I stare straight ahead, uncertain. I don't want to ruin tonight. I don't want to argue with her, either.

How do I talk to Wren without something stupid falling out of my mouth?

"Thanks for tonight," she says softly.

"No problem." I hesitate, then add, "It wasn't a date, though."

"Obviously." But still, she doesn't move.

Neither do I.

The silence should be awkward, but it's not. It's heavy. Charged. Like the pause before a crash… or a kiss.

We just sit there, staring at the windshield, breathing the same space. After a long moment, I glance over. She's already looking at me. Long red hair, glossy pink lips, green eyes wide and steady.

Before I can stop myself, I reach out and brush her cheek. Her lips part slightly. I know, before I even lean in, that I'm going to kiss her again.

This one is different. My lips find hers, soft and searching. She sighs into the kiss, then her hand curls into my hoodie, pulling me closer, deepening it.

Like she means it.

Like she wants it.

Her lips are soft, but there's hunger in the way she kisses me back. It guts me. Because this isn't just a kiss. It's something bigger. Something I'm not ready for.

God, I want to find out if that could possibly be true. But I can't. She's off-limits in her very special, very dangerous way.

I untangle myself gently and pull back.

She blinks up at me, studying my face.

"Still not a date," she whispers.

Good. Because if it were? That would mean I have something to lose.

I grin. "Hell no."

She rolls her eyes and gets out of the car. But she's smiling. She grabs her bag and heads toward her brother's house, just across the hedge and fence.

I sit there a minute longer. My heart's pounding. My brain's buzzing. My lips are still tingling.

All I can think is, God, I'm so screwed.

I think I might have the beginnings of a crush on my best friend's little sister. If I'm not careful, she's going to become someone I can't afford to lose.

What do I do about it, though?

thirteen

WREN

AFTER ALL THE ICE SKATING, I'm exhausted. Even if I got all amped up from kissing Ryan and practically skipped up to the spare bedroom. By the time I've changed into pajamas and my head finally hits the pillow, I'm out cold.

When I wake up the next morning, it's on the late side. The clock says twelve past ten. I shuffle to the bathroom, then lock my bedroom door and climb straight back into bed.

I touch myself while thinking of Ryan.

It doesn't take long. My fingers know exactly where to go. My brain is full of him. His mouth, his hands, the way he said *little girl* like he was tasting the words. I come fast and hard, biting my lip to stay quiet. But I don't stop there. I do it again. Then again.

Three times. Because I'm greedy. Greedy for him.

It's not just sex. It's the way he looked at me, the way he kissed me. That's what wrecks me. That's what I can't stop replaying. It felt like he wanted me. Me. But that can't be real, right?

Why I think that arrogant, smug asshole is a good thing to fantasize about, I don't know. I have no explanation for it. If anyone knew—Jay, the girls on set, Ryan himself. I think I'd dissolve into a puddle of humiliation. He can never know. No one can.

I think about what Elena said to me when she pulled me aside at the end of the night last night. *Be memorable or be gone.* Every single move I make now feels like it might be the one that gets me fired.

It certainly makes staying in bed much more appealing.

When I finally emerge from my bedroom at noon, Jay and Calla have deserted the house and left me to figure out my own schedule.

That works for me, honestly.

I climb back into bed and spend the rest of the early afternoon watching *Bob's Burgers* reruns. It's nice to just veg out. No eyes on me. No pretending. Just stillness. This is the only time I feel like I get to exist without performing. No microphones, no dates, no pretending. Just a blanket, cartoons, and the satisfying ache between my legs.

Eventually, I drag myself into the shower. Afterward, I dry my hair and quietly tuck away Ryan's special jersey. The one I stole a few years ago, the soft one he never lets anyone touch. Into the bottom of my bag like it's contraband.

It smells like him, like cedar and mint and a hint of whatever cologne he's always worn. I used to curl up in it at night and pretend he'd given it to me. Now it feels dangerous to keep.

I change into a black crop top with The Kills scrawled across the front in pink, then pull on a stretchy pair of black leggings that sit high on my waist. I crown the look with my black Converse and my same coat.

I feel… hot. All this time, I thought you had to feel

powerful to wear clothes like this. But in actuality, wearing these clothes gives me a weird, heady sense of power.

Like, for once, I can be the one who turns heads and breaks hearts.

Ta-da. Time to go try out my new outfit on a soft, receptive audience. I am ready to hang out with my big brother.

It's Saturday night. I already know what Jay's plans are. He's always at the Tin Shed Pub on Saturdays for trivia. I try to join him as much as possible.

The Rustin siblings are many things. Stubborn, impetuous, absolutely unwilling to admit that we're ever wrong. But we're an unstoppable trivia team. We're usually joined by a few of Jay's friends too, so I know it'll be a casual night of shouting answers over greasy bar food.

A small part of me kind of expects to see one particular giant hockey player sitting right next to him. I promise myself I won't be disappointed either way.

He probably won't be there. But if he is... what will I say? What will I do? What if he acts like last night meant nothing?

When I show up at the Tin Shed, I'm surprised by the crowd. The pub is packed. As I slip in the door, an old vinyl record spins in the corner. A dozen mismatched tables are already full of shouting regulars. It's hot and bright in here. I have to wade all the way to the back of the room to find Jay and Calla.

Every step into the pub feels like I'm walking across a stage. My coat's too warm, my leggings feel like sandpaper. I already regret the lipstick. What was I thinking? I'm not Calla. I don't float into rooms and own them.

But a year ago, I would've been somewhere in the background, hiding behind my laptop. Hoodie up. Eyes down.

Now I'm standing here in a pair of glittery Converse and

an outfit that turns heads. I don't shrink away from it. I don't apologize for it.

This version of me doesn't fade into the wallpaper. She's a little scary, but she's also mine.

"Hey," I say, giving Jay a quick hug before turning to Calla. I pull her into a longer, more satisfying one. Her curvy body is made for hugging. Not like mine. Skeletons make jokes about how gaunt I am.

Me, I'm all elbows and flatness. No one ever looked at me like I was built for anything but disappearing. Sometimes I'm pretty sure even Jay forgets I'm in the room.

I slide into the chair beside Calla. Jay shifts his gaze to his wife.

"Hey, babe," he says. "Can you give me and Wren a sec to catch up?"

Calla rises from the table and nods. "Of course. Bennett asked me to talk to him about wedding cake for an event they're having, so I'll just go do that."

She slips off. Jay moves into her seat and smiles at me.

"What's up, sis?" he asks. "I haven't heard a word from you in days. Are you all right?"

I take a deep breath and nod. "Yeah, absolutely. I'm sorry I didn't text you back. Work has been crazy."

Jay raises an eyebrow. "How are things at *The Last Kiss* set? Hope it's not too hectic for you."

That gives me pause.

"Well... funny you should say that. I thought I'd be pulling my hair out running around as a production assistant, but it turns out that's not what they need me for."

Jay stills and gives me a hard look.

The moment stretches between us. For a second, I hate lying. But I also hate that if I tell him the full truth, he'll try to fix it. That's what big brothers do. I can't afford to be fixed. Not right now.

"No," I say quickly. "Not like that. I'm actually filling in for a contestant. Hanging out in front of the camera. It's... surreal."

"Whoa. How did they talk you into that?" His brow furrows. "You've always been extremely camera shy."

I bob my head. "Yeah, I still am. But the head executive producer promised me a big fat bonus and a promotion if I played along. She and I have a plan. It's kind of fun to be the secret mole, so to speak."

I trail off for a second.

"Ryan is on the show," I add quietly.

I don't say the other part. That I kissed Ryan. That I can still feel it. That every time I look at him, my stomach flips like I'm sixteen again and hiding a stupid crush in my diary.

Jay's face screws up. "Wait. You guys are on the same show? I thought maybe they shot multiple seasons at once or something."

I can feel heat spreading up my neck and across my cheeks.

"He is the bachelor. And I'm playing along. Pretending to try to win him over. It's... silly."

That is an understatement if I've ever heard one.

"Wait. You and Ryan are supposed to be...?" Jay squints.

"We're not supposed to be anything, really," I say quickly. "Technically, I am supposed to be competing for him. To keep me on the show. But really, I'm just making him mad. You know how pissed off I make him."

Jay's shoulders relax a little. "Oh. I see. So it's just business as usual between you two, huh?"

I make a face, instantly feeling bad about the lie. It was a little white one, at first. But now it's grown into a big, hairy monstrosity. Still, I've already said it. So I just let it lie.

"Yup."

Jay cocks his head. "Do I need to straighten Ryan out?"

"No, no," I say, shaking my head and patting him on the arm. "I'm fine. I swear. We're just playing pretend in front of the camera. Honestly, nothing physical has even happened between us."

Which is not even close to the truth.

I blush, but Calla returns to the table just in time, still talking to Bennett about a cake. Jay's shoulders relax a little more.

"If you need me to, I'll straighten Ryan out," Jay repeats. "I can talk to him. Tell him to watch out for you."

"Please don't do that," I say quickly. "This is my job. It's only for another seven weeks. Then I'll have a promotion and be well on my way to a career in executive producing."

He wrinkles his nose, but nods. "Come here."

He pulls me into a hug, warm and solid. I let myself sink into it for a long moment. Jay is a good big brother and he gives great hugs.

Then, chaos arrives.

My friend Iris shows up with Cora. They're Calla's sisters. Cora, cool and intimidating in a sleek black dress and sharp heels that scream "courtroom drama." Iris in vintage boots and a cropped jacket, looking like a hurricane of fun.

Calla waves them over. I catch Bennett rising from his seat to offer it to Cora, but she pointedly ignores him and takes the empty seat beside Iris instead. Iris squeals, pulling me into a quick hug.

"Where have you been?" she demands. "You have *so much* to tell me about working on a reality show."

I smile and wiggle my eyebrows. "Later. I promise. Let's just get settled in and ready to play."

"Okay." She winks and moves closer to Cora. "Just let me know when you're ready to dish."

Bennett gets up to grab us menus while Jay proudly displays his clipboard, trivia quiz already printed out and color coded. "Are you ready for some sibling duo power?" he asks.

"You've got all three of the Nikolakis sisters here," Cora says, dry as ever. "We *still* might not stand a chance against table six."

She jerks her thumb toward a table of clipboard-wielding older women in matching baseball caps that read *Table Six Trivia Warriors*.

It's funny, but also terrifyingly nerdy.

Jay and I exchange a look.

"We're not losing to table six again," I mutter.

"No, we're not," Jay agrees. "I won't stand for it."

Ryan does me the massive disservice of sneaking up behind me. I guess my back is to the door. But when he comes around the table and drops into the seat next to me, sandwiched between me and Cora, he doesn't so much as glance in my direction.

He looks extremely casual. Henley, backward cap, smug grin. Like he didn't kiss me senseless with my brother right next door less than twenty-four hours ago.

"What's up, guys?" he says.

"'Sup," Jay replies with the briefest acknowledgment.

Bennett returns, sliding menus across the table. I head to the bar to grab drinks. It's so packed in here, I know I'll get served faster if I ask Ernie, the bartender, to just sneak me in rather than wait for our table ticket to come up.

I'm halfway through waving Ernie down when Iris slides in next to me, resting her chin on her hand.

"Give me updates," Iris says, so demanding it's almost funny.

I wave Ernie down and rattle off the drink order. Three pitchers: one cider, one beer, one Coke. Then I turn to my friend. She's still batting her lashes at me like I'm holding out a state secret. I can't help but smile.

"What do you want to know?"

"How is it working with Ryan?" she asks. "I never figured you guys would be more than nemeses, but it seems like with the show and all, you're going to have to get close."

I roll my eyes. "You need hobbies. Knitting. Bike riding. Soccer."

"You're my hobby," she says, deadpan. "You're glowing, so I want to know what you've been doing that gives you that look."

"I got new clothes." I point down to my shirt as a way of dodging her question.

She gives me a once-over and smirks. "That crop top looks amazing on you, by the way. I've never seen you wear anything like it."

"Must be the lighting in here," I say, brushing it off. "Seriously, there's nothing to know. I'd tell you if there was. It's just work, work, work."

Ernie arrives with the pitchers. I gather them carefully as he slides a stack of plastic cups toward Iris. She pouts but grabs them anyway, cradling them like treasure.

Iris ends up squeezing between Cora and Bennett, which is a whole vibe of its own.

I set the pitchers down and pour myself a cup of cider. Ryan opts for the Coke, because of course, he does. He's always been annoyingly responsible. Still, it surprises me that he hasn't even looked at me since he sat down.

Until now.

"You still intense about trivia?" he asks, lifting his glass slightly.

"Yes," I say, giving him a wicked grin. "Some people train for marathons. I train for this."

He shakes his head. "Nerdy and competitive. It's such a dangerous combination."

My mouth goes a little dry. I meet his gaze and bite my lower lip, slow and deliberate.

"You have no idea."

I could be wrong, but I'm pretty sure his ears turn a little pink. He smirks and looks away. But he doesn't push it.

Ryan is staring at me. But it's not like before. This time, it doesn't feel like pity. It feels like he actually sees me.

And I kind of like it.

The first round starts: classic movie quotes. "You had me at hello." "You're gonna need a bigger boat." "Here's looking at you, kid." "There's no crying in baseball." "I'll have what she's having."

Jay's always the strongest at this round, but Calla and I lean in, whispering answers to him as he scribbles them down. Iris completely forgets the rules and yells out "She doesn't even go here!" before anyone can stop her.

"Iris! Don't yell out the answers," Calla whispers, shushing her.

Iris pouts and folds her arms.

Round two is geography. I am dead weight. Cora and Calla dominate. Correcting pronunciations, rattling off obscure capital cities like they've been training for this since birth. Bennett looks personally wounded every time Cora beats him to a buzzer.

"You memorize an atlas?" he grumbles.

Cora's smile cuts like a knife. "I like being right."

Round three starts with spider trivia. I blank on the first two questions. Biology is also not my thing. Hello, liberal arts degree. But then the host pivots.

"Who was turned into a spider after defeating the goddess Athena in a weaving contest?"

My hand shoots up. I lean toward Jay, starting to whisper, "Arach—"

"Arachne," Ryan says first.

I blink. "What?"

He shrugs. "What? I listen sometimes."

I stare at him. He doesn't smirk. Doesn't tease. Just meets my eyes.

Calla notices. Of course, she does. Her eyebrows inch up just slightly, but she doesn't say anything.

I tell myself I'm sitting here because it's the open seat. Not because I want to be near him. Not because I want him to smell my perfume and remember touching me. But the truth is, I don't know why I do anything around Ryan anymore.

"How do you know about Arachne?" I ask.

"Greek mythology's the only thing you ever talk about," Ryan says casually. "I remember that one because you told me that horrifying story about Athena turning her into a spider."

My stomach flips. "You remember that?"

He nods. "It was dark."

"You're dark," I shoot back, soft but automatic.

The rest of the round, we go back and forth like that. Less bite, more spark. Every time I toss something his way, he returns it lighter than I expect. He doesn't call me Chirp. Doesn't needle me at all. Just keeps shifting closer until our elbows are brushing at the table.

At one point, Jay gets up to hand in our answer sheet. Calla leans toward me.

"So," she murmurs, flicking her eyes toward Ryan. "What's happening there?"

"Nothing," I say too quickly.

"Oh, you like him."

"I do not."

Jay returns and Calla sinks back into her seat, grinning like the damn Sphinx.

When the final tally comes in, we lose by two points. Jay frowns and pushes back from the table, muttering something before heading outside.

Calla sighs, grabbing their coats. "Drama," she mutters, and follows him out.

Ryan lifts his glass toward me. I shake my head and lift mine in return.

We linger after the loss. Long enough for Iris to eat the rest of the fries. For Bennett and Cora to fall into a whispered, half-playful argument about whether malicious compliance is a legitimate workplace strategy. Whatever that means.

By nine thirty, Iris and Cora are getting ready to go, still laughing as they pull on their coats.

Iris points at me. "You better call me."

"I will," I say, nodding.

Cora flashes us both a brief smile. "Night, guys."

I stand and grab my coat. The crowd has thinned. Bennett is long gone. Ryan follows me toward the front door, quiet.

Outside, the air is cold and clear. He holds the door

without saying anything. We walk a few steps together, not looking at each other, but not walking away, either.

The gravel crunches under our feet. Behind us, the Tin Shed's neon sign flickers.

Ryan stops first.

"You didn't yell at me tonight," he says.

That surprises me a little. But he's right.

"You didn't deserve it," I say. "Even when you stole my favorite category."

"You knew the answer," he says. "You earned it."

He snorts softly, then looks at me for a long beat. "You okay?"

"I'm fine. Just because I'm competitive..."

"That's not what I'm asking."

I go still. "Oh."

"Day before yesterday," he says, voice low. "When I called your name... you flinched."

I dig my toe into the gravel. I was trying to forget that. But now that he's said it, I can't avoid it.

He sticks his hands in his pockets, not pressuring me. Just... waiting.

I glance at him, trying to read his expression. But there's nothing on his face. Just patience.

"I flinched because it felt like a joke," I admit. "Like you were about to say something awful. I braced for it."

"I wasn't," he says softly. "I mean it."

"Maybe you didn't mean to..." I trail off.

He reaches out, fingers brushing my arm, pulling me gently toward him. We're not exactly embracing, but we're close.

"I can be nice," he says. "I try to be nice to other people. I could try with you."

That makes me smile. "That would be okay."

"You walking home?"

"Yeah. It's only a few blocks."

"Me too," he says. "So... maybe we can walk together."

He stares at me. I nod. "That would be good."

God help me, this conversation sounds like two people who've never spoken English before.

I shove my hands into my coat pockets and walk beside him.

"You were good tonight," he says.

"I'm always good."

He snorts. "Yeah. You really are."

It's weirdly sincere, the way he says it.

I look up. He's watching my mouth. That fact burns a hole straight through me.

So that's what Ryan wants. He's not the only one.

I reach out, touch his arm gently, and pull him to a stop.

"Wren," he says, almost warning.

I shush him. "You know you want to."

"I want to do a lot of things," he murmurs, voice thick. "Dirty things. Stuff you wouldn't be interested in."

I lick my lips and step closer. "Who says I wouldn't be?"

Thank God it's dark and there's no streetlight nearby, because I'm blushing like a maniac. His eyes widen.

"You..."

A horn blares.

Cora's Mercedes rolls up. Iris leans out the passenger window. "Hey! You guys want a ride?"

I drop my hand and turn toward the car. "You go ahead," Ryan says, stepping back. "I forgot something inside."

He walks off fast. Like, faster than I've ever seen him move.

I turn toward the car, disappointment practically

tattooed across my face. Iris sees it immediately and murmurs, "Well. Shit."

I shoot her a glare and climb into the back seat, hands still shaking.

I don't know what's worse. That Ryan didn't kiss me...

Or that I wanted him to so badly.

I've been called many things. Stubborn. A know-it-all. *That weird girl who lives in my dorm*, according to the irritating roommate I was paired with freshman year.

But reckless isn't one of those things. Yet now, I am downright self-ruinous. And over what? A hot guy with dreamy blue eyes and a smile that won't quit?

I have to get my head on straight or I'm doomed.

RYAN

WAFFLE HOUSE IS EXACTLY the same as it's always been, with crowded booths and a few stools at the bar facing the kitchen. No matter how broke I was as a kid, I could usually afford a cup of coffee and a plate of hash browns. I've been meeting Coach T here since before my parents split up, before my mom walked out and left us alone, before I tried to make it on my own, before being placed with the coach.

He's a man who knows everything about me. All the messy, ugly bits. Still shows up when I call. There's something priceless in that.

He's the only man who ever looked at me like I wasn't broken. Like maybe I could become someone. When I was a kid, Coach T treated me with a firm respect that resonates with me to this day. Even now, part of me wants him to fix it, to tell me what the hell to do.

He slides into the booth across from me and inhales. "Smells good in here."

The scent of fried bacon and fresh coffee hangs thick in

the air. It's all familiar. Too familiar, really. I hate how much I need that right now.

Last night, I walked away from her. Because staying? Letting myself have what I wanted? That would've wrecked me. Hell, it already has.

I sip my coffee just as the waitress comes over for our order. She tops off Coach's mug, then hurries off to the line cook, calling it in.

Coach sips and gives me a once-over. "Well, you look terrible. What happened to you?"

"Thanks," I say sarcastically. I know Coach T hates sarcasm, so I try to pivot. "You still mad about that offsides call last week?"

He grunts. "It was bullshit. But you know what else is bullshit? You trying to bait and switch. I asked you here to talk."

I've always been good at pivoting. When I was a kid, I learned fast that if you change the subject fast enough, people stop asking about bruises or empty cupboards.

I shake my head and try to deflect. "Is it the hockey team? The league giving you problems?"

Yes. Let's talk about that. Let's talk about anything other than the girl I almost kissed and definitely can't stop thinking about.

I press my lips together and sigh. "No. I'm doing a side gig of sorts. I got a call from *The Last Kiss* reality TV show. They wanted me to be the bachelor this season. Offered a nice chunk of change, so I'm filming the show during the summer break."

His brows go up. "I didn't know you were doing that. Isn't that a lot of stress?"

I wave away his concern. "It's really not stressful. It's

just... you know. I'm supposedly dating all these women. They're all driving me nuts."

I pause and stare into my coffee mug. "Jay's little sister is on the show, too. One of the bachelorettes."

Just saying it makes something twist inside me. She's not supposed to be here. Not in my space. Not tangled up in my head.

Coach knows who Jay is. Jay does a lot of charity work with middle and high school hockey teams, so Coach just bobs his head. "You don't get along with that girl, if I remember correctly."

"She's always been a thorn in my side. Sharp, sarcastic, impossible. Now we're on the show together. There are cameras. There are dates."

Wren herself. All sharp edges and soft eyes. She sees too much. Feels too much. She's everything I avoid, wrapped in the one person I can't push away.

I hesitate. "The other night... I sort of kissed her."

Even saying it aloud feels dangerous. Like I'm naming something that shouldn't exist. Coach's silence is heavy. Not judging. Just waiting.

Coach raises an eyebrow. "For the cameras?"

It started that way. Or maybe it didn't. Hell, I don't know anymore. She messes with my head. I can't see straight when she's around.

I slowly shake my head. "No. Off camera."

"And she wanted you to kiss her?"

I think about the way Wren looked at me, how her fingers curled in my shirt and pulled me closer.

"Yeah," I say eventually. "I'm pretty sure she was into it."

"Well, you're a big boy. You're a grown man. You know

what you're doing. Just be careful. You don't want to mess around with her and break her heart. She's Jay's little sister. He'll probably kick your ass if you do."

It stings more than it should. Not because he's wrong. But because he's right. Because I don't know if I could stop myself even if I wanted to.

"Yeah. I know. I'm handling it. I think," I lie.

Coach nods slowly, thoughtful. Then he changes the subject. It's like he can feel how close I'm getting to saying too much.

"How's the money?"

I tense. I don't like talking about this. Not even with him. Money always makes things weird. But I'm not going to lie to Coach. He knows me. He's probably the only person who can understand.

"I've got like two million on hand."

The waitress appears suddenly with our breakfast. Steak and eggs for both of us, fulfilling the ritual. I pick up my fork and knife and point them at the steak.

"I've got about twenty million invested in low index funds," I add. I still check my bank app every night. I still wake up sweating from dreams where the money's gone and Ellie's little again, crying because we're out of cereal. I can't stop running from that version of my life. I finish with, "But I still feel like it's not enough."

Coach takes a bite of his toast and asks, "Not enough for what, exactly?"

I sigh. "I don't know. For Ellie. For me. For everything. What if my career ends tomorrow? What if I can't get another sponsorship deal? I thought if I had five million, I'd feel safe. Then I thought another five, or another ten would do it. But it turns out I always worry. What if I make a terrible mistake and my hard work vanishes overnight?"

Coach doesn't look up from his steak as he cuts it into careful pieces.

"You've done more than enough, son. You should feel secure at this point."

"I don't know if there is any 'feeling secure.' Something can always happen."

He's quiet for a beat. Then gently, he says, "You can't control everything, Ryan. You can try, but someday something's gonna hit you sideways. It won't matter how much money you've got saved."

That's the only way I've survived. Controlling everything. My image. My game. My goddamn feelings. Especially the ones that wear eyeliner and call me an asshole with a mouth like honey and venom.

His words piss me off more than I want to admit. I hate when he's right.

"Let's change the subject," I say. "Tell me about your Little League team. How's that going?"

His eyes light up. Coach T isn't the most talkative person. He's never been that way. But he's animated when he talks about the types of players he's working with and his plans for them.

He carries most of the conversation while I demolish my steak and eggs. Then I push the plate away, toast untouched.

He snags my toast and smiles. "I love Waffle House toast. I don't know what kind of bread they use, but it's so buttery and crisp. Always perfect."

It's an important part of the ritual. Meeting for lunch here.

I smile as I get out of the booth and pull out my wallet. "I should go. Gotta get some shut eye. I have an elimination tomorrow on the reality show. Have to send two girls home."

He eyes me carefully. "You sure you're okay?"

"I'm good."

I pick up the check and he looks at me, pinning me in place with his gaze.

"Ryan," he warns.

I shake my head. "Are you kidding? You took me and Ellie in when we were kids. Paid for meals and hockey and Ellie's ballet. I can certainly cover one little meal after you raised a hockey superstar."

He looks like he wants to argue but lets it go.

I go up to the register and pay, then we walk out of the Waffle House together.

He stops by his car and looks me up and down. "You know you can always call me, right?"

I nod.

He claps a hand on my shoulder. "I love you, kid."

I freeze. Those three words are sacred. Dangerous. The last time I said them, my mother left and never came back. I can't risk putting them on anyone else's shoulders.

It's not that I don't want to say it back. I love Coach. I try to make it obvious through my actions. But that word is only for Ellie. No one but my little sister gets to hear it come out of my mouth.

So I just nod again. "Thanks, Coach."

He squeezes my shoulder and then lets me go.

I head for my car and get in. My stomach is in a knot. My chest is tight. I feel worse than I did before lunch.

But I can't afford to fall apart. Not now. Not ever.

The late afternoon shoot is set at what's supposed to look like a fancy spa. There's a large Jacuzzi bubbling on the left with steam curling into the air. A cold plunge pool is on the right. The backdrop is a spa-type thing, all polished wood and soft lighting. Wooden benches surround the pools on three sides.

Luckily, the set is warm, so when Rich suggests I hit the Jacuzzi shirtless, I only roll my eyes and toss my shirt to him. I tug a towel around my waist and start toward the water.

"Actually," Rich says, stopping me. "I want you on the bench here. If you want in the Jacuzzi, you've got to do the Compatibility Plunge first."

I sigh.

The producers are calling it the Compatibility Plunge. Cute. Rich hands me a stack of cards with messy handwriting. The girls wrote answers to personal prompts. I'm supposed to guess who said what.

If I guess right, we get in the hot tub together. If I guess wrong, the girl takes a plunge in the freezing water and has to answer a tough question on camera.

It's classic reality show drama. I get it. It's entertaining. But still, I take a breath and try to center myself.

The girls start coming out one by one, all wrapped in identical white silk robes. Bare legs, nervous smiles. I spot Wren clutching her sash like it personally offended her. She's already glaring at the setup like she's seconds away from dismantling the entire production with sheer force of will.

My mouth goes dry. I've seen what's under that robe before. Bathing suits, beach days on Lake Lanier. But something feels different this time. Maybe it's because I hadn't kissed her then. Those were simpler times.

Now, I can't stop thinking about how soft her lips felt against mine. I shift slightly on the bench, trying to get my head in the game.

Rich waves a cue card at me. "Let's go, Romeo."

Right. Showtime.

I'm unraveling. Slowly, silently. Because if I fall apart now, if I admit I care, then I've already lost.

And I can't stand for that.

RYAN

I STAND and open my arms, gesturing to the girls. "Ladies, welcome."

I pause and glance at Rich, who's standing off camera. He makes an encouraging face.

I continue. "This is a little adventure we like to call the Compatibility Plunge. I have here..." I hold up the index cards. "The answers to the questions you wrote down earlier. If I can guess which one of you wrote the quote on this card, then you and I spend some quality time together in the hot tub.

"If not, you walk straight to that pool over there and take a cold plunge. After you dunk your head under and come up for air, I'll ask you a question."

I smile, trying to lighten the mood. "The goal tonight is to give me a better idea of who I'm compatible with. First week, I got rid of Trinity right away because she didn't share the same values. I knew we were never going to be romantic.

"This week, I've spent a little more time with all of you.

I'm looking forward to seeing whether we're actually compatible."

"Are you ready to go?"

The girls applaud lightly, but no one looks thrilled. I can't say I blame them. This setup is borderline insane.

I glance at Wren. She has one brow cocked while she stares off into the distance. I don't know what she's thinking, but I'd bet good money it's something foul about me.

"All right. Let's begin."

I brandish the cards and read the first one aloud. "What's your biggest fear in a relationship?" I pause. "This one says, 'Getting ghosted again.'"

I scan the group, considering. No one's mentioned being ghosted before, so I go out on a limb. "Daisy."

Daisy ducks her head in her hands. She raises her hand, looking scared.

"Okay. So I go in the cold plunge pool?"

"Yep, that's exactly what you do."

She shrugs off her robe and lays it on the wooden bench. Her glittery swimsuit does very little to keep her warm. She squeals on her way in but takes the plunge, surfacing with a shiver and hugging herself.

I read the follow-up. "I'm supposed to ask: What do you look for in a guy?"

Daisy, still dripping and breathless, answers, "Right now? Someone that's warm-blooded."

The girls laugh, but her answer feels lazy to me. Still, I nod.

She scrambles out of the pool and a PA hands her a plush terry cloth robe.

"Ready for the next question?" I smile. The girls murmur and nod.

"What's one thing you've lied about in the last week?" I

read, "'I told the crew I'm okay sharing a bathroom, but I'm not.'"

What a self-centered little revelation. I keep that bit to myself.

I look around and bite my lip. "I'm going to say... Nikki."

Nikki makes a face and shakes her head. "Wasn't me."

Divya steps forward, looking sheepish. "That was me. I didn't realize you were going to read them out loud."

"Fair enough. Into the pool you go."

She throws her white robe carelessly on the floor and stalks over to the plunge. Her barely-there bikini is white, matching her light brown skin perfectly. After hemming and hawing, she finally forces herself to jump in, splashing water over my legs and hitting a few of the girls nearby.

Of course, she's making a scene. Again.

She surfaces, and I glance at the next question. "What's the last thing you did that scared you?"

Divya doesn't hesitate. "I drove a car on the Autobahn last month and redlined it the whole way. It was insane. I almost hit someone."

Yeah. I don't know what kind of image she's trying to project here, but I'm definitely never dating someone that self-absorbed.

She hurries out of the pool before anyone even hands her a robe. I turn back to the group, card in hand.

"Okay, ladies. I guess I'm not compatible with some of you, but there are still plenty of questions left to be answered."

In truth, the challenge is harder than it probably should be. I go through Mei, Nikki, and Raven before I finally hit on a question I can guess.

"What's something you'd never tell me to my face?"

The answer reads, "You make my stomach do stupid shit."

It's charming. My gut says JacqLyn. "JacqLyn."

She throws up her arms and does a little dance before stripping out of her robe and handing it to Heidi. She makes a beeline for me.

She's voluptuous and wearing a bright orange bikini that barely holds in her boobs. I don't really want her to touch me, but I go along with the plan. We both walk into the bubbling Jacuzzi.

She uses the moment to her full advantage. Hooks her arm in mine, brushes her feet against my legs, and kisses me.

It's stiff. Not because of JacqLyn. She's doing her best to make it sexy. But I feel like I'm made of concrete when she presses her lips to mine. There is absolutely zero physical chemistry there.

Interesting. I would normally pick a zany, outgoing girl like JacqLyn to hook up with. I guess you can never tell who you're going to have weird vibes with.

When JacqLyn finally backs off, I swallow and make eye contact with Wren. She's pointedly looking in the other direction. Two cameramen are actively filming her reaction. Subtle, it is not.

JacqLyn sighs. "I wish we could stay here forever."

Rich holds up his hand, tapping his wrist like he's pointing to a watch.

I jump out of the Jacuzzi, then force myself to turn and help JacqLyn out.

"Yeah, maybe some other time," I say vaguely.

JacqLyn is gorgeous and fun. But honestly, she's way too much for me to handle. It takes a man with balls of steel to tame a filly like her.

"Okay, last question," I say, grabbing the index cards again. "How would someone know you were falling in love with them?"

That's a heavy one.

The answer: "I stop pretending not to care. I let them see the weird parts, the dark parts, the too much parts."

My eyes travel to Wren. She's looking at me like a trapped mouse.

Yeah. That one's hers.

But I don't want to call her out, so I point at Letitia. "Letitia, I think you said that."

Letitia puts her hands on her hips. "You know I didn't say that. I'm way too firm for all that."

"So who did?" I ask.

For a second, no one responds. The girls glance at each other, some murmuring. At last, Wren raises her hand.

"I said it."

She strips quickly, revealing a bright pink bikini that hugs her curves perfectly. She walks straight into the cold plunge like she doesn't even feel it. She dips herself under, then stands up, water running down her body.

She's so fucking attractive. I can't *stand* it.

I glance at the card, my mouth twisting like I've bitten a lemon. "What's something you'd never tell me?"

Without missing a beat, Wren answers, "High school. All of it. Burn it down."

Yeah. That sounds about right.

"All right. You can..."

She submerges herself one more time before climbing out of the cold plunge. I cock a brow. Wren would be the one who enjoyed a cold plunge. Her icy inner core probably loves the chill of it.

I invite the girls to join me in the Jacuzzi for a few

minutes. A few of them do. Most head upstairs to change before the elimination.

When the time comes, I stand at the edge of the set, towel slung low around my waist. Steam curls around my ankles and my heart thuds like I just finished a game.

I'm only supposed to send home two girls, but I already know I won't get along with a handful of them.

Divya probably shouldn't be eliminated. She's what the producers keep calling a villain. But some of the girls are still question marks. If they haven't made an impression by now, I'm ready to let them go.

I gather up my roses and hand them out to everyone except for Brooke and Letitia.

"Brooke and Letitia, if you'll step forward."

Brooke doesn't look surprised. Letitia puts her hands over her mouth and starts crying, but I'm pretty sure she's faking it.

This is standard reality show stuff. I should quiz all three of the women, act conflicted, and then keep one for drama. But I clear my throat.

"I'm opting to send you home."

Brooke looks stunned. "But I thought we were connecting!"

"I realize I've reached the end of the road with you." I shrug. "I'm sorry."

I don't even get to finish before Brooke flips her hair and storms off in a fury. Letitia just offers me a hug. I accept it, wishing her luck. She vanishes and the director calls cut.

I'm very careful not to look at Wren. But it's hard.

I know I shouldn't care what she thinks. But I can feel her gaze burning into me as she witnesses my charades.

What would she say if she knew how I felt?

sixteen

WREN

WE FINALLY WRAP FILMING AROUND 11 p.m. Everyone is pretty tired. We all veg out for a few minutes in the living room without saying a word to each other. Eventually, I head upstairs and change into my pink silky shorts and white tank top. Then I grab an Atlanta Ice Storms hoodie and pull it on, zipping it quickly.

I keep replaying the way Ryan looked at me during the challenge. There was something hot in his eyes. Curious. Like he was starting to wonder who I really am.

Who am I? That's the question. I feel like I've been changing, molting, like I'm almost ready to emerge from my cocoon.

Wait. Did I just compare myself to a butterfly? I really must be out of my mind.

I lie down on my bed and try to read a little, but my mind won't stop spinning. Mostly, I'm thinking about Ryan. The way he looked at me right before I took the cold plunge. Like he saw straight through me.

My brain won't stop spinning. I need quiet, I need stillness, but mostly, I need to stop remembering the way his eyes tracked me like I was something worth seeing.

No one's ever looked at me like that. Of course, the one person who finally does is my big brother's best friend. One man that I absolutely can't have. Figures.

I sit up and decide to take my book downstairs. A few people are still watching TV in the living room. Ryan is nowhere to be found, which kind of makes sense. He's probably not looking to hang out with one of the bachelorettes right now.

I scrunch my face and try to think of where I can go, somewhere without cameras but with good light. Somewhere comfortable. Like the confessional trailer.

It's only a few steps from the house. It's fully powered. I climb the steps and flip the lights on. At one end of a long modern pink couch, a huge lens faces it. That's where we're supposed to sit and relay everything that's happened to us each day. So far, I've only been in here once, but I'm sure the producers will start dragging me in soon enough.

I close the door behind me and settle on the couch. There are a lot of snuggly pillows. I prop myself up on them. At first, I look at the camera, remembering every stupid lie I've told in confessional. But then I open my book and try to relax.

I manage maybe two pages before I hear the door creak open. My heart leaps into my throat, but I should have known who it was.

Of course, it's him. Of course. My pulse taps a frantic rhythm as he closes the door behind him, sealing us inside.

Ryan. The only person who might be gently stalking me.

"I figured you were out here somewhere."

I lick my top lip and look at him. Silence stretches

between us. He doesn't come closer. Just stands there, watching me.

I'm not exactly sure what he wants.

I exhale. "You sent home two girls."

"I did."

"Why? Why them, I mean?"

"Because two of them were lying, and one of them didn't even try to get to know me."

I tilt my head a fraction. "You're not supposed to break the rules."

The second the words leave my mouth, I flush. Breaking the rules is apparently going around lately.

His lips lift into a smirk. "Neither are you. Can I sit?"

I wave at the pillows beside me. "It's a free country."

He sprawls close, not so close that I can feel the heat of his body, but close enough that I can smell the shampoo in his wet hair. He's wearing dark gray sweatpants and a black T-shirt, casual as hell.

I nibble my bottom lip and close my book, squinting a little. "What I said earlier..." I trail off. I'm not exactly sure how to say what I mean.

But he nods like he already knows. "Yeah. Me too."

I huff. "You don't know what I meant."

He studies me. "Try me."

"That stuff I wrote on the card. I didn't realize it would be read out loud. I've never actually said any of that before. Not even to myself."

It's terrifying to admit I meant every word. That the performance is blurring. That he's starting to feel danger-ously real.

Ryan absorbs my words. I can see it in the way he doesn't rush to speak.

"It didn't sound fake," I say. "Because it wasn't."

I shift on the couch and my knee bumps his. I peer at his handsome face, like I'm trying to decode an enigma.

"Do you think I'm still pretending?" I ask softly.

He doesn't answer. Just looks at me for a long time, his gaze steady on my face.

"Maybe I'm not," I whisper.

The truth sits between us, heavy and unnamed. I want to believe he's not just playing. But wanting and believing are two very different things.

My heart pounds. I reach out and touch his forearm, tracing a pattern on his skin with my index finger. "I'm tired of pretending. Aren't you?"

His skin is warm under my fingertip, a low hum of tension thrumming between us. I don't know what I'm asking for. Maybe I just want to be close to someone who sees me.

Ryan casts a glance around the room like he's checking for hidden cameras. I keep tracing little shapes on his hot skin and add, "There are no cameras. No one to watch what happens."

He leans in so slowly it's almost painful. I guess he's giving me a chance to pull away.

But I don't want that.

I fist my hand in his shirt and pull him toward me.

He brushes his lips against mine. I kiss him back. My lips are hungry, searching. The kiss is deeper than before. Slower. More real.

His hand spreads out on my back and pulls me closer. He tilts his head and deepens the kiss.

I sigh into his mouth. He pauses for a moment before whispering against my lips, "I love that fucking sound you make when I kiss you. I swear I can't get enough of it."

His words make my breasts tighten and my nipples

harden. I ache for him to cup my breasts. I kiss him and then whisper a plea, "Touch me, Ryan. Make me feel good."

He meets my eyes for a long second before grabbing my hips and pulling me onto his thighs, his lips trailing down to caress my neck. I throw my head back, releasing a guttural groan I didn't know was hidden inside me. His hands wrap around my waist, drawing me in tightly, while his big hand slowly explores my back. I unzip my hoodie and fling it off.

I arch my back and thrust my hips, a subconscious gesture driven by growing impatience. My pussy bumps against his hard cock, triggering a shuddering moan. He kisses my clavicle and murmurs, "I want you to make that sound again."

"Yeah?" I feel a flutter of nervous excitement. Despite my reservations about many things in this world, I trust that if I do anything wrong, Ryan will tell me. I guide his hand to my aching breast. His eyebrows shoot up as he deliberately caresses it, molding my nipple through my shirt.

I rock my hips against him once more and murmur, "That feels good." When his hand drifts near my breast, I let out an exasperated sound, only to realize he's teasingly trailing his fingers over the strap of my tank top, tempted to pull it down.

I think if he doesn't put his mouth on my tits soon, I'll combust. I pull the tank top over my head, leaving my bare skin exposed to his intense gaze. My nipples, now proudly standing in the cool air, captivate him as if hypnotized.

"This is... something else," he whispers, as if to himself.

Frustration bubbles inside me. "Aren't you supposed to be the one who's done all these things with so many girls?"

He responds softly, "Yeah, but none of them were you."

His eyes darken as he adds, "What if I fuck this up? What if I go too fast?"

I shake my head and offer a nervous smile. "You won't. Just touch me. Please."

He leans in and captures my lips with a passionate kiss. His hand returns to my breast, teasing my nipple yet again before his mouth drifts downward, closing over the tip. In that moment, a spark ignites inside me, as if a light bulb has gone off in my brain. I buck against him as the sensation of his tongue, white-hot and deliberate, trails from my breast down toward the molten passion between my legs.

"Please, Ryan." I squirm.

He pauses, then looks up at me and asks, "What do you need, sweetheart?"

I falter for a moment, my voice a soft whisper. "I... I don't know. I want more. I want you to touch me here." I guide his hand along the front of my silk shorts. He asks, "Have you ever been touched here by anyone?"

I shake my head. "No," I admit, though I add, "I have masturbated, if that's what you mean."

"It's not." A faint smirk passes his lips as he cautions me, "If I do anything wrong or go too fast, promise you'll tell me."

I shrug. "Okay."

He takes both my wrists in his hands, his gaze intense. "You're so perfect, Wren."

I bite my lip, finding his earnestness irresistible. I brush my hand through his hair as he closes his eyes for a moment. Then, with gentle deliberation, he starts pushing my pants down. I help by shifting and kicking away the shorts, revealing that I was wearing nothing underneath except a white cotton thong.

He bites his lip. As I stand before him, he breathes,

"Jesus, Chirp. Do you know how hot you are?" His words make me blush and I shake my head in disbelief. Locking eyes with me, he carefully peels my panties down my thighs.

Before I know it, he guides me to straddle his lap once more. Now that I'm completely bare, every sensation near my super-sensitive pussy is amplified. The soft brush of his cotton pants, the cool caress of the air, and the steady, hot throb of anticipation building deep within me.

His fingers, hesitant but sweetly curious, trace a path along my thigh. A shiver runs through me as he gets closer to the source of my desire. His eyes flicker up to mine, seeking permission. I give it with a nod. I watch as he swallows hard, his Adam's apple bobbing up and down. Then, with a shaky breath, he moves his fingers closer to my core, hovering right on the edge.

I let out a soft whimper of anticipation, pushing my hips forward in silent invitation. The moment his fingers graze over my folds, I gasp, a wave of pleasure washing over me.

"Ryan," I whisper, my voice husky. "Oh god..."

He moves his fingers against me with a newfound boldness. "Does it feel good?" he murmurs, his voice low and raspy.

I nod, too caught up in the sensation to speak. His fingers continue their exploration, tracing lines of pleasure that have me writhing in his lap. His other hand wraps around my waist, keeping me steady as he slowly and deliberately teases me.

A soft moan escapes my lips as he finds a sensitive spot. His eyes darken with desire.

"Again," I breathe out, pushing my hips against his hand. He obeys instantly, finding that spot again and again until I'm gasping for breath, my body trembling with the intensity of the pleasure. His thumb finds my clit. I nearly jump out of my skin as he starts to rub it in slow circles.

"You're so wet," he whispers, his voice filled with awe. "Is this all for me, Chirp?"

His pet name for me sends a thrill down my spine. I nod, unable to speak.

He leans forward, capturing my lips in a deep, passionate kiss as his fingers continue to move against me. The way he touches me, coupled with the intensity of his kiss, has me on the brink of a sensation I've never experienced before. My body tenses, my breath hitches, and then everything goes white as an orgasm rips through me. I cry out, clinging to him as wave after wave of pleasure rolls over me.

After what feels like forever, I slump against him, completely spent. He takes his fingers out my pussy and smells them, his eyes rolling back in his head for a moment. Then he licks them clean as methodically as a cat grooming itself, taking his time and smacking his lips. I watch breathlessly, wondering if he would do the same thing to my pussy, which tingles at the sight.

"Good?" I ask.

Ryan shakes his head. "No. Fucking delicious. I thought you would taste good, but I wasn't prepared for you to taste like heaven."

His words take me aback, making me blush fiercely. "Really?" I ask, my voice coming out as a small squeak.

"Really," he confirms, his dark eyes blazing into mine. "You're amazing, Chirp."

As he leans in for another kiss, he wraps his arms around me, pulling my body close. His heart pounds against mine as if catching the rhythm of my own racing pulse. He kisses me gently on the forehead, then on the nose, then finally on the lips. Slow, languid kisses that make me melt into him.

"You okay?" he asks, his voice tender.

I manage a nod, still too overwhelmed to form coherent words. His thumb brushes gently against my cheek, his eyes soft with concern.

"That was... wow."

"Yeah," he agrees, his lips curving into a satisfied smile. "Wow is right." He strokes my hair gently, his fingers tangling in the soft strands.

I let out a content sigh, leaning into his touch. "I've never... I mean, that was my first time," I admit, a little embarrassed. "I've... uh... touched myself. Made myself come. But I've never... um... done anything with another person involved."

His gaze softens as he looks at me, his thumb brushing gently over my lower lip. "I'm glad I could be of service."

I turn my head and bite his thumb gently, then run my tongue over the place I just bit, soothing the sting. He watches intently, sucking his lower lip into his mouth.

"What can I do to be of service to you?" I ask. I rock my hips against his, reassuring myself that he's still hard. His cock lies rigid between the press of our bodies.

Ryan slowly shakes his head. "Nothing, sweetheart. Even if this were the time and place. Which I assure you, it is not. I wouldn't expect anything in exchange for making you come. You needed a release. I provided that."

I wrinkle my nose. "What do you mean?"

"I mean exactly what I just said. Getting you off is the hottest thing I've ever seen. I'd be lying if I said I wasn't going to dream about feeling you come on my fingers. But that's as far as this can go." He frowns and brushes a strand of hair from my face. "If you were a stranger, it would be different. But you're not. You're my friend—"

I cut him off mid-sentence. "If you start to say that I'm Jay's little sister, I will throttle you."

He chuckles at my threat, the sound vibrating through his chest and sending a pleasant shiver down my spine. His touch sends warmth flooding through me. I find myself craving more of him.

"Such a little tiger. Let's just say there are rules in place, social rules, that mean I shouldn't even touch you. I'm already breaking rules just being here. We can't push any further or go any deeper."

I cross my arms over my chest and narrow my gaze at him. "As you pointed out, you've already broken those rules. So why stop now?"

His eyes flicker with an unreadable emotion before he meets my gaze. "I broke them because you needed me to. But there are lines I won't cross."

I go cold. "What a dumb thing to say."

Ryan starts to stroke my hair, but I bat his hand away. He grabs my hips and holds me against him when I try to move away.

"Don't." His eyes bore into mine. "Don't ruin it."

"It's too late for that." I shove at his chest. "You're an arrogant bastard, you know that? Now let me the fuck go."

For one second, Ryan's grip increases. I suck in a breath, thinking that he isn't going to free me. But then his hands fall away.

"Whatever you want, Chirp." His words sound hollow. "I'm just here to serve."

I snatch up my shorts and stuff my legs into them, then find my tank top and hoodie. I'm feeling embarrassed, yes, but also irrationally angry. How dare he act like he's the one in control, the one making all the decisions? How dare he just dismiss me like that?

"You kissed me. You touched me. I saw the look in your eyes as you took my panties off. If you think you're not as guilty as I am, you're crazy."

Ryan opens his mouth to protest but I don't stick around to hear what he's got to say. I flee the trailer, glad that I make it outside before tears begin to prick at the corners of my eyes.

If he kisses me again, I don't think I'll stop him. If I let him in, I don't think I'll survive when he inevitably walks away.

seventeen

RYAN

WE'RE TRAVELING in two vans to a day hike. The van I'm in is quiet, most of the bachelorettes and camera people either looking out the window at the scenic view or buried in their phones. As we turn off the highway onto a smaller road, the van bumps along. I'm not paying a bit of attention to my surroundings, though. Last night's rose ceremony keeps looping in my head. The way Wren blinked when I said her name. Like she still didn't believe she belonged here.

The idea doesn't sit right with me. How can I fix that?

"We're here!" Rich calls. He slides open the van's door.

When I climb out into a large gravel parking lot, the place is empty. We're in the middle of the woods. The only thing around is a large sign saying CLEAR SPRINGS TRAIL-HEAD. There's a well-worn path that leads off to the right. Behind us, the ground rises up steeply to form a sharp incline. I haven't been here before, but I know this area is right at the beginning of the foothills, where the hill country of the Piedmont above Atlanta meets the sloping terrain of the Blue Ridge Parkway.

I've never really been anywhere around here, but I look at Rich expectantly.

"Is this today's date?" I ask.

"You said that you liked to hike, so here we are." He extends a hand toward the woods. "Once the rest of the girls are here, we should have good weather all day for shooting."

I look up. He's seemingly correct. The sky is bright blue above us, not a cloud in sight. That doesn't guarantee anything when it comes to Georgia weather, but hopefully the hiking won't be too uphill.

I crack my knuckles as Rich opens the back of the van, revealing two backpacks stuffed with hiking gear. He unzips one and shows off the contents. Tons of granola, Clif bars, bandages, and bottled water. He produces a Nalgene bottle and offers it to me.

I take it, twist off the cap, and sniff the contents. It's just water, as far as I can tell.

He points to the bottle. "Water with a little bit of electrolyte solution. The gold standard."

I change into my own hiking boots. I didn't know Rich had asked for them specifically for this date, but I'm not terribly surprised.

The other van pulls up. As soon as the doors open, the other contestants swarm around me. I try not to look at Wren. Or think about how it felt to have my fingers inside her last night. Immediate thoughts of her slam into me anyway.

I glance over the crowd of girls and am instantly entertained. If the TV audience isn't, I don't know what can help them.

Nikki is wearing a black bodycon dress that barely covers her ass and a pair of brand-new hiking boots. She tosses her hair and announces that she doesn't do sweat. As a concept. Whatever that means.

Raven looks around and pulls out a can of bug spray, coating herself and offering it around. Mei is recording everything. She's in denim cutoffs and an oversized plaid workman shirt. I have no idea what she's saying to her phone as she talks and films, but someone somewhere is probably entertained.

Raven and Divya both wear hiking shorts and long-sleeve T-shirts. Raven's biting her lip and looking around like she's unsure. Divya, on the other hand, stays quiet. She keeps looking up at the mountain like it doesn't impress her.

"Okay, everyone." Rich claps his hands, pulling our attention. "Today is a hiking date. For your safety, please take a lightweight pack with granola, water, and a tracking device. Just in case something goes terribly wrong. Once you're ready, we'll have you head out as one group. You'll naturally fall into your own pace. Some people will be faster and move toward the front, others slower and drift toward the back. Doesn't matter. This isn't a race. We're only going a few miles."

He turns to me. "Ryan, anything you want to say?"

I smile at the group and shrug apologetically. "Sorry you got dragged out here. This is one of my favorite off-day activities. Although I usually like my hiking to be a bit more strenuous. Rich assures me this should be an easy out and back. Don't be afraid to speak up if you need anything. Water, food, a break. Whatever. I won't think less of you. Promise."

JacqLyn, who's wearing hiking pants and a loose long-sleeved T-shirt, grins. " Ready to go, Captain."

I smile and walk over to her. "You wanna accompany me as we walk?"

"Yeah, I do." She beams. "I love to hike. This is, like, the perfect date to me."

I cock a brow. "Really?"

"Yeah, it actually is. All my friends think I'm crazy because I adore hiking."

Raven walks up and holds out her can of bug spray. "You guys are crazy for wanting to do this, but can I please spray you down first?"

I nod. Definitely didn't think about bug spray. Internally, I admit I usually don't. Spray matters more in swampy areas, but I don't expect to need it much today. Still, they say good luck is ninety percent preparation, ten percent perspiration. Or whatever.

JacqLyn, Daisy, and I start down the trail. For a long while, it's pretty flat with only a little elevation as we go. JacqLyn hikes with us for a while before breaking away and moving faster. If it were a date with just the two of us, I'd try to keep pace, but as it is, Daisy and I are already ahead of most of the contestants.

As we walk, Daisy tells me about her hometown. Nashville, Tennessee. How the city throws a huge country music festival each spring. She goes into a long, funny story about the antics she and her friends got into this year. I laugh. I can't even see JacqLyn anymore by the time she finishes.

Eventually, I slow down.

"I'm going to wait for some of the others to catch up."

She makes a face and says, "Okay, slowpoke. I'll try to catch up with JacqLyn. See you at the top." A cameraman breaks off and goes with her, so I feel pretty good about letting her go.

Wren and Raven are the next pair of hikers. I wait for

them. They're laughing at a joke Wren just made when I fall into step with them.

Raven looks me up and down. "Okay, I just have to say. Those are some serious hiking boots you've got on."

I glance at my black boots and laugh. "They're pretty metal. They're for more serious hiking than this, but it's what I had."

"I thought for a second you were turning goth like me. You know I love a goth boy."

Wren snorts and I laugh.

Divya seems unbothered by the exercise, but when a bee buzzes near her head, she screams and shoos it away frantically.

"Are you crazy? Don't do that," Wren says. "That probably makes it more interested in you."

"For sure," I add.

"Nobody told me I'd be going on hikes into the wilderness for a man," Divya says primly. "Especially a man that hasn't even kissed me." She arches a brow and crosses her arms.

I shrug and smile. "So sorry to bother you, my lady. Dost thou needeth a piggyback ride?"

Divya shoots me a glare. "Hardly," she says.

I turn my head to look at Wren, who's fallen a bit behind. She's making it all right, but she's sweaty. The boots she's wearing look like something Gene Simmons would wear onstage.

"What's up, Buttercup?" I ask gently.

She looks off into the woods and screws up her face. "Nothing is up."

"No?"

She looks at me, then at the camera, then back at me. "No," she says heavily.

That gets my mind working. Obviously, there are some things she wants to say, but won't. Not with the cameras on her. That's more than fair.

But that doesn't stop me from trying to figure out what she's thinking.

I hike ahead as the trail starts to incline more. She's flushed, breathing a little heavier than usual. When we hit the switchback, she slows down a lot. I pause and let her catch up a few times before she shoots me a crabby look.

"You don't have to stop for me," she mutters.

"We're on a date. A group date, sure, but still a date. If I don't stop for you, then I'll just hike this whole trail alone. Not really interested in that."

She juts her chin. "You could just go a little faster. Catch up with Divya and Raven."

"But I don't want to. I want to stay here and talk to you."

Wren purses her lips. When the trail hits another steep switchback, she stops and stares up the slope like she's not so sure about it.

I grab my Nalgene from my backpack and unscrew the cap before handing it to her.

She blinks at me like I've just offered her a kidney. "You need water," I say. "You're not looking very good."

For a second, I think she's going to fight me on it. But then she surprises me. She takes the bottle and drinks slowly, her throat moving, lashes fluttering slightly.

I swallow. Why is that attractive? I don't know.

When she finishes, she hands it back. "Thanks," she says.

"So, what do you think about hiking in general?"

"I think it sucks. I'm sorry that this is one of your favorite activities, but it gets a zero out of ten from me."

"Even if you get to spend the afternoon with me?" I ask quietly.

That pulls a smile from her. She grunts. "You're the worst. The actual worst."

There's no bite to her words. I walk beside her again, matching her slower pace.

She doesn't push me away. She just mutters something about pine needles and toe blisters. As we start to climb a steeper incline, the shade stretches long overhead.

"You okay?" I ask.

She gives me a little look. "I'm okay. I don't need you to check on me."

"That's just what I do. I like to make sure my girls are okay."

"Your girls, huh? Is that what I am?"

I shrug. "Maybe you could be."

She narrows her eyes at me. I think she's about to let me have it. But before she can, someone shouts from the trail below us.

I can't see anyone, but whoever it is sounds close. I turn and start back down the trail.

Around the next switchback, I find Letitia and Mei trying to help Nikki stand. One of the producers is whipping a cameraman into place, but I bark out, "Are you serious? You guys aren't helping her? Come on, this is a medical emergency!"

Nikki's knees give out and she crumples, dragging Mei down with her.

I call out, "Rich! Get Divya! We need a doctor!"

Wren passes me and kneels beside Nikki, who is flat on the ground now. She feels Nikki's forehead and tries to talk to her.

Nikki's eyes flutter open. She responds, but I can't hear what she says.

Before I can issue another command, Divya comes barreling down the trail. She pushes past me and takes over.

"Okay, move aside. Let me see her."

She all but pushes Mei out of the way and kneels down, checking Nikki's pulse and talking to her a little. Wren gets a bottle of water out of her backpack and hands it to Nikki, but Nikki doesn't seem to be aware of it. Wren tries to coax her into taking a drink.

Divya looks around, then locks eyes with me. "We need to call for medics. Now."

I turn my head. One of the PAs waves at me. "I'm already on the phone with them."

"Can we move her down to the trailhead?" he asks Divya.

Divya looks around and then nods. "I think so. Could two of you come in and take her arms and help her walk? There isn't anything obviously wrong with her, but she's extremely tired. Maybe dehydrated, maybe a little low blood sugar. Her pulse is very fast."

Two contestants take Nikki by the arms and start guiding her down the trail.

JacqLyn and Daisy fall in line behind. I hang back as we start to follow her down the mountain. The cameras are rolling, but most of the group is silent as we descend.

Down at the bottom, the paramedics are already there. They're closing up the back of their truck, ready to take Nikki to the emergency room.

Divya goes with them, her lips pressed into a thin line. I have to give it to her. She held it together really well today. Didn't lose her shit for a second.

That's the closest she's come to knocking my socks off.

There's a picnic set up for us on the other side of the parking lot, but I'm not feeling it anymore. I find Rich and apologize but firmly tell him the date and the shooting are over for the day. He doesn't like it, but he eventually concedes, giving the orders to pack it all in.

On the ride back, Wren sits beside me and stares out the window. It's nearly impossible for me not to brush her pinky with mine.

I swallow. Who am I becoming? Where did the cocky hockey player go?

I wish like anything that Wren didn't make me feel so damned needy.

RYAN

WHEN THE PRODUCERS told me there was a surprise guest today, I figured it would be someone's mom. Maybe a former contestant. Not someone that might make my stomach do something close to a nervous backflip.

Standing right in the middle of all the girls, making them die with laughter, is my best friend Jay. Also, coincidentally, Wren's big brother.

My gut clenches. If Jay's here, I need to be twice as careful. He doesn't know about me and Wren. I can't let him find out.

Well, there's nothing for him to find out. Not *really*.

Steeling myself, I stroll up to the gaggle of people. Jay is gently ribbing his sister.

"You're gonna lose, buddy. Just like you did when you were in third grade."

She screws up her face. "I hardly think that something more than ten years ago should be admissible in this event."

Jay slides his arm around her shoulders and gives her a

squeeze. "Sorry, kid. That's the field you'll always be playing on when you play with someone my age."

Something about the easy way she leans into it makes my throat go tight. She looks safe with him. Protected. Like the rest of the world hasn't touched her yet. Including me.

She rolls her eyes and spots me. "Oh look, there's Ryan," she says. "Let's all look at him now."

I don't miss the sarcasm in her tone. Neither does Jay. He's wearing a whistle, a pair of aviator sunglasses, and he's holding a pair of red and blue flags. He looks like he's coaching a high school football game.

"What is all this?" I say. "Also, hi."

"Hey, man." He gives me a side hug. "I've just been chatting with your lovely bachelorettes here."

Daisy laughs and steps closer to Jay, patting him on his six-pack abs. "You know, if Ryan doesn't pick me..."

She trails off. She's kidding, I think, but Jay steps away and points at his ring finger, which glistens with gold.

"Sorry, ladies. I'm married. You would all love my wife, though. She's the best. Also, she makes amazing cupcakes. In fact, I brought a tray of them for you guys to enjoy later."

The girls exclaim as I give him a questioning smile. "So what's with the getup?"

"Capture the flag, baby," he says.

"I'm amazing at capture the flag!" JacqLyn crows. "Y'all are going down."

"Who's gonna be on what team?" I ask.

"I'm so glad you asked," Jay says. "I'm gonna be on a team with Raven, Letitia, and Nikki. You're on a team with..."

He pauses. "Actually, Wren's team will be paired with JacqLyn, Mei, and Divya."

I glance at Wren. She doesn't flinch, but I know her well

enough to recognize the tiny tick of her jaw. She'll handle it. Of course she will. But that doesn't mean I like it.

I don't know whether that's good news or not for her, since those are the three most chaotic players on the field. But judging from JacqLyn and Divya's serious expressions, I feel like Wren's going to be okay.

Jay explains the rules very briefly. They're not complicated. Capture the flag and run it back to the home team's side. It's not an exceptionally well-thought-out activity.

Jay, of course, revels in it. As far as I can tell, he's always been this way. He's not chaotic himself, but he likes to amplify whatever is already going on.

Five minutes in, the whole field is a jumbled mess, women strewn everywhere. Jay is trash-talking Wren the whole time.

"You sure you don't need a fast pass, little girl?"

The look she gives him would level a normal man, and she just dishes it right back. "You sure you don't need a walker, old man?"

Jay lunges. Wren fakes left, then ducks. Jay trips past her and she sprints right. Straight to the flag.

Her team wins, which is a total surprise. I thought my girls were going to take home the flag.

She's radiant. Mud on her knees, grinning triumphantly. For a second, I forget where we are. Forget that she's off-limits. Forget everything except how goddamn beautiful she is when she's winning.

Wren's in competitive mode now. Fierce. I keep thinking about that first day. Quiet, awkward Wren. That girl's gone. And I miss her. Except I kind of don't.

Jay plays it off like it doesn't sting, but I've known him too long to think he takes losing any competition lying down.

After we all have a bit of water and a cupcake from Jay's wife, we all turn to look at Jay.

"What's next, old man?" I ask him.

He narrows his eyes at me. "You're six months older than I am, first of all," he says. He's as quick as he is sharp. "Second of all, we're going to play a little no-holds-barred Q&A with Jay. That means the girls can all settle under the old oak tree right here and ask me anything they want to know about your life."

Mei squeals. Divya and Raven chuckle. Wren looks downright haughty.

Yeah. I'm already sweating. We haven't even gotten to the meat of this challenge.

We all settle down and the cameras take a couple minutes to center us. During the downtime, Jay answers questions about his own job.

He is a well-known influencer. Most of the questions are about how he got so many Instagram followers. Wren is looking at her nails like she's bored. Raven whispers something in her ear and makes her snicker. God knows what that's about.

Rich and the director get out of the camera line, then the director calls action. JacqLyn is already leaning close to Jay and smiling very widely. She bats her lashes. "Tell us the worst thing that Ryan's ever done on a date."

Jay laughs. Loud and unhelpful. "Which one? God, honestly, too many things to count. He's ghosted a lot of girls while they were on the date. But there was also one time in Vegas when he picked up another girl while he was already on a date with the first... and didn't tell her right away. That was awkward."

The bachelorettes all burst into excited murmurs.

I clear my throat, raising my hands like I'm admitting

my faults. "That was over ten years ago, I'll have you know. I'm a changed man. I swear."

Jay laughs and elbows Divya, who glares at him.

"Has Ryan ever been in love with anyone?" Daisy asks. "Has it ever been serious?"

Jay just snorts. "I don't know... does hockey count? Because if not, he is solo as fuck."

That one lands harder than it should. I laugh it off, but there's an ache behind my ribs. I've given so much to the game. Maybe too much. Maybe I don't know how to give anything else.

I shrug, not seeing any reason to defend myself against that one. It's true.

Raven butts in. "What about hookups? Has he had a lot?"

To his credit, Jay falters here. Clearly, he doesn't want to outright make fun of me. But he and I definitely got up to no good together in college. And out of college, really, until right up until the moment Jay met his wife.

We were man sluts together. A proud tradition.

I don't really know how I want him to answer that question.

"I'm going to say more than a few and leave it at that," Jay says. "Bro code says that you don't rat out your fellow bro."

All the girls start laughing. I grimace. I am dying inside.

Jay swings his gaze over to Wren. "How about you, little sister? You got any dirt you wanna dig up on your boy Ryan?"

She's quiet at first. Then she shrugs. "I already know him, I guess."

JacqLyn purses her lips. "Come on. You must have some questions about the man."

Wren nips her bottom lip with her top teeth. "Okay... well, what kind of girl does he usually go for?"

My heart fucking stops. She's looking at Jay, but I can feel the question burning through me. What is she really asking? What does she want the answer to be?

Jay smirks, spreads his hands wide, and leans back. "Honestly? He likes hot messes. Pretty girls with bad boundaries."

Wren turns bright pink. I nearly choke on the bottle of water I was sipping.

Goddamn it, Jay. I want to reach across the space between us and take it back. Reassure her. Tell her that she's not a mess.

She's the opposite. She's... everything.

Jay doesn't notice. He just keeps going. "Usually, the girls he likes are clingy and dramatic. They're fun for, like, a week. Then Ryan just ghosts them. Hard."

Wren's eyes go wide. I can see her doing some kind of mental math, recalculating everything she's ever thought about me. Goddamn it.

This is the most horrible experience of the show so far.

After a few more questions and answers, the director calls it a day. The girls head toward the house. For a second, I think about catching up with Wren. Making sure she understands that I only ghosted girls who couldn't understand that I just wasn't interested anymore. But I can't exactly follow her right now. Not with Jay lingering nearby.

"Beer?" I offer. "I have a nice little private patio."

"Totally," he says.

We head inside my room. I open the mini fridge that I keep stocked. Mostly bottles of water, but a few Modelos. I pop two and step out onto the deck.

We're only on the first floor, so the courtyard isn't

impressive by any means. But we settle down in the two chairs sitting there and sip our beers.

Jay looks over at me. "You doing all right, man?"

No. Absolutely not. I am sweating bullets, drowning in secrets, and trying not to spiral. The one girl I shouldn't touch is the only one I can't stop thinking about. She happens to be Jay's innocent little sister.

I automatically nod, even though it's more like a shrug if I'm honest. "Yeah, totally. I'm just ready to be done with this whole TV show. I'm doing it because they offered me a lot of cash, but it's a drag on my summer."

Jay nods. "I got you. It's a little wild to me that Wren ended up on the same show you did."

"It was totally by accident. Just... coincidence."

"Right." Jay pauses for a long moment. "Listen. I think Wren still has a crush on you."

I freeze. How the hell would he know that?

I try to look casual. "Oh yeah?"

He nods. "I'm not worried about it or anything. I know this is all just for TV. You'll keep it professional. But it's clear to me that she's still into you. Actually, I should've known the first second I saw you guys in the same location and she wasn't yelling at you."

I roll my eyes to disguise my true feelings. "Yeah, I think that's just down to being stuck in the same room all day, every day for the better part of a month. I wouldn't give it much thought."

"Well, you know," he says, "just treat her gently. You may not have feelings for her, but I don't know. She's never really had a boyfriend or anything. I'm worried that she'll just fixate on you. She's not like the types of girls you usually mess with. She's quiet. She's delicate. She's been through a lot more than you know. More than people think."

I can't quite bring myself to disagree with that sentiment, so I just nod. Jay's told me I'm reckless before. He didn't say it like a joke. And now that I'm starting to care, I finally understand what he meant.

"Anyway." Jay claps me on the shoulder and then takes another draw of his beer. "Maybe this job will help Wren come out of her shell. Meet someone her own age. You know, someone less you-coded."

I swallow hard. I sure as hell hope that's not what's coming down the pipe for us. "Sure. That'd be good," I answer.

"Come on. What are these producers thinking, anyway?" Jay shakes his head. "Pairing you and Wren up? That's a disaster waiting to happen."

"Yeah, uh… total disaster," I agree.

My stomach feels like a black hole.

A few minutes after we finish the beers, Jay leaves me on the balcony. I sit there. I stare out into the sunset, thinking about the way Wren looked at me when Jay called me a perpetual ghost. It was like she suddenly wasn't sure about me. She had to do the math. Figure out whether I was worth the risk.

Honestly, she probably should stay away. I should definitely push her away. But all I want is to touch her again, to hear her moan in my ear, to watch her fall apart just for me.

That might be the problem. The worst part? I don't even want to stop. I just want her.

nineteen

WREN

WEEK FOUR IS OFFICIALLY OVER. Thank *God*. The rose ceremony was incredibly tense, with Ryan sending a highly dramatic Mei home.

I'm *wiped*.

The camera pans toward me and my brain short-circuits. Should I smile? Wave? God, why am I like this? I cross my arms and pretend to be fascinated by a potted plant.

What I am not doing is staring at Ryan while he talks quietly to Raven. The way he touched her elbow shouldn't matter. But it does. God, I hate that it does.

"That's a wrap for today!" an EP calls. The scene froths with lighting techs and sound guys all suddenly moving heavy equipment.

The next day is scheduled to be a rest day, so I'm out the door before Elena can even say another word to me. I am completely exhausted. Not just from the show, which, let's be honest, sleeping in a room with other girls is not conducive to getting eight solid hours of sleep at night.

Divya snores like a madwoman. Raven murmurs in her sleep.

By the time I'm dropped off at Jay's house in greater Georgia, I'm dragging. I thank my driver and pull the strap of my overnight bag over my head as I walk up to Jay's house. Strangely, it's dark inside. I see no lights. When I try the front door, it's locked. They might be out getting a bite to eat or something.

Shit. I don't have my keys. I dump my purse out on the ground, searching through pens and crumpled napkins and loose Tums. Yeah, my purse is gross. And it doesn't have my keys.

I swing around and fumble for my cell phone, ready to call Jay. I wasn't exactly expecting to have the day off and now I'm locked out of his house. I try Jay's phone, but it goes straight to voicemail.

I can't summon the energy to figure this out right now. I look up the street and think about what I should do. I could head for Java Monkey, our local coffee shop, and shovel cake in my face while I plot my next move. I guess that's what tonight is going to have to be.

As I step off the porch, I see a car coming down the street. It pulls in at Ryan's house and the lights flash. I don't know what that's about exactly. I stare as I cross the sidewalk behind the car.

Ryan gets out and looks at me, his face crinkling. "What's going on?" he asks.

"Nothing, exactly," I say, gesturing to Jay's house. "I'm locked out of the house..." I let my sentence trail off.

"So where are you going?" Ryan asks.

I shrug. "I don't know. Java Monkey, I guess. Then maybe Iris's place."

He rolls his eyes like I'm a wayward, difficult child. "No," he says.

"You won't allow that? Since when are you the boss of me?"

He starts to make his way over. "Come on." He waves toward his house. "Come inside. You can stay here until Jay gets back. But he could be gone all night."

Ryan gives me a side-eye.

"Yeah, that's fine. You're not just wandering around in the middle of nowhere."

It's the first time we've been alone since we hooked up. Honestly, I'm not in the mood for him right now. I just want to sleep. But Ryan's house is right here. His couch is certainly more comfortable than an air mattress at Iris's.

I sigh, deflated. "Fine. Lead the way."

He gives me a questioning look. "That's it? That's all you're gonna say? You're not gonna push back?"

I shake my head. "Nope. I don't have the fucks to give. I'm extremely tired."

Rather than say anything else, Ryan just herds me into his house. It strikes me that I've actually never been here before, even though he and Jay have been friends for years. We walk up his front steps. He unlocks the door, ushering me into the living room.

It's nice in here. Not what I expected at all. Decorated with dark, heavy furniture and maps on the wall. I toe off my shoes and pad over to his couch, still wearing my bag. I let it sink to the floor beside me and sit on the couch.

It's actually pretty comfortable. Nice and bouncy. Cushiony, and deep.

"I don't mean to intrude on your sanctuary here." I crack a joke.

Ryan finishes taking off his shoes and putting his keys

and wallet in a dish by the front door. He smirks and walks over.

"It's not that big of a deal," he says. "I'm just really careful about my privacy. Jay's been here, if it helps."

"Yeah, I don't think I'm getting serial murdered here. I was just kidding."

Right. This is awkward. As awkward as awkward can be.

I press my lips together. He pats down his pockets. It's something I've seen him do before when he's at a loss for what to say or do, so I guess he's feeling the tension just like I am.

"Should I order some takeout? From anywhere you want," he asks. "Maybe we can watch a movie, if you're up for it."

His tone is sincere. It's an effort not to make fun of him. I just flush and agree.

"I feel like a weird knockoff Barbie in this outfit," I mutter. "Like one of the ones they only made a hundred of, with a tragic backstory."

Ryan's eyes trail over me, slow and unhurried. "You look hot."

I snort. "You'd say that if I showed up in a potato sack and heels."

He shakes his head. "You've always been pretty. Now the rest of the world just finally sees it."

My throat tightens. For once, I don't fire back. I just let myself feel it.

I sit in the living room while he orders from the Tin Shed. He doesn't ask me for my order, so I just assume I'm getting a burger or chicken fingers. He briefly goes upstairs to change into gray sweats and a dark T-shirt. He also brings a shirt and a pair of oversized shorts and offers them to me.

"What is this?" I ask.

He holds them out. "Something to change into. Don't be weird about this. You're making me jittery."

"Weird, huh?" I take them and look at my bag. Technically, I have my silk shorts and thin tank top in there, but it's been a while since I've washed them. I kind of want the opportunity to wear Ryan's clothes. As weird as that sounds.

There's something vaguely comforting about his jersey that I stole, so I can bet his overnight stuff will be soft and warm as well.

"Okay," I say.

I head into the bathroom and change into them. When I come back, he looks me up and down, his lips curling upward.

"Wow."

"Are you serious?" I ask. "You just gave me this to wear. Are you really picking on me already?"

"I'm not, actually. I was just going to say that shirt looks good on you."

I look at it. The old Atlanta Ice Storms T-shirt.

"It's comfortable," I admit, shrugging a shoulder.

Ryan has taken up what I assume is his usual spot, spread out on the right side of the couch. So I move to the left side and sit down with my hip completely flush with the sofa's arm.

Ryan gives me a funny look but doesn't say anything.

Instead, he says, "So you're here in my house, sitting on my couch, and yet you're not going for my throat. Is that being friendly, where you're concerned?"

His teasing remark pulls a laugh from me.

"I admit, I'm too worn out to have the energy to have enemies right now. Honestly, I was thinking about having a date with a spare bed at Jay's."

He smiles, that impish smile that always gets me in trouble. "Well, I hope you don't mind staying up with me for a while. I need to wind down."

"As long as tonight is relaxing, I don't care what we do."

The moment the words are out of my mouth, I realize that could be misinterpreted.

"It's cute how you go all quiet around everyone else," Ryan says, eyes gleaming. "Why am I the only one who gets the smartass version of you?"

"You're just lucky, I guess," I sass.

He opens his mouth to reply, but just at that moment, the doorbell rings. The food has arrived.

Ryan goes to the door and brings back two big brown bags.

"Hope you're hungry," he says.

He hands me one bag and moves around to sit down, dumping out the other with no regard for the well-being of the expensive-looking coffee table before him.

I open my bag with more care and find french fries. Extra crispy, the way Brick Store does them. A burger. I don't make a face because he got me food, but I don't really like hamburgers. Eating cows just seems wrong after watching so many videos of people playing with cute cows and cows running around with puppies.

So I don't say anything. But when I unwrap my burger, I find that he placed my order exactly the way I like it: a turkey burger, extra Swiss cheese, barbecue sauce, and brown gravy.

I gape at my food for a moment, surprised he would even know that.

Ryan pauses, about to take a bite of his burger. "Is everything okay?"

I nod. He relaxes. He takes a bite. It's literally a third of the whole burger. He chews, a little messy. I can't help but smile.

"I can't believe you knew what I liked."

He frowns and chews a little more. "Are you kidding? You've only ordered that exact thing in front of me, like, a hundred times."

"Well, yeah, but I didn't think you noticed," I say.

He tilts his head to the side and swallows. "I notice everything you do, Chirp."

My ears start to burn. I turn to eat my weird burger. I'm a little freaked out by the fact that Ryan has seen me. Like, actually seen me. Not just the odd little sister that I've been for so long.

This big, hunky guy thought I was interesting enough to keep tabs on. Huh. Well, that doesn't bode well for my crush on him. I'm actually starting to really like him as a person. RIP me.

We eat in silence for a moment before I attempt conversation again.

"Good sandwich."

He has now finished his. Even though he's had it for less than four minutes. He's currently stuffing french fries in his mouth. He just nods.

I feel like right now I am just tired enough and just catty enough to ask about my brother's visit to *The Last Kiss* set.

"So... I didn't realize I was your type."

Ryan coughs on a french fry and then chews and swallows, scrunching his face up. "What are you talking about?"

I take a bite of my turkey burger and chew, giving him a

few moments to think. Then I say, "Well, you know. Hot messes. Bad boundaries. Fun for a week."

Basically... everything I'm not. Or maybe I secretly am, but just quieter about it.

His shoulders deflate. "Yeah, fucking Jay. I know he's your brother, but I could've killed him for that."

"It was interesting, that's for sure. Especially the part about ghosting."

He sighs and pulls the last few french fries from the container, then points them at me. "Don't be dramatic."

"He exaggerated, did he?" I finally look at him because it sounded pretty rehearsed.

He shakes his head. "I haven't ghosted anyone in a while. Like, probably a couple years at least."

"Wow. What a glowing record," I say.

He finishes the fries and sits back, eyeing my untouched container of them. I push them toward him and he takes a couple out but then pushes the rest back.

"So, what? You think I'm proud of that?"

I thumb a little barbecue sauce from my lower lip and watch him noticing. It's funny how once a guy notices you, he keeps doing it.

"I think you're fine with it," I say.

"Wren, I know you're not like those girls."

"Who says I'm not? Are they aliens or astronauts or something else unreasonable? Because if not, you don't know what I am or what they are not."

He shakes his head. "No, I'm pretty sure I've got you pegged."

"Oh yeah? I'm not looking to be a fling or a plot twist or a deleted scene."

That gives him pause. He frowns and hesitates for a second. "You're not."

"No."

I inhale, my breath shakier than I want it to be. "If this is just a bit for the show, it ends the same way all your stories seem to end."

"It won't," he says. "It can't."

I arch a brow. "Do you tell all your one-night stands that, too?"

He just shakes his head. "Nope. Only you."

That makes something in my chest lurch. I hate it.

"So what happens when the cameras stop filming? Does that mean this, whatever this is that's going on between us, is done?"

He doesn't answer.

I sigh and take another bite of my burger. After a minute, he slides along the couch until he's close to me. He catches my wrist gently, not enough to stop me but enough to make me pause.

"I don't know how to do this, okay? I know I shouldn't, but I can't help it."

My lip catches between my teeth. I look up. His eyes spear right through me. God help me. I have feelings for this guy, don't I?

"Just don't lie to me," I whisper. "I couldn't handle that."

He moves to touch my hair, tucking a strand back behind my ear. I almost believe him.

I don't know if he knows what he's saying, but it's clear that my brother was playing up Ryan's past.

Ryan says, "I know we're caught in a world of rights and wrongs, but I would like just one night where I don't have to play by the rules. Anybody's rules."

I look up at him, breathless. "Then take me."

RYAN HAART IS KISSING ME. And oh, does he know how to kiss.

I open my mouth. Ryan crashes into me, tasting like fresh air and danger. It's greedy, messy, and perfect. I arch against him, his pulse heavy on my lips. My skin prickles with desire. Before I know it, I am straddling him. The friction between us makes my head spin. I'm grinding against him, feeling him, hard through his jeans. All I can think is *more*. He groans against my mouth, the sound vibrating through me.

"You're killing me, Chirp," he murmurs, breathless, leaving me breathless, too.

"I'm killing you?" I whisper, a laugh bubbling up, the tension electric between us. I'm surprised by how bold I feel, emboldened by everything that's happened tonight. "Then why don't we take this to the bedroom?"

He pulls back slightly. I can see his eyes gleaming in the dim light, wild and mischievous. He scoops me up over his shoulder like I'm a sack of flour, but it feels more like I'm his prize. I'm so surprised I let out a tiny, involuntary squeak that makes him chuckle as he carries me down the hallway. He deposits me on his bed with a grin that makes my stomach flip.

I laugh and flop back, catching my breath, trying to make sense of this.

"You're such a caveman, Haart," I tease. But there's heat in my voice, in the room, everywhere. This is happening.

He hovers over me, his breath hot on my skin. I pull at his shirt, needing it off, needing everything off. He complies, a flash of his bare chest in the dim light. I think about how I am undressing him again with more than just my eyes this time.

We fumble with my shirt, our fingers tangling, my hands shaking with urgency. When I tug it off, he pushes it down my shoulders. It feels like a small victory, but I want so much more.

He stops, breathes, takes me in. His eyes are like a touch, moving over my skin. I want to cover myself, but more than that, I want him to finish what he started.

"You're staring," I say, my voice coming out soft and impatient.

"I won't be rushed." His gaze is unwavering, full of want. "Let me memorize you, Chirp."

The way he says it makes my heart stutter. It's like he's waiting for permission, like he means every word.

I arch my back and part my thighs, wide, while my cheeks blaze. His eyes, hungry and bright, never leave me, like I'm the last game of the season and he must win. My deliberate display breaks the last of his resolve. He growls, lunges, and is on me. His mouth finds my breasts, kisses trailing down my stomach. I am slick and ready when he touches me. It's like a fuse igniting.

"Is that all for me?" he asks, breathless.

"That's what you do to me," I manage, not quite a whisper, not quite a shout.

Ryan shifts between my legs, his touch like fire. His fingers rub over my clit in the slowest of circles. Pleasure pulses through me, my head tipping back.

"Please," I beg, writhing under his hands. "I need more."

He's smiling, I can hear it in his voice. "You'll get it, Chirp. But first this."

Then his mouth is on me, kissing my thighs, kissing my wet heat. I'm dizzy, delirious, and already close. His tongue does something that makes me cry out, makes my fingers tangle in his hair, makes the world around me dissolve. I'm not used to this, not used to him, my body on fire, barely able to breathe.

"Fuck," I gasp. His low laughter rumbles against me.

I didn't know I could want anything this much. "Please, Ryan," I plead, words escaping like gasps. "I want your cock."

He doesn't let up, just intensifies, his mouth and hands like sin. My body arches, a bow pulled tight. I explode against him. I see stars. I can't hear my own cries. It doesn't stop, keeps going, again and again. He moves up my body, holding me as I shudder, and captures my mouth with his, letting me taste the wild and wicked flavor of myself.

I don't know how I'm even alive after that. I feel molten, barely holding it together. His weight is on me. It feels incredible. I reach down, fumbling for him, desperate to touch him.

"Ryan," I breathe.

"Do you even know what you want?" he teases, breath hot on my neck, hands making the rest of my body catch fire.

I shift and press against him. His erection is so hard against my thigh I can't help but moan. I catch his lips again, tasting myself on him. "Yes, I do."

My hands grip Ryan. I pull him down onto the bed, straddling him. His eyes are wild, but I'm wilder, my legs tangling with his. I'm bold, so bold. I tug down his briefs, freeing his cock. It's huge, daunting, and beautiful. I want it, all of it; I want him.

I position myself above him, feeling reckless and slick, then his length is hard against me. He thrusts upward, making me dizzy with wanting.

"Fuck me properly," I gasp, my hands pressing into his chest, needing it all. When he hesitates, I lean down to whisper in his ear.

I want him to know I'm serious. I want him to know that I want this, want him.

"Ryan," I whisper, lips brushing his ear. "I want you to be my first."

His eyes are wide, wild. He's never looked more perfect to me. He's staring like I've said something shocking, like he can't believe it.

"Are you sure, Chirp?" He groans. "You could do so much better."

I laugh. "What are you talking about, Ryan? Look at you. You're a walking wet dream with a hockey stick."

That makes him chuckle.

"That doesn't mean anything. You should want someone your own age."

I roll my eyes. "You're not that old. Get ahold of yourself."

"But—"

I silence him with a finger against his soft lips. "I know you'll do it right."

This revelation makes him move, all restraint shattered. He flips us, my back hitting the mattress. His mouth is on mine again, kissing me like he means it, like he's claimed me and can't get enough. He reaches for the nightstand, one hand holding me close, grabbing a condom with the other. He's so fast but so careful. When he rolls it on, I'm arching, needy, feeling like my whole life has led to this.

But Ryan doesn't just fuck me like I want. He takes his time, kissing my neck, sucking on my nipples, teasing my slit until I'm drenched. My hands roam his body and explore his smooth skin, his hard muscles, the way that he tenses and his breath stills when I run my fingers across different spots.

Ryan closes his eyes when I run my nails up the back of his neck. He tenses when I kiss and suck his fingertips. His breath stutters when I run my tongue over the delicate shell of his ear and nibble his earlobe.

Interesting. I make careful notes of what he seems to like as I navigate the parts of his body I can reach. The second I try to touch his cock, though, he stills my hand and shakes his head.

"Not yet," he husks out. He gathers my curious hands and pins them back, holding them with one hand while he sucks my nipples and runs his fingers along the cleft of my pussy. It only takes a solid minute of his torturous, wonderful touches before I'm bucking my hips and biting my lower lip.

"Ryan..." I whine. "You're killing me."

He flashes me a grin and rubs his thumb against my clit. My back bows and if he wasn't holding me in place, I think I would shoot off the bed.

"Okay, baby. I'm going to take care of you. Trust me."

I do, but I'm going crazy right now. He has me all

worked up. I can feel how wet I am, that my thighs are drenched in my excitement, that some of it has pooled on the bed beneath me.

I need *more*.

Ryan parts my thighs and rubs the head of his cock along the seam of my pussy. I gasp and grip his broad back, my nails digging into his flesh.

He enters me, so slow. My breath catches. I know his cock is big, but it isn't until right this moment that I'm actually worried it's not going to fit. It's too much and not enough all at once, stretching me in ways I didn't know I could stretch.

And it *hurts*. I wince and let out a sound. He freezes.

His voice is ragged, unsure. "Do you want me to stop?"

I shake my head, more frantic than I intend, more desperate than I can hide. I want to laugh because he's not the one who gets to decide to stop right now. I want to scream because it's so much, so real. I'm finally his.

"I'm dying for you," I breathe. "Keep going."

He groans and kisses me hard, burying the sound, burying everything else as he moves. The ache turns sweet, the fullness overwhelming and amazing.

"Fuck, Wren," he gasps. "You're so tight."

I want him to know how much I'm enjoying this, how perfect it is, how incredible he is. He's so careful with me. I can feel the tension in his muscles as he keeps his thrusts slow and intentional.

I warm up fast, my hips snapping against his. I've never had sex before, but my body moves in time with Ryan's.

"Baby." I don't even recognize the needy, breathy voice when it leaves my chest. "Please. I need it... harder."

"You only had to ask." A dimple flashes in his cheek and he obliges.

He starts going faster and deeper, gripping my hips as he drives into me. His hand finds me again, finds my clit. He touches me, drives me wild, drives me to the edge.

"Just like that," I moan, nails raking down his back, claiming him back, pulling him in. "Fuck, Ryan."

"You're amazing," he says, breathless, intense, words a hot rush against my neck. "Your pussy's so perfect. I've dreamed of this moment for so long and you're better than my imagination."

He's holding back, tensing, but I don't want him to. I want him to give me everything.

"Don't stop," I plead. "Don't hold back."

His thumb on my clit presses firmly. He doesn't hold back anymore, pushing us both over the edge, feeling my pussy walls begin to spasm. He slams into me, filling me, stretching me, finishing me in a way I've never been finished before.

I explode around him, muscles tightening, everything going white and bright and hot. He cries out, spilling into me, the pulse of it intense, real, fucking incredible. We keep moving, together, until there's nothing left to give, until we're both drained and panting and boneless, holding onto each other like the whole world could crumble and we wouldn't care.

We're caught in this, tangled together, hot and slick, until it's almost too much. I hold him. He holds me. I don't want to let go.

Our breathing finally slows. He's still inside me. I feel full, replete, entirely his. When his lips find mine, soft now, urgent in a new way, something shifts, something deep. He kisses me everywhere. When he pulls out, I'm not ready to be empty.

I can't help but smile when he insists, "Go to the bathroom. I don't want you getting a UTI."

I cock a brow at him. "Really?"

He kisses me, long and slow, then pulls away from me with a groan, giving me a nudge.

"Go on," he says, more of an order than a request. "Trust me, Chirp."

It's a little gross, but kind of sweet. Even in this, he's thoughtful, protective. I could get used to this side of Ryan.

I don't know why I'm so thrilled that he's looking out for me, but the warmth that floods my chest is undeniable. I roll my eyes like I think he's being ridiculous. Still, I do what he says, running to the bathroom, then back to him, breathless with the realization that this feels more than just incredible. It feels like more than I ever thought it could.

He's waiting on the bed, his eyes half lidded and dangerous. I like this sleepy, sexy version of him. He reaches for me, pulling me close again.

"Chirp," he murmurs against my skin. "I can't get enough of you." Then his head is between my legs, his tongue against my clit. It's gentle, urgent, nothing like before.

I'm not used to him like this. I'm not used to anyone like this. I should care that I'm falling apart under him, that he's got all the power. I should care that my body's greedy and needy and helpless. But I don't. It's incredible. I'm coming undone all over again, but slower, softer, with a kind of intensity that makes me gasp, makes me think maybe there's something here I didn't expect.

This changes everything.

Or does it? Maybe it's just another game. Maybe it's a way to pass the time while Jay's away. Maybe I'm kidding myself that this could be more.

He's murmuring things I can barely hear, barely stand to hear. About how good I taste, how amazing I am, like he means it. His hands and mouth are all I can think about. My body's an instrument only he knows how to play. Everything trembles, the edges blur. I don't know what happens after this, but I know what I want. I know that I'm close, so close, so ready.

I don't want to stop.

I don't have to tonight.

But what about tomorrow?

twenty-one

WREN

I WAKE up to warm skin, tangled sheets, and the soft sound of Ryan breathing next to me. I don't open my eyes right away, because I know when I do, the real world will rush in. I just want to stay right here, in the bubble of being not quite awake.

Last night clings to me. Ryan... His voice, his hands, the way he looked at me like I wasn't just some girl on a reality show. It was everything. I roll over and find that Ryan is on his side.

Surprisingly, he doesn't snore. I guess I figured that someone as big as he is would snore like a trucker.

His arm is slung over my waist like it belongs there. My face is tucked under his chin. He's still asleep, but I can feel the way his chest rises and falls. Steady, warm, grounding.

I should feel smug or maybe satisfied. I should feel powerful. This man, this hockey god, got on his knees for me last night.

Instead, I feel like I might throw up. Because now it's real. Not just a fantasy I could rewrite in my head a hundred different ways. Now he's seen me. Touched me. I don't get to take that back.

Last night was the best night of my life so far. This morning is easily the second best.

That's the problem.

This wasn't supposed to feel good. Not this good. Not heart-in-the-throat, nerves-on-fire, what-if-I-let-myself-fall good.

I stare at his pretty face. His hair falls gently over his forehead and into his eyes. The urge to reach out and brush it back is almost overwhelming.

Yeah. I have to get out of here before he wakes up and bursts my bubble.

Ever so carefully, I ease myself out of his arms, gently placing his arm on the bed. Then I sit up and move over to the edge. For some reason, my heart's racing.

What's wrong with me? That I liked it that much? That I wanted it to mean something?

No one ever looks at me and sees forever. I'm the foot-note. The afterthought. The nice girl who's never quite enough.

It meant something to me. But I know better than to think I meant something to him.

I rub my hand over my face, trying to control my heart rate. But it's too late. The spiral's already happening.

I like fucking him too much.

I like *him* too much. Goddamn it.

I think he saw me last night. Really saw me. Instead of running, he stayed. That's what's messing me up the most.

The second he wakes up, he'll decide it was just a onetime thing. Just a showmance gone too far. I will be the punchline.

My mouth twists like I've eaten something bitter.

This feeling? This is the reason I haven't ever slept with anyone.

The sheets rustle behind me. A hand slides across my back to my hip, pulling me gently backward.

Ryan's voice is low, still rough and sleepy. "Hey. Where'd you go?"

I hate myself more than I can say, but I automatically collapse back into bed. Tears prick my eyes. I have to take a deep breath to control myself.

"Just say it," I whisper.

"Say what?"

"Say that you think it was a mistake," I answer. "I know you do."

The words scald my throat on the way out, bitter and humiliating. I hate how small I sound. How hopeful.

I brace myself for the dismissal. For the part where he shrugs and says, *cool story, kid*. Because that's what always happens. I expect him to act like I'm lucky to be noticed at all.

He puts his finger under my chin and tips my face toward him. "What are you talking about?"

His touch is gentle. Too gentle. Like I might shatter. Which is ironic, since I'm already shattering inside.

I shake my head. "You don't have to pretend. I get it. It got heated. We got caught up in it. Now you're…"

"Wren, stop." His palm rests on my chest, just above my heart. "Breathe."

I suck in a deep breath, but it doesn't seem to help. His big body shifts so he's half on his side, but half holding me down with one thigh.

"Stop deciding how I feel before I've even had coffee," he teases. His voice is gentle.

I let out a strangled laugh. His lips twitch with humor,

but he sounds perfectly calm as he says, "We slept together. That's not something I take lightly. Well, not with you, at least."

I mumble, "But you basically hate me."

He looks as shocked as if I had just slapped him. "You think I could hate you?"

"You've said worse."

"I've said stupid shit because you get under my skin," he says. "But hate you? No. Never."

I press my lips together. I thought for sure that I knew how Ryan felt about me. Now uncertainty claws at my belly.

We lie there for a few beats. Then he mutters, "I don't know what I'm supposed to do or feel right now. Should I sneak over to your brother's house and break in? Let him punch me in the face when he finds out I slept with you?"

I roll my eyes, even though my throat is still tight. "God, no."

Ryan's hand comes up to my face and he brushes several strands of my hair back. "I don't want to do that. I want to stay here. I want you to stay here with me, in bed all day."

Last night we broke the rules. Maybe we should just keep breaking them. For today, I mean.

My breath hitches. He might think what we did was a mistake, but he doesn't seem overly ashamed or anything.

I lick my lips and ask, "Can we fuck again?"

His mouth curves upward into a grin. "You're asking?"

I nod, biting my lip.

"Come here," he says.

He pulls me under him, kissing me slow and deep.

Afternoon light spills across the bed. I'm in his T-shirt

and nothing else, curled against his side, half asleep and wholly content.

My stomach growls. He brushes a kiss over my lips and murmurs, "I should order food. You hungry?"

My stomach growls again and he laughs. "Never mind, don't answer that. I'll be right back."

He pads to the bathroom and then grabs his cell phone to order food. "Java Monkey okay?" he asks.

"Since when have I ever turned down my favorite food from my favorite coffee shop?" I ask.

He smirks and places the order.

Twenty minutes later, the doorbell rings. I assume he placed a contactless delivery. That's the only thing I've ever done anyway, so I run downstairs after pulling on a pair of panties. I'm already fantasizing about the coffee and carbs that are about to be in my hands at home.

As I open the door, the only problem is, I come face-to-face with Ellie. Ryan's younger sister.

She's standing on the front stoop holding our takeout. Her eyes widen as she takes me in.

"Wren," she says, her tone surprised.

I swear I turn six shades of purplish red. "I thought you were the food delivery," I explain awkwardly.

She holds out a bag. "Yeah, I ran into the delivery girl. She looked pretty overwhelmed. I was happy to take the order off her hands. I guess I should've let her come to the door, huh?"

"Yeah, ha!" I swallow. "Right. Uh, thanks."

I accept the bag. She smirks and looks me up and down.

"You should go back upstairs before your legs give out. Tell my brother that I'll call him later."

"Thanks," I say, not knowing what else I could say. I close the door and bolt upstairs, my face on fire.

When I burst into Ryan's room, I practically yell, "It was Ellie."

"Delivering food?" he asks, his voice quizzical.

"She took the delivery. Accepted the delivery from the delivery girl."

He groans. "Ah. Of course she did."

I set the paper bag on his bed, the paper cups on the bedside table, and then look at him. "Why are you not freaking out more? She knows. She saw me in this."

I indicate his T-shirt hanging off my body.

He sits up, pulls a face, and stretches. "It's not the greatest thing, but Ellie won't tell anybody. She knows how to keep a secret."

I cock my hips and put my hands on them. "What if she tells Jay?"

"She won't. Even if she did, it could've been worse. Jay could've been at the door."

I groan and flop down beside him.

"We'll be all right," he says. He grabs the brown bag and opens it. "I think we got away with it this time."

He hands me a large paper cup.

"If this is drip coffee, I don't really want it. I only like sweet, milky coffee. Preferably—"

"A tall white mocha?" He arches a brow. "Yeah, I know. It's what you always order at Java Monkey. I even got it with caramel drizzled on top."

My mouth opens and closes. Ryan knows my regular order? How?

"Don't look so surprised." He smirks. "I've only seen you order it like five hundred times. I'm telling you, Rustin. I know you."

"Uh... thanks." I blush as I grip the cup in both hands, like I need the warmth. Sure, it's the middle of summer. But my head is spinning and I feel like I need to hold onto something to anchor me.

I wonder again if he has been paying more attention than I thought. Ryan contentedly sips what I think is an iced Americano or a black iced coffee. Not what I would've guessed.

Then he looks into the bag, eyeing the variety of bagels and cream cheese packets. "This looks good. Should we go downstairs?"

"Are you kidding? I am never leaving this bed again."

He gives me a sharp look. "Eating in bed is disgusting."

I ignore him and pluck a cinnamon raisin bagel from the bag. I take a bite.

"I'm still doing it," I declare.

He smirks. "Gross."

I sip my coffee and then recline, stretching out and smiling at him. "What if I said you could eat it off me, if you'd rather?"

"That's the best suggestion you've ever had," he growls.

He pounces immediately, knocking the bag of bagels to the floor and tackling me into the pillows.

I don't disagree.

twenty-two

RYAN

I'M LYING in bed just as dawn begins to break, changing the light pouring in the window from heavy and blue to a swirl of gray. Wren is tucked up against me. I swear to God, it feels like some kind of trick. Like if I move too fast, she'll vanish.

I spent so long fantasizing about having sex with her that I never realized how fulfilling the other part would be. The part where she fell asleep in my arms. Her skin is warm, her breathing steady. Her face is pressed against my chest and her hand curls against my hip like I'm someone she trusts. That wrecks me a little bit.

That trust burns in my chest. Not because I deserve it, but because I desperately wish I was the sort of man who did.

It's unexpected, but the fact that she's been so unabashedly needy for the last thirty-six hours blows my mind. I stay still and watch her for longer than I should.

When her eyes flutter open, she gazes up at me. For just a moment, the combative version of Wren is gone. She kisses my jaw, then my neck, then my chest. Each kiss is like a fuse, lit and burning slow. I want to explode.

My heart nearly stops every time she does it. My body hardens. I skip ahead in time, anticipating that she'll want me. That she'll straddle my hips and grind into me. My body reverberates with need.

But then her phone buzzes.

Wren groans and hesitates. Then she reaches for it. Looking at the screen, she screws up her face. "There's a 7 a.m. production meeting," she says. "Top secret, of course. I have to go."

"Are you sure?" I kiss her bare shoulder. She shivers.

She smiles at me and bites her lip. Of course, I get it. I already know that she's the producers' behind-the-scenes plant, the secret crew member embedded in the cast. I just hate that it means she has to pretend.

Pretend we're not combusting. Pretend I'm not already ruined for anyone else. Pretend that we're enemies. Pretend that nothing's changed between us.

It certainly feels as though things have.

She kisses my lips and then gets up. She pulls on a fresh pair of panties and a bra from her duffel bag. I watch her move around my room like she belongs here. In another life, when she wasn't Jay's sister, this could be normal.

Then she looks over her shoulder. "Can I borrow a shirt?" she asks.

"You can wear anything of mine, anytime," I say.

She drags on a pair of jeans and pulls my shirt on. It swallows her frame. But somehow, it fits better on her than it ever did on me.

"It smells like you," she says. "I mean that in the best way possible."

I grab her and kiss her lips again. She leans in and kisses

me back for some time, but before I can deepen the kiss and start taking her clothes off, she backs away.

"I really have to go now. I'll see you later tonight."

I almost say *don't go*. Almost. But I bite it back and let her choose.

She blushes as she bolts out the bedroom door. Then I'm alone.

I hate it.

My body is primed for sex. It's not going to happen. But I lie in bed for much too long, refusing to do anything about it. I talk myself down. I tell myself that it was just sex. Just two nights of pretending and breaking the rules.

But the echo of her laugh in my head, the way she looked wearing my shirt. That doesn't feel casual.

I picture her face, the way she looked at me when I went down on her for the first time. The way she looked at me like I was good. No, I wasn't good. I was the best thing she'd ever had. Like she wanted me for more than a hookup or a headline. Like I was safe. Like I was enough.

If I start to believe any of that is true, I'm terrified of the outcome.

I shower and dress before I grab a bowl of oatmeal. My phone is full of texts and missed calls. Jay wanted to grab lunch yesterday. Jay asking if I had plans last night. Then my sister Ellie, sending me several blushing emojis and suggesting I call her.

I text,

> So Wren got a makeover. As you can see, it's… a lot.

The dots appear instantly.

> Hot girl transformation?

My lips curve upward.

> She looks like the kind of woman who'd eat me alive.

Sounds like your type.

I stare at the screen for a second too long.

> She had heels on. Eyeliner. A crop top. How was I supposed to resist?

You poor thing. Did you faint?

> No, but I forgot how to use my legs for a minute.

Be honest. You've been into her since she wore that nerdy little Greek mythology shirt to your birthday party.

> That was three years ago.

Exactly.

I pause. How do I dodge her accusation?

> I'm going to eliminate someone. Someone other than Wren, obviously. Pray for me.

The reply comes fast.

Do you remember how weird it was when you first moved into the dorms at Emory and had to make friends with Jay? You survived that. You thrived. You'll be all right.

The difference is that no one was going to cry on national television.

You heartbreaker.

I've certainly been called worse.

I remember how stiff Wren was the first night we were on set. She bristled when anyone so much as looked her way. Now she's laughing and wearing my shirt to set. And it's wrecking me in ways I can't admit.

Checking my watch, I see that I don't have to be on set for several hours, later tonight.

There's a group date and then an elimination. I should go to the gym and then rest.

Instead, I text Coach T.

Skate?

We meet at the ice rink. It smells like chilly air, sweat, and hard work. I walk down the stands and see Coach T sitting and watching young hockey players skate before him. His arms are crossed. He's outwardly emotionless, but his eyes dart back and forth, carefully monitoring the activity on the rink.

When I sit down, Coach hands me a brown paper lunch bag.

"Evelyn made you a sandwich," he says gruffly.

That's how you know Coach cares. He doesn't ask questions. He sends food. He shows up.

Emotion wells in my chest. I don't know whether I'm going to laugh or cry, but I accept the paper bag with reverence.

"Tell her she's still my favorite woman."

He eyes me for a moment and then gives me the tiniest smile.

"She knows."

I sit beside him and unwrap the sandwich. I'm not starving, but when Mrs. T offers me food, there's no way I'm going to skip that. I unwrap the sandwich and find it's turkey, cheddar, and mustard. Same thing I used to eat in Coach's kitchen after school.

I used to inhale these while Ellie sat beside me, swinging her feet and trying to copy my stick tape job. The familiarity and comfort the first bite brings me are an anchor, fixing me in time.

I watch the kids skate on the ice before me. They're little messes with oversized helmets and untied laces. I can't stop the flood of memories. Begging Coach to take us in. Promising I'd work, clean, run drills, tape sticks, do anything if it meant keeping Ellie close. We had been split up by CPS. I didn't know where she was sleeping. I didn't know how to protect her.

When Coach and his wife Evelyn finally agreed to take us both in, Ellie was quiet and shell-shocked for weeks afterward. I was afraid I'd taken too long. That some kind of fracture had already formed in her personality. She eventually warmed up and returned to her usual easygoing self, but I still wake up in the dead of night sweating and shaking, afraid she isn't safe.

I'm a grown man now. I've got twenty-five million in the bank and a trophy case with my name on it. But that fear? It never left. It just got quieter.

Coach T is the best. Mrs. T is second only to him in my book, but she's the only woman who has that designation. Every other woman in my life has been a flicker. Gone before I could even get warm.

Women often leave and say they're coming back, but they never do. They always leave.

I stop eating my sandwich and put it down because it suddenly seems like I'm eating ashes.

They always leave.

Wren felt too good. Too easy. I know she will leave at some point. If I let her mean something, if I let the relationship between us grow, it'll ruin me when she goes.

Because she will.

They always do. Wren will smile. She'll tell me it meant something. Then she'll walk away like she never touched me at all.

Coach T slides his gaze to me.

"There something wrong with the sandwich?"

I shake my head. "No, it's not that. I just ate before I came here."

Not exactly true, but the white lie makes me feel a bit better.

He eyes me. "You're moody today. Is this about a girl?"

I sigh and drop my gaze. I don't say anything, but I feel like Coach sees right through me. He's not a big talker. He's more of a listener, so he lets the silence stretch between us, like he always does.

Eventually, I say, "There might be someone."

"Might?"

I purse my lips. There is someone, but it's not, you know. It's not gonna work. She's too young. She's too sweet. She deserves better than me. I can't afford to lose focus.

Coach arches a brow. "No?"

I shrug.

We lapse into silence for another minute before he surprises me by breaking the tension.

"You don't let yourself have good things, do you?"

I stare at the ice and clamp down on any show of emotion. I'm not interested in letting Coach see the ins and outs of my relationship with Wren just now. I haven't even begun to process it.

Coach stands up and jerks his head toward the ice.

"Come on. Come down and talk to the kids. They'll be excited to see to you. Talk to a real professional hockey player."

I wrap up the rest of my sandwich and take it with me. As the kids' practice ends, a dozen of them run up to us, yelling my name, asking for autographs and selfies. One kid asks for tips on his slapshot.

Coach hands me a Sharpie and claps my shoulder again. I'm off the hook for now, but one thought keeps crawling back in as I sign jerseys and ruffle sweaty hair.

If Wren makes me feel like I'm enough... what happens when she realizes I'm not?

What happens when she leaves and I can't pretend I never needed her?

twenty-three

WREN

IT'S three minutes to seven in the morning when I drag myself into *The Last Kiss* production offices. Most of the crew aren't around yet, but as I scurry down the hall toward the meeting room, I pass by the wardrobe office. The light is on. I slow down, spotting Jennifer as she organizes some cosmetics on the counter closest to the door.

She looks up and smiles warmly. "Hey, what are you doing here so early?"

I know I'm going to be late but fuck it. I haven't seen Jennifer in a week. Catching up with her for a few minutes won't hurt anything.

She swirls a makeup brush in the air.

"I'm here for an early meeting with Elena," I explain.

She nods, then looks me up and down. "You look comfortable."

I glance down and realize I forgot to change out of Ryan's shirt. It's oversized and soft and worn in. Definitely not from wardrobe. Or my closet.

My stomach lurches. Before I can say anything, Elena's voice rings down the hall.

"Wren! Get in here. Now." Her voice cracks down the hallway like a whip. "Some of us are trying to run a show."

I stiffen and look toward Jennifer. She gently shoos me on.

"We'll talk later."

I nod and then approach Elena, trying not to fidget with the hem of the T-shirt like a guilty teenager sneaking in after curfew. Elena looks like a million bucks in a red wrap dress and white heels. She waits for me until I reach the doorway, then marches into the conference room, sitting down and kicking her heels up on the table.

Marcus is right beside her with a tablet, chewing gum and scrolling with an intense expression on his face. He raises his eyes and smirks. He's watching me like I'm a bug under glass and he's going to trap me. I plunk down in the seat across from his. Elena turns to me.

"Let's talk about how this season nearly went off the rails."

I hesitate. "I think it's going well, don't you?"

She waves her hand like she's irritated by everything. I brace myself. Elena never wastes time on meetings unless she's about to detonate something.

"That depends on what your definition of 'well' is. It's the most boring season of *The Last Kiss* I've ever witnessed. I've been here for twelve years."

My eyebrows rise. "What do you mean, boring?"

"I mean the bachelor isn't horny enough."

Marcus snorts and looks up. "There's more action in the B-roll between Raven and JacqLyn."

"Exactly," Elena says. "He hasn't kissed half the girls. Don't even get me started on the fantasy suite buildup. If this season tanks, we blame blue balls."

I press my lips together, trying not to visibly react. Elena slaps me lightly on the hand.

"You know him, Wren. You guys go way back. Any idea how to get his mojo flowing?"

It just so happens I have exactly every idea of what will get his mojo flowing. But I can't exactly share that with her.

"He's, um... private. I've never seen him hit on anybody. I think girls mostly chase him around and he just accepts. Even on New Year's Eve... and Cinco de Mayo... I've never seen him drunk."

Maybe he's just a slower burn than the usual contestants.

"Why hasn't he ever been drunk, do you think?" Elena asks before I consider it. The answer is out of my mouth.

"Well, his mom... she had problems with addiction. Specifically, alcohol."

Marcus looks at Elena, his expression worried. "Shit, really?"

I nod, wishing I hadn't said anything at all. If he knew I had blabbed about his mom, Ryan would be really upset.

Elena tilts her head and taps a finger against her lips. "Interesting. Still, if the girls are drunk enough, maybe he won't have a choice. Then maybe they'll make the moves for him, like you suggested."

I blanch. "I wasn't suggesting anything like that."

Elena waves me off. "I want you to come up with three activities guaranteed to make him loosen up. Horny is the goal. Think flirting. Think touching. Think jealousy, even."

I nod quickly. "I'll, uh... I'll think about it."

"Good," she says. "Get to work."

I get up and leave the room quickly, pretending that Ryan's shirt isn't burning my skin.

* * *

Tonight's group date starts with everyone doing a shot of tequila together. I wince as it burns down my throat. I'm not much of a drinker. Tequila reminds me why. Liquor makes me too honest, too messy, too likely to reveal every secret I've ever kept.

It's what the producers call a low-stakes bonding night. Which is code for dress casual but slutty, because we're going to pump you full of alcohol and give you a reason to be stupid.

We sit on the back patio in a loose circle. Everyone is already buzzed. Ryan sits three spots away, beer bottle in hand, looking a little too serious for a man surrounded by tittering drunk women. He hasn't looked my way once, like last night evaporated with the morning sun.

I haven't spoken to him all day. He texted once earlier. *Sleep OK?* Then nothing. I didn't answer because I didn't know what to say. How do you casually respond after your entire heart unraveled in someone's arms?

So now he's acting like I don't exist. Fine.

Two can play at that game.

JacqLyn spins the bottle and it lands on Raven. There's a big bowl full of questions and dares. She waves her hands over it.

"What will it be? Truth or shot?"

Raven eyes her, then takes a shot before the question is even read. "I don't trust you with any of my secrets. None of you."

That gets a laugh. Next, it's Nikki's turn. I see that she has recovered from the hiking excursion and is gamely trying to act like it never happened. Okay, then. She chooses to take a gamble on the contents of the bowl...

Raven's lips curve up as she reads the card.

"Do a lap around the patio wearing nothing but a beach towel."

Nikki stands up looking jubilant. "I think a beach towel would be more than I'm wearing right now." She looks down at her micro skirt and tube top. "What do you think, Ryan?"

Ryan smiles and tilts his head. "I think you're right."

Nikki does a quick lap and Raven takes a shot. The game is chaotic and loud. Divya lets Letitia eat whipped cream out of her belly button, which is hysterical for everyone.

Then it's my turn.

"Truth or shot?" Raven asks.

I've had two shots so far and that's too many for me, so I opt for the other choice. "Truth."

Raven asks, "Who here do you think is faking it the most?"

I think about it for a second, look around the circle, then opt to take the shot. Because the person faking it most here is me, pretending Ryan hasn't hollowed me out.

The whole group *oohs* and *aahs*. Ryan doesn't look at me, though. He just takes a long pull from his beer.

The cameras circle as Ryan is up at the plate. JacqLyn reads a card to him.

"Kiss someone that you haven't kissed on the show yet."

He smiles but doesn't move. He thinks about it for a moment and then shakes his head and takes a shot.

Everyone laughs, but there's a ripple of uncertainty. My stomach twists uncomfortably. I refuse to believe that his hesitation has anything to do with me. But God, I hope it does.

I lean in, emboldened by the three shots of expensive

tequila. "What's the matter, Haart? You running out of eligible victims?"

Now his gaze finally cuts to me. "I just didn't feel like faking anything tonight. Is that all right with you, Wren?"

Ouch. With a capital O.

I raise an eyebrow. "Is cryptic and broody your new personality trait, or are you saving that just for me?"

"You practically whisper around half the crew, but the second I walk in, you're roasting me like I'm a marshmallow. Explain that."

"Oh, fuck off." I stick my tongue out at him and he grins.

The game moves on and JacqLyn takes her turn. As she enacts her dare, I move seats, slipping in next to Ryan and whisper, "Are you okay? Or are you just trying to pretend that I don't exist again?"

His jaw tightens. "Maybe don't start with me tonight."

"Oh, I'm so sorry," I whisper. "Did you wake up cuddling someone you didn't want to deal with the morning after?"

He blinks, stunned. I can tell he wasn't expecting that.

"I didn't say that," he murmurs, voice gone to gravel, as if the words cost him something.

"You didn't have to. You've been treating me like a PR liability all day."

Like I'm something to hide. Something regrettable.

He stares at me hard. For a moment, something unguarded flashes in his eyes. Hurt, confusion, regret. Then it's gone.

Raven shrieks about JacqLyn picking strip truth or dare and the moment between us breaks.

We turn back to the circle, both pretending nothing just happened. But I can feel the pressure of his attention, like a bruise forming where his gaze touched me. My cheeks are flushed, my chest is tight. Ryan hasn't taken his eyes off me once.

I shiver with the realization that once we're alone, there will be no stopping him from taking what he wants.

twenty-four

RYAN

AFTER DRINKING TOO MANY SHOTS, there's still an elimination ceremony. We make it through the beginning pretty quickly with Raven, Divya, and Nikki. Nikki is sobbing and JacqLyn is clearly plastered. I am trying to keep my face blank while handing out roses like I'm emotionally available and not falling apart inside. Being tipsy while I supposedly make life-altering decisions isn't really sitting well with me.

Wren is near the back of the crowd. Her chin is up, her shoulders are squared, but I can tell she's tense. Her eyes keep flicking toward me like she's looking for something and then looking off into the distance. I hand her a rose second to last.

She grips the stem so hard that it breaks on the way back to her spot. She stumbles slightly, her heel catching on the uneven tile. I move without even thinking about it. One step forward and my hand is on her elbow, steadying her.

She looks up at me, surprised. "Thanks."

I swallow. "Of course."

My hand lingers a half second too long. She peers up at

me, her breath catching. Then I force myself to move away. The cameramen circle us, catching every moment. I taste bile at the back of my throat.

She used to blend in so much I'd forget she was even there. Now I can't stop tracking her. Every damn move.

I end up sending Letitia home. Not anything personal against her. I just... I can tell we don't mesh together. By the time I'm done, I'm exhausted. Wren doesn't even meet my gaze as she flees.

I storm back to my room, slamming the door and pressing my palms to my eyes. I'm not sure what happened today. I wonder if the alcohol caused me to be soft toward Wren, that instinct to help her, to touch her in front of everyone.

It's going to ruin both of us. The cameras are hungry for any sign of me showing even the vaguest interest in any of the girls. Wren deserves someone better. Someone stable. Someone who doesn't have a job where they're on the road all the time. Most importantly, someone who doesn't mind people watching their vulnerable moments.

I get changed out of my clothes that still kind of smell like tequila, then take a shower, chugging a bottle of water while I clean my body. When I get out of the shower, my phone lights up as it lies on my bed. I wrap a towel around my waist and pad over to it, looking down at the screen.

It's her, of course.

Wanna talk?

I hesitate and then type back.

About what?

I change into a pair of track pants and a fresh T-shirt. Then I see a new text from Wren.

I'm outside. I killed the room cam. Let me in.

My eyebrows fly up. She's making a big effort and putting herself out there to talk to me in private. I open my bedroom door and she's there, wearing her silk sleep shorts and my T-shirt. Her hair is wet and she smells freshly showered. She's not wearing any makeup or any of the crazy punk rock trappings. She gives me a mischievous smile.

Without saying a word, I let her in. Because of course, I do. How could I say no? She strides into my room and flops down onto the couch. I sit beside her and try not to look at her legs, but then I'm caught staring at her mouth.

She tilts her head. "You've been weird."

"I'm always weird," I grunt.

She pauses for a moment. "You're being distant. It's not just me. What's going on?"

"It just feels like everything changed." I let out my breath in a long stream. "I'm not particularly good at hiding any of it, so it's easier to just keep my distance."

We're halfway through filming. Halfway to the end. And all I can think about is what happens if she walks away from me at the end of this.

She nods like she understands. "So let's not make it a big deal. Let's call it what it is. We're two people who happen to get along only when we're naked, that's all."

Her tone makes me laugh, which only encourages her. She scoots closer and drops her head to my shoulder. I don't mean to relax at her touch, but it's hard not to. I lean back against the couch and inhale a full, deep breath. Her scent grazes my nose, honey and lemons. I touch her hair with two fingers, flicking it away from her face.

Wren's lips part and she looks up at me. Our faces are only inches apart.

"Can I be sweet to you?" she asks. "Just right now. No one can see."

Has any man ever been so sorely tempted?

My body hardens. I hate the way her words make me feel desperate for her touch. I clench my jaw, but nod. She wraps her hand around my jaw and presses her lips against my neck, my shoulder, my lips. I know what we're doing is wrong. I know Jay will kill me if he ever finds out, but damn if I can stop myself.

I press my lips against hers and deepen the kiss, stroking her tongue with mine. She's warm and soft and smells like shampoo and bad ideas.

Without thinking, I grab her waist and pull her onto my lap, needing to feel her closer, needing more of her.

"Ryan," she whispers, her soft voice gone husky.

I capture her mouth with mine, swallowing whatever she was about to say. Her lips are sweet and eager, opening for me like she's been waiting her whole life for this moment. Maybe she has. The thought makes something tighten in my chest, something possessive and primal.

Her satin sleep shorts slide against my track pants as she settles on my thighs. The thin material of my t-shirt that she's wearing does nothing to hide her hardened nipples or the flush spreading across her chest. I can feel the heat between her legs through the fabric of my shorts. It's driving me insane.

"Fuck, Chirp," I murmur against her mouth, hands gripping her hips firmly. I guide her against me, setting a rhythm that makes us both gasp. "You feel so good."

Her fingers dig into my shoulders, holding on tight as I control her movements. I grind her down onto my hardening cock, feeling her wetness seep through both layers of our clothing. The knowledge that I've made her this wet, this ready, sends a fresh surge of desire through me.

I pull back just enough to see her face. Her cheeks are flushed, her lips swollen from my kisses. She bites her lower lip, a gesture so innocent and yet so provocative that I have to stifle a groan. Her eyes meet mine, pupils blown wide with desire.

"It's supposed to be my turn," she whispers, her breath warm against my face, "to make you feel good."

Something about her words, about her wanting to please me, makes my cock twitch against her. I thrust upward, pushing against her core.

"You are making me feel good," I grate out. "So fucking good."

Her head falls back, exposing the delicate line of her throat. I take advantage, pressing my lips to her pulse point, feeling it race under my tongue. My hands stay firmly on her hips, guiding her movements as she rocks against me. Each thrust brings me closer to the edge. I realize with a start that I could come just like this, with both of us still mostly clothed.

"Jesus Christ," I mutter, lifting her slightly to adjust our position. When I settle her back down, the head of my cock brushes directly against her pussy through our clothes. The contact makes her gasp, her hands tightening on my shoulders.

This girl is making me crazy. I've been with women before. Plenty of them. But none have affected me like Wren. None have made me feel like I'm losing my mind with just a look, a touch, a whispered word. It's both terrifying and exhilarating.

I'm practically dry humping her now, rutting against her like a teenager getting his first taste of action. I should be embarrassed, but all I feel is desperate need. I'm ready to come in my shorts like a virgin, but I'm too deep in the moment to be able to control myself any better than this. What has Wren done to me?

She seems to sense my desperation because she tightens her thighs around me and starts to move with more purpose. Her hips roll in a motion that can only be described as sinful, riding me like I'm a bucking bronco she's determined to tame.

"Ryan," she moans, her voice breaking on my name. The sound goes straight to my groin, making me harder than I thought possible.

I can't take it anymore. I need to see her, all of her. With trembling fingers, I grab the hem of her borrowed shirt and pull it upward. She raises her arms, helping me strip it off. The sight of her, braless, flushed, perfect, knocks the breath from my lungs.

Her breasts are smaller than what I usually go for, but they're perfect for her frame. Perfect for my hands. Perfect, period. The soft pink of her nipples makes my mouth water. I waste no time cupping them, feeling their weight in my palms. They're so fucking soft.

"So beautiful." I brush my thumbs over the hardened peaks. She shivers at my touch, arching into my hands.

I pinch one nipple gently, then with more pressure when she responds with a moan. The sound sends a jolt straight to my cock. I pull and twist the soft rosebuds, learning what makes her breath catch, what makes her push harder against my erection.

"I never knew," she gasps, eyes closed in pleasure. "I never knew it could feel like this."

Her words remind me that this is all new to her, that I'm the first man to touch her this way, to see her come undone. The thought fills me with equal parts pride and terror. I want to be worthy of this trust she's placed in me.

"I'm going to make you feel so good, Chirp," I promise. "So fucking good that you'll never forget."

"As if I ever could." She smiles then, a smile so genuine and trusting that it makes my heart stutter in my chest.

I pull her closer, our skin finally touching. I lose myself in the sweet heat of her mouth once more.

After a few more strokes of my thumbs across her nipples, Wren pushes against my shoulders. I back off immediately, worried I've gone too far or hurt her somehow. But the look in her eyes isn't pain.

It's determination. She slides off my lap and sinks to her knees between my legs, her hands resting on my thighs. The sight of her looking up at me, lips parted and cheeks flushed, nearly stops my heart.

"I want to try something." Her fingers play with the waistband of my track pants, sending jolts of electricity across my skin.

I swallow hard, unable to form words as she tugs at the elastic. I lift my hips slightly, helping her pull down both my pants and boxer briefs in one smooth motion. My cock springs free, harder than I can ever remember being. Her eyes widen slightly. I fight the urge to preen under her gaze.

Nah, fuck it. I give my cock a stroke, fisting it as I stare at her swollen lips. She runs her tongue over those lips and I think I might faint. I want her so badly right now.

Wren wraps her fingers around the base of my cock tentatively. I inhale sharply at the contact. Her touch is light, exploring, nothing like the confident handling I'm used to. But somehow, this gentle curiosity is more arousing than anything I've experienced before.

Wren leans forward, pressing her lips against the tip in a soft kiss. The teasing contact makes my thighs tense, my fingers digging into the couch to keep from grabbing her hair. She places another kiss along the shaft, then another, each one sending sparks of pleasure up my spine.

"Show me," she whispers, looking up at me through her lashes. "Show me how you like to have your cock sucked."

Fuck. I should not be this turned on by her inexperience, by those innocent words coming from her mouth. But goddamn, I want her. I want to teach her every filthy thing I know, want to watch her learn and grow confident with my cock.

"You sure?"

She nods, her expression eager and trusting. "I want to make you feel good, Ryan. Like you made me feel. I want to make you come."

I reach out, burying my hands in her hair, cradling her head gently. "Start with just the tip," I instruct, surprised at how hoarse my voice sounds. "Use your tongue. Lick around it."

She follows my direction immediately, her tongue darting out to circle the head of my cock. The wet heat of her mouth sends pleasure shooting through me, but I try to hold myself in check. This is about her learning, not me losing control.

"That's it," I encourage as she takes me deeper, her lips stretching around my girth. "Now suck gently while you move up and down."

Wren complies, establishing a slow rhythm that has me biting my lip to keep from groaning too loudly. She's clumsy at first, teeth occasionally grazing me, but she's a quick learner. Within minutes, she's found a pattern that has my toes curling in pleasure.

Her eyes flick up to mine, watching my reactions carefully. There's something incredibly intimate about that eye contact, something that makes my chest tight with an emotion I'm not ready to name.

"You can go faster," I tell her, my fingers tightening slightly in her hair. "Take as much of my cock in your mouth as feels comfortable."

She tries, but after a few attempts, she pulls back, a small frown creasing her forehead. "I can tell you're holding back," she whispers. "I want all of you, Ryan. Don't treat me like I'll break."

Her words hit me like a physical blow. I've been treating her gently because she's new to this, because she's Wren. My best friend's little sister, the girl I've watched grow up, the woman I've secretly wanted for longer than I care to admit. But she's right. I'm holding back, and not just physically.

"Move back," I say, my voice rougher than intended. She looks confused but scrambles backward. I stand, then guide her back to my cock. "Open your mouth for me, Chirp."

Her lips part without hesitation, trust evident in her eyes. I hold her in place with one hand firmly tangled in her hair, the other guiding my cock to her waiting mouth. The position change shifts the power dynamic, putting me in control. I watch her carefully for any sign of discomfort.

"I'm going to fuck your throat," I warn her, my cock twitching at the mere thought. "Tap my thigh twice if it's too much."

She nods. I slowly push forward, feeding my length into

her warm, wet mouth. The sensation is incredible. I have to force myself to go slowly, to give her time to adjust. Her throat constricts around me as I push deeper. She gags slightly before relaxing.

"Good girl," I praise, pulling back slightly before pushing in again. "You're taking my cock so well, Chirp. That feels amazing."

She hums against me, the vibration sending pleasure racing through my body. The sound isn't one of discomfort. It's arousal. The knowledge that she's enjoying this, that she's turned on by pleasuring me, nearly sends me over the edge.

"Fuck, you're so hot," I groan, establishing a rhythm now, my hips moving more confidently. "The way you're taking all of my cock... I'm going to remember this forever, Chirp."

Her eyes water slightly as I hit the back of her throat, but she doesn't tap out. Instead, she hollows her cheeks, sucking harder, her tongue working against the underside of my shaft. The sensation is overwhelming, pushing me closer to the brink.

She slurps around me, the obscene sound making my toes curl and my eyes roll back. It's too much. Her eagerness, her trust, the wet heat of her mouth. I feel the familiar tightening in my balls, the building pressure that signals I'm close.

"I'm going to come," I warn her, trying to pull back. "You don't have to..."

She grabs my ass, preventing my retreat, her eyes locked on mine in silent communication. The message is clear. She wants this, wants all of me. The realization pushes me over the edge.

"Oh fuck!" I grit out. "Fuck, baby..."

I come like a freight train, my entire body tensing as pleasure rips through me. I spill into her mouth, pulse after pulse, my vision blurring with the intensity. Through it all, Wren stays with me, swallowing every drop like an angel sent to destroy me.

When the last aftershock passes, I carefully pull out of her mouth, my legs trembling with the effort to remain standing. She looks up at me, lips swollen and shiny, a small smile playing at the corners of her mouth. There's a hint of pride in her expression, and something else.

Something that makes my heart race for reasons entirely unrelated to physical pleasure.

"Was that okay?" she asks. I nearly laugh at the absurdity of the question.

Instead, I reach down and help her to her feet, pulling her against me in a fierce embrace. "That was fucking perfect," I tell her. I mean every word.

I can't resist kissing her again, tasting myself on her lips. The intimacy of it should be strange. I never kiss women after they service me. But somehow, the gesture only fuels my desire for her.

I walk her backward until her legs hit the edge of the bed, our mouths still connected, our hands exploring like we have all the time in the world.

"Let me taste you," I murmur against her lips, feeling her shiver at my words.

She nods, eyes wide and trusting. I pull my T-shirt over my head, carelessly tossing it aside. Her hands immediately find my chest, fingers tracing the contours of my muscles with fascination. The gentleness of her touch contrasts with the hunger in her eyes, making my heart race.

I hook my fingers into the waistband of her pink silk sleep shorts, looking into her eyes for permission. She lifts her hips slightly. I slide them down her legs, my knuckles brushing against her smooth skin. She's left in just a pair of plain white cotton panties.

Somehow, they're sexier than any lace or silk pair I've ever seen.

"You're beautiful," I tell her, meaning it more than I've ever meant those words before.

Her cheeks flush. She tries to look away. I catch her chin gently, bringing her gaze back to mine. "I mean it, Chirp. Every inch of you."

I lay her back on the bed, her hair fanning out across my pillow like a halo. The sight of her there, in my bed, wearing nothing but those innocent white panties, makes my recently satisfied cock twitch with renewed interest. But this isn't about me. This is about her.

I start at her neck, pressing soft kisses along the column of her throat. Her pulse flutters beneath my lips, rapid and strong. I work my way down, paying special attention to her collarbones, the hollow between them, the slope of her shoulders. Her scent is intoxicating, like vanilla and something uniquely her.

"Ryan," she sighs. Her fingers tangle in my hair as I move lower.

I take my time with her breasts, remembering how responsive she was before. I circle one nipple with my tongue before drawing it into my mouth, sucking gently. She arches beneath me, a soft moan escaping her lips. I give the same attention to her other breast, alternating between gentle suction and light grazes of my teeth.

Her stomach trembles beneath my lips as I continue my journey downward. I can smell her arousal now, sweet and musky, making my mouth water in anticipation. I press open-mouthed kisses to her hipbones, her lower belly, deliberately avoiding where she wants me most.

"Please," she whispers, her hips lifting slightly.

I smile against her skin, moving lower to kiss her inner thighs. The soft flesh quivers beneath my lips. I nip at the sensitive skin, leaving marks that no one but me will see. The thought is oddly satisfying.

"Patience," I murmur. "I want to savor you."

"You're driving me insane." The frustration in her voice makes me smile again.

"Turnabout is fair play. Shh, Chirp. Be a good girl for me."

She squirms but doesn't respond, which I take as encouragement. I continue my teasing, alternating between gentle kisses and light bites along her inner thighs. Her legs fall open wider, an unconscious invitation that makes my cock throb. I glance up at her face and find her watching me, lips parted, eyes darkened with desire.

Finally, I brush my fingers over the damp spot at the apex of her thighs. The cotton is soaked through, evidence of her arousal. The sight sends a fresh wave of desire through me. I did this to her. I made her this wet, this ready.

She groans at the contact, her hips bucking slightly. "Ryan, please," she begs, voice cracking. "I need more."

I press my mouth to the wet spot on her panties, inhaling her scent before licking the fabric. The taste of her, even filtered through cotton, is exquisite. Her cry of pleasure encourages me. I lick again, this time with more pressure.

"Oh god," she gasps, her hands clutching at the sheets.

I continue this torturous pace, licking and sucking at her through the thin fabric until the wet spot triples in size.

Her thighs tremble on either side of my head, her breathing becoming more erratic with each pass of my tongue.

When I judge that she's right on the edge, I hook my fingers into the waistband of her panties and slowly peel them down her legs. She lifts her hips to help, her eagerness making me smile. Once the fabric is gone, I take a moment to just look at her, spread out before me, completely bare.

Her pussy is pink and perfect, glistening with her arousal. I lick my lips, anticipation building as I lower my head. The first swipe of my tongue against her bare flesh makes us both groan. She tastes sweet and tangy and uniquely Wren.

I explore her with my tongue, memorizing what makes her gasp, what makes her moan. When I find her clit, swollen and sensitive, she cries out, her back arching off the bed. I circle the small bud with my tongue, varying pressure and speed until I find the rhythm that has her panting my name.

While my mouth works on her clit, I slowly slide a single finger into her dripping pussy. She's tight around me, her inner walls clenching as I curl my finger to find that special spot inside her. When I hit it, she buries her hands in my hair, pressing my face harder against her.

"Ryan," she moans. "Right there. God, please don't stop."

As if I could. I add a second finger, stretching her gently as I continue to work her clit with my tongue. Her thighs begin to tremble, a sure sign she's close. I increase the pressure, curling my fingers more firmly against her G-spot.

"I'm going to come," she warns, voice high and tight with pleasure.

I hum against her in encouragement, the vibration making her gasp. Her fingers tighten in my hair, almost painful but so fucking worth it. I can feel her pussy start to contract around my fingers, her entire body tensing as the orgasm builds.

When it hits, she cries out my name, her back arching sharply. Her pussy clenches rhythmically around my fingers, her clit pulsing against my tongue. I work her through it, gentling my touch as the waves subside, but not stopping until she pushes weakly at my head.

I place one final kiss on her sensitive flesh before moving up to lie beside her. Her eyes are closed, her chest rising and falling rapidly as she catches her breath. A light sheen of sweat covers her skin, making her glow in the dim light of my bedroom.

"You okay?" I ask, brushing a strand of hair from her forehead.

She opens her eyes slowly, a lazy smile spreading across her face. "More than okay," she murmurs. "You're so good at that. Like, too good. I can't think about how you got so good at eating pussy."

"It's a natural talent. I was born this way." I chuckle, oddly pleased by her crassness. "Glad to hear you like how I do it, though."

She snorts, which is about the cutest reaction I've ever seen. "You liar."

I watch her face as she comes down from her high, trying to memorize every detail of this moment. The flush on her cheeks, the softness in her eyes, the way her lips curve into a smile of pure satisfaction. I've been with other women, plenty of them, but this feels different. Special. I want to remember every second of it, lock it away somewhere no one can touch it.

My body is still humming with the afterglow of her

pleasure but watching her come apart has renewed my hunger.

"Are you ready to go again?" I ask.

She arches a brow. "Can you... you know?"

"I've been hard since I saw you in those panties."

Wren's cheeks flush as she nods slowly. "I want you, Ryan. I always do."

Her words make something tighten in my chest.

I reach over to my bedside table, pulling open the drawer to grab a condom. The foil packet crinkles between my fingers as I tear it open, a sound that seems impossibly loud in the quiet room. Wren watches me with curious eyes as I roll the latex down my length with practiced ease.

Instead of positioning myself over her as she might expect, I shift onto my back, resting my head against the pillows. Her brow furrows slightly in confusion.

"Come here," I say, my voice gentle but firm. I pat my thighs in invitation. "I want you to ride me."

Her eyes widen, a flash of uncertainty crossing her features. "I... I don't know how," she admits, a blush spreading across her cheeks.

I reach for her hand, tugging her toward me. "I'll show you. You'll be a natural."

She moves hesitantly, straddling my thighs just as she did earlier when we were still clothed. The difference now is that there's nothing between us, and the heat of her core hovers tantalizingly close to my cock. I run my hands up her thighs, settling them on her hips.

"Take your time," I tell her, fighting the urge to thrust upward. "Go at your own pace."

Wren nods, determination replacing the uncertainty in her eyes. She rises up slightly on her knees, reaching between us to grasp my cock. The touch of her fingers, even through the condom, makes me inhale sharply. She positions me at her entrance, the head of my cock brushing against her slick folds.

Slowly, so slowly it's almost torture, she begins to lower herself onto me. The tight heat of her pussy envelops the head of my cock. I have to bite my lip to keep from groaning too loudly. She pauses, her breath catching, adjusting to the intrusion.

"You okay?" I ask, my voice strained with the effort of holding still.

She nods, a small smile playing at her lips. "It just feels... different like this. Deeper. Your dick is huge, in case you missed the memo."

My dick throbs as though pleased by her words.

I guide her with my hands on her hips, helping her take me inch by inch. The sight of her above me, her hair falling around her shoulders, her lips parted in concentration, is the most erotic thing I've ever seen. When she finally settles fully onto me, taking my entire length, I realize I've never been harder in my life.

"Christ, Chirp," I murmur, my fingers digging into the soft flesh of her hips. "You feel amazing."

She experiments with a small roll of her hips. The sensation pulls a groan from deep in my chest. Her eyes widen at my reaction, a flicker of pride crossing her features. She does it again, this time with more confidence.

"That's it," I encourage, helping her find a rhythm. "Just like that."

She throws her head back, her hair cascading down her back as she begins to move in earnest. Her hands rest on my chest for balance as she rises up before sinking back down, taking me deeper each time. The sight of my cock disappearing into her pussy, slick with her arousal, is almost enough to send me over the edge.

I force myself to focus, to stay present. I want to make this good for her, want to watch her come apart around me again. She's riding me harder now, her confidence growing with each movement. Her breasts bounce with the motion, her nipples hard peaks that I can't resist reaching up to tease.

She moans when I pinch one nipple lightly, her rhythm faltering momentarily before resuming with renewed vigor. Her hips snap against mine, the sound of skin against skin filling the room along with our mingled breaths and moans.

I slip my hand between us, my thumb finding her clit among her slick folds. She gasps at the contact, her eyes flying open to meet mine. I rub gentle circles around the sensitive bud, watching as pleasure transforms her features.

"Ryan," she begs, voice breaking. "Please, more."

"I know what you need, sweetheart. Let it build. Don't rush."

I increase the pressure slightly, matching the rhythm of my thumb to the motion of her hips. Her movements become more erratic, less controlled, a sign that she's chasing her pleasure.

"God, it's so fucking good," she says. "I love the way you touch me."

Watching her fuck me is the hottest thing I've ever seen, her inhibitions completely gone as she uses my body for her pleasure. Hearing her say that makes it hard to keep a steady rhythm.

"That's it, baby," I encourage. I feel her pussy start to

contract around my cock. "That's it. Are you going to come?"

She nods, her eyes squeezed shut in concentration, her hips snapping in a crazed rhythm that tells me she's close. The sight of her like this, uninhibited and beautiful in her pleasure, makes something in my chest tighten.

"Eyes on me, Chirp," I command softly. "I want you to know who's making you come."

Her eyes open, hazy with pleasure but focused on my face. The connection between us in that moment feels almost tangible, like a physical thing binding us together beyond just our bodies. I press my thumb more firmly against her clit.

That's all it takes.

She falls apart with a cry that might be my name, her pussy clenching around my cock in near-violent waves. The sensation of her orgasm, combined with the sight of her face in ecstasy, pushes me right to the edge. I thrust upward, meeting her movements, chasing my own release.

So. Fucking. Perfect.

After a few more strokes, I follow her over the cliff, splintering inside her so hard that I see spots dancing at the edges of my vision. My orgasm tears through me with an intensity that leaves me breathless, my hands gripping her hips hard enough to bruise as I empty myself into the condom.

Wren collapses onto my chest, her body trembling with aftershocks. I wrap my arms around her, holding her close as our breathing gradually slows. Her hair is damp with sweat where it sticks to my chest. Faintly, I can feel her heart racing against my own.

We lie there, neither of us speaking, neither of us needing to. The silence is comfortable, filled with the kind of contentment that comes after not just sex, but connection. I stroke her back lazily, not ready to break the spell that seems to have settled over us.

I've broken plenty of hearts. Been called every synonym for asshole in the book. But none of it ever mattered. Not until now. Not until Wren.

Eventually, she shifts slightly, propping herself up on one elbow to look at me. Her expression is soft, open in a way I've rarely seen from her. There's a vulnerability there that makes my throat tight.

"What are you thinking?"

I could lie, could give her some generic response about how good she was or how much I enjoyed it. But something about the moment, about the way she's looking at me, demands honesty.

"I'm thinking that was the best sex I've ever had," I tell her, tucking a strand of hair behind her ear. "I'm thinking I want to fuck you again. A lot."

Her smile in response is like the sunrise, gradual and warm and full of promise. She leans down to press her lips against mine in a kiss that's gentle but somehow more intimate than anything we've shared tonight.

* * *

Sometime just before sunrise, she wakes me with a kiss on my lips.

"Hey," she whispers. "I should go before people start waking up around here."

My arms slide around her waist and pull her closer. I kiss her like she is the air and I am thirsty for oxygen. My body stirs and she runs her hand down my flat abs, moaning just a little.

"Let me have you again before you go," I ask.

She smiles against my lips but shakes her head. "I waited too long because I wanted to spend every last second in bed with you. But I really have to leave now. The EP is expecting the bachelorettes to start waking up in less than an hour. Believe me, I know."

I sigh and release her. "Maybe the next time you come in here, you just leave the cameras on, huh? Then we can take as much time as we want."

She flashes me a wicked smile. "That's the worst idea I've ever heard. But I'm glad to hear that you think there will be a next time."

She gets up and starts hunting around for her shorts. I grab her and pull her to the edge of the bed, kissing her.

"Is there not going to be a next time?" I ask.

"I hope there will be," she says. "That is, if you want it."

Of course I want it. How could I ever refuse? I kiss her again and she sighs.

"I have to plug the cameras back in. Try not to miss me too much, huh?"

She slips out my bedroom door and I turn my head toward the bed. Not missing her will be more of a challenge than I thought.

twenty-five
WREN

THIS ISN'T JUST A GAME. It's a spectacle. A whirlwind. A high-stakes, end-of-the-season, star-studded charity event with a magnitude that feels like the Super Bowl. Everywhere you look, there's a camera rolling: from the massive film crews ready to capture every blink and gasp, to phone-wielding fans anticipating the next viral moment.

It's a mad house. Intense.

Swarming with fans and camera crews, the producers have gone all out to make sure this isn't just an event but a full-on reality TV extravaganza. The entire cast has front-row seats, faces pressed against the glass like kids at the zoo, all in pursuit of chaos, drama, or maybe even love. Shiny boom mics dangle just out of the frame. Countless GoPros are tucked into flower arrangements on the ledge, capturing our every move. Every breath. Every awkward pause. We're being recorded again. Story of my life.

I'm still breathing hard from fucking Ryan. Again. This isn't just amazing, terrible timing. It's starting to feel like fate.

There they are in a row, like synchronized swimmers: all the contestants, each wearing crisp new hockey jerseys. We're supposed to look like a team, unified in blue and white. Excited to catch the cameras' attention. Every contestant has HAART printed on the back in stark, bold letters, along with the number sixteen. I can practically hear the producers snickering about how clever they are. Here we all are, looking like one big happy family, the kind you see on TV but never in real life.

Except me.

I stare down at my jersey, a relic from another time. *The* jersey. The one with frayed edges and a stubborn stain that never quite washed out. The ancient one I stole years ago right after Ryan carelessly left it at our house. I swiped it off the couch, gave it a new home, and never looked back. While everyone else is decked out in fresh-off-the-press gear, mine is almost nostalgic, a reminder of days long passed. It's thin as paper, softer than it has any right to be, a paler blue than it used to be.

I paired it with a dark gray pleated skirt and my platform Mary Janes. It's a look, but I'm uncertain that I got it right.

I squeeze in beside Raven. The cotton of my jersey rustles against my skin. I can't help but think about all the times I fell asleep in it, wrapped up like it was some kind of security blanket. Maybe it was. I could almost be a teenager again in this faded jersey.

I should have more shame, but I don't.

"Is my makeup okay?" I ask Raven.

"I wouldn't say that." She lights up and touches a strand of my hair. "I would say that you look like a knockout."

I feel my cheeks heat. "Thanks. I got a serious makeover

for this show and it's taking some time for me to come to terms with it."

"Whatever it is, it's working."

"Thanks. That means a lot coming from you. You always look so put together."

Raven grins. "Thanks, babe."

I lean forward and look onto the rink before us where the players zoom around. The energy around us is super-charged. Raven is practically bouncing, her barely-contained excitement fizzing like soda out of a freshly cracked can.

"He's hot!" she announces, eyes glued to the players warming up on the ice. Her voice rings with more surprise than she'd probably care to admit. "I'll say it now. This was a genius date idea!" She jostles me with her elbow. "Major win for the producers. They must be losing it right now."

Heidi bobs her head in agreement. Determination flashes in her eyes, a readiness to see the drama unfold. "Oh, I'm gonna scream so loud if he gets in a fight," she declares, the prospect as thrilling as a front-row seat at a rock concert.

"He won't," I say instinctively, the words tumbling out with less certainty than I'd like. A small, nervous part of me can't rule it out. "At least, I hope not. He was given a red card last season right before the playoffs, and I think that's kept him in line this year."

My mind drifts to all the times I've seen him go from zero to sixty, fists curled, ready to face anyone who thinks they can take him. He fights clean, his punches more preci-sion than rage. But it still makes me flinch when he drops the gloves. He can't help himself sometimes.

It's so Ryan.

Though maybe he'll surprise me. He's got a whole

bunch of bachelorettes to impress tonight, even if it's mostly for the TV show.

The crowd buzzes with anticipation, a low rumble undercutting our conversations. The lights dim. The crowd quiets, then erupts again as the team is introduced. One by one, players burst from the tunnel in a blur of sharp blades and adrenaline. Ryan skates out last.

The crowd loses it.

He's a streak of blue and white, moving with terrifying ease, his shoulders squared and his jaw set with determined precision. That stupid little smirk tugs at his mouth, as if he already knows he's the one they came to see, the main attraction, the headline act. As he flies past our corner of the rink, he slows just a notch, a fraction of a second that feels impossibly long.

Heidi waves.

Raven squeals.

Ryan's eyes find mine. Just for a breath. A flash of heat, intense but fleeting. A flicker of something that makes my pulse skip. It's enough to make me lean forward, to stand up, to feel like maybe this is a story with me in it. Then he's gone, speeding off into the frenzy.

I'm left clutching the railing and pretending I didn't just melt into the floor.

When the puck drops, the game starts with a jolt.

I know it's just for charity, but you wouldn't know it from the way they're playing. The pace is relentless. They don't hold back. The collisions are sharp, players careening off the walls and into each other like they have something to prove. Ryan controls the puck as if it's part of him. Flicking passes, darting through traffic, skating backward like it's no big deal.

Because to him, it isn't. He's in hyper-focus mode, his eyes searching the ice like he's reading minds.

The first period flies by in a blur of thundering skates and crashing bodies. Ryan moves like water flowing around rocks, finding gaps where none should exist. When he's got the puck, he's untouchable. His stick work is poetry in motion, quick little taps and nudges that send the puck exactly where he wants it to go. I watch him fake left, pivot right, and slip past two defenders like they're standing still.

"Did you see that?" Raven shrieks beside me. "How did he even do that?"

I want to explain that Ryan's been doing moves like that since he was twelve, that I've watched him practice the same sequence a thousand times in our neighborhood rink. But I just nod and cheer along.

The opposing team starts targeting him. I can see it happening. Extra checks when he's near the boards. Subtle slashes across his wrists that the refs don't catch. A late hit that sends him sprawling into the corner. My stomach clenches every time someone lines him up for a hit.

"They're going after him," I mutter, gripping the rail tighter.

"Who?" Heidi asks.

"Number twenty-three. The big guy in white. He's been gunning for Ryan all period."

Sure enough, the next time Ryan touches the puck, number twenty-three is right there, throwing his shoulder into Ryan's ribs. Ryan absorbs the hit and keeps skating like it's nothing. But I see the way he stretches his back afterward. The way he flexes his fingers around his stick.

Then Ryan gets his revenge in the most Ryan way possible. He scores.

It happens so fast I almost miss it. A face-off in the

attacking zone. The puck comes back to the point. Ryan drifts toward the net, looking casual, almost lazy. The defenseman passes to him without thinking. Ryan onetimes it, top shelf, bar down. The goalie doesn't even move.

The red light goes on. The horn blares. The crowd explodes.

Ryan doesn't celebrate like the other players. No fist pumps or stick raises. He just skates in a slow circle, that infuriating smirk tugging at his lips like he knew it was going in before he even shot it. Show-off.

"THAT'S MY BOY!" some guy behind us screams.

I want to turn around and tell him that no, actually, that's my… what? My what exactly? My brother's best friend? My secret hookup? My complicated whatever this is?

The second period is more of the same. Ryan sets up two assists with passes so perfect they look scripted. He draws a penalty by being faster than the guy trying to hit him. He even drops back to play defense when their center gets a breakaway, skating backward at full speed and somehow stealing the puck without even looking like he's trying.

"He's everywhere," Heidi breathes.

She's right. Ryan is everywhere. Covering for his teammates. Making plays. Being the kind of player who makes everyone around him better just by existing on the same ice.

But it's the little things that really get to me. The way he taps his stick on the ice to call for a pass. The way he adjusts his helmet between shifts. The way he stretches his neck, rolling his shoulders to work out the kinks. I know all these habits. I've been watching them for years.

During the second intermission, they show highlights on the Jumbotron. Ryan features in about half of them. The crowd cheers louder every time his face appears on screen. I catch myself smiling like an idiot when they replay his first goal in slow motion.

"You're so obvious," Raven teases, nudging my shoulder.

"I don't know what you mean." My neck grows hot.

"Girl, you light up every time he touches the puck. It's adorable."

I want to deny it, but she's probably right. There's something hypnotic about watching Ryan play hockey. It's like seeing him in his natural habitat. This is who he really is underneath all the cameras and producers and artificial drama. This is Ryan at his most pure.

The third period starts differently. Both teams are tired now. The hits aren't quite as crisp. The passes aren't quite as sharp. But Ryan looks like he could play three more periods. He's one of those players who gets stronger as the game goes on. More focused. More dangerous.

With five minutes left, the other team scores to tie it up. The crowd deflates a little. Even I feel the disappointment settling in my chest. But Ryan doesn't look worried. If anything, he looks more determined.

He wins the next face-off cleanly. Draws the puck back to his defenseman. Then something magical happens. Ryan and his linemates start passing the puck like they're playing keep-away from a bunch of kids. Quick little passes. One touches. Tic-tac-toe until the defense is spinning in circles trying to keep up.

It's beautiful hockey. The kind that makes you forget you're watching a charity game.

Ryan has the puck behind the net. He looks up, sees

something I can't, and makes a pass that shouldn't be possible. Through three sets of legs, off the boards, right onto his teammate's stick. The guy barely has to move to redirect it into the net.

Goal. Pure Ryan Haart magic.

This time when the crowd erupts, I don't hold back. I scream until my throat is raw. Jump up and down until my feet hurt. Hug Raven and Heidi until we're all laughing and breathless.

Ryan, the super athlete. Ryan, the undefeatable. Ryan, the ridiculous, irritating, adorable show-off. He's in his element, tearing up the ice with impossible speed and shining under the lights like he was born there.

The noise is deafening.

Fans are on their feet, shouting themselves hoarse. I catch no fewer than five different signs with his name on them. A group of college girls, squeezed together in the row just above us, scream "RYAN! RYAN!" with the kind of enthusiasm usually reserved for rock stars and royalty.

Then I remember my jersey, the craftiest wardrobe choice yet. The rooting becomes a little easier. When he almost scores a third goal, I scream right with them. I'm in the moment, in the crowd, hugging Raven and Heidi until we're an impossible tangle of arms and ponytails.

Even though it's just a stupid game, I find myself sucked in, feeling the pull, the thrill of it all. I'm in the front row of the Ryan Haart show. With the way he's playing, there's zero chance of changing the channel.

By the end of the game, people start whispering. Pointing. Wishing they had binoculars. At first, it's just a trickle of curiosity, a handful of voices rising above the noise. But then a few heads turn our way. It snowballs.

"That's the guy that's going to be on *The Last Kiss*, right?"

"Yeah, number sixteen. He's the bachelor this season."

"He's into the one with the blonde hair, right? Heidi?"

"No, I think it's the redhead. The tiny one."

They must be talking about me. How *embarrassing*.

"That's the one he keeps looking at!" a voice exclaims.

The words echo, growing louder, a rumor gathering steam. The cameras circle, catching all the rumors. *This* is what the producers had in mind.

I almost hate that I'm playing right into it.

Raven leans over and stage-whispers, "They're talking about you, if you hadn't noticed."

I roll my eyes, but my stomach flips over with nerves.

Ryan gets the puck, weaves through a wall of defensemen like it's nothing, then rips a pass across the ice. One of his teammates snaps it into the net. Goal. Game.

The arena explodes.

I jump up, shrieking with everyone else. Raven grabs my arm, whooping. Heidi shouts something unintelligible. The scoreboard flashes. The crowd stays on its feet long after the final buzzer.

It's electric. I catch my breath, but my pulse is still racing. It's impossible not to smile. For one second, I let myself enjoy it. Just for a second.

Afterward, we're swept into a single-file line. I lag behind, dragging my feet like a child who doesn't want to follow the group. The thrill of the moment hangs over me, but I need space. A pause. Just to breathe. Just to be.

Mostly I am thinking about what it would be like to actually be a hockey player's girlfriend. Would I be under constant surveillance by everyone? Something tells me I wouldn't handle that well.

Two voices, sharp and blatant, slice through the air with the kind of clipped tones meant for secrecy. The words hit harder than I expect.

"She's so boring."

"Which one?"

"Wren. It's like, go on girl, give us absolutely nothing. She's a complete wet blanket. You can just tell."

"She's the virgin, right?"

Both women crack up.

"He's only keeping her around because she's Jay Rustin's baby sister."

"I didn't know that! Makes sense why the show keeps her on. She's a nepo baby."

There's a beat before one voice says, "Girl, that's not what a nepo baby is. But you're right, she has zero personality."

The sound of laughter follows.

I freeze, every syllable of their conversation gluing me to the spot. My hands clench around the hem of my jersey.

I know I shouldn't let it get to me. I know I should laugh it off. But the words sink in, heavy as anchors. I don't cry. I don't move. I just press my lips together in silence and refuse to shed a single tear.

Ryan is off-limits for so many reasons. But this is the biggest one. This sort of treatment is what I should expect if I were ever foolish enough to let Ryan sweet-talk me into dating him.

I have to protect my heart. No matter that he's a battering ram of a man, threatening to break down the careful walls I've put up.

twenty-six

RYAN

WE'RE SUPPOSED to be filming part of the new reality tv show at the arena's after-party, but it's not exactly the glamorous scene you'd imagine. The place is pretty chill, filled mostly with charity donors who pretend they're not excited to be here and production people rolling their eyes at the signage.

A couple of the other players linger around, all trying to look casual as bait for reality TV gold. Everyone has plastic cups filled with weak cocktails. There's a not-so-subtle effort from the crowd to act like they don't notice the clunky cameras hovering in every corner.

I should be playing the amiable jock, chatting people up, but I'm barely interested in the charade.

Because Wren is here. She's laughing with someone else.

Hunter Huxley, a left wing from the Seattle Havoc. A guy who is so fucking cocky that he wouldn't shake my hand at the end of the charity game. We're supposed to be raising money for sick kids and he's so full of himself he can't even see straight.

He runs his fingers through his dirty blond hair and smirks down at Wren. I was just on the ice with the guy and can confirm that he's a giant.

But he's also a huge dick. What does Wren see in him?

She's different now than she used to be. Stronger. More visible. Part of me is proud. The other part is spiraling.

She's got this soft, pretty laugh that cuts through all the noise. She has unintentionally reprogrammed me, changed my brain chemistry to be so attuned to her voice, her laugh, her every damn nuance.

I can tell she actually thinks whatever he's just said is really funny. I'm not proud of the way the sound of her giggling knots me up. I try to pretend I don't see it.

Like that's possible. She's not mine, not really. Not yet. But watching her smile at someone else like that? It feels like being benched during the most important game of my life.

I attempt a little small talk with Rich, feigning interest in his endless theory about last season's finale. He goes on and on about how it could have had even more drama if only the producers had known about that secret hookup.

But my attention keeps slipping. I'm not even sure if I'm nodding at the right parts when he pauses expectantly.

I strain to hear her voice, even when it gets drowned out by the background noise. Finally, I give up pretending and let my gaze drift back to where she stands.

Wren's always had this way of pulling focus. It used to drive me nuts, the way she'd steal the spotlight from whatever I was supposed to be paying attention to without even trying. Now, it's more like she's got a target on my heart and doesn't even know it.

The guy Wren's talking to? He's looking slick, standing there like he's already made the team and the highlight reel. He's got that effortless swagger that makes him hard to ignore and he's still in his practice gear, half-unzipped like he's too cool for shirts that fit and manners that matter.

The worst part? He's charming, throwing Wren a grin that must work on half the population.

I know his type. Hell, I *am* him.

I don't miss the way Huxley looks at her legs in that short gray skirt. She shouldn't be allowed to wear anything so sexy while other hockey players are around.

Most hockey players are dogs. Hunter Huxley is the worst of them all. My fists bunch as I think of how I'd like to deal with this situation: with violence.

I take a sip of my Coke, wondering how a drink with no alcohol can feel so bitter. I watch from across the room, pretending I'm totally fine, that I'm not glued to the sight of them like it's some slow-motion car wreck I can't tear my eyes from.

The guy leans in, says something that makes Wren tilt her head, brushing her hair behind her ear. She gives him a smile that's not supposed to be meant for strangers. I see it.

I know it's not an act.

I don't move, just stare across the room like maybe the force of my gaze will interrupt. It doesn't. She's into whatever he's saying. I'm hating every second of it.

Just as someone shoves a camera in my face, I decide I've had enough. I cut across the room, ignoring the flash of a production assistant's camera like it's a pesky gnat. I'm only half aware of the people I squeeze past, the scattered conversations I bulldoze through. I can still see them, the way he's so obviously holding her attention.

She's stepping away from the bar, drink in hand, looking almost too pleased. Her cheeks are pink, whether from the rum punch or the attention, I'm not sure. Either way, I'm there before she's gone more than a couple of steps.

"You flirting now?" I hear my own voice come out louder than I'd intended. My words hang in the air between us. For a second, I think I see her flinch.

She startles a little, looking genuinely caught off guard.

"What?" she says, her eyes wide as if she hasn't been on my radar this whole time.

"That guy. Huxley. From the other team. You're really gonna go with him?"

I don't even recognize my own voice. It's got this raw edge I can't control. But there's a needling ache in my chest that's pushing me. I'm not about to back down now.

Wren narrows her eyes and I know I've struck a nerve.

"What's your problem?" Her voice sharpens, a defense mechanism I know too well. She tilts her chin, daring me to accuse her of anything more.

For a moment, I almost waver, but then I remember the way she laughed at the guy's jokes.

I fold my arms, trying to look like I'm the one with the upper hand here, though I'm not so sure I've got any hand at all. "You're doing this on purpose. Laughing. Touching his arm. Trying to get a reaction."

It sounds desperate, even to me, but I can't stop. Her cheeks are still flushed. I know I'm the reason now, not some rum punch.

"Why would I?" she asks softly, dropping the bravado. "He was telling me a funny story about his niece. That's all. What would I get out of flirting with him?"

Her eyes search mine.

I wonder if she's right, if I'm the only one clinging to some idea that we're both in on this game.

A muscle tics in my jaw. I realize how hollow my words

sound. "To drive me crazy? I'm not sure what I did to deserve it, though."

There's a vulnerability that creeps in, a crack in my armor that shows her how much she gets to me.

"You didn't do anything, Ryan." Her voice is so soft it almost drowns in the noise. "Honestly. I was just being friendly."

I lower my voice so she's the only one that can hear me. "Wren…"

She licks her bottom lip. It takes everything I have to focus on the words and not the motion. "We both know what a terrible idea this is."

A fresh wave of adrenaline hits, a rush of something I can't identify. Suddenly, I'm feeling too much all at once. She's giving voice to the fear I'm constantly working so hard to silence, the one that breathes down my neck at every turn, that worries she might slip through my fingers before I can even get a firm grip.

Wren peers up at me, her eyes emotional. There's a flicker of suspicion and regret. She's scanning my face, searching for something. I can't look away.

It's like I'm staring down everything I've ever wanted. It's staring back like it's trying to decide whether being with me is worth the hassle.

I cup her neck just at the juncture of her shoulder and stare down into her eyes. Does she have any idea what she does to me?

"It's risky. But I'm willing to take the risk."

She swallows, her lips parting like each breath is suddenly a struggle. "Ryan…"

I'm afraid of what she'll say next. Before she can finish the thought, I run right over it, desperate to change the script. "I'm not messing around. You think I'd risk Jay hating me if this was just for fun?"

Maybe I'm overplaying my hand, but it's all I've got. The words hit the air before I can stop them.

Wren freezes.

Her lips part like she wants to say something, but she doesn't. She just stands there, staring at me, a hundred questions in her eyes and not a single one making it to her mouth.

Then, before I can even guess what's coming, she grabs my sleeve and pulls me away from the crowd. I stumble behind her, half in shock, half in something else. My heart pounds against my ribs like it wants out.

We squeeze past a group of interns arguing logistics for tomorrow's shoot. She pulls me into a hallway and it suddenly gets quieter and darker. We turn the corner by the coat check. It's half lit, almost impossible to see straight. Jackets hang in bunches, casting weird shadows over the floor, but I barely notice. I'm too busy trying to figure out if I'm dreaming this whole thing.

She closes the door, flips on the light, and spins to face me. She's breathing hard, eyes locked on mine. Maybe it's the adrenaline, or maybe it's something else, something she's been holding back, too.

"You're the one acting weird," she accuses.

A nervous laugh slips out of me.

"Maybe I am. Because I like you, Wren." I've never let the words out before. I'm not even sure how they sound. "Okay? I know I'm not supposed to, but I can't help it."

That shuts her up. She just stares at me, long and unblinking. Waiting, presumably, for the other shoe to drop. But I am certainly not trying to trick her. I don't have a lot to offer her, but she can have my honesty.

Her hand curls into my shirt and everything changes.

Wren pushes me backward into the wall of jackets and kisses me.

It's not sweet. It's not slow. It's fast and hot and a little angry. There's the rough crush of her mouth on mine, the tangle of her fingers in my hair. I barely have time to react before I find myself pulling her closer, pulling her in.

I grip her hips and kiss her back hard, teeth knocking, breath short. She's in my arms, against me, closer than I ever thought possible. My head spins with the feel of her, the heat of her, the electric charge of something I've been dying to touch.

I should stop. I should pull back. I should do a lot of things.

I don't.

Her mouth is warm and needy, hot like she's pouring all her frustration and longing into the kiss. She tastes like ripe berries and total recklessness. I'm feeling lightheaded from the rush of it all.

I'm not sure if she'll change her mind, if she'll let the reality of what this means sink in, so I pull her in tighter, holding on like it's my only shot.

I'm against the wall. She's right there with me. Right there and wild in a way I've never seen. She kisses me back with an intensity I've only dreamed about, like she's making up for all the times we couldn't.

My fingers slide under the hem of her jersey, finding her skin soft and warm. I don't even know when I decided to let go like this, but I can't remember a time it didn't feel inevitable.

I can't stop, won't stop, not this time.

She breaks the kiss first, breathless. "We shouldn't…"

I kiss her again, greedy for all of it, greedy for more. She groans. My fingers tremble as I push her skirt up and yank her panties down her thighs. She wriggles out of them and I slip them into my back pocket.

"I'm keeping these," I whisper. "If you think I'm not going to jerk off with these on my face, you're crazy."

"Perv."

"You love it."

Wren smirks at me and pulls me closer, her fingers fumbling with the laces at the front of my hockey pants. I catch her hand and shake my head, kissing her lips again. Then I drop to my knees and press her back against the wall of coats, lifting her thighs, one at a time. She presses into the coats until her back hits the wall and I nuzzle her damp pink pussy.

God, I can't decide if she tastes or smells better. Don't even get me started on the sounds she makes. I'm already hard and I've only begun to taste her.

She groans and rocks her hips impatiently. If we were anywhere else, I would tease her, draw it out and make her orgasm two or three times. But we're at a party and someone is bound to come looking for us sooner or later. So I run my tongue over her slit, which is dripping wet, and moan at the taste of her. Sweet and faintly metallic.

She drives her hands into my hair and I kiss her clit. She makes a low *mmm* of pleasure as I circle the tender bud with my tongue. I shift her thighs so they are wider apart, giving me better access, and suck on her clit. Lightly at first, then with increasing vigor. She's panting and moaning and whispering, "Fuck, Ryan! Right there..."

Her hips rock against my chin as she runs her nails over my scalp in a way that makes me shudder. I hum as I lick and suck, wishing that we were in bed so I could fuck her with my fingers, too.

"Oh yes... oh yes!" she chants. She's lost in the moment, not thinking about being overheard. My face is too deep in her pussy to remind her. Oh well.

Her excitement dribbles down my chin. Her fingers tighten in my hair. She goes still, crying out. "Fuck! Ryan... Fuck, I'm going to..."

Slavishly, I lick and suck her clit. She starts to disintegrate, my name on her lips as the orgasm hits. She's panting as it seems to go on and on. I help her ride it out by running my tongue around her clit in lazy circles.

God, she's fucking beautiful when she comes. I love watching her orgasm. It's a little like an out-of-body experience. All I can do is watch.

At least when I'm eating her out, I know I'm giving her something good. It's the only time I don't feel like a mistake.

Then someone calls a name. Loudly.

"Stacy?"

A woman's voice. She's not looking for us, but she is looking for someone. We could easily be exposed.

We both freeze, caught. I feel her body go rigid. For a moment, the world slips back into focus. The muffled sounds of a party in full swing crash around us. She pushes at my shoulders, wild-eyed, like she's been jolted back to reality.

I don't her let go that easily. Not yet.

She draws a shaky breath and smooths her jersey down, her fingers trembling. I desperately want to keep her here, in this moment.

She pushes at my shoulders harder, snapping me out of my thoughts. "Put me down, Ryan!"

I do as she asks, reluctantly letting her go. She pulls down her skirt and blushes.

"Thanks," she whispers.

I grab her hands and kiss her wrists, like she's fragile and I'm the reason. Then I look at her earnestly. "I love the way you taste, Chirp. I'd eat that pussy for breakfast, lunch, and dinner if you'd let me. I'd starve to death, but I'd die grinning."

Wren shakes her head, but I can see a smile on her lips.

"You're insane. You should be examined by a professional."

"They'd just tell me I have pussy mania. I already know that. The only cure is more of you, sweetheart. All day, every day."

"Yeah, right." Her lips twist with humor and she shakes her head again. "Now get up before someone figures out where we disappeared to."

I climb to my feet. Wren holds out her hand. "Panties, please."

"I don't think so. That's my price for wrecking your pussy like it was dessert."

"What?" Her eyes bulge slightly. "You can't leave me commando!"

"I'm willing to take the risk." I wink at her. "I wasn't kidding. As soon as I'm alone, I'm going to lay down with your panties on my face and jerk off furiously."

"You're ridiculous," she whispers. There's a note of panic in her voice.

"I know." I force the words out, even though they sting, even though they don't come close to what I really want to say.

"We have to go. I'm going first. You wait a minute before following me."

Like that's going to fool anyone. But I just nod.

She disappears around the corner. I'm left alone under

the overhead lights, my back pressing against the jackets. I'm dizzy, off balance, like the ground's crumbling beneath me.

I'm wrecked. Inside and out. All I can do is lean my head back against the coats and try to remember how to breathe.

I like her. No, scratch that. I am *obsessed* with her. All I want is to be around this girl.

This isn't just a hookup. This is the beginning of the end. Because if I want Wren for real... I might lose everything else.

Fuck. Do I have feelings for Wren?

twenty-seven

WREN

IT STARTED AS A GAME. A way to stay on the show. But now I don't know where the fake ends and the real begins.

I feel like Ryan doesn't know where the borders are, either.

When he asks me to spend the weekend with him, I mean to say no. At least I *think* I mean to. I've spent years saying no to myself. To the wild, selfish parts of me that want things I'm not supposed to want.

But Ryan leans in at the end of a long, brutal day, all cocky grin and tired eyes, and murmurs, "Let's get out of here this weekend. Just you and me. Somewhere nobody can find us."

I blink at him. "What?"

"No cameras. No producers. No contestants fake-laughing at everything I say. Just quiet. Just us." He says it like it's simple. Like the answer should be easy.

And the worst part is... it is.

I can't quite bring myself to turn down the chance to be

somewhere secret and safe with him for a whole weekend. My world has been reduced to cameras and those who wield them like weapons. To people like Rich, who see everything but never truly see me.

I try to laugh it off. "Jay would kill you."

"What Jay doesn't know won't hurt him." He's teasing, but I see something serious flicker in his eyes. Something tender. Something that scares me more than the rest.

"Come on, Rustin." His voice drops. "Let me steal you for forty-eight hours. Just to see what it feels like when it's not a game."

I'm supposed to be running the other way. Supposed to be throwing myself fully into untangling my life, not knotting it tighter. But when Ryan says, "You want this, too. I know you do," there's a treacherous, exhilarating *yes* that comes flying out before I can even think.

"Yeah." My voice is soft. "I want to."

And God help me, I mean it.

I'm already too attached, thinking of how good it will feel to be off the grid, then back on it again. Already too attached to the image of twenty-three missed texts from Jay, half of them in all caps.

WHERE ARE YOU

WHY IS RYAN GONE TOO

CALL ME RIGHT NOW

I imagine walking back into the studio, my skin sun-warmed and smile impossible to hide. And it won't be as someone's assistant. Or someone's little sister. It'll be as someone who did something wild and dangerous just for herself.

Already too attached to the idea of vanishing. Driving to the coast with the windows down, sneaking into overpriced hotels with Ryan's hand in mine and not a single plan in place. Already too attached to the picture in my head of Jay huddled over his phone next to Calla, too anxious that I'm gone to be angry for real.

I say yes. Because I know better. But I decide it's worth the risk to find out if I mean it at all.

Even though Jay is going to freak if Ryan disappears and I vanish at the same time. Even though I've known Ryan practically my whole life. Even though I'm already too attached.

Too attached to this overwhelming feeling of freedom. This wild, reckless chance to turn my back on everything pristine and expected for a little while.

Ryan doesn't tell me where we're going. I lie awake the night before with butterflies the size of planets in my stomach. He just texts me the name of a hotel and a time.

10 a.m. sharp. Pack something soft. Something that'll make me regret ever teasing you.

I stare at my phone until it fades to black. And then I smile. Because for once, I don't want to say no. Not even a little.

When I show up, I'm nervous. My bag's too full. I know I'm going to freak when I have to drag it around and Ryan sees how ridiculously overpacked it is.

This is a mistake. But I can't alter my course now. Not when I'm so close.

I knock twice, then open the door, expecting a decent suite. I bite my lip and breathe in deep and order myself not to care if it's small or smells like old sandwiches or something.

What I find is luxury. Like... luxury, luxury.

The room has vaulted ceilings, a king-sized bed that

looks like it belongs in a movie, a private patio with a firepit, and a view of the mountains that makes my stomach drop a little. It's beautiful and wild and totally surreal.

The private patio with a firepit seals the deal. I feel a little unsteady in my own skin, like I'm trapped inside a dream where everything's impossibly perfect.

Ryan's already here, lounging on the couch as though he ordered up this luxury like room service, looking infuriatingly edible in casual gray sweatpants and a T-shirt that hints at a fresh shower. He throws a lazy smile that makes me way too self-conscious.

His eyes drag over me, slowly taking in every detail.

"You wore that on purpose."

I glance down at myself. Black jeans. His old jersey from college. Oh.

"You asked for casual," I say, my voice doing this little squeaky thing that gives me away.

"I didn't ask for psychological warfare."

I kick off my shoes, trying to act cool, even when I feel anything but.

"This place is insane."

He shrugs, making it look effortless, like all of this just fell into his lap.

"Team sponsors comped it for the offseason. I just made a call."

I raise an eyebrow, pretending I'm not impressed, while secretly I'm reeling from how easy he makes it sound.

"Must be nice."

"So you're not mad?" he teases, leaning back like he's got all the time in the world to wait for my answer.

I want to be mad. I want to pretend I'm not already too

attached to the idea of disappearing into this life with him, but it's a losing battle.

It's a mistake to spend more time with him. I know it is. But there's a defiant pulse in my blood that whispers *maybe it's not.*

He studies my face, looking almost nervous.

"Is this okay? We don't have to stay here. I just... I wanted us to be somewhere safe. Somewhere that doesn't feel like a set."

The soft, unsure way he says it makes me melt.

"Yeah. It's okay."

We spend the afternoon outside wrapped in blankets, bundled up tight against the mountain chill, sitting by the firepit. I'm already savoring the way the world feels when it's just the two of us.

There's no one else around, just us and a big expanse of wild scenery. It's kind of incredible. I didn't even know Ryan liked marshmallows, let alone that he's an absolute menace with a roasting stick. He laughs at the mess, the crispy black blobs that drip into the glowing red-orange of the fire if you hold them over the flame for too long.

"I like them burnt," he exclaims. He holds a skewered bit of charcoal as evidence.

"You're a monster."

There's a flash of his grin. It's the best one, the kind that makes my pulse race.

"You say that like it's new information."

I make a valiant, tragic attempt at getting one marshmallow to turn a little golden, at least before it catches fire. Ryan tosses another failed attempt into his mouth and laughs at me.

"Very professional," he says, nodding with sarcastic approval.

"Shut up," I mumble. I go silent, thinking how much I like him. He treats me like a queen. Like what I think matters. Maybe I more than like him.

Okay, definitely more than that.

"You're quiet. You usually have a burn-a-minute ratio with me," he teases. "Where did you go?"

My heart beats faster. Does he not know that he's the reason? His smile, the way he lights up when I give him shit. His obvious and genuine enjoyment of the stupid little insults that come out of my mouth and keep them coming.

Ryan sees me. He knows my nature. He likes *me*.

"You want to know why I'm not shy around you?" I cock my head. "Because you've never looked at me like I was background noise. You've been a pain in my ass for most of my life, but you always saw me. I think I like that. Even when I hate it."

His mouth opens, his eyebrows shooting up. But for several seconds, he has no response. I chuckle.

"You had to know that already."

"I didn't. Believe it or not, I'm not a mind reader."

"Hmm." I put another marshmallow on my stick, not willing to discuss it further. We are wading into dangerous, deep waters here.

I feel a little reckless, a little electric, like maybe we've escaped into some weird daydream where nothing and no one else matters. I let myself sink into it.

It's okay to let myself feel like this could be real. Just for tonight.

Eventually, we head back into the ridiculous luxury of the room. I steal his hoodie because it's cozy and big on me and it smells like him. I curl up in the corner of the couch, pretending not to stare as he stretches, the T-shirt lifting just enough to make my breath catch. I try to act cool, even as my brain short-circuits watching him move like he belongs here. With me.

He tosses me a bottle of water when he comes back. "So. You like stars, right?"

"I like them a lot better than charcoal marshmallows."

He rolls his eyes in mock offense. "I've got a million of those if you want to retry."

I'm still smiling when I answer his question. "How do you even know about my love of the stars?"

He shrugs like maybe he's as surprised as I am. "You talk about them. Or you used to."

Is it possible he was paying attention all those years ago? I squint at him, suspicious and charmed.

"I was obsessed with astronomy for, like, a month in middle school. I thought I was going to be an astrophysicist."

He flops down beside me, looking way too pleased with himself. "Well, I thought I was going to be a zookeeper. Life's weird."

I can't help it. I laugh and lean into his side, feeling all fluttery and nervous and giddy at once.

We spend the rest of the night watching *Contact* and *Interstellar*, the glow from the TV flickering around the luxurious hotel room. We share a giant bowl of popcorn and bombard it with a ridiculous amount of butter.

The sarcastic commentary I expect gives way to something else.

An easy quiet. A comfortable sort of silence that's even better than I'd imagined.

Around midnight, I stretch and yawn, legs tucked up under me and head resting on his shoulder.

"You tired?" he asks, his voice low and warm.

I nod, the word coming out on another yawn. "Kinda."

"Come to bed."

It's an invitation, nothing more. No heat, no teasing, just a soft expectant look. He stands and stretches. I feel like I might vibrate right out of my skin.

He heads to the massive bedroom. I follow him, heart hammering, pulse going a million miles an hour. The covers are crisp and inviting. I slide under them, barely even getting the lights turned out first.

I know this isn't real life. But for once, I want to see what it feels like to be someone's first choice. Someone worth breaking the rules for.

When he pulls me into his arms, I go willingly. His body is warm and solid against mine. I already know I'm in trouble.

I tell myself it's just for now, just one night where we can forget about everything waiting for us back home, one chance to let our guards down and pretend none of it matters.

The way we tangle around each other is instinctive, like we both know this is something we shouldn't be doing, but I'm not brave enough to pull away.

Ryan doesn't give me any reason to. He holds me close. I fit myself against him like we belong, like we've always belonged. We don't talk about what this is.

We don't say the word "feelings."

Just a comforting, beat-heavy silence and the steady rhythm of his breathing.

I listen to it like it might stop at any moment, but it never does. Eventually, I fall asleep.

I sleep better than I have in months. Maybe ever.

When I wake up, light is spilling over the mountains. Ryan hasn't let me go. I haven't moved away. He's still wrapped around me, like he's afraid I'll disappear if he loosens his hold.

When I wake up to him tangled around me like he belongs there, I don't question it. Not yet.

But I just know that tomorrow morning, things will be back to normal. I just don't know that I'll be the same girl when dawn breaks.

twenty-eight

WREN

WE DON'T LEAVE the hotel room all morning. We
don't even think about leaving. Who cares about the rest of
the world when you've got a king-sized bed, room service,
and a morning like this?

It's a bubble for two, where the only important thing is
how close we can be, how many times lips can meet before
they go numb, and which limbs can tangle together in the
most delicious knot. It starts with lazy kisses and sleepy
bodies meshed together. My face is tucked into Ryan's chest
while he sleep-mumbles something unintelligible and rolls
us over, squeezing me so tight I giggle into his chest.

Then his lips find my neck. His weight presses me into
the mattress. I forget how to breathe. I can't believe this is
happening. I can't believe this is still happening. I can't
believe time can pass like this, hours slipping away like
they belong to someone else.

Eventually, the real world starts to elbow its way back
into focus. I finally pull myself out of bed and shuffle
toward the bathroom, though I don't want to be away from
Ryan for even a second. My legs feel like Jell-O.

My hair looks like a cautionary tale of what happens when you spend hours tangled up with a man like him. I catch a glimpse of myself in the mirror and see the small dark hickey blooming under my collarbone.

A reminder and a promise that this morning was not some cruel delirium. Giddy and dazed, I splash cold water on my face until I'm sure I'm fully awake, then I stumble back out of the bathroom.

Ryan's already made himself busy ordering food. He's still shirtless, sitting cross-legged on the bed like he owns the world, like he owns this moment, his casual confidence almost enough to make me blush all over again.

"I thought you'd be hungry," he says.

As if breakfast in bed is the most normal thing in the world. As if this whole morning is just another morning for us. As if this is what normal looks like for Ryan and me.

"I'm starving," I admit. I crawl back under the covers, still wrapped in his hoodie, still soaking up his warmth.

It doesn't take long for room service to arrive. He uncovers a stack of pancakes with an exaggerated flourish and hands me a fork. "You want syrup on or around?"

"Don't you dare pour it like a psycho."

He snorts, eyes alive with teasing. "So demanding."

I roll my eyes at him, but I can't help smiling like an idiot. There's something so easy and so impossible about sharing breakfast with him like this. So dangerously close to a world where I'm not just tolerated but chosen. The way he's already tossing the syrup my way, already saving the strawberries for me because he knows I'll want them later.

This is all a strange dream and Ryan is just a figment of my imagination. If I'm in an insane asylum and hallucinating him, that's fine. I just don't want to wake up quite yet.

It's easy.

Dangerously easy. So easy, there are moments I forget this isn't normal for us.

Later, we make a fire in the small hearth near the bed, the room flickering in warmth and light. We play cards by the warmth of the fire. I beat him at rummy three times in a row before he accuses me of cheating with a wounded sigh.

"Admit it, Haart," I say, holding up my winning hand. "You're just mad you lost."

"There's no way you aren't cheating," he insists, shuffling the cards again. "Nobody's that good."

"My dad would beg to differ."

Ryan glances up, curiosity flickering in his eyes. I look down at the cards, suddenly focused on organizing them by suit. I don't tell him I learned from years of playing as a kid. That it's all muscle memory now, ingrained like a reflex. I can't lose if I try.

But saying any of that would invite questions about childhoods and families. Things I don't want to talk about. They might break the spell of this perfect day by reminding us of the real world waiting outside the door.

When it starts getting dark, we wrap up in blankets and end up on the patio, the air cool and the world outside finally nudging its way back into our bubble, the one we've been floating in all day. I'm not sure what the time is anymore. I don't really care. As long as I'm here with him, none of those numbers matter. None of those numbers are real.

He's quiet.

I'm not used to quiet Ryan. Not really.

"What are you thinking?" I ask, my voice barely above a whisper. Ryan is uncharacteristically silent. It makes me nervous, as if saying something out loud could puncture the fragile perfection of this evening and send it crashing into reality.

He shrugs, a small, almost uncertain gesture. "Just... this is nice." His words hang in the air between us, soft and tentative as if he's testing them out, not quite sure if he trusts them. It's nice, but it's also terrifying.

I bite my lip, afraid of what the answer might be but needing to ask anyway.

"Too nice?"

I don't mean to sound so vulnerable, but I can't help it. It's so delicious and unbearable to be this open with him.

He glances my way, eyes searching mine. "That a trick question?"

"No." The answer is simple, but the feeling behind it definitely isn't.

We're both scared. We both have way too much to lose.

There's a silence, thick and telling. I know neither of us wants to be the first to say what we're both thinking, what lurks behind this easy intimacy we've been pretending feels so natural.

Ryan looks away first, the movement quick and almost defensive. "Nice is dangerous."

I get it.

We're both horrible at good things. At letting things be simple and accepting that something warm and rich can last without turning into a mess. At trusting that this isn't a dream, that we won't wake up and find out that everything's fallen apart once again.

"I know what you mean," I say.

I really do. I've spent weeks now wondering if this is only temporary. When will Ryan suddenly decide he's made a mistake and move on like he always has before? It's safer to expect that, easier not to give my heart to something that might evaporate or explode without warning. Safer not to end up like the small, dark bruise on my collarbone.

Impermanent.

But there's another part of me, a softer and more hopeful part, that thinks maybe this time it's not just a mistake, not just a passing phase for both of us. This part of me wants so badly to trust that it's real, that it's right, that it's more than some fragile illusion. That Ryan won't leave. That I won't end up alone, picking pieces of my life off the floor and trying to fit them back together.

He reaches over and tangles our fingers together under the blanket.

Neither of us says anything else.

But we sit like that for a long time, wrapped up in the quiet, the only sounds the occasional hum of traffic from the street and the rustling of leaves in the breeze. We're both waiting for it to feel less fragile and more certain, wondering if we're brave enough to let it. Wondering what will happen if it gets even better than this. Wondering what will happen if it doesn't.

For once, I let myself believe this could be more than pretend.

* * *

Later that night, we're curled up in bed again, the room swathed in shadows that dance over the walls as the fireplace flickers and dies down. I'm cocooned in his hoodie, swamped in warmth and Ryan's scent. He lies bare-chested beside me, careless and content, like he hasn't a worry in the world. But I know better.

I can feel it. The subtle shift from comfortable silence to

something that feels more jagged. He's retreating somewhere behind his eyes. I'm not sure if I should follow.

Finally, words escape him like an admission, startling in the quiet of the room. "Of course it had to be you." It's a confession and a defeat all at once. The implication sends a shiver through me.

I freeze, not sure I heard him right. "What?"

He turns his head just slightly, enough for his eyes to meet mine with a look that's resigned and almost somber. "I'm probably self-sabotaging. I've done it before."

I sit up on my elbow, something snagging in my chest at this unexpected honesty. "Is that why you've...?" I start to ask, but the words stick. I can't finish without sounding like I've been keeping track of his history.

Ryan arches an eyebrow, catching my hesitation. "Why I've what? Slept my way across the lower forty-eight?"

I wince, not wanting to be that blunt. "That's not what I meant."

But it's true enough, giving voice to the worry that's been gnawing at me all day. That I'm just one on a long list, that this is a temporary stop on his usual route, one that ends with me being nothing more than a footnote. Not wanting to become vulnerable, the same useless mark I was left with last time. I try to sound lighthearted, but my voice wobbles.

"I just meant, is that why you never... you know?"

I can't bring myself to say the word commit, as if saying it out loud will destroy this fragile thing between us. It's a terrifying relief, hearing him say he's falling for me, but more terrifying is the thought that he might not mean it. That he might be sabotaging both of us without even knowing it.

He shrugs, lazy and unbothered on the surface, like it

doesn't matter, like he doesn't care. But I can see it. I can see the struggle beneath the calm facade.

"You're not wrong," he finally says, his voice almost too casual. "It's easier when it doesn't mean anything." There's an edge to his words, but I hear it. I hear the truth slipping out.

"But don't you want something real?" I ask, leaning in closer, trying to make him look at me..

Trying to make him see that I'm here, that I won't disappear. That I'm not the one he needs to worry about leaving. My voice is soft, tentative. Terrified of what his answer might be.

He doesn't answer right away. The silence stretches between us. I can feel him wrestling with it, wrestling with himself and what he might say. The air in the room grows thick. I think he's not going to respond at all.

Then, he says softly, "Love's just another line people use before they leave." The words hang there like a challenge, like a heartbreak waiting to happen.

I blink, startled by the rawness of the confession, by the fear I hear behind it. Fear and something else, something that cuts much deeper.

"What do you mean?" I ask, but I think I already know.

His mouth tightens. I see him try to pull the words back inside, try to move past this sudden exposure. But he can't.

His voice is even, but something sharp flickers behind it, something that twists in my chest and makes my heart hurt. I want to say that he's wrong, that I'm not like that, that he doesn't have to be so afraid, but nothing comes out.

I want to ask more. I want him to tell me everything he's been keeping hidden, everything that makes him think this way. I want to know how to make it better, how to convince him I won't be like everyone else. How to convince him it can be different this time.

I don't.

Instead, he clears his throat and glances at me like he's trying to steer us somewhere safer.

"Your turn," he says, his voice daring me to be as open as he's been. "Please, make up a story. Or maybe tell me something that happened a long time ago. Make me feel like less of an idiot."

I hesitate. A second passes. Then another. What exactly is Ryan looking for?

"It's hard having Jay as a big brother."

I'm not sure how he'll react to that. I hold my breath, waiting. Ryan's brow furrows, caught off guard.

"He's so... big," I go on, trying to find the words. "Loud, charming, unforgettable. He walks into a room and owns it. Me? I've always just been the kid in the corner with a book."

Ryan watches me, those eyes of his soft as he takes it all in, lets it all sink in.

"I spent years trying to figure out why that made me feel small. I'm still not totally sure. I think I'm just the less special sibling."

He doesn't respond right away. My heart beats faster in that silence. Maybe I said too much. Maybe he doesn't understand. Then, finally, he speaks, his words so quiet I almost miss them.

"I've seen you do it," he says with a kind of certainty. "The magic trick."

"What magic trick?" I ask, confused.

"The one where you're sitting right there, not even moving, but you vanish. Like... emotionally disappear. Slip out the side door without anyone noticing."

I huff a laugh, surprised at how well he sees me, how

much he's noticed. "Yeah. I do that when Jay starts show-boating."

Ryan's eyes don't leave mine. There's a warmth in them that makes me feel like maybe he really is different, like he really does see me in a way no one else does. "I always saw you, Wren. Even when Jay was sucking all the air out of the room."

I turn away, fast.

Because that? That one hits too hard.

My eyes sting and I don't want him to see. I blink down at the blanket instead.

"Can we watch a movie?" I ask, voice a little too bright.

He doesn't push.

"Yeah," he says. "You pick."

I scroll through the movie menu, past the action flicks and rom-coms, while Ryan watches me with a mix of curiosity and apprehension. I know exactly what I'm going to pick. I can practically hear his unspoken protest as my finger hovers over the screen.

"Oh, come on," he says when I land on *Pride and Prejudice*, the Keira Knightley version. "You're killing me."

I flash him a grin, feeling much lighter than I did a few minutes ago. "You said I could choose."

He shakes his head, but there's a smile tugging at his lips. "Here I was hoping for at least a car chase."

But he doesn't argue, doesn't put up any real fight as the opening scene flickers onto the screen. I settle in closer to him.

It doesn't take long for me to get completely drawn in, forgetting everything else as the familiar story weaves its spell. About halfway through, the letter scene comes on, the part where Elizabeth realizes how terribly wrong she's been, how completely she misjudged Darcy, and all the emotions I've been holding back start to bubble up. I can't help it.

I start crying, tears tracing down my cheek as my chest tightens with the intensity of it all. Elizabeth got it all wrong at first, too. And still, Darcy stayed. Maybe people don't always leave. Maybe sometimes they stay and let you try again.

Ryan notices right away. I wait for him to tease me, to make some crack about women and their feelings, something to soften my embarrassment at being so deeply affected.

But he doesn't.

Instead, he pulls me closer, his arm wrapping around my shoulder and drawing me into the safety and warmth of his chest. "Come here," he murmurs, his voice gentle. It feels so good, so right to be held like this, to let myself be vulnerable without fear of what it might mean.

We sit like that for a long time, the movie playing on, while something subtle and important shifts between us. It tightens my throat and makes my heart beat faster. Suddenly, I know.

I know that maybe this is as real as I've been secretly hoping it could be. Maybe we're not self-sabotaging. Maybe we're actually doing the opposite. Maybe we're not fooling ourselves after all.

We don't talk again for the rest of the movie.

But something between us shifts. Quietly. Almost imperceptibly. His arm around me tightens. Not possessive. Just sure. Like he's not going anywhere.

I think he feels it, too.

Does Ryan have feelings for me?

twenty-nine

RYAN

WE'RE BACK ON SET, and it feels like whiplash. Three days ago, Wren was tangled up with me in bed, whispering my name like it meant something. Now? She won't even look at me. I'm not heartbroken. I'm furious. Which feels suspiciously like the same thing.

Is she pretending now? Was she pretending when she came around my cock and whispered her secrets to me? My mind is fragmented and it's impossible for me to tell. I can't come close to being objective with her.

Everything about being back in this house sucks. The other contestants are too loud, the lights are too hot, and Wren acts like I'm a stranger. I mean, she looks at me when she thinks I'm not watching. But the second our eyes meet, she flushes and glances away fast, like I'm too bright, too hot, like maybe I burned her or something.

It's like I dreamed the whole weekend at the hotel. Like it was all in my head. I imagined every single kiss, every slow morning in bed, every time she laughed against my chest like she belonged there. I thought things were going to be different. Better. More.

But things are exactly like they were before. She's back to acting like I'm a stranger. It's driving me out of my mind.

What did I do wrong? I can't figure out what happened. One minute, it felt like she was falling as hard as I was. The next, she froze me out. No explanation, no goodbye. How am I supposed to know what she's thinking when she won't even talk to me?

I keep catching myself staring across the set, searching for her face like an idiot. If she sees me looking, she changes direction and acts like she was planning to walk that way all along. If someone else stands too close, she ducks behind a bigger contestant and uses them like a human shield.

I should look away. She's laughing, all sunlight and a glittering smile. And it's killing me because I want to be the one making her do that.

At least, that's what it feels like. I thought she'd hate how fake everything seemed back on set.

I pull out my phone and text Ellie.

I told Wren something real. Like, real, real.

That's huge. Are you okay?

I think so. She didn't run.

There's a pause. Then:

Then maybe it's finally safe to stop running too.

I stare at that line longer than I probably should.

Now she might be avoiding me. What if I screw this up?

Then you'll apologize and fix it. You're not
Mom. You won't disappear.

I don't want to lose her.

Then don't. Start acting like you deserve
her. Because I think you do.

I twiddle my thumbs, considering my response.

I hate this. I hate being on this show.

A moment later, she replies.

Because it's fake?

Because it feels like lying.

You've never been good at faking feelings.
That's not a bad thing.

It is when all the bachelorettes are looking
at you like you're their last shot at love.

You're not a villain. You're just a dumb
hockey player who got dropped into a rom-
com and forgot his lines.

I stare at that one for a second.

Yeah, well. The blooper reel's gonna be
brutal.

Don't worry. You're still the emotional
support himbo of my heart.

I almost smile. Almost.

Today's group activity is something ridiculous. An obstacle course set up like a Tough Mudder. There's a mud pit, a climbing wall, a tangle of ropes, and of course, cameras everywhere to catch every fall and flop. At the starting line, the crew is doing their best to rev up the energy, directing contestants like it's the season finale. Some are buying it.

I'm just here to observe. Stand on the sidelines and pretend I'm not dying inside while Wren army-crawls through sludge like I didn't have her pressed up against a hotel window three nights ago.

Wren's terrible at it. She falls twice in the first minute and nearly gets tangled under the net. I bite the inside of my cheek to keep from going over to help her. Raven's right behind, glaring at the mud like it personally insulted her. Everyone's playing their part, hamming it up for the lens.

Except for Wren. She looks like she's fighting an entirely different battle. Somehow, she's still adorable, even when she's struggling to get back up from the last fall. I catch a flash of crimson in the corner of my eye. Before I know it, she's back on her feet and moving faster than before, pony-tail bouncing through the chaos.

Wren's the star of the scene. She's laughing, throwing a quick glance over her shoulder to see who's catching up, face lit up like she's having the time of her life. The complete opposite of the weekend, where she couldn't even fake a smile the last time I saw her.

She's laughing like it's easy. Like this means nothing. But I know that laugh. I know when it's real. This isn't it.

Unless she's faking it. Unless she's trying to play it safe. But why? Why freeze me out when we were finally real?

Now she's back to acting like she loves every minute of this. The thrill, the competition, the set. I'm the only one who seems to remember how she acted when it was just her and me. Is she really over it already? Over me? Am I the only one still frozen in that hotel room, thinking there was more?

The thought drops like a weight in my gut. What was I expecting? That she'd quit the show for me? Jump into my arms and announce we're soulmates on national television? I'm the idiot here. She's right back in the game. I'm the one stuck wondering what's real and what's for show.

I'm so wrapped up in my own thoughts that I don't notice Raven catching up to them. She's got dirt smeared across her face and a determined look that says she's not giving up, no matter what kind of craziness happens. Everyone else might be in on the drama, but Raven is laser focused. This is the closest I've seen her to having fun since we got back.

I keep my eyes on them, just far enough away that I can pretend her laughter isn't needling at me. Wren and Raven trade teasing shoves. It feels like Wren's actually enjoying this. All the mud and madness.

Raven jokes through the whole thing. "If I survive this, I want a drink and a tetanus shot." I hear her say it and snort.

Raven's perfect, of course. No surprise there. She takes it like a personal challenge, her blonde ponytail whipping in the wind as she scales the climbing wall without a single hesitation. Raven's a little ball of athletic fury, an Amazon packed into a five foot two frame. She probably finishes the course in record time.

Meanwhile, JacqLyn is a machine. Loud, strong, and hilarious. She's barreling through the obstacles, whooping like a cowgirl as she tears through the mud pit. She actually doubles back at one point to help Raven out of the sludge, shouting "Yeehaw!" like she's riding a bucking bronco.

Divya... refuses to crawl. She stands on the sidelines for a second, hands on her hips, and scowls like someone's made her touch garbage. Then she literally walks around the obstacle, mud-free and defiant. I swear one of the producers gives her a thumbs-up.

The whole thing's over in about an hour. To me, it felt like ten. I towel off, even though I wasn't the one competing. Sweat clings to my back anyway. Watching Wren trip over a tire and mutter "Jesus take the wheel" under her breath was almost too much. My pulse was pounding like I'd run the course myself.

As the crew collects cameras, I can't stop sneaking looks at Wren, who's standing in a circle with JacqLyn and Raven. She's laughing too loud, like she has to convince them and herself again that she's over me.

After everyone clears out, Rich finds me near the trailers.

"We need to talk about who you're eliminating," Rich says, walking right up to me with that smug producer grin, like we're best buds and nothing's wrong. Just like that. No lead-up. No easing into it. He gets straight to the point. He's not subtle about it. Typical. The guy's relentless. He wants an answer.

I already know what he's about to say. That I have to choose between cutting Wren and cutting Raven. That the girl I'm sacrificing my sanity for has to be the one I send home. He doesn't give me a second to breathe before he says it.

"Wren or Raven. They both underperformed." He crosses his arms over his stupidly defined chest and acts like he's offering me some great advice.

My jaw tightens. My face probably looks like it belongs on a missing person poster. I don't say anything. I can't say anything. I look off toward the catering tent, pretending I didn't hear him.

"You have to cut someone," he says, voice lighter now. Friendly. Manipulative. "We're getting to the point in the season where feelings might start getting in the way." Rich is piling it on, the way only he can. All I feel is the pressure to pick one of them and the certainty that I can't win here.

I lie and say I don't know yet. That I haven't decided. That I'll think about it. His face is unreadable. For a second, I wonder if I've convinced him. If I've convinced myself. How am I supposed to cut Wren when I'm the only one who seems to remember what this whole thing was supposed to be?

It's the world's worst situation. I can't see a way out.

Rich gives me a long look, like he's waiting for me to crack. I don't give him the satisfaction. Instead, he jerks his head toward the confessional trailer. He's already turning around, assuming I'll follow like he's got me on a leash. "Let's get a few takes while the day's still fresh."

I go along for the walk of shame, following him in. I can't believe I'm doing this. The confessional trailer reeks of fresh paint and desperation. All I hear are ghosts. This is the same trailer where we... where I pressed Wren... where I thought... My head spins with the intensity of that night, with the memory of her moan still lingering in my mouth.

I sit down on the bench, stiff as hell, and try to swallow down the regret clawing its way out of me. Rich gets comfortable right across from me, acting like we're on some kind of buddy cop mission to save America from being bored. He flips open a notepad and looks at me like he's expecting an entire season's worth of drama to pour out of me.

It's classic Rich. Straight to the point, relentless and

cunning. "Okay, talk to me about Raven. And Wren. Anything special going on there?" He's fishing with dynamite. He knows it.

I try to play it cool, keep my voice as neutral as a Switzerland postcard. "They're both funny," I say. "I like being around them." I almost say more, but I catch myself before too much spills out. No way am I giving him what he wants. Not yet.

Rich acts like I've just handed him a season finale wrapped in a bow. He lifts a brow, ready to pounce. "More than the others?" It's a direct hit. He knows it.

I shrug, trying to make it look effortless, like my entire sanity isn't on the line here. "I enjoy both of them. I'd rather keep them than, say, Divya." Maybe that's a mistake. I already know how this game works, but I have to try.

Rich doesn't even let me finish. "Can't lose Divya. She's the villain. Ratings love her." It's like he's saying water is wet. My teeth grind together. I nod, trying not to explode. I knew it before he said it but hearing it out loud makes me want to punch the wall, the world, or maybe just my own idiot self for thinking I could control any of this.

I'm on the edge of cracking. On the edge of giving him everything he needs.

"Okay," Rich says, already standing and giving a thumbs-up to the camera crew. "Now give us a take. Look right at the camera and say you're torn. You have no idea who to send home. You're emotionally exhausted from the decision." His hands move like a conductor leading an orchestra, in total control. He doesn't even sit back down. He's already planning his next ambush. He clicks his pen, ready to jot down the next scoop.

I stare straight into the lens and say the words. I make

my voice quiet, thoughtful, convincing. Try to sound like I'm baring my soul.

"She's…" I stop myself. Not now. Not like this. "She's entertaining. People like her."

But it feels fake as hell.

As soon as they call *cut*, I lean back in the chair and stare at the ceiling. All I can think about is Wren's face when she turned away from me this morning. Like we were strangers. Like none of it meant anything.

Her laughter echoes in my ears.

If we meant something to her, anything at all, I didn't get the memo. She was so quick to forget, to move on like I was just another stage prop. I remember her bright face, the way she laughed and tossed her hair in the wind. It stabs at me. It's impossible to believe it was the same Wren who wouldn't even look at me in the hotel room, eyes downcast and voice a whisper.

How did I end up being the one who got played? How did I let myself fall so hard when she barely fell at all? Here I am, following Rich like some desperate dog, trying to decide which one of them I can stand to lose the least.

I don't even know how I ended up in this trailer, trying to breathe through the mess I made. I was convinced she felt it, too. The connection. The spark. I thought it was real, but now… now I'm the one sitting in this claustrophobic room, trying to figure out where the hell I went wrong.

Here I am, lying through my teeth, pretending I don't know who I want to stay.

Maybe I was wrong. Maybe I'm the only one who ever believed this could be more. How do I sort out the truth?

RYAN

THE SUN'S already slipped beyond the horizon, leaving behind dusky hues. Everything around us smells like the sharp mix of lavender-scented disinfectant and astringent lemon soap.

We've finally been liberated from the grimy clutches of the obstacle course, each of us emerging one by one from the chaos, victorious in cleanliness. Everyone's been scrubbed, polished, and repaired, ready to brave another evening in the artificial romance wonderland. Hair is back in place like nothing ever happened. Makeup, flawlessly reapplied.

Now we've traded the wild frenzy of the day for a bougie, low-key atmosphere. Instead of wet and wild, we're back to pretending we're a group of sophisticated folks having a civilized glass of wine and nibbling on artisan cheese. Acting more like casual friends than cutthroat competitors. As if we aren't in the middle of a dating circus that airs weekly on national television.

Elena's determined to set a scene tonight. She's turned off half the lamps and lit candles across every table, the flickering flames casting romantic shapes against the walls. The cameras, ever-present but trying to stay invisible, have been pulled back to give the illusion of privacy.

It's supposed to be the moment in the show where it feels organic. Like we're not all aware of the microphones pinned to our collars. More intimate. Relaxed. Real.

I can practically hear Elena talking to the crew. "We need the audience to see how much this group connects."

The girls trickle in slowly at first. This time a little more polished than usual, as if the invitation said cocktail party instead of last rose standing. They ease into the room like it's a friend's loft apartment, posing with glasses of wine and clutching their sides in laughter.

Everyone's dressed up just enough to look effortless.

I relax against the giant L-shaped sectional as a couple of girls sit at the other end, leaning close to whisper conspiratorially. Nobody wants to seem too eager, even though that's the whole point of why we're here.

I'm trying to melt into the cushions when I spot Wren arriving.

She appears in the doorway, framed by the dim light and the shadowy background of the hall. She's in soft black. Nothing flashy, but she looks beautiful. Simple. Unapproachable.

I grit my teeth.

She's been doing this all day. Sending signals, then clamming up and keeping her distance. Playing this maddening game of push and pull that's driving me insane.

She pauses as she comes in, scanning the scene with those unreadable eyes. My pulse picks up and I shuffle a little, half expecting, half hoping she'll make a move my way.

Wren seems to spot me, but it's like nothing registers

on her face. She just gives a slight shrug, like she's got no idea I'm even here.

She heads for the far end of the room, her chin up, making a point to sit as far away from me as possible.

Elena calls out across the room. "Wren! Sit beside him, would you? Everyone move over and make room."

It's an order. Not a request. Elena's eyebrows arch with expectation as she gestures insistently to the cushion on my left, the empty spot beside me that might as well be blinking with neon arrows.

Wren hesitates, caught in the spotlight, while Heidi dramatically scoots closer on my right. She smirks as she stakes her claim by practically gluing her thigh to mine. Her perfume hangs thick in the air.

I start to feel like I'm trapped in the world's most awkward sandwich.

Wren's face flickers with something. Indecision, maybe. Frustration. Then she lets out a sigh so quiet it's almost inaudible and gives a small nod.

She finally sits next to me with a silent huff. So close yet so far away. Her body stiff, tense. A tightly wound coil ready to spring at any second.

Her leg bounces once, then goes still. She looks everywhere but at me, like the candles and cheese trays have suddenly become wildly interesting.

I shuffle uncomfortably, caught between the jubilant giggles on my right and Wren's icy indifference on my left.

We start talking, though it's more like a play. The kind the producers want us to perform, complete with a suggested script and prompt cards.

The cameras hover nearby, eager for a soundbite, as we throw ourselves into the kind of forced conversation that's supposed to seem deep and interesting. About love, about life, about dating in the public eye. It's all calculated to sound breezy and intimate and relatable, but it's anything but that.

The phrase *hockey god's girlfriend* comes up, just like I knew it would.

I cringe so hard my entire body tightens, retreating instinctively behind a gulp of wine.

When someone says that dreaded phrase, Wren glances at me with a sideways look. Just briefly. A quick flash of something. Then she smothers it with a nonchalant shrug and turns away, feigning indifference like it didn't mean anything at all.

I know it's only a matter of time before someone derails this cozy little chat we're supposed to be having.

Heidi doesn't bother with subtlety.

She turns to me halfway through a bite of cracker and says, "Are you ever gonna kiss me, or are you scared I'll be too good at it?"

Someone hoots. A few of the girls chime in with catcalls and teasing nudges, egging Heidi on with barely suppressed giggles.

I shift uncomfortably, feeling the heat rise to my cheeks, and look toward Elena. She's nodding emphatically from behind the cameras. All "do it for the footage."

I know there's no escaping this moment.

Yeah. This is happening.

Heidi waits expectantly, her eyes practically daring me to back down. I give her a sideways grin, then lean in and kiss her.

It's quick. Almost clinical. I barely let it last ten seconds. The whole thing has a wine-flavored aftertaste and feels more like an obligation than passion. Just enough to satisfy the cameras. Probably Heidi's ego, too.

She pulls away with a triumphant smile like she's just won a challenge.

Everyone claps and someone whistles as the pressure breaks. The conversation picks up again, full of manufactured intimacy and playful banter.

I steal a glance at Wren, but she's still looking coolly uninterested. Ignoring the kiss entirely.

My heart sinks a little and I throw myself into more meaningless chatter about cheese and poorly matched wine pairings. I almost convince myself I'm relaxed, but I know the veneer won't last long.

Raven, who has clearly been refilling her glass more often than anyone else, leans forward with the inebriated persistence of someone who's got a truth bomb to deliver.

Her cheeks are flushed. She hiccups a little before blurting, "Okay, but like... why haven't you kissed Wren more? She's right there."

The words hang in the air. Bold and unrestrained. Much like Raven herself on a tipsy night.

I freeze. So does Wren.

Elena's smiling again from the shadows. Waiting.

Wren mutters, "You don't have to..." But I'm already leaning in.

It's a reckless urge. A runaway impulse. And it takes over completely, pulling me across the invisible line.

I'm sure I'll regret it. I'm sure it's a terrible idea.

But I don't care. Not in this instant.

I breathe in the scent of her. Sweet and soft and impossible. Just as our lips meet.

Everything else blurs. Everyone else vanishes. There's no show. No competition. No awkward sandwiching to escape from.

There's only Wren.

It's like I'm kissing her for the first time.

She doesn't pull away or start with another protest. She doesn't freeze up or brush it off like I halfway expected.

Instead, her mouth opens against mine like she forgot there were people watching. Her fingers curl into the cushion between us.

I seize the moment, tilting her chin to deepen the kiss.

It's suddenly more than I thought it would be. Hotter. Wilder. More real. It tastes like fear and longing, not cheap wine.

It's wrong. It's dangerous. There are a thousand reasons why we should stop.

But we don't stop.

We don't hold back.

We don't break away until the whisper of silence falls over the room.

We just made out for a solid minute in front of everyone.

I look around and realize most of the girls are pretending it didn't happen. Wren looks like she wants to sink through the floor.

I reach for my wine again, trying to cool off after the kiss. After the whole crazy scene. After that one blazing moment when everything else disappeared.

I try to shake off the awkwardness of returning to reality, taking a shaky breath as conversations resume around me. Wren is still beside me but miles away. Silent and distant. The tension hangs between us like smoke.

I'm pretty sure Elena's got a whole new plan now and won't stop until she gets exactly what she wants.

She paces behind the cameras, hatching new schemes, while I sit there dazed and drained and not sure how to handle this latest insanity.

Later, after everyone's been herded out to the back patio for the fastest rose ceremony we've done all season, I call the names like I'm supposed to.

They're expecting dramatic tension, lingering shots, and suspenseful pauses, but I power through it at warp speed instead. I get through the names like I'm ripping off bandages. Fast, clumsy, and hoping the sting won't last long.

Wren's name leaves my lips with more force than necessary. I can't stop thinking about that kiss. About how it felt. About how she wouldn't look at me afterward.

Nobody misses my hesitation. My pause is monumental as her name echoes in the night.

Her eyes find mine for a fraction of a second as I hand her the rose.

I'm not sure if she's angry or confused or both. Maybe she hates what just happened.

Maybe she's scared she didn't hate it enough.

When I say Ravn, I pause again. I don't mean to, but I can't help it.

She looks at me with big, playful eyes and that mischievous grin, already knowing what it means.

"I'm sorry," I say. I hand her a goodbye rose. "You're not the one."

She nods, hugs me, and makes a joke about dodging a bullet. Because that's Raven. Always the life of every party, even her own farewell.

Elena's thrilled with the unexpected drama and is probably brainstorming how to make Wren and me even more of a spectacle next week.

I'd put money on her sending us on the dreaded two-on-one date. The ultimate showdown. Guaranteed humiliation.

My mind spins in a million directions, but I can't shake how close I just came to messing everything up.

Wren doesn't look at me. Not directly.

Every time I think she might, she turns away at the last second, avoiding my gaze like it burns.

I feel the sting of it as the rest of the girls gather inside. Full of whispers and speculation now that the biggest cat is out of the bag.

I catch sight of a few producers punching notes into their phones and scrambling to adjust the storyline.

Everyone looks a little frantic as we file back in. A little too eager to build on the segment they never saw coming.

The whole house heaves with so much noise, it feels like the walls will burst. A thousand voices. A thousand excited whispers. Everyone's alive with the sound of what just went down.

I lose track of Wren in the chaos. I'm not sure if she's avoiding me or just caught up in the surge, but Elena's voice carries over it all.

"Keep rolling!" she shouts, full of manic energy, ready to capitalize on the madness. "We're getting it all on camera!"

Her words push the crew into a frenzy, desperate to capture more shocking moments. More sizzling drama.

I barely have time to think before I get swept away in it again. Thrown right back into the storm of glittery chaos.

That's when it happens.

A sputter. A flicker. A buzz.

Then nothing.

The lights die out. The whole set is dark. I can still make out the shadowy faces of people, but I'm not certain who I'm looking at.

For a second, we're all frozen. It's like someone hit

pause on our very own reality TV, leaving us in a void that's as silent as it is sudden.

Stunned confusion ripples through the room, a wave of uncertain murmurs.

"What the hell?" I hear someone say, and it's as if that breaks the spell.

The air snaps with bewildered voices, all at once.

"Did someone trip over a cable?" one of the guys calls out, trying to lighten the mood.

Some of the girls laugh like they think it's part of the show. Another crazy twist to shake things up.

But then a metallic clang echoes, and the laughter falters.

I reach awkwardly in the dark, bumping into elbows, knees, and a body I hope is Heidi's.

Accusations fly.

"Who touched me?"

"Wasn't me."

"Very funny, guys."

A crash sounds from somewhere close, followed by a panicked "Watch out!"

It feels like the world's starting to tilt. To turn on its head. To slip out of control.

A chorus of voices, high-pitched and frantic, starts rising over the din. The sound builds and builds, gaining momentum like a runaway train. Like everyone's about to lose their minds.

"Is this a joke?"

More shouts. More random guesses.

"Come on, you guys!"

"Um, are we gonna die?"

"Not cool!"

Even the crew's yelling, fumbling to figure it out, as chaos spreads like a quickly catching fire.

I hear feet scuffling across the floor. Bodies jostling for position. Everyone crowding toward the nearest windows. Anywhere there might be some light. Some relief from the sudden plunge into uncertainty.

Then Elena's voice cuts through.

"Power's out! Something electrical is definitely on fire!"

It's loud. Authoritative. It sucks up the noise like a vacuum.

What follows is dead silence. Like we're all holding our breath.

"We're halting production until further notice," she announces.

The finality of her words hangs in the air. Dimming our panic, but not by much.

Everyone murmurs and starts scattering.

I glance at Wren. Her hands tremble at her sides.

When I take a step toward her, she flinches.

She's not just startled.

She's afraid.

For the first time, I'm not sure it's only the dark she fears.

WREN

THE DARKNESS SWALLOWS EVERYTHING
WHOLE.

Girls are shrieking. Someone crashes into a table. I hear Heidi yelling about her ankle and JacqLyn demanding to know if this is part of the show. The crew is shouting orders that no one can follow because we can't see a damn thing.

I can't tell where the walls end or the voices begin. Someone's crying. Someone else is shouting orders that don't make sense. A chair crashes against something hard and metal. For a second, I swear I hear a scream.

That's when I feel the hand.

I press myself against the wall, heart hammering, trying to get my bearings. The emergency lighting should kick in any second. It has to. This is a professional set, not some backwoods cabin.

A couple of phone flashlights go on, sweeping through the murkiness. A warm hand closes around my wrist in the darkness.

I know that touch immediately. The size of his fingers,

the rough calluses on his palm from years of gripping hockey sticks. Ryan.

"Come with me," he whispers, his breath hot against my ear.

I should pull away. I should tell him to let go, that we can't keep doing this. But the chaos around us is terrifying and he's the only solid thing in a world that's suddenly tilted sideways.

He tugs me toward what I think is the service hallway, away from the panicked voices and stumbling footsteps. I follow blindly, my free hand stretched out in front of me to avoid walking into a wall.

"Where are we going?" I whisper.

"Storage room. End of the hall."

His voice is steady, confident. Like he's mapped out this entire house in case of emergency. Of course he has. Ryan's the type who notices exit signs and counts steps without realizing it.

We bump into a door and I hear him fumbling for the handle. It clicks open and he pulls me inside, closing it softly behind us. The sound cuts off most of the chaos from the main room, leaving us in thick, heavy silence.

I can't see him, but I can feel him. The heat radiating from his body, the whisper of his breathing. We're standing close, too close, in what feels like a tiny space.

"Your phone," he says quietly. "Do you have it?"

I pat my pockets and find it, my fingers shaking slightly as I turn on the flashlight. The beam illuminates a small storage closet filled with cleaning supplies and towels. And Ryan, standing right in front of me, his eyes dark and intense in the harsh white light.

"Better?" he asks.

I nod, though I'm not sure anything about this situation

is better. We're alone. Actually alone. No cameras, no microphones, no producers lurking in the shadows. Just me and Ryan and the weight of everything we've been pretending doesn't exist.

This is a mistake. A trap. A moment that doesn't belong to me. I shouldn't want this. But his voice pulls me in like gravity and I can't find a single reason to resist that doesn't sound like fear.

He takes a step closer and I back up until my shoulders hit the shelves behind me. A stack of towels shifts and tumbles to the floor.

"Wren."

The way he says my name makes my stomach flip. Soft and rough at the same time, like he's been holding it in his mouth too long.

I can't stop thinking about when he told me that love don't mean anything. *Just because they say it, doesn't mean they stay.* His voice went flat, but I could hear the hurt in it. I don't think he's ever said that out loud before.

My heart aches for him. I want to be the one to change that for him. To make him whole. I smile and tilt my head, taking him in.

"We shouldn't be here," I whisper.

"I know."

"Someone will notice we're both missing."

"I know."

I flush under Ryan's gaze. I used to fade into the background. Now people look. I'm not ready... but I'm not hiding, either.

He reaches up and brushes a strand of hair away from my face. His fingers linger against my cheek, and I lean into the touch before I can stop myself.

"I can't stop thinking about the hotel," he says quietly.

My breath catches. "Ryan…"

"You've been avoiding me all day."

"I haven't been avoiding you."

He raises an eyebrow and I flush, caught in the lie.

"Okay, maybe I have been. But you know why."

"Actually, I don't. Everything was perfect and then we came back here and you turned into ice."

I look away, but there's nowhere to go in this tiny space. The light from my phone casts strange shadows on the walls, making everything feel surreal.

"It wasn't real," I say finally.

"What?"

"The hotel. The weekend. It was like… like playing house. But this is real life, Ryan. This is your job and my job and cameras are everywhere and my brother who would literally murder you if he found out."

Ryan's jaw tightens. "So what, we just pretend it never happened?"

"Yes."

"Bullshit."

The word comes out sharp and I flinch. He immediately softens, stepping even closer until I can smell his cologne mixed with something that's just him.

"You're…" I search for the right word. "You're dangerous."

"Dangerous how?"

"You make me forget things. Important things. Like the fact that this is temporary and you're Ryan Haart and I'm nobody."

His expression darkens. "Don't say that."

"It's true."

"It's not." He cups my face in both hands, forcing me to look at him. "You're not nobody, Wren. You're everything."

The words hit me like a physical blow. I want to believe them so badly it hurts. My chest aches like something's breaking open inside.

"You don't mean that."

"I do."

"You'll change your mind. When the show ends and you go back to your real life, you'll realize this was just..."

"Just what?"

"A distraction."

He stares at me for a long moment, his thumbs stroking across my cheekbones. I'm trembling and I hope he can't feel it.

"Is that what you think this is? A distraction?"

I can't answer. Because if I say yes, I'm lying. And if I say no, I'm admitting something I'm not ready to admit.

"Wren." His voice is softer now, almost pleading. "Talk to me."

"I can't."

"Why?"

"Because I'm falling for you and it's terrifying and I don't know how to stop."

The confession tumbles out before I can stop it. Ryan goes very still, his hands still framing my face.

"Don't stop," he whispers.

"What?"

"Don't stop falling for me. Because I'm already gone."

And then he's kissing me, desperate and hungry like he's been starving for days. My body answers before my mind can form a protest. There's no world in which this is smart. But I don't care. Not when he kisses me like this. Like I'm the only thing he's ever wanted and the only thing he's ever lost.

I should push him away. I should remember where we

are and what we're risking. But his mouth is hot and demanding and I melt into him like I always do.

He presses me back against the shelves, his body caging me in. I can feel every hard line of him, the way his chest rises and falls with his breathing. My phone falls from my hand, the light spinning crazily before settling on the floor, casting strange angular shadows across the ceiling.

"I missed you today," he murmurs against my lips.

"You saw me all day."

"Not like this. Not touching you."

His hands slide down my sides, skimming over my ribs, my waist, coming to rest on my hips. I'm wearing a simple black dress and tights, nothing fancy, but the way he looks at me makes me feel like I'm dressed in silk and diamonds.

"We can't do this here," I whisper even as I arch into his touch.

"I know."

But neither of us moves to stop it. If anything, he kisses me harder, one hand tangling in my hair while the other slides around to the small of my back, pulling me flush against him.

I can feel how much he wants me, hard and insistent against my stomach. It sends heat spiraling through my core and I make a soft sound that gets swallowed by his mouth.

"Fuck, Chirp," he breathes. "The sounds you make."

He trails kisses down my throat, finding that spot just below my ear that makes me gasp. His stubble scrapes against my skin and I shiver, my hands fisting in his shirt.

"Ryan, we have to stop."

"I will. In a minute."

But he doesn't stop. His mouth works its way down to my collarbone, and I tip my head back to give him better access. One of his hands slides up to cup my breast through the thin fabric of my dress.

His thumb brushes over my nipple and every part of me locks up like a live wire. I shouldn't want this. I shouldn't need this. But I feel like I've been starved of touch my whole life and suddenly he's the only thing that feels real.

I bite my lip to keep from crying out, but a whimper escapes anyway. The sound seems to snap something in him because suddenly his mouth is back on mine, more urgent than before.

"I want to take you home," he says against my lips. "I want to strip you naked and spend hours learning every inch of your body."

The image his words paint makes my knees weak. "Ryan..."

"I want to make you come so many times you forget your own name."

"Stop."

"I want to wake up with you in my arms every morning."

"Stop," I say again, but there's no conviction in it.

He pulls back to look at me, his eyes dark with desire and something deeper. Something that makes my chest tight.

"This isn't just... I'm not screwing around. Not with you."

"What is it then?"

He's quiet for a moment, his forehead resting against mine. "I don't know. But it's more."

The words hang between us, heavy with possibility and terror. Because more means complications. More means risk. More means the possibility of getting my heart shattered into a million pieces.

A loud bang echoes from somewhere in the house, followed by shouting. The emergency lighting must have finally kicked in because I can see a faint glow under the door.

"They'll be looking for us," I whisper.

Ryan nods but doesn't step away. "Probably."

"We should go back."

"Probably."

Neither one of us moves. We just stand there, breathing hard, staring at each other in the dim light from my phone on the floor.

"This is crazy," I say finally.

"I know."

"We're going to get caught."

"I know."

"Jay will kill you."

"I know."

"And then Elena will kill both of us."

He smiles at that, the first real smile I've seen from him all day. "Worth it."

"You're insane."

"About you? Completely."

The words send a thrill through me that I try to ignore. I bend down to pick up my phone, grateful for the excuse to break eye contact. When I straighten up, Ryan is watching me with an expression I can't read.

"What happens now?" I ask.

"I don't know."

"That's not helpful."

"I've never... Christ, I've never done anything like this before. Never fallen for someone like you."

I snort despite myself. "When you put it like that, it does sound pretty stupid."

"The stupidest."

But he's smiling when he says it, and I can't help smiling back. Even in this tiny storage closet with cleaning supplies and chaos outside, he makes everything feel lighter.

"We really should go back," I say.

"I know."

This time he actually steps away, giving me room to breathe. I smooth down my dress and try to finger comb my hair into something that doesn't scream "I was just making out in a closet."

"How do I look?" I ask.

His eyes rake over me slowly, lingering on my mouth. "Like I want to kiss you again."

"That's not what I meant."

"You look beautiful. You always look beautiful."

The simple honesty in his voice makes my heart skip. I duck my head, suddenly shy.

"You go first," I say. "I'll wait a few minutes."

He nods and moves toward the door, then stops. "Wren?"

"Yeah?"

"This isn't over."

<h1 style="text-align:center">thirty-two</h1>

RYAN

I CAN'T SLEEP.

It's been three hours since the power came back on, two since Elena finally called it a night and sent everyone to their rooms, and one since I heard the last giggling conversation die down in the hallway. The house is finally quiet, but my brain won't shut up.

Every time I close my eyes, I'm back in that storage closet with Wren pressed against the shelves, her breath hitching when I touched her. The way she looked at me when I said this wasn't over. Like she wanted to believe me but was too scared to try.

What if I made it worse? What if she regrets it already? What if Jay finds out and I have to explain why I've been in love with his sister since before he even realized she was hot?

We've crossed too many lines. There's no walking this back. Not when every glance feels like a question neither of us wants to answer.

I roll onto my back and stare at the ceiling. The emergency lighting left weird shadows that are still burned into my retinas. Or maybe that's just the image of Wren's face in the glow of her phone, her lips parted and eyes wide with want.

This is insane. I'm lying here like some lovesick teenager, replaying every second of a ten-minute conversation in a closet. But I can't help it. She finally admitted she's falling for me. Instead of making things easier, it's made everything a thousand times more complicated.

Because now I know she feels it, too. This pull between us that's been driving me crazy for weeks. It's not just me imagining things or projecting my own feelings onto her. She's scared, yeah, but she wants this as much as I do.

That terrifies me.

I sit up and scrub my hands over my face. My room feels too small, too hot, too quiet. I need to move, do something other than lie here obsessing over every word she said, every touch we shared.

I sit on the edge of the bed, phone in hand, staring at the same text for five minutes before finally sending it.

> I think I'm catching feelings for someone.

Ellie doesn't even hesitate.

> Oh, so we're being sneaky now? Duh. You have feelings for Wren.

I run a hand through my hair and reply.

> Yes. She makes me insane.

> Yeah, but she also makes you shut up and listen. That's rare for you.

> She makes me want to be a better version of myself. Even when I don't know how.

> Then maybe you're finally in the right story.

> Maybe. What are you doing up so late, early bird?

> I'm hanging out with a sick dog at the clinic. It's touch and go. Speaking of... I should get back to her. But good luck with your Wren situation.

> Thanks.

My mind wanders back to Wren. I grab my phone and check the time. It's almost 3 a.m. Everyone should be asleep by now. The cameras in the common areas shut down at midnight according to the production schedule I memorized week one. If I'm careful, I could probably sneak down to the kitchen for some water without anyone noticing.

I pull on a T-shirt and ease my door open. The hallway is dark except for the dim emergency lighting they left on after the power incident. I can hear someone snoring through one of the doors. Probably JacqLyn. That girl could wake the dead.

I pad barefoot down the hall, avoiding the spots where the floor creaks. Years of sneaking around my aunt's house as a teenager taught me how to move silently. Some skills you never lose.

The kitchen is empty and peaceful. I grab a bottle of water from the fridge and lean against the counter, letting the cool air wash over my face. The silence is a relief after the chaos of earlier.

"Couldn't sleep either?"

I nearly jump out of my skin. My head jerks toward the hallway, expecting someone to catch us. Nothing. Just my pulse pounding in my ears. Wren is sitting at the breakfast bar in the dark corner of the kitchen, curled up in an over-sized hoodie with her knees pulled to her chest. I didn't even see her when I walked in.

"Jesus, Chirp. You scared the hell out of me."

She smiles, and even in the dim light I can see it reach her eyes. "Sorry. I've been sitting here for like an hour. Figured you'd show up eventually."

"Why?"

"Because you're predictable. When you can't sleep, you eat. When you're stressed, you eat. When you're thinking too hard, you eat."

I raise an eyebrow. "I came down for water."

"Uh-huh. Check the pantry. I bet you were planning to grab some of those granola bars you've been hoarding."

Damn. She's not wrong. I was absolutely going to grab a granola bar after the water. Maybe two.

"How do you know about my granola bars?"

"I pay attention."

The simple statement hits harder than it should. She pays attention. To me. To my habits and patterns and the stupid little things I do when I think no one's watching.

I twist the cap off my water and take a long drink, using the time to study her face. She looks tired but alert, like her mind is running in circles just like mine.

"So what's keeping you up?" I ask.

"You really want to know?"

"Yeah."

She unfolds herself from the bar stool and walks over to me, stopping just close enough that I can smell her shampoo. Some kind of vanilla and honey scent that always makes me want to bury my face in her hair.

"I can't stop thinking about what you said."

"Which part?"

"That you're already in too deep." She looks up at me. There's something vulnerable in her expression that makes my chest tight. "Did you mean it?"

The question hangs between us like a live wire. I could deflect, make a joke, turn this into something lighter. But she's looking at me like my answer matters more than anything else in the world.

"Yeah," I say quietly. "I meant it."

She nods, like she was expecting that answer but needed to hear it anyway. "That's what I was afraid of."

"Afraid?"

"Because I'm in too deep, too, Ryan. Completely, stupidly deep. I have no idea what to do about it."

The confession hits me like a slap shot to the chest. All the air leaves my lungs at once. She's gone. She said it. Out loud, with no cameras rolling and no producers listening and no one to perform for except me.

"Wren…"

"I know it's crazy. I know there are a million reasons this won't work. But I can't pretend anymore that this is just physical or just for the show or just anything other than what it is."

"And what is it?"

She takes a shaky breath. "I'm not saying I'm in love with you. I'm just saying I think about you all the time, and everything feels heavier when you're not around, and…"

She trails off, flushing.

Her words slice right through every defense I've ever

built. I set my water bottle down on the counter with hands that aren't quite steady.

"You're terrifying, Wren. I'm scared shitless of what you could do if you wanted to hurt me."

Her eyes probe my face. When she speaks, her voice is a whisper. "I would never do that."

I scrunch my face up. "Maybe not on purpose. But you have me wrapped around your finger, sweetheart."

I reach for her before I can think better of it, pulling her against my chest. She comes willingly, wrapping her arms around my waist and pressing her face into my shoulder.

"So we are agreed. This whole situation is insane."

"It's not insane," I murmur into her hair.

"It's not?"

"Well, it is. But not for the reasons you think."

She pulls back to look at me. "What do you mean?"

"I mean I've been half in love with you since college, Chirp. Watching you grow up, seeing you become this incredible woman, trying to convince myself you were off-limits because you're Jay's sister. The insane part isn't that we're having feelings for each other. The insane part is that it took us this long to do something about it."

Her eyes widen. "Since college?"

"You remember that night freshman year when you came to visit Jay and we all went to that party at Delta Chi?"

"Vaguely. I was pretty drunk."

"You were wearing this blue dress and you kept laughing at everything Jay said, trying to fit in with us. I spent the whole night watching you and thinking about how much I wanted to kiss you."

"Why didn't you?"

"Because you were barely eighteen and I was almost

twenty-six. And because Jay would have murdered me in my fucking sleep."

She's quiet for a moment, processing this. "So all this time...?"

"All this time."

"But you dated other people. A lot of other people."

I shrug. "None of them were you."

The simple truth of it sits between us. All those years of me convincing myself I was protecting her, protecting Jay, protecting myself. All those hookups and short relationships that never meant anything because I was always comparing them to a girl I couldn't have.

"I was so stupid," she whispers.

"You were a kid."

"No, I mean now. This week. Pulling away from you after the hotel, trying to pretend it didn't mean anything. I was scared."

"Of what?"

"Of this." She gestures between us. "Of wanting something I couldn't have. Of getting my heart broken when you realized I'm not worth the complications."

I cup her face in my hands, forcing her to look at me. "Hey. Listen to me. You think you're not worth the risk? Wren, I've built my whole life around the wrong things because I didn't think I could have you. You are worth every complication, every risk, every consequence that comes with this. You understand me?"

Tears pool in her eyes and she nods.

"I don't care about Jay's reaction or the cameras or Elena or any of it. I care about you."

"Jay's going to lose his mind."

"Probably."

"The show is going to milk this for everything it's worth."

"Definitely."

"We could both end up getting hurt."

"Maybe." I brush my thumbs across her cheekbones. "But I'd rather get hurt loving you than spend the rest of my life wondering what if."

She makes a sound that's half laugh, half sob. "You can't just say things like that."

"Why not?"

"Because it makes me want to do stupid things."

"Like what?"

She rises up on her toes and kisses me, soft and sweet and full of promise. It's different from the desperate kiss in the storage closet. This one feels like a decision. Like a beginning.

When she pulls away, she's smiling. "Like that."

"That wasn't stupid."

"It was if someone sees us."

I glance around the empty kitchen. We're standing in the shadows by the refrigerator, mostly hidden from view even if someone did walk in. But she's right. We're taking a huge risk.

"We should probably go back to our rooms," I say, even though it's the last thing I want to do.

"Probably."

But neither of us moves. We just stand there, holding each other in the dim light of the kitchen, pretending like the rest of the world doesn't exist.

"Ryan?"

"Yeah?"

"When this is all over, when the show wraps and the cameras go away... what happens then?"

It's the question I've been avoiding, the one that keeps me awake at night. Because the truth is, I don't know. My life is hockey and travel and a schedule that doesn't leave room for much else. Wren deserves better than someone who's gone half the year.

But looking at her now, seeing the hope and fear warring in her expression, I know I have to try. We have to try.

"I don't know," I admit. "But I want to find out."

She nods, like that's enough for now. Maybe it is. Maybe we don't need to have all the answers tonight.

"I should go," she whispers.

"I know."

She starts to pull away but I catch her hand, threading our fingers together.

"Wren?"

"Yeah?"

"I'm glad you couldn't sleep."

She smiles, the real one that makes her whole face light up. "Me too."

I watch her walk away, disappearing into the shadows of the hallway. When I can't see her anymore, I lean back against the counter and close my eyes.

Jay's going to kill me. Elena's going to spin this into a ratings monster. And I'd do it all again just to hear her say my name like that.

I'm in love with Jay's little sister.

Somehow, miraculously, she might be in love with me, too. I can't say it to her. Not yet. I don't want to scare her off. But the truth is still wrapped around my heart, gripping it impossibly tight.

We're completely screwed.

But for the first time in years, I don't care. I just need her to keep looking at me like that.

thirty-three

RYAN

THE HELICOPTER RIDE to the resort feels like it lasts forever and no time at all. I'm sitting across from Wren, pretending to look out the window at the coastline below while really watching her reflection in the glass. She's gripping the armrests so tight her knuckles are white. I want nothing more than to reach over and take her hand.

But there are cameras rolling and Elena is sitting right next to the pilot, occasionally turning back to check on us with that predatory smile of hers. This whole setup screams manipulation, from the romantic sunset timing to the overnight bags the crew loaded without asking what we wanted to pack.

"An overnight escape with Ryan." That's what the date card said. Like we're going on some dreamy romantic getaway instead of another carefully orchestrated scene in Elena's twisted love story.

The resort comes into view as we descend. I have to admit, it's impressive. Infinity pool, private beach, the kind of place that costs more per night than most people make in a month. The producers aren't messing around with this one.

We land on a helipad that's been decorated with rose petals and candles. Because of course, it has. Elena's nothing if not thorough in her pursuit of maximum cheese factor.

"Welcome to paradise," the pilot announces as we touch down.

Wren shoots me a look that says "kill me now" and I have to bite back a smile. At least we're on the same page about how ridiculous this is.

Elena climbs out first, gesturing for us to follow. "Ryan, Wren, welcome to your romantic overnight date. You have the entire resort to yourselves until tomorrow afternoon."

The entire resort. Jesus. I knew the show had money, but this is next-level.

"The dining room has been set up for a candlelit dinner," Elena continues, checking something on her clipboard. "After that, you're free to explore. Your rooms are on the second floor."

"Rooms?" Wren asks. "Plural?"

Elena's smile sharpens. "Well, yes. We can't very well put you in the same room, can we? What would the viewers think?"

Right. Because heaven forbid the audience actually believe we might want to sleep in the same bed. That would be too real for reality TV.

"The cameras will be capturing your dinner and some ambient shots around the property," Elena goes on. "But you'll have plenty of private time to… connect."

The way she says *connect* makes my skin crawl. Like our relationship is just another plot point for her to manipulate.

"Any questions?" she asks.

"How long do we have before the cameras start rolling?" I ask.

"Fifteen minutes. Just enough time to freshen up and get into character."

Get into character. As if my feelings for Wren are just another performance.

Elena and her crew disappear into the resort, leaving Wren and me alone on the helipad. The sun is setting over the ocean, painting everything in shades of gold and pink. It would be romantic if it weren't so obviously manufactured.

"Well," Wren says, adjusting the strap of her overnight bag. "This isn't subtle."

"Elena doesn't do subtle."

"The woman once told me to cry prettier for a confessional. Prettier. Like my tears weren't aesthetically pleasing enough."

I laugh, despite the tension coiling in my shoulders. "Rich told me to look more conflicted during last week's rose ceremony. Apparently my face wasn't conveying enough inner turmoil."

"Were you having inner turmoil?"

"About sending Raven home? I don't know. I guess."

Wren's expression flickers with something I can't read. "Right. Raven."

There's an edge to her voice that makes me pause. "What about Raven?"

"Nothing. Just... you two seemed close."

"We were friendly. That's it."

"Friends who had a lot of chemistry on camera."

"Chirp." I step closer, lowering my voice even though there's no one around to hear us. "Are you jealous?"

"No. I'm just... I mean, it's not like you didn't have options." She's avoiding my eyes. "It was easy to imagine you picking someone like her."

"Someone like her?"

"Fun. Outgoing. The type of person you usually go for."

"Is that what you think?"

She finally looks at me. "I'm scared that when all this is over, you're going to realize you picked the wrong girl."

The vulnerability in her voice hits me like a punch to the gut. Here we are, on this ridiculously romantic date, and she's worried I'm going to change my mind about her.

"Wren, look at me."

She does, reluctantly.

"There is no wrong girl. There's only you."

"But Raven was more..."

I cut her off by kissing her, quick and soft but firm enough to make my point. When I pull back, her eyes are wide.

"Raven was great," I say. "But she wasn't you. And you're the only one I want."

Pink spreads across her cheeks, and she looks down at her feet. "Okay."

"Okay?"

"Okay, I believe you. For now."

"I'll take it."

A crew member appears from somewhere, waving us toward the resort. "Five minutes to places!"

Wren sighs. "Showtime."

"Hey." I catch her hand before she can walk away. "Just because they're filming doesn't mean it's not real. What's happening between us... that's not for the cameras."

She squeezes my fingers. "I know. It's just hard to remember sometimes."

"Then let me remind you."

The dinner setup is exactly what I expected. Candles everywhere, rose petals scattered on the table, and an infinity pool glowing blue in the background. It's beautiful in that expensive, try-hard way that someone spent a fortune on to make this look effortless.

Wren emerges from wherever they took her to get ready. I nearly swallow my tongue. She's wearing a flowing white dress that makes her look like some kind of goddess, her hair loose around her shoulders and catching the candlelight. She hesitates at the edge of the terrace like she's not sure she's allowed to take up this much space.

"Wow," I breathe.

She ducks her head, but I catch her smile. "Elena's team. They said I needed to look more 'romantically available.'"

"Well, mission accomplished."

The cameras start rolling and suddenly we're back in performance mode. I pull out her chair, and she thanks me with that camera-ready smile. We settle into our designated roles. The perfect bachelor and his potential bride, falling in love over expensive wine and artfully plated food.

I lace my fingers with hers under the table. The camera won't catch it, but maybe the producers will. Maybe they'll zoom in. Maybe they'll cut it entirely.

Except it doesn't feel like a performance when she laughs at something I say, her whole face lighting up.

"So," she says, twirling pasta around her fork in a way that shouldn't be sexy but absolutely is. "If we were on a normal date, what would we be doing right now?"

"Normal date?"

"You know. Without cameras and producers and a location that costs more than my college tuition."

I consider this. "Probably arguing about where to eat."

"Arguing?"

"You'd want some hole-in-the-wall place with authentic atmosphere and I'd want something with a decent beer selection and burgers that don't come with sprouts."

"I like sprouts."

"I know. It's disgusting."

She throws a piece of bread at me and I duck, grinning. The cameras eat it up, but it's real. This is how we are together when no one's watching. This easy banter, this comfortable friction.

"Where would we go to compromise?" she asks.

"The Tin Shed. They have those loaded potato skins you're obsessed with."

She pauses, fork halfway to her mouth. "You remember that?"

"I remember everything about you, Chirp."

The words come out more intense than I meant them to. Something shifts in her expression. The playful energy turns charged, electric.

"Everything?" she asks quietly.

"Everything."

We're staring at each other across the candlelit table. I forget there are cameras rolling. I forget we're on a TV show. I forget everything except the way she's looking at me, like I'm something precious and terrifying all at once.

"Cut!"

Elena's voice shatters the moment. Wren jerks back like she's been burned. I have to resist the urge to tell Elena exactly what I think of her timing.

"Beautiful work, you two," Elena says, approaching the

table. "Really lovely chemistry. We'll pick up after dessert for the transition to your evening activities."

Evening activities. Right. Because even our alone time has to be scheduled and scripted.

"What happens now?" Wren asks.

"Now you have about two hours of private time. No cameras, no crew. Just the two of you and this beautiful setting." Elena's smile is sharp as a blade. "Try to make the most of it."

That's the problem. I already am. I don't want any of this to be hers to use.

She disappears with her team, leaving us alone on the candlelit terrace. The silence feels heavy after all the direction and movement of the crew.

"Two hours," Wren says.

"Two hours."

"That's not very long."

"No, it's not."

She stands up from the table, smoothing down her dress. "I should probably change. This thing is beautiful but not exactly comfortable."

"Don't."

She pauses. "Don't what?"

"Don't change. You look..." I trail off, searching for words that won't sound like a line. "You look incredible."

"Elena's team gets the credit."

"Elena's team didn't make your eyes light up when you laugh. Or the way you bite your lip when you're thinking. Or how you get this little wrinkle between your eyebrows when you're concentrating."

She touches her forehead self-consciously. "I do not get a wrinkle."

"You do. Right there." I reach out and smooth the spot with my thumb. "It's adorable."

"You're ridiculous."

"About you? Completely."

She rolls her eyes, but she's smiling. I count that as a win.

"So what do you want to do with our two hours of freedom?" she asks.

I could suggest a dozen things. We could walk on the beach, explore the resort, sit by the pool and talk. But there's only one thing I really want to do.

"I want to kiss you," I say honestly. "Without cameras. Without wondering who's watching or what they're going to do with the footage. I just want to kiss you because I want to, not because it makes good television."

It's all coming apart now. The plan. The persona. All the decisions I've made that led me right here. And I still want her like it's the only thing that makes sense.

Her breath catches. "Ryan…"

"I know it's not much of a plan. But I've been sitting across from you all night, watching you in that dress, listening to you laugh. All I can think about is how much I want to touch you."

I don't want to rush this. But I also can't stop thinking about that dress hitting the floor.

"The cameras could come back early."

"They won't. Elena's too professional to mess with her own schedule."

"Someone could see us."

"Let them."

She stares at me for a long moment. I can practically see her internal debate playing out across her face. Caution warring with desire, fear fighting with trust.

Finally, she steps closer. "Okay."

"Okay?"

"Kiss me, Ryan. Kiss me like you mean it."

I don't need to be asked twice.

thirty-four

WREN

THE KISS STARTS soft and sweet, but it doesn't stay that way. Ryan's hands slide into my hair, tilting my head back as he deepens it. I feel that familiar flutter low in my stomach that only he can cause. We're standing on this ridiculously romantic terrace with candles flickering around us and the ocean stretching endlessly in the background, but all I can focus on is the heat of his mouth and the way he's holding me like I'm something he can't live without.

"God, I missed this," he murmurs against my lips.

I laugh, but it turns into a gasp when he trails kisses down my throat. The stubble on his jaw scrapes against my skin and I shiver, my hands fisting in his shirt to keep myself steady.

"We should go somewhere more private," I whisper.

"Why? No one's watching."

"Because if you keep doing that, I'm going to forget we're supposed to be acting professional."

He pulls back to look at me, his eyes dark with heat.

"Professional went out the window the moment I saw you in that dress."

"This old thing?" I flick the dress out with my fingertips.

"That old thing is going to be the death of me." His hands slide down to rest on my hips. "Do you have any idea what you do to me?"

The raw honesty in his voice makes my breath catch. "Show me."

Something fierce flashes in his eyes. "Come with me."

He takes my hand and leads me through the resort. Past the infinity pool with its underwater lighting, past a hot tub that's definitely going to feature in tomorrow's filming, past what looks like a spa area with massage tables set up under a pergola. Everything is beautiful and expensive and designed to make people fall in love on camera.

But I'm not thinking about cameras right now. I'm thinking about the way Ryan's thumb is stroking across my knuckles, the way he keeps glancing back at me like he can't quite believe I'm real.

"Where are we going?" I ask.

"My room."

"Ryan, we can't. If Elena finds out..."

"Elena said we had two hours of private time. What we do with it is our business."

We reach a set of stairs leading to the second floor. Ryan pauses at the bottom, still holding my hand but not pulling me forward.

"If you want to stop, we stop," he says quietly. "No questions, no pressure. We can go sit by the pool and talk about the weather if that's what you want."

I look up at him, this man who's been driving me crazy for weeks, who kissed me in a storage closet and made me feel things I didn't know I was capable of feeling. His hair is mussed from my fingers, his shirt wrinkled from my hands. He's looking at me like I'm the only person in the world.

"I don't want to talk about the weather," I say.

His smile is slow and devastating. "Good."

His room is just as over-the-top as everything else about this place. Massive bed with white linens, floor-to-ceiling windows overlooking the ocean, a balcony with what looks like a private hot tub. Rose petals are scattered across the comforter and there are more candles than a church.

"Subtle," I mutter.

Ryan closes the door behind us and suddenly, the space feels different. Intimate. Real. We're alone. Actually alone. No cameras, no crew, no one watching our every move.

"Second thoughts?" he asks.

I turn to face him, taking in the way he's standing there so still, giving me space to change my mind if I need to. Not pushing, not assuming. Just waiting.

"No second thoughts," I say. "Just... are you sure about this? About us?"

He's on me in two strides, his mouth crashing into mine with desperate hunger. His hands are everywhere, sliding down my back to grip my ass, pulling me against him so I can feel exactly how hard he is.

"Fuck, I need you," he growls against my lips.

"Then take me."

His hands find the zipper of my dress and he drags it down slowly, his knuckles brushing against my spine. The dress pools at my feet, leaving me in just a white lace thong and the heels Elena's team picked out.

"Jesus Christ," he breathes, stepping back to look at me. "You're fucking perfect."

I should feel exposed, but the way he's looking at me

makes me feel powerful. Like I could bring him to his knees with just a look.

"Your turn," I say, reaching for his shirt.

But instead of letting me undress him, he catches my wrists and pins them above my head against the wall.

"Not yet," he says, his voice rough. "I want to taste you first."

Before I can respond, he's dropping to his knees in front of me. He hooks his fingers in my thong and drags it down my legs, his breath hot against my inner thighs.

"Spread your legs for me," he commands.

I do. He wastes no time burying his face between my thighs. His tongue finds my clit immediately, circling it with just the right pressure to make me cry out.

"Oh god, Ryan!"

He hums against me, the vibration sending shock waves through my core. His tongue is relentless, licking and sucking until I'm grinding against his face, chasing the orgasm that's building low in my belly.

"You taste so fucking good," he murmurs between licks. "I could eat this pussy all night."

"Please," I gasp. "I'm so close."

He slides two fingers inside me while his tongue works my clit. That's all it takes. I come with a scream, my legs shaking as waves of pleasure crash over me.

But he doesn't stop. He keeps licking, keeps finger fucking me through the aftershocks until I'm begging him to stop because it's too much.

"One more," he says against my swollen flesh. "Give me one more."

He adds a third finger, stretching me, curling them to hit the spot that makes me see stars. His mouth is relentless on my clit. Before I know it, I'm coming again, harder this time, my vision going white around the edges.

When I finally come back to myself, Ryan is standing in front of me, his face glistening with my arousal, his eyes dark with satisfaction.

"I've been thinking about this all day," he murmurs against my lips.

"Just today?"

"Okay, fine. I've been thinking about this since the hotel. Since the storage closet. Since that first night when you came to my room and we talked until sunrise."

"Fuck," I breathe. "That was…"

"That was just the beginning," he says, lifting me easily and carrying me to the bed.

He tosses me down on the rose petals and I bounce slightly, laughing breathlessly. But my laughter dies when I see him stripping off his clothes, revealing inch after inch of tanned skin and hard muscle.

When he pushes down his boxer briefs, his cock springs free, thick and hard and already leaking precum. I lick my lips, suddenly desperate to taste him.

"Come here," I say, crooking my finger at him.

He joins me on the bed, but when I reach for his cock, he catches my hand.

"Not yet," he says. "I need to be inside you. I've been thinking about your pussy all day."

He reaches for his wallet, fumbling for a condom. I help him roll it on, my hands trembling with anticipation.

When he finally settles between my thighs, I wrap my legs around his waist, pulling him closer. Then he's pushing inside me in one smooth thrust.

We both groan at the sensation. He's so thick, stretching me perfectly, filling me completely.

"Fuck, you feel incredible," he gasps. "So tight and wet for me."

He starts to move, setting a rhythm that's deep and hard and perfect. Each thrust hits the spot inside me that makes me see stars. I can already feel another orgasm building.

"Harder," I beg. "Fuck me harder."

He complies, driving into me with a force that makes the headboard slam against the wall. The sound of skin slapping against skin fills the room, along with our moans and gasps.

"You like that?" he growls. "You like when I fuck you hard?"

"Yes! God, yes! Don't stop!"

He reaches between us to rub my clit with his thumb. I nearly scream at the added stimulation.

"Come for me," he commands. "Come on my cock."

I do, exploding around him with a force that surprises us both. My pussy clenches around him rhythmically. He curses as he follows me over the edge, spilling himself inside the condom with a hoarse shout.

We collapse together, hearts racing, skin slick with sweat. I trace lazy patterns on his chest while he plays with my hair.

"You're incredible," he whispers against my skin. "Perfect."

"Not perfect."

"Perfect for me."

The words make my heart skip. We lie tangled together, hearts racing, skin damp with sweat.

"That was..." I start.

"Yeah."

"We're in so much trouble."

He tightens his arms around me. "Worth it."

"Elena's going to know something happened."

"Probably."

I prop myself up to look at him. "And you're okay with all that?"

He reaches up to cup my face, his thumb stroking across my cheekbone. "For you? I'm okay with anything."

The show is nearly over. I'm almost at the end of this journey. I should feel strong. Instead, all I can think is, what if I'm still just the girl nobody picks?

The sincerity in his voice makes my chest tight. I want to tell him I feel the same way, that I'd risk everything for this, for him. But the words stick in my throat.

Instead, I kiss him again, pouring everything I can't say into the touch of my lips against his. He kisses me back just as fiercely. I know he understands.

But what if he crushes my heart by accident?

RYAN

I SIT in the confessional chair, arms crossed, watching the producer across from me with what I hope looks like my usual cocky smirk. The lighting in here is harsh, designed to make people look vulnerable and exposed. It makes me feel like a bug under a glass.

I've let three more girls go in one ceremony: Heidi, Divya, and Whitney. Letting Divya go was a huge weight off my shoulders, even if it wasn't what the producers wanted. But now I'm left with three finalists.

JacqLyn, Daisy, and Wren. I think the producers are expecting me to pick Wren at this point. What I don't know is why Rich is being so nice about it.

There are only two weeks of the show left and suddenly I can't tell what's real anymore.

"This is starting to feel like an interrogation," I say.

"Just a check-in. The audience is really invested in you and Wren."

I clock the way Rich keeps glancing at his notebook like he's checking off boxes. Not a check-in. A setup.

"Yeah?" I lean back, stretching my arms behind my head like I don't have a care in the world. "What's the verdict?"

Rich tilts his head, studying me with those beady eyes that remind me of a hawk circling prey. "They're wondering if it's real."

I roll my eyes. "Define real."

And there it is. The real reason I'm here. The trapdoor under the chair creaks open.

"Are you falling for her?"

The question hits harder than I expect it to. I open my mouth to laugh it off, to give him some charming nonanswer that'll keep everyone guessing. But the words get stuck somewhere between my brain and my throat.

Rich watches me, waiting. The silence stretches longer than it should.

My knee bounces once, then twice. I stop it. I don't want to give anything away, but my body already has.

"She's a pain in my ass," I say finally.

His grin spreads wider. "That's not a no."

I don't respond. Can't respond. Because the truth is sitting right there in my chest, heavy and undeniable. I think about her all the time. The more I try not to, the worse it gets. I'm not about to hand that over to these vultures.

"Let's try a different approach," Rich says, flipping through his notes. "Tell me about last night. The overnight date."

My jaw tightens automatically. "What about it?"

"How did it go? Any... developments?"

I know what he's fishing for. He wants me to spill about what happened between Wren and me on that balcony, in my room, in the hours when the cameras weren't rolling. He wants details he can twist into whatever narrative Elena's cooking up.

"It was nice," I say carefully. "We talked."

"Just talked?"

"Is that a problem?"

Rich laughs. "Of course not. It's just... the viewers are expecting more. You two have so much chemistry. They want to see that connection deepen."

My throat goes dry. Jay's going to see this. He's going to see all of it.

Chemistry. Like what's happening between Wren and me is just some chemical reaction they can manipulate for ratings. The thought makes me sick.

"Maybe the viewers need to be patient," I say.

"Patience doesn't make for good television, Ryan."

"Neither does forcing something that isn't there."

But even as I say it, I know it's a lie. What's between Wren and me isn't forced. If anything, I've been fighting it since the moment she walked into that first rose ceremony wearing that punk rock outfit and glaring at me like I'd personally offended her.

"So you're saying there's nothing there?" Rich presses. "No feelings developing?"

I stare at him for a long moment. "I'm saying that if there were feelings developing, they'd be private. Between me and her. Not entertainment for people sitting on their couches eating popcorn."

"Fair enough." He makes a note on his pad. "But you have to admit, the dynamic between you two is compelling. The way you challenge each other, the banter, the obvious attraction."

"Obvious?"

"Come on, Ryan. I've watched the footage. The way you look at her when you think no one's watching. The way she responds to you. It's electric."

My chest tightens. If it's that obvious to the producers, who else can see it? Jay's going to watch this show when it airs. He's going to see every glance, every touch, every moment I've failed to hide how I feel about his sister.

"Like I said," I tell Rich. "She drives me insane."

"The kind of insane you'd miss if it was gone?"

The question catches me off guard. Because the answer is yes, absolutely, I would miss her if she was gone. I'd miss her sarcasm and her stubbornness and the way she challenges everything I say. I'd miss the way she looks at me when she thinks I'm being ridiculous. I'd miss the sound of her laugh when I actually manage to say something funny.

I'd miss all of it.

But I'm not about to tell Rich that.

"We're almost done here," he says, closing his notebook. "Just one more question. If you had to choose right now, today, who would get your final rose?"

My heart starts pounding. "It's too early for that."

"Hypothetically."

"I don't deal in hypotheticals."

"Ryan." His voice gets sharper, more insistent. "The audience needs to see that you're taking this seriously. That you're genuinely looking for love, not just going through the motions."

I am taking it seriously. More seriously than I've ever taken anything in my life. But the person I'm taking seriously isn't someone I can talk about in this room, with these cameras rolling and these producers hanging on every word.

"I'm here to find my person," I say finally. "When I do, everyone will know."

Rich nods, seemingly satisfied with that nonanswer. "Great. I think we got what we need."

I stand up to leave, but he stops me with one more question.

"Off the record," he says. "How much trouble are you in?"

I pause with my hand on the door handle. "What do you mean?"

"With Jay. Wren's his sister, right? How crazy is he going to go when he finds out that you've been... *talking* to her? Are we going to have to call the cops?"

His tone suggests he would very much like to get that on film. The fact that he knows about my relationship with Wren, that the producers all know, makes my stomach drop. "I don't know what you're talking about."

Rich smiles. "Sure you don't. But Ryan? When this all comes out, and it will come out, make sure you're ready for the fallout. Because it's going to be big."

I leave the confessional feeling like I've been run over by a truck. The producers know about Wren and me. They're probably planning to use it as their big, dramatic twist, the moment that'll have viewers glued to their screens.

Jay... fuck, Jay's going to lose his mind.

I came into this room thinking I could keep lying. That I could spin some charming soundbites and walk out clean. But I can't. Not anymore. I've already chosen her. The only question now is, what's that choice going to cost me?

I need to talk to Wren. Need to warn her that our secret isn't as secret as we thought. But first, I need to figure out how to protect her from the storm that's coming.

It started as a stupid reality television show. Now I'm

standing here rehearsing what I'm going to say to Wren when I tell her how much she means to me... and praying she doesn't walk away.

Because Rich is right about one thing. When this all comes out, the fallout is going to be massive.

thirty-six

RYAN

MY PHONE BUZZES JUST as I'm finishing up another pointless conversation with Rich about "opening up emotionally for the cameras." I glance down and see Coach T's name on the screen.

> Thinking about you, kid. Hope you're remembering what we talked about. You deserve good things. Ellie's doing great, by the way. Says to tell you she's proud of you.

I stare at the message for a long moment, something tight loosening in my chest. Coach always knows exactly when to reach out, like he has some sixth sense for when I'm spiraling. The reminder about Ellie being safe, being proud of me... it hits harder than it should.

I type back quickly:

> Thanks, Coach. Needed to hear that today.

His response comes almost immediately:

> Trust your gut. And stop overthinking everything.

Trust your gut. Easier said than done when your gut is telling you to do something that could blow up your entire life. But Coach has never steered me wrong before.

I pocket my phone and go looking for Wren.

I find her in the kitchen, washing dishes that she definitely didn't use. It's one of her nervous habits, cleaning things when she's stressed. She does it at Jay's house, too, scrubbing counters that are already spotless when she's anxious about something.

"Hey," I say quietly.

She looks up. I can see the tension in her shoulders, the way her mouth is set in a thin line. "Hey yourself."

"You okay?"

"Peachy. Just enjoying the lovely evening conversation with my housemates about what a fraud I am."

I move closer, lowering my voice even though there's no one else around. "They're just scared. They can see which way this is going and they don't like it."

"Can they? Because I sure as hell can't."

She turns back to the dishes, scrubbing a plate with more force than necessary. I want to touch her, to pull her into my arms and tell her everything's going to be okay. But we're in the common area of the house and there are cameras everywhere.

"Meet me upstairs in ten minutes," I murmur. "Third door on the right. It's empty."

She doesn't turn around, but I see her nod slightly.

The unused bedroom is small and sparse, clearly meant for crew or storage rather than contestants. But it has a lock on the door and no cameras, which makes it perfect for what I need right now.

Wren slips in exactly ten minutes later, closing the door softly behind her and turning the lock. She leans against it for a moment, her eyes closed.

"This is insane," she says.

"I know."

"We're going to get caught."

"Probably."

"Elena's going to have our heads."

"Most likely."

She opens her eyes and looks at me. "And you're still okay with all that?"

I cross the room in three strides, backing her up against the door. My hands frame her face and I can feel the way her breath catches when I touch her.

"I got a text from Coach T today," I say quietly. "He reminded me that I deserve good things. That I shouldn't overthink everything."

"What does that have to do with us?"

"You're a good thing, Wren. The best thing that's happened to me in years. I'm tired of overthinking it."

Before she can respond, I'm kissing her. It's desperate and hungry and full of all the things I can't say out loud. She melts into me immediately, her hands fisting in my shirt.

"This is a mistake," she whispers against my mouth. "If we get caught..."

"Then we'll deal with it," I say. "Together."

That's what does it. Not the kiss. Not the promises. The *together*.

"Ryan," she breathes against my mouth.

"I need you," I tell her. "Right now. Right here."

"Someone could come looking for us."

"Let them."

I can see the exact moment she gives in, when the worry leaves her eyes and gets replaced by want. She reaches for the hem of my shirt and pulls it over my head, her hands immediately going to my chest.

"You're going to be the death of me," she murmurs.

"Good. I want to ruin you for anyone else. I don't want you to ever be satisfied by anyone else. Only *me*."

The words come out rougher than I intended, but I mean them. I want to mark her, claim her, make sure she never forgets what it feels like to be touched by me.

I lift her easily, her legs wrapping around my waist as I carry her to the narrow bed. When I lay her down, she's looking at me with an expression I've never seen before. Vulnerable and trusting and so beautiful it makes my chest ache.

"Tell me what you want," I say.

"You. Just you."

I take my time undressing her, pressing kisses to each inch of skin as I reveal it. I wait. Just long enough for her to nod. Just long enough for her to tell me without words that she's sure. When I finally settle between her thighs, she's trembling and breathless.

"Please," she whispers.

"Please what?"

"Touch me. Make me forget everything else."

I do. I worship her body with my hands and mouth until she's writhing beneath me, my name falling from her lips over and over. When I finally push inside her, we both go still for a moment.

"Fuck," I breathe. "You feel incredible."

She pulls me down for a kiss that's all teeth and tongue

and desperation. She doesn't just reach for me. She clings. Like she's finally letting herself need someone. "Move," she demands.

I set a rhythm that's slow and deep, taking my time, despite the urgency clawing at my chest. This feels different from our other encounters. More intense. More real.

I don't know when it happened. Somewhere between the sarcasm and the stolen kisses, this thing stopped being fun and started feeling like everything. The words claw at the back of my throat. They terrify me. But they won't stay down.

"I'm so gone for you," I tell her, the words torn from somewhere deep in my chest. "I've fallen so fucking hard it scares me."

Her eyes go wide and she cups my face in her hands. "Ryan…"

"I know it's crazy. I know there are a million reasons why this won't work. But I can't stop it."

"I'm falling for you, too," she whispers, and the admission sounds like it costs her something. "I tried not to, but I can't help it."

The confession breaks something open in my chest. I kiss her harder, moving faster, losing myself in the heat and tightness of her body.

"You're mine," I growl against her throat. "Say it."

"I'm yours," she gasps. "God, Ryan, I'm yours."

When she comes apart beneath me, it's with my name on her lips and her nails digging into my shoulders. I follow her over the edge, burying my face in her neck as the orgasm rips through me.

We lie tangled together afterward, hearts racing, skin damp with sweat. I trace lazy patterns on her back while she presses soft kisses to my chest.

"We're in trouble, aren't we?" she says quietly.

"Deep trouble."

"I should probably care more about that."

"Probably."

She lifts her head to look at me. "Do you regret it?"

"Not a single second."

"Even when Jay finds out and murders you in your sleep?"

"Especially then."

She laughs. Really laughs. For the first time all day. "You're insane."

"About you? Hopelessly."

We stay like that for as long as we dare, wrapped up in each other and pretending the rest of the world doesn't exist. But eventually, reality intrudes, and we have to get dressed and sneak back to our separate rooms and pretend like nothing happened.

"Same time tomorrow?" I ask as she's fixing her hair in the small mirror.

"You wish."

But she's smiling when she says it. I take that as a yes.

I want to say yes. Hell yes. But part of me is already counting the cracks in the walls we just built this on. How long before it all comes down?

thirty-seven

WREN

IT'S two days later and I'm stuck in a loop of Ryan admitting, *I'm so gone for you.* The words play over and over in my head, piling up till there isn't room for anything else. I sit stiffly on the couch, my hands clasped so tightly in my lap that my knuckles are white. The other contestants are chattering around me, but their voices sound muffled, like I'm underwater.

The host walks in with that megawatt smile that always means trouble. He's wearing a suit that probably costs more than my rent. His teeth are so white they could blind someone.

"Ladies," he announces, clapping his hands together. "Tonight, we have a twist."

The room goes quiet except for the nervous shifting of bodies on leather couches. I feel my stomach clench because twists on this show are never good. They're designed to create maximum drama and minimum comfort for everyone involved.

"For the next forty-eight hours," the host continues, his

grin getting wider, "Ryan will be spending time with one contestant. Exclusively."

Murmurs ripple through the group. Heidi actually gasps and presses her hand to her chest like she's having a heart attack. JacqLyn mutters something under her breath that sounds distinctly unflattering.

"This contestant will have full access to Ryan, outside of cameras, outside of scheduled dates. Just the two of them."

My stomach drops straight through the floor. Oh no. No, no, no. This is exactly the kind of setup that Elena loves, the kind that forces people into impossible situations and then films the fallout. I can already see where this is going and I hate every second of it.

The host turns toward the doorway where Ryan is presumably waiting. "Ryan, who are you choosing?"

For one split second, I let myself hope it won't be me. Anyone that wouldn't make me the enemy of the house.

Ryan walks in looking like he owns the place, which I suppose he kind of does. His eyes scan the room briefly before locking onto mine. There's something in his expression that makes my pulse stutter.

"Wren," he says without hesitation.

The air gets sucked out of the room. I can feel every pair of eyes turning to stare at me, some shocked, some angry, some calculating what this means for their own chances. The whispers start immediately, a low buzz of speculation and resentment.

My pulse is hammering so hard I'm pretty sure everyone can hear it. I expected some kind of setup, but this? Forty-eight hours alone with Ryan while the other contestants stew in their own jealousy? Elena really went all out on this one.

"Wren and Ryan," —the host beams— "pack your bags. You're leaving tonight."

I look at Ryan and panic starts creeping up my throat. He just smirks and leans back in that casual way he has, like he planned this whole thing. Like he knew exactly what was coming and decided to roll with it.

"This is bullshit," Divya says loudly. "She already has an unfair advantage because of her brother."

"Totally unfair," Heidi agrees, though she's trying to keep her voice sweet. "Some of us are actually here to find love."

They're not wrong. I am here under false pretenses. I am paid to be here. But the feelings... those weren't part of the job description. I didn't mean to want him.

The implication stings even though I know it shouldn't. Because the truth is, I'm not here to find love. I'm here to do a job. But somewhere along the way that job got complicated and now I'm sitting in a room full of hostile women who think I'm cheating my way to the final rose.

"Ladies," the host says with fake sympathy, "I know this is disappointing. But Ryan has made his choice."

More grumbling. More pointed looks in my direction. I want to sink through the couch cushions and disappear completely.

"Pack light," the host tells us. "You'll be leaving in an hour."

I stand up on shaky legs, my mind racing. Forty-eight hours alone with Ryan. No cameras, no other contestants, no buffer between us and whatever this thing is that we've been dancing around for weeks.

I'm completely screwed.

I should be angry. Embarrassed. But underneath all of

that? I'm a little bit thrilled. I wanted him to choose me. And he did.

"Wren," Daisy calls out as I'm heading for the stairs. When I turn back, she gives me a thumbs-up and a wink. "Have fun."

At least someone's on my side.

I make it to my room and start throwing things into my overnight bag with hands that won't stop trembling. Clothes, toiletries, the book I've been trying to read but can't concentrate on. I have no idea where we're going or what we're supposed to be doing for two whole days.

"Hey."

I spin around to find Ryan leaning against my doorframe, his own bag slung over his shoulder. He looks completely calm, like this is just another day at the office.

"Are you insane?" I hiss, glancing around to make sure none of my roommates are within earshot. "What were you thinking?"

"I was thinking that I'm tired of pretending I don't want to spend time with you."

"Ryan, this is going to make everything worse. The other girls already hate me."

He steps into the room and closes the door behind him. "So what? Let them hate you. In two weeks this whole thing will be over and none of their opinions will matter."

"You're not the one they're calling a fraud."

"You're not a fraud, Wren."

"Aren't I? I'm not here for the right reasons, Ryan. I'm here because Elena paid me to be here. The other contestants, they're actually looking for love. I'm just playing a role."

"And what about now? Are you still just playing a role?"

The question hangs between us and I can't answer it

because I don't know anymore. When I signed up for this job, it was supposed to be simple. Play the villain, cause some drama, collect my paycheck. But nothing about this feels simple anymore.

"I came onto this show with no goal in mind other than to get a promotion. But lately, all I've been able to think about is you," I admit quietly. "You're in my head. You're what I think about before I go to sleep at night. What would you say that is?"

His gaze sharpens. "Well, whatever it is, we've got forty-eight hours to figure it out."

A PA opens the door, clipboard in hand. He looks between us then waves us out the door. "Ready to go?"

I shoulder my bag and follow them downstairs, trying to ignore the stares and whispers from the other contestants. Ryan walks beside me, close enough that our arms brush with every step.

"Where are we going?" I ask.

"It's a surprise," the PA says cheerfully.

Of course it is. Because this whole situation isn't stressful enough without adding mystery destinations to the mix.

The car is waiting outside, black and sleek and probably worth more than I'll make in five years. Ryan opens the door for me and I slide onto the leather seats, my bag clutched in my lap like a shield.

The car door shuts with a soft click that sounds like a lock. I swallow hard. It feels like a trap disguised as a getaway.

"You okay?" he asks once we're both settled and the driver pulls away from the mansion.

"Define okay."

He reaches over and takes my hand, threading our

fingers together. It should comfort me, but instead, it makes everything feel more real. More dangerous.

"It's going to be fine," he says.

"You don't know that."

"No, I don't. But I know that I want to find out what happens when it's just you and me without all the noise."

I look out the window at the city lights flashing by. "What if we don't like what we find?"

"Then at least we'll know."

His thumb strokes across my knuckles and I try not to think about how good it feels. How right. Because in forty-eight hours, this little bubble is going to burst and we'll be back to reality. Back to cameras and eliminations and the inevitable moment when Ryan has to choose someone.

"Wren," he says quietly.

"Yeah?"

"Whatever happens this weekend, I want you to know... picking you wasn't just easy. It was inevitable."

My throat goes tight and I have to look away before I do something stupid like cry. Because as terrifying as this all is, part of me is relieved. Part of me has been waiting for this moment since the first time he kissed me.

Forty-eight hours to figure out if what we have is real or just really good television.

I guess we're about to find out.

thirty-eight

RYAN

THE VILLA IS EXACTLY what I expected from Elena's team. Over-the-top, romantic to the point of being ridiculous, and designed to make people fall in love on camera. The whole place screams "fairy-tale romance" in a way that would normally make me roll my eyes.

But watching Wren step inside, her eyes wide as she takes it all in, I have to admit, it's pretty impressive.

Her fingers tighten around the strap of her bag like it's the only solid thing in the room. She takes a step forward, then freezes again when her gaze lands on the bedroom visible through the open doorway. One king-sized bed dominating the space.

She's tense, though. I can see it in the set of her shoulders, the way she's scanning the space like she's looking for an escape route.

"You gonna relax anytime soon, Rustin?" I tease.

She crosses her arms and gives me a look that could melt steel. "This is a nightmare."

I grin because her attitude is so perfectly Wren. "Come on. We've had worse."

"Have we?" She gestures around the villa, then stops. "Tell me you didn't know about this."

I shrug, trying to play it casual even though my pulse kicks up at the sight of that bed, too. "I mean, it is a romance show."

"Oh my God." She puts her face in her hands. "I hate everyone."

"Including me?"

She peeks at me through her fingers. "Especially you."

But there's no real heat behind it. I can see the corner of her mouth twitching like she's fighting a smile.

The breakfast is beautiful but untouched. The pool is cool but quiet. We go through the motions, pretending we're in a fairy tale. But under it all, the tension is unbearable.

I catch Wren watching me when she thinks I'm not looking. The way her eyes follow my movements when I'm getting out of the pool, water running down my chest. She catches me staring, too, when she's drying off her hair and the towel rides up to show a strip of skin at her waist.

Neither of us acknowledge it. But it's there.

As the day stretches on and we're sitting by the pool with drinks we're both nursing slowly, Wren finally breaks.

"This isn't going to end well," she sighs.

I tilt my head, studying her profile in the soft lighting. "You always assume the worst, huh?"

She turns to look at me. There's something in her expression I can't quite read. Resignation, maybe. Or fear.

"You don't?"

I think about that for a second. "I don't know what happens after this." I pause, watching her closely. "But I know what I want right now."

Her breath catches and her lips part slightly. The

tension that's been building all evening suddenly feels like a live wire between us.

I lean in, just enough to test the waters. Close enough that I can smell her shampoo, feel the warmth of her skin. Close enough to kiss her if she lets me.

She doesn't pull away.

"Ryan," she whispers.

"Yeah?"

"I need to tell you something. About before. About when we were kids."

I settle back slightly, giving her space but not moving away entirely. "Okay."

She takes a shaky breath and suddenly the words start pouring out of her.

"You made me feel like such a loser," she says, her voice quiet but intense. "All those years, the way you'd tease me, the way you'd look at me like I was this annoying little kid who didn't know anything. I spent so much time trying to be cool enough, smart enough, pretty enough to make you stop seeing me that way."

I feel like she's punched me in the gut. "Wren…"

"I would practice conversations in my head, trying to think of something clever to say that would make you actually see me as a person instead of just Jay's dumb little sister."

"You think I hated you?" The words come out quieter than I intended. "Wren, I never…"

"I don't even know why I'm telling you this."

"Because it matters."

"I used to hate how you looked through me. Like I didn't matter. And then I hated how much I wanted to matter." Her voice cracks slightly. "I used to steal your hockey jerseys because they smelled like you and I was so pathetic that even negative attention from you was better than being invisible."

I'm staring at her now, this woman who's been driving me crazy for months. Years, even. I'm seeing her completely differently. Not as the confident, sarcastic girl who gives as good as she gets, but as the kid who felt overlooked and ignored.

"You were never invisible to me," I say.

"Right."

"I'm serious. Wren, you were Jay's little sister. You were off-limits. Untouchable. I had to push you away."

"Why?"

"You think I didn't notice you? You think I didn't see how smart you were, how funny, how beautiful? I noticed everything about you. That's why I had to be such an ass. Because the alternative was admitting that I had feelings for my best friend's little sister.

"I thought I was protecting you by keeping my distance. But all I did was make you feel small. I fucking hate that."

We stare at each other across the small space between us. I can see her processing this. Reevaluating everything she thought she knew about our history.

"I'm fucked up," I tell her. "I'm broken in ways you don't even know about. But being with you... it helps. You make me feel like maybe I'm not as damaged as I thought."

"I'm just as broken as you are," she says quietly. "We're two half people, trying our hardest to become whole."

The honesty in her voice undoes something in my chest. This conversation, this moment, it's the most real thing that's happened to me in years.

This is the first real choice we've been allowed to make. No cameras. No producers. Just us.

"So what do we do?" I ask.

"I don't know."

I reach out, tracing the edge of her knee with my thumb. "Want to figure it out together?"

She looks at me for a long moment, then nods.

"Yeah," she whispers. "I'd like that."

thirty-nine

RYAN

THE DAY HAS LEFT us both sun-drunk and salty, sprawled across the villa's oversized couch like we've been shipwrecked and finally found ashore. Wren stretches next to me, her skin still warm from hours in the sun, and makes this little groaning sound that goes straight to my cock.

"I'm so sandy," she complains, running her fingers through her hair. "And sore. I think I pulled something at the beach."

"Where?" I ask, sitting up with interest. "I could take a look. I'm practically a medical professional."

She gives me a look. "You play hockey. That doesn't make you a doctor."

"I've had a lot of sports injuries. I know about muscle strains."

"Uh-huh. And I'm sure your examination would be very thorough."

"Extremely thorough."

She rolls her eyes but she's smiling, which I count as progress. "I should probably shower. Get all this sand and sunscreen off."

"I could assist with that."

"You could assist with a lot of things. Doesn't mean you should."

But her smile gives her away. There's something different about the way she's looking at me now, post-fight and post make up. Like she's decided to stop overthinking everything and just let herself want what she wants.

"Actually," I say, remembering something the villa host mentioned during the tour, "there's a hot tub on the upper deck. Might be good for those sore muscles."

Her eyes light up. "Now you're talking."

Twenty minutes later, we're slipping into the bubbling water, the night air cool against our damp skin. Wren groans as she settles back against the jets, her legs floating over mine under the water.

"Okay, this was a good idea," she admits.

"I have them occasionally."

"Very occasionally."

I slide my hands up her calves, massaging the muscles there. "Better?"

"Mmm." Her eyes drift closed. "That's nice."

"Just nice?"

"Don't fish for compliments, Haart."

But she's relaxing under my touch, the tension from our earlier fight finally leaving her shoulders. We sit in comfortable silence for a while, just enjoying the heat and the bubbles and the fact that we're alone. Really alone.

"So," I say eventually, "on a scale of one to ten, how much did you hate parasailing?"

"Before or after I stopped thinking I was going to die?"

"After."

She considers this. "Maybe a seven. The view was incredible."

"Just the view?"

"Well, the company wasn't terrible, either."

"High praise from Wren Rustin."

She opens her eyes and looks at me. "Don't let it go to your head."

"Too late. I'm already planning our next adventure."

"What makes you think there's going to be a next adventure?"

"Call it optimism."

She snorts. "That's not what I'd call it."

"What would you call it?"

"Delusion."

I laugh and pull her closer, until she's practically in my lap. "Come here, you."

"Ryan..."

"What? I'm just adjusting the seating arrangement."

"Is that what we're calling it?"

"Among other things."

She's straddling me now, her hands resting on my shoulders, and the playful energy between us is shifting into something else. Something charged.

"This is dangerous," she murmurs.

"How so?"

"Because I'm starting to think you might actually be as charming as you think you are."

"Only starting to think?"

"Don't push it."

But she's smiling when she says it. When I lean up to kiss her, she doesn't pull away. The kiss starts soft, teasing, but it deepens quickly. Her lips part under mine and I can taste the wine we had with dinner, sweet and intoxicating.

My hands slide up her back, tangling in her wet hair. She makes this soft sound that drives me crazy. I want to devour her, right here in this hot tub under the stars, but I force myself to go slow. To savor this.

"We should probably go inside," she breathes against my lips.

"Probably."

But neither of us moves. We just keep kissing, hands exploring, the heat building between us until I'm hard enough to cut glass and she's grinding against me in a way that's going to make me lose my mind.

"Wren," I groan. "You need to either fuck me or I'm going to have to excuse myself to go upstairs and masturbate furiously for all of five seconds."

She laughs, throwing her head back. "Five seconds? That's optimistic."

"You've been driving me crazy all day. I'm hanging on by a thread here."

"All day?"

"The bikini. The sunscreen. The way you kept licking mango juice off your fingers. Do you have any idea what you do to me?"

She looks at me like she's weighing a decision. Not just about sex. About whether to let herself want this. Want me. With nothing held back.

Her eyes go dark. "Show me."

"Here?"

"No. Upstairs. In that ridiculous shower."

"The one that's bigger than my first apartment?"

"That's the one."

I don't need to be asked twice. I lift her out of the water, her legs wrapping around my waist as I carry her toward the villa. She's giggling and kissing my neck and generally making it very difficult to navigate the stairs without tripping.

"You're going to drop me," she says.

"Never."

"You're not that strong."

"Are you questioning my athletic ability?"

"I'm questioning your coordination while distracted."

"I'm not distracted."

"Liar."

She nips at my earlobe and I nearly stumble. "Okay, maybe a little distracted."

We make it to the bathroom without incident, though I have to set her down to figure out how to work the shower controls. The thing has more buttons than a spaceship.

"Here," Wren says, reaching around me to adjust the temperature. "Like this."

The water starts flowing, multiple showerheads creating this perfect cascade of warmth. Steam immediately begins fogging the glass walls.

"This is ridiculous," I say.

"Ridiculously amazing."

"I feel like I'm in a spa commercial."

"Less talking, more washing," she says, pulling me under the spray.

The hot water feels incredible after the chlorine from the hot tub. Wren reaches for the shampoo, working it through her hair. I just watch for a moment. The way the water runs down her body, the way she moves, completely unselfconscious and beautiful.

"You're staring again," she says without opening her eyes.

"Can't help it."

"Make yourself useful. Wash my back."

I take the body wash and start working it across her

shoulders, down her spine. My hands slide over her skin, slick with soap and water. She leans into my touch.

"That feels good," she murmurs.

"Just good?"

"Fishing for compliments again."

"Always."

I work my way down her back, taking my time, mapping every inch of her. When I reach the curve of her ass, she turns in my arms.

"My turn," she says.

Her hands on my chest, sliding through the soap, is pure torture. She's thorough, washing every inch of me with careful attention. When her soapy hands wrap around my cock, I nearly come on the spot.

"Jesus, Wren."

"Too much?"

"Not enough."

Her hand moves in slow strokes, her thumb brushing over the head. I have to brace myself against the shower wall to stay upright.

"You said you could go more than one round," she says.

"I can."

"Prove it."

Her hand moves faster now, more confident. I'm lost. The heat, the steam, the feel of her touching me like she owns me. I come hard, spilling over her fingers with a groan that echoes off the tile walls.

I laugh, but inside, I feel a little unraveled. Like I gave her something I didn't know I was holding onto.

"Five seconds was generous," she says with a smirk.

"Smart ass."

But I'm already recovering, already reaching for her. I lift her against the wall, the cool tile against her back making her gasp. My mouth finds her throat, her collar-bone, working my way down.

"Ryan…"

"Say my name again."

"Ryan."

"Again."

"Ryan, please."

My hands slide between her thighs, finding her already wet and ready. She cries out when I touch her clit, her head falling back against the wall.

"That's it," I murmur against her skin. "Let me hear you."

I work her with my fingers, my mouth on her breast, until she's shaking and begging and saying my name over and over. When she comes, it's with a cry that goes straight to my cock.

"I need to be inside you," I tell her.

"Yes."

I lift her higher, lining myself up at her entrance. She's so wet, so ready. When I push inside her, we both groan at the sensation.

"Fuck," I breathe. "You feel incredible."

I start moving, hard and fast, the sound of skin slapping against skin mixing with the rush of water. She wraps her legs around my waist, pulling me deeper. I lose myself in the heat and tightness of her.

"Wait," I pant, suddenly remembering. "Condom."

"I'm on birth control," she gasps. "Have been for years. I'm religious about it."

I should stop. Should do the responsible thing. But she's here, wrapped around me like a prayer. For once in my life, I want to believe in something without backup plans.

I know her well enough to trust that completely. Have

known her long enough to know she's careful about things that matter. So I don't pull out. Instead I fuck her harder, deeper, until she's coming again with my name on her lips.

I'm not just fucking her. I'm letting her see me. All of me. It scares the shit out of me.

I don't stop. I just plow right through, and she does nothing to stop me. The second time she clenches around me, raking her nails down my back and screaming my name, I let her push me over the edge. I follow her down, spilling inside her with a groan that probably wakes the neighbors.

We stand there for a moment, breathing hard, the water still cascading around us. Then Wren starts laughing.

"What's so funny?" I ask.

"I can't believe we just did that."

"Which part?"

"All of it. Any of it. This whole weekend."

I set her down carefully, my hands steadying her as she finds her footing. "How are you feeling?"

"Fine." Wren gives me a suspicious look. "Why?"

"Because I'm not done with you." I kiss her neck, her collarbone, suck on that one spot between her neck and her shoulder that makes her shudder.

Her eyes open just a slit. "We should probably get out before we prune."

"Probably."

But first I kiss her again, slow and deep, tasting the water on her lips. When we finally step out of the shower, we're both breathless and laughing, wrapped in towels that are way too soft and expensive.

I scoop her up again, carrying her to the bedroom, and toss her onto the massive bed with a growl. "You drive me crazy."

She grabs my towel and pulls me down with her. "Good crazy or bad crazy?"

"The best kind of crazy."

We should be exhausted. We should be done. But I can't get enough of her. The way she tastes, the way she feels, the way she looks at me like I'm the only person in the world.

This time we take it slow. Face-to-face, hands everywhere, nothing held back. I tell her she's beautiful. Tell her I've never felt like this before. She doesn't stop me. Doesn't pull away. Just lets me worship her body with mine until we're both shaking and spent.

Afterward, we lie tangled in the sheets, her leg thrown over my hip, her fingers tracing patterns on my chest. I kiss her forehead, her eyelids, the spot just below her ear that makes her shiver.

"I don't want to go back," she murmurs against my chest.

"Then don't."

"Ryan..."

"I'm serious. We could just stay here. Forget about the show, forget about everything else."

"And do what? Live in this villa forever?"

"Why not? The view's nice. The shower's incredible. The company's not bad."

She pinches my side. "Be realistic."

"I am being realistic. This is the most real thing I've felt in years."

She's quiet for a long moment, her fingers still moving across my skin. "What happens when we go back?"

"I don't know."

"That's not very reassuring."

"I don't have all the answers, Wren. I just know that I don't want this to end."

"You really think we can figure it out?"

"I think that what we have here, right now, is worth fighting for."

"Even if it means dealing with Jay?"

"Even then."

"He's going to lose his mind."

"Probably. But he'll get over it."

She lifts her head to look at me. "You sound very confident for someone who's about to tell his best friend he's sleeping with his little sister."

"I'm not just sleeping with you."

"No?"

"This is more than that."

The words hang between us, heavy with meaning. I can see her processing them, trying to decide whether she believes me.

"What is it then?" she asks quietly.

"I don't know yet. But I want to find out."

She smiles, soft and real. "Okay."

"Okay?"

"Let's find out."

I pull her up for a kiss, tasting the promise on her lips. Outside, the night is quiet except for the distant sound of waves. The firepit on the terrace is still glowing, casting warm light through the open windows.

Her fingers rest over my heart. For the first time in years, I don't feel haunted by all the things I've lost. I don't feel empty or broken or like I'm just going through the motions.

I feel home.

Wren's breathing evens out against my chest. I know she's falling asleep. I should probably sleep, too. In two days, we have to go back to reality. Back to the cameras and the other contestants and all the complications we've been avoiding.

But for now, there's just this. The weight of her in my arms, the scent of her hair, the way she fits against me like she was made for this spot.

I won't think about tomorrow. All that matters right now is getting more of this girl, inhaling her, injecting her into my veins. I can't think further than that.

forty

RYAN

I WAKE up with Wren curled against my side, her hair spread across my chest. For a moment I let myself pretend this is normal. That I wake up next to her every morning. That we're not stealing time we don't really have.

The sunlight streaming through the villa's floor-to-ceiling windows makes everything look golden and perfect. Like we're in a movie or a magazine spread instead of reality TV contestants sneaking around behind everyone's backs.

"Morning," she mumbles against my chest, her voice thick with sleep.

"Morning yourself."

She lifts her head to look at me, and her hair is sticking up in about twelve different directions. It's the most beautiful thing I've ever seen.

"What's the plan for today?" she asks.

"I was thinking we could try wakeboarding."

She makes a face. "You want me to get dragged behind a boat on a plank?"

"I want to see you crush it."

"That's not crushing it. That's drowning with extra steps."

I laugh and roll us over so she's pinned beneath me. "Come on, Rustin. Where's your sense of adventure?"

"I left it in my other pants. The ones I'm not wearing because Elena's team packed me nothing but dental floss disguised as swimwear."

"I like the dental floss."

She swats at my chest. "You would."

But she doesn't say no. She grumbles about it, makes increasingly dramatic complaints about the tiny bikini she'll have to wear, but she doesn't actually refuse. Because Wren's never backed down from a challenge in her life, and she's not about to start now.

An hour later we're on the beach. I'm trying not to stare as she strips off her cover-up. The bikini is barely there, just scraps of bright blue fabric that make her skin look like honey and her legs look impossibly long.

"Stop looking at me like that," she says, but she's smiling.

"Like what?"

"Like you want to eat me."

"I do want to eat you."

Her cheeks go pink and she throws her cover-up at my face. "You're impossible."

The wakeboarding instructor is a guy named Carlos who looks like he spends more time in the gym than on the water, but he knows what he's doing. He gets us into life jackets, explains the basics, and walks Wren through how to get up without snapping her spine.

"People do this every day," he tells her.

"People do a lot of stupid things every day," she mutters back.

When it's her turn, she stares down the water like it's a personal enemy. I offer to go first, but she shakes her head.

"If I wait, I'll talk myself out of it."

I stay on the boat while she gets into position. The rope goes taut, the boat roars forward, and for a second it looks like she's going to eat it. But then she pops up, wobbling, fighting for balance, and somehow finds it. Her knees bend, her arms steady, and suddenly she's carving across the wake like she's done it before.

"Oh," she breathes, shouting over the sound of the engine. "Oh wow."

Her grin is wild. Her hair is flying. Her entire body radiates joy. I can't stop watching her. Not the water. Not the horizon. Just her.

"This is amazing," she calls out.

"Yeah, it is."

She catches me staring and grins. "You're not even looking at the view."

"I'm looking at the best view."

She rolls her eyes but she's still smiling. When she hits a wave and nearly loses it, she yells and throws her arms up when she recovers like she just won a gold medal.

That's the moment I know I'm completely screwed. Watching her laugh like that, fearless and beautiful and completely in her element. This isn't just attraction. This isn't just physical.

I'm falling for Jay's little sister while she's skimming across the ocean behind a speeding boat. There's not a damn thing I can do to stop it.

After we finish, we take the jet ski back to the villa's private beach. Wren sits behind me, her arms wrapped around my waist, her chin resting on my shoulder. I could get used to her holding on like this. But I don't know how to ask her to stay.

"That was incredible," she says into my ear.

"Better than drowning with extra steps?"

"Significantly better."

We hit a wave and she laughs, the sound vibrating through my chest. Her hands are splayed across my abs and every time we bounce, she grips me tighter. It's torture and paradise all at once.

Back at the beach, we collapse onto one of the oversized lounge chairs. Wren immediately starts digging through the bag the villa staff packed for us, pulling out water bottles and snacks and enough sunscreen to coat a small army.

"Come here," she says, patting the space next to her. "You're already turning red."

I settle beside her and she starts working sunscreen into my shoulders. Her hands are cool against my sun-warmed skin. She's being completely practical about it, but every touch sends electricity shooting through me.

"Turn around," she orders.

I do. Her hands smooth across my back, working the lotion in with slow, thorough strokes. When her fingers trace the scar from the shoulder surgery I had two years ago, I tense.

"Hockey?" she asks quietly.

"Shoulder separation. Nothing dramatic."

Her fingers linger on the spot for a moment longer than necessary. "Does it hurt?"

"Not anymore."

She doesn't say anything else, just continues spreading sunscreen across my back with careful attention. When she's done, she caps the bottle and settles back against the chair.

"My turn," I say, reaching for the sunscreen.

"I can do it myself."

"Where's the fun in that?"

She gives me a look but hands over the bottle. I squeeze some into my palm and start with her shoulders, taking my time, letting my hands glide over her skin. She's trying to act casual about it, but I can see the way her breath changes when I work the lotion down her arms.

When I get to her legs, starting at her ankles and working my way up, she goes very still.

"You're being very thorough," she says, her voice slightly breathless.

"Don't want you to burn."

My hands slide up her calves, over her knees, along her thighs. The bikini bottoms she's wearing are practically nonexistent. When my fingers brush the edge of the fabric, she makes a soft sound that goes straight to my cock.

"Ryan."

"Hmm?"

"You're supposed to be putting on sunscreen, not trying to get me naked."

"Can't I do both?"

She laughs and pushes my hands away. "Behave yourself."

But she's smiling when she says it. When I lean back against the chair, she curls up next to me, her head on my shoulder.

We spend the next few hours just talking. She tells me about her obsession with Greek mythology in middle school, how she used to check out the same books about ancient civilizations over and over until the librarian started saving them for her.

"I wanted to be an archaeologist," she says. "I had this whole plan to discover some lost city and become famous."

"What changed?"

"Reality. Turns out archaeology involves a lot more dirt and cataloguing pottery shards than discovering lost civilizations."

She pauses, looking out at the water. "Don't get used to this," she says quietly, almost to herself.

"What?"

"Nothing." She shakes her head, forcing a smile. "Tell me about your worst hockey injury."

I tell her about the time I broke my wrist trying to impress a girl in high school by jumping off the roof of the gym onto a snowbank that turned out to be mostly ice.

"You're an idiot," she says, but she's laughing.

"Yeah, well, teenage boys don't make good decisions."

"Some of you never grow out of it."

"Hey."

She grins and pokes me in the ribs. "Present company excluded, obviously."

"Obviously."

She gets animated when she talks, using her hands to gesture, crinkling her nose when she's trying to remember details. All I can think about is how badly I want to keep her exactly like this. Happy and relaxed and mine.

The thought scares the hell out of me.

By the time we head back to the villa, the sun is starting to set and we're both exhausted from the day. We rinse off the salt and sand in the outdoor shower, which is basically just an excuse for me to watch water run down Wren's body while trying to keep my hands to myself.

"You're staring again," she says, wrapping a towel around herself.

"Can you blame me?"

She rolls her eyes but she's smiling. "Come on, I'm starving."

We raid the kitchen still wrapped in towels. I watch Wren hop up onto the counter and start devouring mango slices and leftover grilled chicken like she hasn't eaten in days.

"You eat like a linebacker," I tell her.

"Shut up, I'm hungry."

"I didn't say it was a bad thing."

She throws a piece of mango at me and I catch it in my mouth, which makes her laugh again. The sound fills the kitchen and I want to record it, keep it somewhere safe for when this is all over and I'm back to my regular life where Wren Rustin doesn't laugh at my stupid jokes.

For a moment, everything feels perfect. Natural. Like this is what we do. Like this is who we are together when no one's watching and there are no cameras and no rules about who we're supposed to be.

But then something shifts. I can see it happen, the way Wren's expression changes, like she's remembered something unpleasant. She gets quiet, withdrawn, pulling that invisible shield over herself that I've seen her use a hundred times when things get too real.

"You okay?" I ask.

"Fine."

But she's not fine. She slides off the counter and wraps her towel tighter around herself, putting physical distance between us that feels like a chasm.

"Wren, what's wrong?"

She shakes her head, not meeting my eyes. "Nothing. I'm just tired."

It's a lie and we both know it. But I don't push because I can see the walls going up, see her retreating into herself the way she always does when she gets scared.

"We can't keep doing this, Ryan."

Something cold settles in my stomach. "Why not?"

"Because it's not real."

The words hit me harder than they should. "Feels pretty real to me."

"That's because you're good at making things feel real in the moment."

"What's that supposed to mean?"

She shrugs, but there's something brittle in the gesture. Something defensive. "Guys like you are always good at this. Making things feel intense and important when they're really just... temporary."

"Guys like me?"

"You know what I mean."

But I don't. I really don't. The fact that she thinks she has me all figured out, that she's already writing the ending to this story before we've even figured out what it is, pisses me off more than it should.

"Actually, I don't know what you mean. Why don't you explain it to me?"

She crosses her arms. "Forget it."

"No, seriously. Tell me about guys like me. I'm curious."

"Ryan, don't."

"You brought it up."

We're staring at each other across the kitchen now. I can feel the energy between us shifting into something dangerous. Something that's going to end badly for both of us.

"You think you know me?" I ask, my voice coming out sharper than I intended. "You think I get bored of people?"

She opens her mouth to say something but I don't let her.

"You know who didn't get bored of you? Me. When your brother was too busy being the golden boy to notice his little sister sitting in the corner with a book, when every other guy our age looked right past you like you weren't worth seeing, I noticed you, Wren. I always noticed you."

She flinches like I've slapped her. Her eyes go bright and her throat works around words she can't seem to get out.

The silence stretches between us, heavy and loaded.

"Tell me how I'd leave you first," I say quietly. "Because I wouldn't."

"Ryan..."

"I'm not fighting with you about this." I run my hands through my hair, trying to keep my temper in check. "Not about something you made up in your head."

But we fight anyway.

The words fly between us, sharp and scared and hot with everything we haven't been able to say. She accuses me of not taking this seriously, of treating her like a game. I accuse her of being too scared to try, of deciding I'm going to hurt her before I've even had the chance.

"You don't understand what it's like," she says, her voice rising. "To always be the consolation prize. The backup plan. The girl guys settle for when they can't have who they really want."

"If you think that's what you are to me, then you're an idiot."

"Am I? Because from where I'm standing, this looks like you killing time until you figure out who you're actually going to choose."

"That's not..."

"Isn't it? You're the bachelor, Ryan. You're supposed to fall in love with someone on this show. We both know it's not going to be Jay's weird little sister who argues with you about everything."

"Stop calling yourself that."

"It's what I am."

"It's not what you are to me."

"Then what am I to you?"

The question hangs between us, heavy and loaded. I realize I don't have an answer. Not one I'm ready to give. Not one that won't change everything.

She wants a name for this. I can't give her one, not because I don't feel it. But because I'm terrified it won't be enough.

The silence stretches too long. Wren's face crumples and then hardens again.

"That's what I thought," she says quietly.

That's when I know I've lost her. When I see her retreat behind those walls, see her convince herself that my hesitation proves everything she's been telling herself about why this won't work.

"Wren, that's not..."

"I'm tired," she says, cutting me off. "I'm going to bed."

She walks away, leaving me standing in the kitchen with my heart pounding. My hands shake slightly from adrenaline and hurt and the terrible knowledge that I just let the best thing in my life slip through my fingers.

I hear the bedroom door close. Then the lock click.

I reach for one of the kitchen chairs, my hand gripping the back of it so hard my knuckles go white. The villa feels different now. Hollow. All the golden light and perfect staging can't hide the silence where her laughter used to be.

All I had to do was say it... but I didn't.
Why am I such a fucking coward?

forty-one

I STARE out the airplane window, arms crossed tight over my chest, watching the coastline disappear beneath us. My heart feels like it's been put through a blender, all torn up and aching in ways I don't know how to fix.

Ryan sits across from me, his body language screaming tension. Jaw set, shoulders rigid, hands clenched in his lap. He hasn't looked at me once since we boarded twenty minutes ago. Not once.

This is the longest we've gone without speaking since this whole mess started. Even when we were fighting, even when we hated each other, there was always something. A snide comment, a sarcastic quip, some kind of verbal sparring that kept us connected.

Now there's just silence. Cold, empty silence that feels like it's swallowing me whole.

If I say something now, it'll just make him hate me faster. Maybe it's better this way. I tell myself this is for the best. I was right to push him away before he could do it first. He'll be fine without me. He'll choose one of the other girls, someone who actually makes sense for him. I'll go back to my regular life where Ryan Haart is just my brother's annoying best friend.

But the thought of him choosing someone else makes the ache in my chest deepen until I can barely breathe. The thought of watching him fall in love with Heidi or JacqLyn or whoever Elena decides is the perfect match for America's favorite bachelor.

The thought of him moving on like this weekend never happened.

"We're beginning our descent," the stewardess says. "Please fasten your seatbelts until we're at the gate."

Ryan finally looks up, but not at me. He stares at the seat back in front of him like it holds the secrets of the universe.

I want to say something. Anything. But every word I think of feels too small or too big or too dangerous. So I stay quiet and watch the ground get closer, knowing that every mile brings us back to reality.

Back to the mansion where we'll have to pretend we're just contestants on a dating show. Where he'll go back to kissing other women and I'll go back to being the weird girl who doesn't belong.

Ryan immediately unbuckles his seatbelt and stands, grabbing his bag from the overhead compartment without a word.

I follow him down the narrow aisle, staying a few steps behind. Like I'm his shadow again. When we reach the bathroom at the front of the plane, he stops abruptly and I nearly crash into him.

"Ryan, I…"

He finally turns, and our eyes meet. Something cracks. Not anger, not lust, just everything we've been holding back exploding all at once.

Before I can finish the sentence, he's backing me into the tiny bathroom, his mouth crashing against mine with desperate hunger.

I should push him away. Should tell him this is exactly what I was trying to avoid. But God, I've missed this. Missed him. My hands fist in his shirt and I kiss him back just as desperately.

"I can't stop thinking about you," he growls against my lips.

"Ryan, we can't..."

"I know. I know we can't. But I can't stop."

His hands slide into my hair, tilting my head back. I'm drowning in him. In the taste of him, the smell of him, the way he's looking at me like I'm the only thing that matters.

"This is insane," I whisper.

"I don't care."

His mouth moves to my throat and I have to bite my lip to keep from moaning. We're on an airplane. The crew is probably wondering where we are. But I can't bring myself to care about anything except the way he's touching me.

"Tell me you don't want this," he says against my skin.

I open my mouth to lie, to tell him exactly that. But the words won't come.

"Wren."

"I can't."

"Can't what?"

"I can't tell you I don't want this. But I also can't do this."

He pulls back to look at me, his eyes dark with frustration and want. "Why?"

"It's going to feel amazing and perfect and real. Then it'll be over. You'll pick someone else. I can't survive that."

He stares at me for a long moment, then steps back, running his hands through his hair. "Right. Of course."

The hurt in his voice makes my chest tight. "Ryan..."

"Forget it. You're right. This was stupid."

He pushes past me and out of the bathroom, leaving me standing there with my heart pounding and my hands shaking.

By the time I make it out, he's already off the plane.

The car ride back to the mansion is even worse than the flight. We sit on opposite sides of the backseat, the space between us feeling like an ocean.

The driver tries to make small talk about the weather, but neither of us responds.

When we pull up to the mansion, Ryan gets out first and walks inside without waiting for me. I sit in the car for an extra moment, trying to pull myself together before facing the other contestants.

"You okay, miss?" the driver asks.

"Tired of everything," I lie.

I drag my bag up to my room, grateful that my roommates are nowhere to be found. The space feels too small and too big all at once. Too small because I can still smell Ryan on my clothes. Too big because he's not here.

I need a shower. Need to wash off the salt air and the memory of his hands on my skin.

The water is scalding hot, exactly how I like it when I'm trying to punish myself. I stand under the spray and try not to think about the shower at the villa. About Ryan's hands sliding soap across my skin. About the way he looked at me, like I was something precious.

But my body has other ideas. My hands drift down, tracing the same paths his fingers took just hours ago. I close my eyes and imagine he's here with me. Imagine what would have happened if I hadn't stopped him in that airplane bathroom. If I'd let him push my skirt up and take me right there, the crew just outside the door.

The thought makes me gasp, my fingers moving faster. I imagine him lifting me onto the tiny counter, imagine the desperate way he'd touch me, the way he'd murmur my name against my ear. His mouth on my throat, his hands everywhere, his voice telling me how much he wants me.

I come hard, Ryan's name on my lips, my legs shaking so badly I have to brace myself against the shower wall.

Afterward, I slide down to sit on the shower floor, letting the hot water run over me while I cry. Because this is what I've done to myself. This is what pushing him away has gotten me.

I'm alone, aching for a man I can't have, masturbating in a shower while he's probably downstairs charming the other contestants like nothing happened between us.

I was right to protect myself. Right to push him away before he remembered I was never the kind of girl men keep. But why does being right feel exactly like being invisible again?

I won't go back to that life. I can't.

RYAN

THE MANSION FEELS LIKE A MAUSOLEUM. Same furniture, same cameras. But now it smells like her shampoo and regret.

I dump my bag in my room and stare at the bed that suddenly feels too big, too empty. Forty-eight hours ago, I was sharing a king-sized bed with Wren in paradise. Now I'm back to this sterile box where everything smells like industrial cleaning products and broken dreams.

My phone buzzes. A text from Coach T:

How's it going, kid?

I stare at the message for a long time before typing back:

It's going.

Not exactly the truth, but not exactly a lie, either. Because it is going. Going straight to hell, but going, none-theless.

I can hear voices downstairs. The other contestants welcoming Wren back, probably fishing for details about our romantic getaway. The thought of facing them, of pretending everything's fine, makes my stomach turn.

But I'm Ryan Haart. I've been pretending things are fine my whole life.

Seven weeks in and I'm one bad move from losing Wren completely.

I change into clean clothes and head downstairs, plastering on the same cocky grin that's gotten me through every uncomfortable situation since I was thirteen years old. The one that says I don't have a care in the world.

"Look who's back," Heidi calls out when I walk into the living room. She's curled up on the couch in tiny shorts and a tank top that leaves nothing to the imagination. Her smile suggests she knows something I don't. "How was your romantic getaway?"

The other girls look up expectantly. JacqLyn, Divya, Nikki. All waiting for details, for some hint about whether their chances just got better or worse.

"It was great," I say, settling into the chair across from them. "Beautiful location. Good food. Can't complain."

"That's it?" JacqLyn presses. "Come on, give us something. Did you guys connect? Was it romantic? Did you…"

"Where's Wren?" Divya interrupts, looking around like she just noticed the obvious absence.

"Upstairs, I think," I say with a shrug. "Probably unpacking."

But that's not why she's avoiding this room. She's avoiding me, just like she has been since our fight. Since I fucked everything up by hesitating when she asked what she meant to me.

The truth is, she means everything. But I couldn't say

that. Couldn't hand her that kind of power over me when she was already looking for reasons to run.

"So things went well?" Heidi asks. There's something calculating in her voice. Like she's trying to figure out if she should be worried.

"We had a good time," I say. It's not technically a lie. We did have a good time. Right up until we didn't.

"You don't look like someone who just had a good time," Nikki observes. She's always been too perceptive for her own good.

I laugh, but it sounds hollow even to my own ears. "Sorry, I don't know what you want me to say. We hung out, we talked, we enjoyed the villa. End of story."

"Bullshit," JacqLyn says bluntly. "You left as a maybe-couple and you both came back acting like strangers. That's not nothing."

"Both?"

"Wren came through here like a zombie twenty minutes ago. Didn't say a word to anyone. You look like someone killed your dog."

Great. So much for keeping our drama private. If the contestants can see it, the producers definitely can, too. Which means this is about to become everyone's business whether we want it to be or not.

"Maybe she's just tired," I suggest.

"Right," Divya says with a smirk. "Tired from all that romantic connecting you guys were doing."

I don't respond. Can't respond without saying something I'll regret. So I just sit there, enduring their speculation and pointed looks, wishing I could disappear.

A PA appears in the doorway, clipboard in hand. "Ryan? Elena wants to see you in the production office."

Fuck. I knew this was coming.

"Now?" I ask, though I already know the answer.

"Now."

I follow the PA down the hallway, my chest tight with dread. Elena's office is exactly what you'd expect from a reality TV producer. Awards on the walls, photos with various celebrities, and a desk covered in papers that probably detail every embarrassing moment of every contestant's life.

Elena looks up when I walk in, her dark eyes sharp and assessing. She's wearing another one of those power suits that make her look like she could eat you alive and not even feel guilty about it.

"Sit," she says, gesturing to the chair across from her desk.

I sit, keeping my expression neutral. Whatever game she's playing, I'm not going to make it easy for her.

"So," she begins, leaning back in her chair. "How was your romantic getaway?"

"Fine."

"Fine?" She arches one perfectly sculpted eyebrow. "Ryan, darling, I've been doing this for fifteen years. I can spot relationship drama from a mile away. You and Wren are practically radiating it."

I shrug. "I don't know what you're talking about."

"Don't you?" She leans forward, resting her elbows on the desk. "Because from where I'm sitting, it looks like you two had some kind of falling out. Big enough to kill whatever spark you had going."

"Maybe there wasn't as much of a spark as you thought."

Elena laughs, but there's no humor in it. "Please. I watched the footage from your overnight dates. I saw the way you looked at each other. The tension, the chemistry. It was electric."

My jaw tightens. "Things change."

"What happened, Ryan?"

"Nothing happened."

"Bullshit." She slaps her hand on the desk, making me jump slightly. "Something happened. Something big enough to turn you both into walking corpses. So I'm going to ask you again: what happened?"

I stare at her for a long moment, weighing my options. I could tell her the truth. About the fight, about Wren pushing me away, about how I'm completely fucked up over a woman I can't have. But that would give Elena exactly what she wants. More drama, more manipulation, more ways to torture us for ratings.

"She got bored." Elena arches a brow. I almost say "I scared her off." Almost say "I didn't tell her what she meant to me until it was too late." But instead, I smile. "Can't win 'em all."

Elena blinks. "Bored?"

"Yeah. Turns out, forty-eight hours of my company was about thirty-six hours too many."

It's a lie, but it's the kind of lie Elena can work with. The kind that makes me look like an ass instead of revealing how much this is actually destroying me.

"Interesting," she muses. "And how do you feel about that?"

"Disappointed, I guess. But not surprised. Wren's always been hard to pin down."

"So you're moving on?"

"What else would I do?"

Elena studies me for a long moment. I can practically see the wheels turning in her head. She's trying to figure out how to use this, how to turn our disaster into compelling television.

"Good," she says finally. "Because we have a group date planned for tomorrow. Time to refocus on the other women."

"Sure."

"And Ryan?" She leans forward again, her voice dropping to a whisper. "Try to look like you're having fun. Dead-eyed bachelors don't make for good television."

I force a smile. "You got it."

She dismisses me with a wave. I walk back toward the living room on autopilot. The other contestants are still there, still gossiping and speculating. They look up when I enter, all fake smiles and barely concealed curiosity.

"Everything okay?" Heidi asks.

"Perfect," I lie. "Just scheduling stuff for tomorrow."

"What's tomorrow?" Nikki wants to know.

"Group date. Should be fun."

The word "fun" tastes like ash in my mouth. Because I know what tomorrow's going to be like. Me going through the motions, pretending to be interested in women who aren't Wren, while she watches from the sidelines and acts like she doesn't care.

Fuck, I need a drink. Or ten.

I excuse myself and head to the kitchen, hoping to find something stronger than the wine they usually stock. But when I push through the swinging door, I stop dead.

Wren's there, standing at the counter with her back to me. She's changed into yoga pants and an oversized sweatshirt that swallows her whole. Her hair is damp from a shower, twisted up in a messy bun that makes my fingers itch to touch it.

She turns when she hears me enter. For a split second,

her mask slips. I see the hurt in her eyes, the exhaustion, the same hollow ache that's been eating me alive since our fight.

Then the walls go back up.

"Oh," she says. "Hey."

"Hey yourself."

We stand there for a moment, separated by about five feet of kitchen tile that might as well be the Grand Canyon. The silence stretches between us, heavy with all the things we're not saying.

I can feel her presence even when I'm not looking. She's making tea. The same kind we had on the terrace at the villa, vanilla and honey that smelled like paradise.

"How was your meeting with Elena?" she asks finally.

"Fine. Yours?"

"I haven't had one yet."

"You will."

She nods, turning back to whatever she was doing at the counter. Her movements are mechanical, precise. Like she's concentrating very hard on not falling apart.

"Wren..."

"Don't," she says without turning around. "Please don't."

"I just..." I swallow. My hand grips the counter. "I couldn't walk past you like you weren't everything."

"I know what you wanted to say. I don't want to hear it."

Her voice is steady, controlled. But I can hear the tremor underneath it, the effort it's taking to keep herself together.

I want to cross the room and pull her into my arms. Want to tell her I'm sorry, that I fucked up, that she means more to me than I've ever admitted to anyone, including myself. But I can't. Because she's made it clear that's not what she wants.

So I grab a water bottle from the fridge and leave without another word.

The rest of the evening passes in a blur of forced normalcy. Dinner with the group, where Wren and I sit at opposite ends of the table and carefully avoid looking at each other. A movie night in the living room, where she curls up in the chair farthest from mine and stares at the screen without really watching.

The other contestants notice. How could they not? The tension between us is thick enough to cut with a knife. We're both doing a shit job of hiding it.

"You two are being weird," JacqLyn observes during a commercial break.

"Weird how?" I ask, though I already know.

"Like you can't stand to be in the same room together."

"Maybe they had a fight," Divya suggests with barely concealed glee.

"We didn't fight," Wren says quietly. It's the first thing she's said all evening.

"Then why do you both look miserable?"

"I don't look miserable," Wren lies.

"Honey, you look like someone ran over your dog," Nikki says gently.

Wren's face flushes, but she doesn't respond. Just gets up and mumbles something about being tired before disappearing upstairs.

The remaining women all turn to look at me expectantly.

"Don't ask," I say.

"Come on," Heidi presses. "What happened between you two?"

"Nothing happened."

"Bullshit," JacqLyn says for the second time today. "You guys had something. Everyone could see it. Now you're acting like strangers."

"Maybe we realized we don't have as much in common as we thought."

It's another lie, but it's easier than the truth. Easier than admitting that we have everything in common and that's exactly the problem.

I make it through the rest of the movie, then excuse myself to go to bed. But sleep doesn't come. I lie in the dark staring at the ceiling, replaying every moment of our fight. Every word, every expression, every opportunity I had to say something different.

Somewhere in this house, Wren is probably doing the same thing. Lying awake, thinking about us, about what went wrong and whether it can be fixed.

I could go to her. Say everything I didn't say in that fucking kitchen. But what if I do and she still walks away?

But every time I think about going to her, about trying to fix this mess, I remember the look on her face when she asked what she meant to me. The hope and fear warring in her expression. How I failed her in that moment.

How I let my own fear of being vulnerable cost me the best thing that's ever happened to me.

Tomorrow's group date is going to be hell. Pretending to be interested in other women while the only woman I actually want watches from the sidelines. Pretending I'm not completely destroyed by our breakup while she pretends she doesn't care.

But that's what we signed up for, isn't it? This whole show is about pretending. About performing emotion for the cameras, about manufacturing moments that feel real but aren't.

The problem is, what Wren and I had *was* real. Is real, despite everything that's happened. Now we have to pretend it never existed.

I roll over and punch my pillow, trying to find a comfortable position. But comfort feels impossible when everything inside me is screaming for the woman who's probably crying herself to sleep three rooms away.

She was right. This whole thing is fake. But what I felt for her never was. Now I have to pretend she never meant a damn thing to me. I know I can do it. I've been pretending disinterest in Wren for years.

For the remainder of the show, I can fake it for the cameras. I just don't know if I can fake it for myself.

What if I don't want it to be fake?

WREN

I'VE NEVER BEEN this nervous at an elimination ceremony before.

The dress is satin. Emerald green. Backless, with a slit that makes me feel powerful. I used to live in oversized sweaters and jeans that swallowed me whole.

But this? This is something else.

Tonight I walk into the room and meet every stare. I don't just wear the dress. I wear everything I've fought for. Every inch of growth. I'm not in anyone's shadow anymore.

I'm me. And I'm not afraid to take up space.

I am, however, insanely anxious about everything else. My hands are shaking as I stand at the end of the lineup, trying to keep my breathing steady. The rose garden looks beautiful tonight, all twinkling lights and dramatic shadows, but I can barely focus on any of it. My stomach feels like it's tied in knots.

There are only four of us left. Me, Nikki, Daisy, and Jacq-Lyn. Four women, three roses. One of us is going home tonight.

I don't know why I suddenly feel cold all over. It's probably nothing. Just nerves. Just cameras. Just... something.

It won't be me. It can't be me. Not after everything that's happened between Ryan and me. Not after last week when he told me he was falling for me. Not after the way he kissed me yesterday during our one-on-one, soft and desperate like he was trying to memorize the taste of my mouth.

But standing here now, watching him pace back and forth with those three roses in his hands, I feel sick with uncertainty.

The cameras are rolling, capturing every micro-expression on our faces. I can feel the lens focusing on me, zooming in on the way I'm biting my lip, the way my hands are clasped too tightly in front of me. I try to relax my face into something more neutral, but it's hard when my heart is beating so fast I'm surprised everyone can't hear it.

"Ladies," Rich says, stepping forward with that practiced TV host smile. "Tonight is one of the most important nights of this journey. Ryan has some difficult decisions to make."

I glance at Ryan, hoping for some kind of reassurance, some sign that I don't need to worry. He does smile at me, quick and soft. I feel some of the tension leave my shoulders. He wouldn't smile at me like that if he was about to send me home, right?

The first part of the ceremony is always the same. They make us watch video packages of each contestant's relationship with Ryan, highlighting all the key moments and emotional beats. It's supposed to build suspense, but mostly it just makes me want to scream.

I have to watch Nikki's package first, full of their early connection and the way she made him laugh during their first one-on-one. Then Daisy's, showing all their intense conversations and the obvious physical chemistry between them. JacqLyn's comes next, focusing on how she challenged him and pushed him out of his comfort zone.

When mine plays, I see our journey from the beginning. The awkward first meeting where I was so nervous I could barely speak. Our first real conversation during that group date where we talked about books and I realized he was nothing like I'd expected. The moment during our overnight date when I finally told him I was scared of falling for him, and he said he was scared too.

Watching it all play out on the big screen makes my chest tight with emotion. We've come so far from those early days when I was convinced he'd send me home any minute. When I was so sure that someone like him could never really want someone like me.

But he does want me. I know he does. I can see it in every clip, the way he looks at me, the way he touches me like I'm something precious. The way he said my name when he told me he was falling for me.

I was sure. I let myself believe this was real.

So why do I still feel like I might throw up?

The video packages finally end, and Rich steps forward again. My throat is so tight I can barely swallow. "Ryan, you have one single rose to give out tonight. When you're ready."

Ryan picks up the first rose, and I hold my breath.

I look at Ryan, trying to read his expression, but his face is carefully neutral. Professional. He's not giving anything away.

"Contestants, we need to take a quick break," one of the producers calls out suddenly. "Technical difficulties."

The cameras stop rolling. Immediately people swarm

onto the set. Makeup artists appear with powder and lipstick for touch-ups. Someone hands me a bottle of water, which I drink gratefully even though my hands are still shaking.

"You okay?" Jennifer whispers as she fixes my lipstick. Jennifer's been my makeup artist since day one, and she's become something of a friend over the weeks.

"Just nervous," I admit.

"Don't be. You've got this." She squeezes my shoulder. "Good luck."

I watch as Ryan gets pulled aside by his producer, Rich. They disappear into the house. A minute later I see Elena and Marcus following them inside. The head producer and director don't usually get involved unless something serious is happening.

I strain to hear what's going on, but I'm too far away. All I can make out are raised voices. At one point I'm pretty sure I hear Ryan yelling, though I can't make out the words.

"What's happening?" I ask Hana, my producer, when she comes over to check on me.

But Hana's not joking with me like she usually does. She won't meet my eyes. Something's off.

"Just some last-minute details," she says. "You need to stay put, okay? We'll be rolling again in a few minutes."

I want to move closer to the house, to try to figure out what's going on, but every time I take a step, someone redirects me back to my spot in the lineup. It's like they're deliberately keeping me away from whatever conversation is happening inside.

When Ryan finally emerges from the house, he looks furious. His jaw is clenched, his hands are in fists at his sides. There's something in his eyes that I've never seen before. Something dark and angry and hurt.

Elena follows him out, clearly trying to manage whatever damage control is needed. I see her mouth something to him, probably telling him to smile for the cameras, but he just stops frowning. He doesn't actually smile.

"Okay, everyone back to places," Marcus calls out. "We're rolling in thirty seconds."

I take my position next to JacqLyn, my heart hammering against my ribs. Something is wrong. Something has changed in the last few minutes, and I don't know what it is.

The cameras start rolling again. Ryan picks up the white rose. His face is back to that careful neutral expression, but I can see the tension in his shoulders, the way his grip on the stem is a little too tight.

"Tonight, I finally get to decide who I'm going to fall in love with," he says, his voice steady but somehow hollow. His words are stilted; I think if I had a moment to let them sink in, they wouldn't make any sense. But he keeps pushing forward. "As you know, this has been an incredibly difficult decision."

He looks at me. For just a second, I see something flicker in his expression. Something that looks almost like an apology.

My stomach drops. What if...?

"JacqLyn," he says.

The word hits me like a slap. I go completely still. Not frozen. Absent. Like my body checked out before my mind could catch up. This isn't happening. This can't be happening.

But JacqLyn is moving forward, accepting the rose with tears in her eyes. Ryan is hugging her while the other women congratulate her. I'm still standing here in shock, trying to process what just happened.

I didn't get the rose. Ryan didn't choose me.

It's happening again. Just like always. I let myself believe I was special. That I was chosen. And once again, I wasn't.

"Wren," Rich says. His voice sounds like it's coming from very far away. "I'm sorry, but your journey ends here. Thank you for being part of this experience."

I nod mechanically, though I'm not sure what I'm agreeing to. My brain feels like it's full of static. Nothing makes sense anymore.

I look at Ryan, waiting for him to say something, to explain what just happened. Waiting for him to tell me this is all some mistake, some terrible joke.

But he just looks back at me, his jaw still clenched, his eyes full of something that might be regret or pain or both. He doesn't say anything. Doesn't even mouth an apology.

How can he look at me like that and not say anything? How can he just stand there while my world falls apart?

"I need to go pack," I hear myself say. My voice sounds strange.

"Of course," Rich says kindly. "Take all the time you need."

I walk toward the house on unsteady legs, barely aware of the cameras following me. This must be great television, watching me fall apart in real time. The heartbroken contestant who thought she had it all figured out.

My room feels too small and too big at the same time. I sit on the edge of the bed for a moment, just trying to breathe, trying to make sense of what just happened.

Twenty minutes ago, I was sure Ryan was going to choose me. I was sure we had something real, something that went beyond the show and the cameras and all the artificial drama. I was sure he felt the same way about me that I feel about him.

But I was wrong. I was so, so wrong.

I start throwing things into my suitcase, not caring if they're folded properly or if I'm forgetting anything. I just want to get out of here. I want to go home and crawl into my own bed and pretend this never happened.

My phone buzzes with a text from an unknown number.

Wait for me.

That's it. Just three words. No explanation, no signature, nothing.

I stare at the message, trying to figure out who it could be from. Ryan? But why wouldn't he use his own phone? And why would he tell me to wait when he just chose someone else?

A stupid part of me wants to believe it means everything. That there's a reason. A plan. A second chance waiting just around the corner. But the smarter part of me. The part that's done waiting to be chosen. Wants to throw my phone out the window.

I wait for another message, some kind of clarification, but nothing comes. Just those three words hanging there, cryptic and meaningless.

I finish packing and drag my suitcase to the front door, where a producer is waiting to escort me to the limo. The same limo that brought me here all those weeks ago, full of hope and excitement and the crazy belief that maybe, just maybe, I might find something real.

"Ready?" the producer asks. I nod because I don't trust my voice.

The ride home is a blur. I stare out the window at the city lights, trying not to think about Ryan, trying not to replay every moment between us and wonder where I went wrong.

But I can't stop thinking about the way he looked at me tonight. The pain in his eyes, the tension in his jaw. He didn't look like someone who had just made the choice he wanted to make. He looked like someone who had just done something that was killing him.

So why did he do it? Why did he choose JacqLyn when everything between us felt so real, so right?

My phone buzzes again. For a second my heart leaps, thinking it might be Ryan with an explanation. But it's just Jay, asking how the ceremony went.

I can't even begin to answer that question.

Instead, I turn my phone off and lean my head against the window. The tears come then, finally, hot and angry and full of all the hurt I've been trying to hold back.

I let myself cry for the boy who made me believe in fairy tales. For the girl who was stupid enough to think she deserved one.

By the time we reach the airport, my eyes are red and swollen, but I feel empty. Hollowed out. Like someone scooped out everything that mattered and left me with nothing but the shell of who I used to be.

The flight home is mercifully quiet. It's late enough that most of the other passengers are sleeping, so no one bothers me as I stare out the window at the darkness below.

I keep thinking about that text. *Wait for me.* What does that even mean? Wait for what? Wait for him to change his mind? Wait for him to decide he made a mistake?

I'm not going to wait. I can't. I've spent too much of my

life waiting for other people to choose me, to see my worth, to decide I'm enough. I'm done waiting.

But even as I tell myself that, I know it's not entirely true. Because despite everything that happened tonight, despite the humiliation and the heartbreak and the complete destruction of everything I thought I knew, there's still a part of me that wants to believe that text means something.

There's still a part of me that loves Ryan Haart, even though he just broke my heart on national television.

And maybe that's the worst part of all. That even after everything, I still love him. Even after everything, I still want to believe there's a reason.

But what if he just smashed my heart into a trillion tiny shards?

forty-four

RYAN

I THROW open the door so hard it slams against the wall.

"What the fuck was that?"

Rich barely looks up from his phone. He's sitting behind the desk like he owns the place, which I guess he does. Elena lounges in one of the leather chairs, sipping from a crystal tumbler full of what looks like whiskey. She doesn't even blink when I storm in.

Wren didn't cry. She didn't scream. She just looked at me like I'd done exactly what she'd expected all along. That's what gutted me the most.

"That," Elena says coolly, "was compelling television."

"I didn't want to eliminate her."

My voice comes out low and tight, but I can feel the rage building underneath. My whole body feels coiled, dangerous, like I'm seconds away from throwing a chair through the window or putting my fist through the wall.

Rich finally glances up, twirling a pen between his fingers. "Well. You did."

"I didn't have a choice." The words come out sharp,

bitter. "You cornered me. You set the whole thing up. She wasn't even supposed to be in the bottom two."

Elena's smile doesn't change, but her eyes go flat, like shutters slamming down. "You always have a choice. But if you'd like to discuss breach of contract..."

"Don't," I snap.

She raises one perfectly sculpted eyebrow. "You think this is about you? This is about her. She's ours now too."

Rich leans forward, folding his hands like we're having a casual business meeting instead of me confronting them about destroying the woman I love. "You agreed to this. Every piece of it. You signed on to be the Bachelor. You signed on to play a part. You agreed to let us guide the arc."

I start pacing in front of them, my hands clenched into fists. I feel like a caged animal, trapped and furious and looking for something to destroy.

"You didn't guide anything," I bite out. "You railroaded me. You ambushed her with that fake cheating footage, then told me it would be 'bad optics' if I kept her. And now she's gone."

"Not gone," Elena says lightly, taking another sip of her drink. "Just... offscreen."

The casual way she says it makes my vision go red. "She looked devastated."

Rich doesn't even flinch. He checks his watch like this conversation is keeping him from something important. "She looked great. That mascara tear down her cheek? That was gold."

I turn slowly to face him. Something in my expression must finally register because he sits back slightly in his chair.

"You think this is funny?"

"No," Rich replies, still cool as ice. "I think this is money.

Big money. And if you want to see any of it, I suggest you sit your ass down."

I don't move. I keep standing there, staring him down, letting him see exactly how close I am to losing it completely.

Elena exhales, sounding annoyed for the first time. "Let's be very clear, Ryan. If you talk to Wren off camera, if you even try to explain anything to her, you're in violation of your contract."

"So what?" I ask. "You're going to sue me?"

"No," Rich says, and now he's smiling. Actually smiling. "We're going to withhold your entire payout. That's seven figures, Haart. And we'll make sure the network lawyers have a fucking field day with your image clause. You'll lose more than money."

Elena adds, "We'll also cut you from the finale. You'll just be a guy who dumped America's sweetheart and disappeared. We'll tank your entire career. Sponsors. Endorsements. Gone."

The threat hangs in the air between us. Seven figures. My entire career. Everything I've worked for.

But all I can think about is the look on Wren's face when I handed that rose to JacqLyn. The way her face went completely blank, like she was shutting down to protect herself. The way she looked at me afterward, waiting for some kind of explanation that I couldn't give her.

"She's not America's sweetheart to you," I say. "You never even saw her."

"We saw her perfectly," Elena says. "Shy, sweet, heartbroken. That was your best moment yet."

I take a step forward. Both of them tense slightly. Good. They should be nervous.

"You ambushed her," I say, my voice deadly quiet. "You humiliated her. You broke her heart to make a promo reel."

Rich shrugs like we're talking about the weather. "This is what you're paid for, Ryan."

I stare at him. Just stare, breathing hard, trying to process the casual cruelty of it all. These people took something real, something beautiful, and they twisted it into entertainment. They took the woman I love and they broke her heart for ratings.

Elena stands up, slow and deliberate. She slides something across the desk toward me.

"Give us your phone."

I don't move.

She smiles, all teeth. "You're not going to call her. You're not going to sneak into her hotel. You're not going to send a friend. We own your time, your image, and your loyalty until the finale airs. You want to fix this? Then make it count. And make it on camera."

I look down at my phone in my hand. My lifeline to Wren. The only way I could possibly reach out to her and try to explain what just happened.

I know that once I hand it over, she's gone. I can't reach her, can't explain, can't apologize. Just silence. Just damage.

The second the cameras cut earlier, I yanked out my phone and texted three words with shaking fingers. No punctuation. No time to explain. Just a Hail Mary to the woman I'd just destroyed.

Slowly, I pull it out and set it down on the desk.

"Smart choice," Rich says. "You've got one episodes left. Just get through the finale and then you're gold. We suggest you lean in. Fake it. Cry a little. Pretend like you're searching for love again."

I turn to leave, but Elena's voice stops me.

"Oh," she adds, and there's something in her tone that makes my chest tighten. "And we will be bringing her back for the finale. Not because you asked. Because we want to."

I freeze. My heart starts pounding.

"She's too valuable not to," Elena finishes with a smirk.

I don't say anything. Can't say anything. Because if I open my mouth right now, I'm going to say something that gets me sued into oblivion.

Instead, I walk out of that room and head straight for my suite. The cameras try to follow me, but I slam the door in their faces.

For a moment, I just stand there in the silence, trying to process everything that just happened. They have my phone. I signed a contract that says that they don't have to pay me a dime if I don't attend every single taping for the duration of the show. They have complete control over my life for the next two weeks.

But the producers don't have my mind. And they sure as hell don't have my heart.

My heart is its own beast. They can't control it or commodify it. And it belongs to Wren.

Assuming that she'll have me in two weeks after I've been paid for this tv show, that is. I have to believe that she will.

I don't punch the wall, even though every instinct is telling me to. I don't scream or throw things or do any of the dramatic bullshit they'd probably love to film.

Instead, I sit down at the desk and pull out a notebook. One of those cheap ones they stock the rooms with for guests who want to journal about *their journey*.

The room feels like a set now. Pristine. Staged. Everything perfectly fake. The only real thing left in it is me and this notebook.

I start writing. Planning.

They want compelling television? I'll give them compelling television.

They want drama? They want a moment that'll have people talking for years?

Fine.

But it's going to be on my terms. And it's going to be real.

I think about Wren, probably getting to Jay's house right now, trying to pretend that her heart isn't in pieces. I think about how she looked at me tonight, like I was a stranger. Like everything between us had been a lie.

I need her to know it wasn't a lie. None of it was.

The finale is in two weeks. That's when Elena said they're bringing her back. Two weeks to figure out how to fix this, how to make it right, how to show her and the entire world that what we have is real.

I start making lists. People I can trust. Ways to communicate without my phone. Loopholes in my contract that might give me some wiggle room.

There's a clause about "off-screen family contact in emergencies." Maybe there's a way in through that door. Maybe I just need to find the right emergency.

It's not going to be easy. These people are professionals at manipulation and control. They've been playing this game a lot longer than I have.

But they made one mistake. They assumed I care more about money and fame than I do about Wren.

They're about to find out how wrong they are.

I write for an hour, filling page after page with ideas, backup plans, contingencies. By the time I'm done, it's quite late. I have the skeleton of something that might actually work.

It's risky. If I'm wrong about any part of it, I could lose everything. My career, my reputation, my future.

But if I'm right, if I can pull this off, then maybe I can get Wren back. Maybe I can show her that what happened tonight wasn't my choice. That everything I told her was true.

That I love her.

I close the notebook and hide it in the bottom of my suitcase, underneath clothes I haven't worn. Tomorrow, the cameras will be back. Tomorrow, I'll have to pretend to be heartbroken about eliminating Wren while also pretending to be excited about the remaining women.

I'll have to lie to everyone, including myself, for two more weeks.

But it'll be worth it. Because at the finale, when Elena brings Wren back, I'm going to tell her everything. On camera, in front of millions of people, I'm going to tell her exactly what happened tonight and why I had to choose someone else.

And then I'm going to choose her. For real this time.

I just hope she still wants to be chosen.

I think about that text I managed to send before they took my phone. "*Wait for me.*" Three words that probably didn't make any sense to her, given what had just happened.

But I meant them. I meant them more than I've ever meant anything in my life.

Wait for me, Wren. I'm coming for you.

I'm going to make this right.

The sun is starting to come up outside my window, painting the sky in shades of pink and gold. In a few hours, the cameras will be here. The producers will be back with their fake smiles and their manipulation.

But for now, it's just me and my plan and the desperate hope that love is stronger than contracts and money and the twisted game these people are playing.

I think about Wren's face when she laughs. The way she looks at me when she thinks I'm not paying attention. The way she says my name when we're alone.

That's what I'm fighting for. Not the show, not the fame, not the money.

Her.

And I'm going to win.

Even if I have to burn the whole thing down, I'm going to show her the truth. That I never stopped choosing her. Not once.

I'm desperate to show her.

HE GAVE the rose to someone else.

It's over.

I'm over.

I've been wearing the same hoodie for four days, not because it's comfortable, but because changing feels like admitting something broke.

It's gray and oversized and smells vaguely like the cereal I've been eating straight from the box, but I can't bring myself to change. The Airbnb I'm hiding out in has blackout curtains that I haven't opened since I got here. Honestly, I prefer it that way. The outside world can stay exactly where it is.

The Simpsons are on auto play on my laptop. I'm not really watching, just letting the familiar voices fill the silence so I don't have to think. Homer's complaining about something, Marge is being patient. I'm sitting on this ugly beige couch eating Frosted Flakes with my fingers because I ran out of clean bowls two days ago and can't be bothered to wash any.

My phone is face down on the coffee table, buzzing

constantly. Emails from producers. Voicemails from the show. Texts from Hana asking if I'm okay, if I need anything, if I'm planning to come to the finale taping.

I answered her once. Just once. Told her I'd be there so she could stop worrying about me. But other than that, I've ignored everything.

Well, almost everything.

There was one text that almost made me pick up my phone. From a number I didn't recognize. Just three question marks. Nothing else. No name, no follow-up, no explanation.

For thirty seconds, my heart hammered against my ribs. This was it. This was Ryan reaching out, trying to explain.

Then reality kicked in and I remembered that Ryan had his chance to explain. He had his chance to fight for me, to tell me what was really going on.

He chose not to.

He chose JacqLyn instead.

So whoever sent those question marks can keep their cryptic bullshit. I'm done trying to decode messages from people who don't have the guts to just say what they mean.

I grab another handful of cereal and try to focus on the TV. Bart's getting in trouble at school. Classic Bart. At least some things never change.

My phone buzzes again. I flip it over to see Elena's name on the screen. A work email. I almost don't open it, but curiosity gets the better of me.

It's just logistics stuff. Asking for my current address for finale-related arrangements. Wardrobe fittings, maybe, or some kind of PR thing. I don't really care anymore, but I send her the address of the Airbnb anyway. Easier than dealing with follow-up emails.

I haven't even asked if I still have my job. Part of me

doesn't want to know. If they fired me because of what happened on the show, fine. I'll figure something else out. The last thing I want is to show up on set and have everyone look at me with pity in their eyes. Poor Wren, who thought she had a chance with the bachelor. Poor Wren, who got her heart broken on national television.

No thank you.

I'd rather eat cereal in the dark and pretend the outside world doesn't exist.

The episode ends and another one starts. I've probably seen this one a dozen times, but it doesn't matter. It's just noise to keep my brain from going to places I don't want it to go. Places where I replay every conversation with Ryan, every kiss, every moment when I thought maybe this was real.

It wasn't real. It was never real.

I should have known better. Of course someone like Ryan Haart was too good to be true. Of course the hockey player with the perfect smile and the perfect life wouldn't actually choose the awkward production assistant who trips over her own feet half the time.

I was just a distraction. Something to pass the time while he figured out who he really wanted.

And apparently, who he really wanted was JacqLyn.

The doorbell rings.

I freeze, a handful of cereal halfway to my mouth. Nobody knows I'm here except Elena, and I just sent her my address an hour ago. There's no way she'd show up in person.

Wait. What if something happened to Jay?

The thought gets me off the couch faster than anything else could. I shuffle to the door in my socks, not bothering to fix my hair or change out of my disgusting hoodie. When I open it, Calla is standing there with a tight smile on her face. Next to her is Jennifer, the costume designer from the show, looking like a fabulous hurricane with several garment bags and a professional makeup kit.

I blink at them stupidly. "What the hell are you doing here? Is Jay okay?"

Calla pushes past me into the Airbnb like she owns the place. "Jay's fine. But you're not answering your phone. So we came."

Jennifer follows her in, carrying what looks like an entire salon's worth of equipment. She takes one look around the dark, cereal-strewn disaster that is my temporary living situation and shakes her head.

"Honey," she says, setting her bags down. "This is worse than I thought."

"Worse than what?" I ask, closing the door. "How did you even find me?"

"You're not getting out of the finale," Jennifer says matter-of-factly, unzipping one of the garment bags. "Ryan sent us."

I feel all the blood drain from my face. "What?"

Calla turns to face me. Her expression is serious now. "Ryan reached out to Jay. Begged him to help find you. Said it was urgent. Said he needed a favor."

My whole body goes rigid. "You can go. I don't want help from a man who dumped me on national TV."

"Wren," Calla starts, but I cut her off.

"No. I'm serious. Whatever he told you, whatever sob story he gave Jay, I don't want to hear it. He made his choice."

Jennifer continues unpacking her makeup kit like I haven't said anything. "You know, for someone who works in television, you sure don't understand how television works."

"What's that supposed to mean?"

"It means," Calla says, settling onto the couch next to my cereal box, "that maybe you don't have the whole story."

I cross my arms. "I have enough of the story. I was there, remember? I watched him hand that rose to someone else."

"And then what happened?" Jennifer asks.

"Then I went home."

"Did he try to talk to you?"

"No."

"Did he call you?"

I hesitate. Those three question marks flash through my mind again. "No."

"Wren." Calla's voice is gentle but firm. "Sit down. Please."

I don't want to sit down. I want them to leave so I can go back to my Simpsons marathon and my denial spiral. But something in Calla's tone makes me sink into the armchair across from them.

"Talk," she says.

"About what?"

"About what really happened. Not the version you've been telling yourself. The real version."

I stare at her for a long moment. Then something inside me just breaks. All the hurt and anger and confusion that I've been stuffing down for the past week comes pouring out.

"Ryan told me he was in love with me. He said we should be together after the show finished filming. And then... the producers pulled him aside right before the rose ceremony. When he came back, he was all angry looking. And then…" I cut off the flow of words, tears pricking my eyes.

Calla strokes the back of my hand. "What happened?"

"He picked another girl! Sent me packing. I was just… stunned."

Calla looks over at Jennifer. "What do you make of that?"

"Seems like the producers made him eliminate you. They do that pretty frequently, you know. They say, 'oh, the final decision is ours, per your contract'. They want surprises. So let's say a bachelor obviously favors one bachelorette… Elena will swing in and force him to choose another contestant or lose all the money from the show."

I suck in a breath. Money is a huge motivator for Ryan. He will do almost anything to make his account balance grow bigger. Even if it hurts him. Even if it's not what he wants.

"It doesn't matter," I say, but even as I say it, I can hear how weak it sounds. "If he loved me, he would have fought for me."

"Maybe he did fight for you," Calla says quietly. "Maybe he just lost."

I stare at her. "What do you mean?"

"I mean that Ryan called Jay at two in the morning, Wren. He was desperate. He said he needed help finding you because they wouldn't let him contact you directly."

"They wouldn't let him?"

"Contract stuff. Legal stuff. I don't know the details, but Jay said Ryan sounded like a man who was crawling. And let me tell you, I've never known Ryan Haart to crawl for anyone."

My heart starts beating faster. "That doesn't change what happened."

"Doesn't it?" Jennifer starts pulling makeup brushes out of her kit. "You think he sent us here for fun? You think he's orchestrating some elaborate plan to humiliate you further?"

"I don't know what he's doing."

"He's trying to get you back," Calla says simply. "And he's using the finale to do it."

"What?"

Jennifer grins. "Honey, you are going to look so incredible tonight that the producers are going to need to bleep Ryan's reaction."

"Tonight?" I shake my head. "I'm not going tonight."

"Yes, you are." Calla stands up and walks over to where Jennifer hung the garment bags. She unzips one and pulls out the most beautiful dress I've ever seen. It's a soft salmon pink, floor length, with full skirts and a delicate layer of hand-stitched flowers that take my breath away. It's elegant and sophisticated and absolutely perfect.

"Where did this come from?" I breathe.

"Ryan had it made," Jennifer says. "Custom fitted. He remembered your measurements from wardrobe fittings."

I touch the fabric gently. It's soft and expensive and clearly chosen with care. "Why would he do this?"

"Because he loves you, you idiot," Calla says, but her voice is fond. "Because he's been planning something, and he needs you there for it to work."

"What if this is just another manipulation?" I ask. "What if I show up and he humiliates me all over again?"

Jennifer shrugs. "Then you'll look incredible while flipping him off on camera."

Despite everything, I crack a small smile. "Thanks. I think."

"That's the spirit." Jennifer claps her hands together. "Now, let's get you cleaned up. We have a lot of work to do."

The next two hours pass in a blur. Jennifer works magic with concealer and foundation, hiding the evidence of my week-long breakdown. She does my eyes in soft, smoky colors that make them look bigger and brighter than they've ever looked. My hair gets styled into loose waves that fall over one shoulder, elegant but not trying too hard.

The dress fits perfectly. Better than perfectly, actually. It hugs my curves in all the right places and makes me look like someone who belongs at a finale taping. Someone who deserves to be there.

"Wren," Calla says when I emerge from the bathroom fully dressed. "You look stunning."

I catch sight of myself in the mirror and barely recognize the woman looking back at me. I look strong. Confident. Beautiful.

I look like someone Ryan Haart might actually choose.

"I don't even look like myself. I look... like someone that expects to be chosen."

Jennifer nods approvingly. "Trust me, you're going to win."

The limo ride to the mansion feels surreal. Jennifer comes with me, chattering about behind-the-scenes gossip and trying to keep me distracted, but my mind is racing. What is Ryan planning? What am I walking into?

As we get closer, doubt creeps back in. What if I'm wrong about this? What if Ryan really did just move on and this is some twisted consolation prize?

The mansion is all lights and cameras when we arrive. There's a red carpet set up for the eliminated contestants. I can see photographers snapping pictures as women in evening gowns pose and smile.

I feel like I'm going to throw up.

"You've got this," Jennifer whispers as we get out of the limo. "Remember, you look incredible. Hold your head up."

I walk through the back hallway like I'm floating. Or maybe drowning. Everything feels distant and unreal. A few crew members nod at me, but mostly I'm invisible. Just another eliminated contestant coming back for the finale.

Hana appears at my elbow as I'm trying to find my seat. "I'm so glad you came," she whispers, squeezing my hand.

"Yeah," I manage. "Me too."

The eliminated contestants are seated in a section off to the side of the main stage. I find my assigned seat and settle in, keeping my posture straight and my face carefully neutral. I'm not going to give anyone the satisfaction of seeing me fall apart again.

The lights dim and the taping begins. Rich takes the stage with his usual polished enthusiasm, talking about love and second chances and the journey we've all been on. I barely listen. I'm too busy trying not to look at the stage where I know Ryan will appear any minute.

When he does, my heart stops.

He looks good. Too good. His hair is perfect, his suit is perfectly tailored. But there are shadows under his eyes that makeup couldn't quite hide. A tension in his jaw that speaks to sleepless nights. He's standing with his back straight, but I can see the way his hands are clenched at his sides.

He looks like a man who's been through hell.

Our eyes meet across the room. I feel that familiar electric shock that always happens when he looks at me. But this time, there's something different in his expression. Something desperate and determined and almost wild.

He starts to move toward me during the first commercial break, but a producer intercepts him before he can get close. I watch as they have a tense, whispered conversation. Then Ryan is dragged back to his mark on stage, but not before I see him mouth something that looks like "wait."

He keeps looking at me. Every chance he gets, his eyes find mine.

My stomach is doing flips, but I force myself to stay calm. To stay controlled. I'm not going to make a scene. I'm not going to give anyone more ammunition to use against me.

The ceremony continues. Daisy is brought out, radiant in a white gown that makes her look like a princess. She's glowing with happiness and anticipation. I can barely stand to look at her. Not because I hate her, but because she's about to get everything I wanted.

Rich begins his final monologue about love and commitment and finding your person. The audience leans forward in anticipation. This is it. This is the moment everyone's been waiting for.

Ryan is supposed to get down on one knee. He's supposed to propose to Daisy and they're supposed to live happily ever after.

I brace myself for it. This is the final blow, and I just need to get through it. Let it come. Let it be over.

But Ryan doesn't kneel.

He starts to lower himself, then stops. Straightens. His eyes find mine across the room.

He doesn't reach for the ring box that Rich is holding out to him.

Instead, he stands tall and looks directly into the audience. Directly at me.

Rich falters. "Ryan?"

The crowd starts to murmur. The energy in the room shifts, becomes electric with confusion and anticipation.

Ryan takes a step forward, away from Daisy, away from Rich, away from the script they've all been following.

"I was never supposed to let her go," he says, and his voice carries clearly through the suddenly silent room.

I hear someone behind the cameras yell "What the fuck?" A headset hits the floor with a clatter.

The cameras whip around to find me in the audience. I feel the heat of the lights on my face, the weight of hundreds of eyes staring at me, but I can't move. Can't breathe.

Ryan steps off the stage.

He walks toward me with purpose in every step, ignoring the chaos erupting around him. Producers are scrambling. Rich is trying to regain control. Daisy is standing frozen on stage, her face cycling through shock, confusion, and something that might be understanding.

Ryan ignores all of it.

"Wren Rustin," he says when he's close enough that I can see the gold flecks in his eyes. "I'm in love with you."

The words hit me right in the chest. After everything that's happened, after all the doubt and pain and confusion, hearing him say it like that, in front of everyone, makes my heart start beating again.

"I let them take you from me," he continues, and his voice is rough with emotion. "I didn't fight hard enough. But I'm not making that mistake again."

Rich is trying to interrupt, trying to salvage the show, but Ryan doesn't even glance in his direction.

"I love your wit," he says, looking only at me. "I love your quiet strength. I love the way you notice details that nobody else sees. I love that you looked at the worst parts of me and didn't flinch."

I'm crying now. I can feel the tears sliding down my cheeks, probably ruining Jennifer's perfect makeup job, but I don't care.

"The last ten days have been hell without you," Ryan says. "I don't care about the money. I don't care about the show. I don't care about any of it. I just want you."

The silence in the room is deafening. Every eye is on us, every camera is recording, but it feels like we're the only two people in the world.

"You don't have to say it back," he says quietly. "You don't owe me anything. But I needed you to know. I choose you. Always."

I sit there for what feels like forever, trying to process what just happened. Ryan just blew up his entire contract, his entire career, for me. He just chose me in front of millions of people, in the most public way possible.

Finally, I stand up on shaky legs.

I walk toward him. With each step, I feel more certain. More sure of what I want and who I want to be.

When I'm close enough to touch him, I stop.

"You complete disaster of a human being," I say, and my voice cracks on the words.

Then I kiss him.

I kiss him like my life depends on it, like he's the air I need to breathe. I bury my hands in his hair and pour everything I've been feeling into that kiss. All the love and pain and hope and fear and desperate, overwhelming relief.

The audience erupts. People are screaming and cheering and crying. Even Rich looks like he's tearing up.

When we finally break apart, Ryan cups my face in his hands.

"I love you, too," I whisper, just loud enough for him to hear. "I've always loved you."

He grins, and it's the most beautiful thing I've ever seen. "Let's get out of here."

I nod, still crying, still smiling, still not quite able to believe this is real.

As we walk toward the exit hand in hand, I can hear the chaos behind us. Producers rushing to figure out how to salvage the show. Cameras trying to follow us. Rich attempting to wrap up the taping.

But none of it matters anymore.

Because Ryan chose me. Really chose me. Not because he was supposed to, not because it made good television, but because he loves me.

And I finally believe it.

It was never fake. None of it was fake.

We don't need the show. We just need each other.

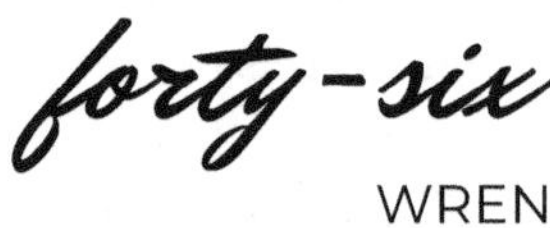

WREN

THE DOOR CLICKS SHUT behind us.

I think about the first day I walked into work. Oversized tee. Scuffed Chucks. Shy, uncertain voice. Invisible.

Now I'm center stage, and I'm not shrinking from the spotlight.

And the reason is this man standing in front of me.

Ryan turns the lock, not because we need security but because I think he wants to keep the outside world out for just a little while longer. The silence hits me immediately, loud in its own way after all the chaos of the finale. I can still hear the buzz of voices and cameras through the walls, producers probably scrambling to figure out what the hell just happened, but it feels far away now.

We just stand there for a moment, breathing. Both of us coming down from whatever that was. My heart is still racing from the kiss, from his declaration, from the way the entire audience erupted when I walked into his arms.

Ryan finally breaks the silence.

"Well, that was dramatic." He rubs a hand down his face. I can see him trying to process everything that just happened. The adrenaline is still coursing through both of us.

I cross my arms and smirk at him, even though I'm still trying to wrap my head around all of this. "What, you didn't love making TV history?"

He grins back. "I think I just earned myself the ultimate villain-to-lover redemption arc."

"Oh, I can't wait to see what Reddit has to say about all of this."

"Reddit's going to lose its collective mind."

We're joking, but there's an edge to it. A nervous energy that comes from doing something completely insane and not knowing what the consequences will be. Ryan just chose me over everything else. He walked away from his finale, from his proposal, from everything he was supposed to do.

For me.

The weight of that hits me all over again. My teasing smile fades into something more serious. I take a step closer to him, searching his face.

"So," I say quietly. "What now?"

His expression shifts too, becoming more serious, more real. "You tell me, Rustin. You gonna wake up tomorrow and pretend none of this happened?"

I look at him, really look at him. This man who just turned his entire world upside down for me. I take a breath, feeling the magnitude of this moment settle between us.

I hesitate. Not because I doubt him, not because I'm not sure about my feelings, but because I'm scared to hope. Because hoping for things with Ryan has hurt me before. I'm not sure I can survive it happening again.

"Wren," he says, and his voice is gentler now. "Talk to me."

"I just..." I pause, trying to find the right words. "When you didn't reach out after the elimination, I thought... I mean, I assumed you'd moved on. That maybe everything between us wasn't as real as I thought it was."

His face falls. "Shit. Wren, they took my phone."

"What?"

"The producers. They confiscated it right after the elimination ceremony. Told me I wasn't allowed to contact you until after the finale aired."

I stare at him. "Are you serious?"

"Dead serious. That's why I had to send Calla and Jennifer. It was the only loophole they couldn't block." His jaw tightens. "I should have found a way sooner. Should have fought harder to get to you."

"The mysterious text," I say, the pieces clicking into place. "The one with just question marks. I wasn't sure who it was. I thought maybe it was a producer messing with me."

"That was me. I borrowed someone's phone for about thirty seconds before they caught me and took that one, too."

Relief floods through me, followed immediately by anger. "Those bastards."

"Yeah. They are." He steps closer, his hands finding mine. "I came so close to just walking away from the whole thing. From the show, from the money, from everything. But I stayed because I needed this. Tonight. The chance to say it on my terms, in front of everyone."

I look up at him, this man who just sacrificed everything for me. I feel my chest get tight with emotion.

A few weeks ago, I was the woman who felt invisible. Who thought she wasn't worth choosing. Now I'm standing here with the most visible man in the world telling me I'm the only one who matters.

"You're insufferable," I say, half laughing, half crying.

"Wren."

"I love you, Ryan. Once you push past the cocky bad boy image, you're gentle and honest and endlessly kind. You make me feel brave. You treat me like I matter. And most of all, when I'm with you, I feel..." I gulp. "Seen."

His smile is instant and brilliant. "You deserve to be seen, Chirp. You're so fucking beautiful, inside and out."

We're standing close now, our hands brushing. I can feel the energy in the room shifting again. Less frantic, more intimate.

"You never ask me to be different. And you're loyal."

"Not to your brother."

"Yeah, and it all but killed you." I spread my hand over his heart. "I'm so glad you chose me."

"Oh, sweetheart." Ryan takes my hand and brushes a kiss against my knuckles. "You see me, too. Even the parts that aren't pretty. And you stay anyway."

I stroke his cheek. "Of course, I do."

"Well, I love you for that." His eyes shine suddenly with unshed tears. "You don't fall for my bullshit. You've never even looked my way when I tried desperately to flirt with you. You made me *work* to impress you. And now that I have, it feels pretty damn special."

"You're a terrible flirt."

"I'm great at it."

"Isn't that what I just said?"

Ryan's eyes sparkle. "You're smarter than me. And it wrecks me."

"I know." I give him a rueful smile. "It's a counterbalance to how soft I am. It's not the strongest quality."

"Gentleness can be powerful." He pulls me closer. "Most of all, I love you because you give me a future. All my life was just banter and fucking and hockey. But with you... I finally know what home feels like."

My heart grows five sizes. I kiss him, because I don't have the words to say how special and magical he is to me. He groans and kisses me back, a hand sifting through my hair.

"Did I mention that you also smell incredibly good?" he whispers against my lips. "Like lemons and honey and sunshine."

Oh god. "You're just lured in by my pheromones."

He bleats a surprised laugh. "I'm happy to say that I don't know what the hell that means."

"I can't wait to teach you all of the made-up bullshit that romance novels have taught me. Seriously, I have some shockingly bad takes on where the clitoris is located."

"I think I've got that one covered," he says, his tone amused.

I place my hand flat on his chest, right over his heart, and feel the steady thud of it under my palm. "We have no idea how to do this."

"So?" he says, covering my hand with his. "We figure it out."

"I mean the real stuff. The after. Where do we go from here? Do we leave tonight? Do we face the press together? Do you have any idea what kind of shitstorm you just created?"

Ryan laughs. "Honestly? I don't care about the interviews or the headlines or any of that. I want pancakes and you in my jersey and Sunday mornings when we don't have to perform for anyone."

The image hits me right in the chest. Simple and domestic and perfect. "That sounds pretty damn good."

"Doesn't it?"

But even as I say it, the fears start creeping in. The doubts that have been living in the back of my mind since this whole thing started.

"What if we're only this good in stolen moments?" I ask. "What if we suck at the real stuff? What if we get bored when there aren't any cameras around to make everything dramatic?"

"Then we suck together," he says simply. "Wren, I don't need drama. I don't need cameras or producers or any of that bullshit. I just need you."

I study his face, looking for any sign that he's not being completely honest with me. But all I see is sincerity and love and a kind of quiet confidence that makes me believe him.

"I felt so invisible," I admit. "When you didn't choose me, when you didn't call, I felt like maybe I'd imagined everything between us. Like maybe I was just some temporary distraction while you figured out who you really wanted."

"You've always been the one I couldn't forget," he says, and his voice is fierce. "There's never been a version of my life where you didn't matter. Even when I was trying to convince myself this was just a show, just a job, you were the thing that made it real."

He reaches up and threads his fingers through my hair, gentle and careful, like I might break. "I'm sorry I couldn't fight harder for you in that moment. I'm sorry they put you through that."

"You're fighting for me now."

"I'll always fight for you."

He leans down and kisses me then, soft and slow and completely different from the desperate kiss we shared in front of the cameras. This one is just for us. Personal and quiet and full of promise.

I lean into him fully, letting myself sink into the feeling of being chosen, of being wanted, of being home.

When we break apart, he rests his forehead against mine. "Stay with me tonight."

"Ryan."

"Not because of the show or the cameras or because it makes a good story. Stay with me because you want to."

"Where would we go?"

"My house. My real house, not some mansion set. I want to wake up with you in my bed and make you coffee and show you what normal looks like with us."

The idea sounds perfect and terrifying all at once. "Will there be pancakes?"

"Only if you wear nothing but my hoodie."

I groan. "God, you're going to be insufferable about this, aren't you?"

"Probably."

"I love you anyway."

"I know," he says, smug as hell.

I wrinkle my nose and hit his arm playfully, but I'm laughing. God help me, I love him for it. "You're the worst."

"The worst guy you're in love with."

"The worst guy I'm in love with," I agree.

He kisses me again, deeper this time. I feel heat start to build between us. His hands slide down to my waist, pulling me closer. I can feel how much he wants me.

"I'm not trying to seduce you," he murmurs against my lips.

"Then you're really bad at failing," I reply, breathless.

He lifts me easily, setting me on the edge of the dressing room table. The cold surface makes me gasp. My heels hit the floor with soft thuds as my legs wrap around him automatically. My dress rides up. His hands find the bare skin of my thighs.

For a moment, we just look at each other. The weight of everything that just happened, everything that's about to happen, settling between us.

"Are you sure about this?" he asks. "Here? Now?"

"I'm sure about you," I say. "I've been sure about you for a long time."

That's all the permission he needs. He kisses me harder, his hands roaming over my body like he's trying to memorize every inch of me. I can feel how careful he's being, how much he's holding back. It makes my heart ache with love for him.

"You don't have to be gentle with me," I whisper.

"I want to be. I want to worship you."

He starts with my neck, pressing soft kisses along the column of my throat. I tip my head back to give him better access. His fingers find the small buttons at the top of my dress and he undoes them slowly, one by one, like he has all the time in the world.

When he pulls the fabric aside and looks at me, really looks at me, I feel beautiful in a way I never have before.

"You're perfect," he says, and I believe him.

He takes his time with me, exploring every inch of newly exposed skin with his mouth and hands. When he pushes my dress up around my waist and drops to his knees in front of the table, I think I might actually die.

"Ryan."

"Let me," he says, hooking his fingers in my underwear. "Let me make you feel good."

I nod, beyond words. He slides the lace down my legs and tosses it aside. Then his mouth is on me, warm and wet and perfect. I have to grip the edge of the table to keep from falling off.

He takes his time here too, licking and sucking and using his tongue in ways that make me gasp his name. When he slides two fingers inside me while his mouth works my clit, I come so hard I see stars.

"God," I breathe when I can speak again. "That was—"

"Amazing," he finishes, looking smug. "I know."

I pull him up to kiss me, tasting myself on his lips, and start working on the buttons of his shirt. "Your turn."

"We don't have to."

"I want to. I want you."

He helps me get his shirt off, then his pants. When he's naked in front of me, I take a moment to just appreciate him. All lean muscle and smooth skin and the evidence of how much he wants me.

"You're not so bad yourself," I tell him.

He laughs. "Thanks. That's exactly what every guy wants to hear."

"You know what I mean."

"I do."

He steps between my legs again. I can feel him, hard and ready against me. "Are you sure?"

"Ryan. Stop overthinking it."

I cup his face in my hands. "I love you. I want this. I want you."

"Okay," he says, and he kisses me as he pushes inside me.

The feeling of him filling me completely makes me gasp against his mouth. He holds still for a moment, letting me adjust. When I rock my hips against him, he takes it as permission to start moving.

It's slow and deep and perfect. Nothing like the frantic, desperate sex we had that night in his suite. This is about love and connection and taking our time because we finally have it.

"I love you," he whispers against my ear.

"I love you, too."

We move together like we've been doing this for years, like our bodies were made to fit together. When I feel my second orgasm building, I tighten my legs around him and pull him deeper.

"Come with me," I breathe.

"Wren."

"Come with me."

He does, burying his face in my neck as he pulses inside me. I follow him over the edge with a soft cry.

We stay like that for a long moment afterward, breathing hard, holding each other close. I can feel him softening inside me, but neither of us moves to separate.

"Are you always going to look at me like that?" I ask when I catch my breath.

"Like you're the only person in the world? Yeah."

"A girl could get used to that."

"Good. Because I plan on doing it for a very long time."

He pulls back to fully look at me. His expression is so tender it makes my chest tight. "Come home with me tonight."

"Is that an order?"

"It's a request. A very heartfelt request."

I pretend to consider it. "Deal."

He grins and kisses me again, soft and sweet. "I love you, Wren Rustin."

"I love you too, Ryan Haart."

"Good," he says. "Because I'm never letting you go again."

"Promise?"

"Promise."

And for the first time in my life, I believe in promises. I believe in love. I believe in us.

As we get dressed and prepare to face whatever chaos is waiting for us outside this room, I realize that the show was never the real story. The cameras and the drama and the roses were just background noise.

The real story was always just this. Just us. Just two people who found each other and chose each other and decided to build something real together.

Relationships, dating, marriage... Everything else is just details.

As long as he's with me, everything else can wait forever.

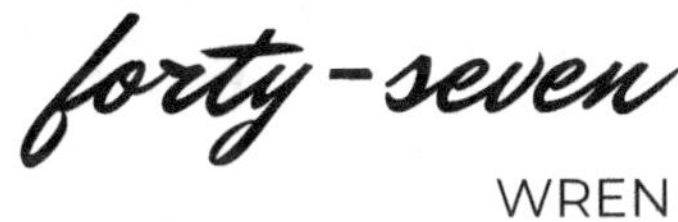

WREN

MY HANDS ARE SHAKING as I park outside Jay's house.

It's been three weeks since the finale aired, three weeks since Ryan and I went public, and three weeks since Jay has spoken to me for more than five minutes at a time. Three weeks of polite text messages and awkward phone calls where he asks about work and I ask about Calla and we both pretend everything is normal.

But everything isn't normal. Ever since the show ended, ever since Ryan and I moved in together, ever since I took the promotion to executive producer on a new reality dating show, Jay has been different with me. Distant. Protective in that suffocating way that makes me feel like I'm sixteen again and asking permission to go to prom.

He texted yesterday asking me to come to dinner. Just me. Not Ryan. Which felt deliberate and pointed and exactly like the kind of power move Jay makes when he wants to have A Conversation.

So I texted Ryan on my way over here and told him to come anyway.

I've been dreading this for weeks, but I can't avoid it anymore. Ryan and I are building a life together. Jay is my brother. These are the two most important men in my life, and if they can't figure out how to coexist, then I'm going to lose my mind.

Plus, if I'm being completely honest, I'm tired of feeling like I have to choose between them. Tired of Jay acting like I'm making some terrible mistake by falling in love with his best friend. Tired of Ryan biting his tongue every time Jay makes one of his passive-aggressive comments about our relationship.

I sit in my car for another minute, trying to work up the courage to go inside. Through the front window, I can see Jay moving around the kitchen. For a second, I'm transported back to being eight years old and coming home from school to find him making grilled cheese sandwiches because Mom was working late again.

He's always taken care of me. Always been the one to fix things when they went wrong. But maybe that's part of the problem.

I can't keep putting this off. Jay and I need to have this conversation. If I'm being honest, I need Ryan here for backup. Not because I can't handle my brother, but because this is about all of us now. About the life Ryan and I are building together.

I take a deep breath and walk up to the front door. I still have my key, but I knock anyway. It feels like the polite thing to do when you're about to have a fight with someone.

Jay opens the door wearing an apron that says "Kiss the Cook" that Calla got him as a joke. He looks relaxed, which is never a good sign when it comes to my brother and difficult conversations. When Jay looks relaxed before a serious talk, it usually means he's already decided how the conversation is going to go.

"Hey, Wren." He hugs me, and for a second, everything feels normal. Like we're just brother and sister having dinner on a Thursday night.

"Smells good in here."

"Calla's recipe for chicken parmesan. She's at book club, so it's just us."

Just us. Right. The way he says it confirms what I already suspected. This isn't a casual dinner invitation. This is an intervention.

I follow him into the kitchen, where he's got sauce simmering on the stove and what looks like enough food for an army laid out on the counter. There's Caesar salad, garlic bread, and a bottle of wine that I recognize as one of the expensive ones from the collection he and Calla started when they got married.

He cooks for four when he only wants to talk to one.

"This is a lot of food for two people," I observe.

"I might have gotten carried away." He doesn't look at me when he says it, which means he's lying.

I notice he's set the table for three. Three place settings, three wine glasses, three sets of silverware. Even though he only invited me.

"Jay." I cross my arms and lean against the counter. "Why didn't you invite Ryan?"

He doesn't even pretend to look surprised by the question. Just keeps stirring the sauce like it's the most important thing in the world.

"Because I wanted to talk to my sister without her boyfriend hovering."

"He's protective. There's a difference."

Jay turns from the stove to look at me. I can see the

concern written all over his face. The same expression he's been giving me since I was five years old and decided I wanted to climb the big oak tree in our backyard.

"Wren, I'm worried about you."

"I know you are. But you don't need to be."

"Don't I?" He sets down his wooden spoon. "You've been with this guy for what, a few months? And now you're living together, you've got a new job, you're all over social media. That's not like you."

"Maybe the old me wasn't the real me."

"Or maybe you're changing yourself for a guy who has a pretty bad track record when it comes to relationships."

There it is. The thing we've been dancing around for weeks.

"Ryan's track record is his business," I say. "What matters is how he treats me."

"And how does he treat you?"

"Like I matter."

Jay sighs. "Wren, you've always mattered. You don't need some hockey player to validate that."

"You're right. I don't need him to validate it. But I spent a lot of years wondering if anyone would ever see me as more than Jay Rustin's little sister. Ryan sees me."

"I see you."

"Do you? Because you invited me to dinner and specifically excluded the man I'm in love with. That doesn't feel like seeing me. That feels like trying to control me."

Before Jay can respond, the doorbell rings. We both freeze.

"Expecting someone?" I ask, even though I know exactly who it is.

"No."

But I can feel my phone buzzing in my pocket with

Ryan's text that he's here. My stomach flips with nerves and relief in equal measure.

Jay gives me a look that's half exasperation, half resignation. "You didn't."

"I did."

"Wren."

"What? He's part of this now, Jay. He's part of my life. You can't just pretend he doesn't exist."

"I'm not pretending he doesn't exist. I'm trying to have a conversation with my sister."

"About my boyfriend. Who should probably be here for that conversation."

Jay stares at me for a long moment. I can see him weighing his options. Finally, he sighs and walks to the front door. I hear him open it, hear Ryan's polite greeting, hear Jay's reluctant invitation to come in.

They walk into the kitchen together. The tension immediately ratchets up about ten degrees. It's not that they hate each other, exactly. They've been friends for years. But Ryan being Jay's friend is different from Ryan being Jay's little sister's boyfriend. Neither of them seems to know how to navigate that change.

Ryan nods at me, then turns to face my brother head-on. There's something different about his posture, more controlled than usual. Like he's ready for a fight but trying not to start one. His hands are clenched at his sides.

"Jay."

"Ryan."

"Thanks for having me."

"I didn't invite you."

"No, but Wren did. And where she goes, I go."

I can see Jay's jaw clench at that. "That's exactly what I'm worried about."

"What, that I love your sister?"

"That you think loving her gives you the right to make decisions for her."

Ryan's laugh is sharp, bitter. "You're not the only one who wants to protect her, Jay. But at least I know the difference between protection and control."

"Okay," I interject before this turns into a full-blown argument. "Both of you, stop. I'm standing right here, and I can speak for myself."

They both look at me. I can see them trying to dial back their aggression.

"Jay," I continue. "You wanted to talk? Let's talk. But Ryan stays."

My brother looks between us, clearly not happy about the situation, but he nods. "Fine. Let's eat first."

Dinner is painful. Jay asks polite questions about Ryan's off-season training schedule. Ryan inquires about Jay and Calla's shooting schedule in the next few months. I push food around my plate and try not to scream at both of them to just say what they're really thinking.

The chicken is perfectly cooked, and the wine is excellent, but I can barely taste any of it. I'm too focused on the undercurrent of tension running between the two men at this table, both of whom I love in completely different ways.

"This is ridiculous," I finally say, setting down my fork. "We're all adults here. Can we please just have the conversation we came here to have?"

Jay and Ryan look at each other, then back at me.

"Fine," Jay says. He puts down his fork and looks directly at Ryan. "Why should I believe you won't hurt her?"

Ryan doesn't hesitate. "I can't promise I won't. People

hurt each other sometimes, even when they love each other. What I can promise is that I'll never do it on purpose. And if I do hurt her, I'll do everything in my power to make it right."

"That's not good enough."

"It's the truth. It's more honest than promising I'll never hurt her, because that would be a lie."

Jay studies him for a long moment. "You have a reputation, Ryan. A pretty well-documented history of not staying with women very long."

"You're right. I do. But Wren isn't just another woman. She's *the* woman. The one I want to build a life with."

"How do I know that?"

"Because I'm here. Because I walked away from a seven-figure contract to choose her on national television. Because I'm sitting in your kitchen letting you interrogate me instead of telling you to go to hell, which is what I want to do."

I reach over and take Ryan's hand under the table, squeezing it gently. He squeezes back.

Jay looks between us and sighs. "I don't like this."

"You don't have to like it," I say. "But you do have to respect it."

"And if I can't?"

"Then that's your choice. But it doesn't change mine."

Jay is quiet for a long moment, clearly wrestling with something. Finally, he looks at Ryan again.

"If you hurt her, there will be consequences."

Ryan smirks. "Wouldn't expect anything less."

"I'm serious."

"So am I."

They stare at each other. I can practically see them

sizing each other up. Finally, Jay nods once, sharp and decisive.

"Okay, then."

"Okay, then," Ryan agrees.

After dinner, Ryan kisses my cheek and tells Jay thank you for dinner. "I'm going to head out," he says. "Give you two some space to talk."

"You don't have to leave," I tell him.

"Yeah, I do. This part is between you and Jay."

He's right, and I know it. As much as I wanted him here for moral support, this conversation needs to happen without him.

"I'll see you at home," he says, and the casual way he says it makes my heart flutter. Home. Our home.

After he leaves, Jay and I migrate to the living room. I curl up in the corner of the couch, the same spot I always sat in when we were kids. Jay takes his usual chair. The room feels different without Ryan here. Smaller somehow, but also safer. Like we can finally say the things we've been holding back.

"You love him," he says. It's not a question.

"Yeah. I do."

"And you're happy?"

"I am."

He nods slowly, like he's trying to accept something he doesn't want to be true. "Then I guess that's what matters."

"But?"

"But I'm having a hard time with this, Wren. Not just Ryan, but all of it. You moving in with him, taking this new job, this whole new life you're building. It feels like you're pulling away from us. From me."

And there it is. The real issue. Not Ryan's reputation or my moving too fast or any of the other surface-level concerns Jay's been voicing. The real problem is that Jay is scared of losing me.

"I am pulling away," I say quietly. The words feel both terrifying and liberating to say out loud.

Jay flinches like I physically hit him. "Why?"

"Because I need space, Jay. Not because I don't love you, but because I've spent my whole life being Jay Rustin's little sister. I don't know who I am outside of that."

"You're Wren. You're brilliant and funny and kind and—"

"In your shadow," I interrupt. "I've been in your shadow my whole life. In high school, I was the girl whose brother was the Insta influencer. At work, I was the girl whose brother knew everyone in the industry."

The words come pouring out of me now, years of suppressed frustration and resentment that I've never let myself fully acknowledge.

"Do you know what it's like to walk into a room and have people light up when they realize who my brother is? To have every conversation eventually circle back to you and your career and your achievements?"

I'm standing now, though I don't remember getting up. Jay looks stricken.

"To feel like I'm just an extension of you instead of my own person?"

"Damn, Wren," Jay says quietly. "I didn't know you felt that way."

"Because I never told you. Because I was scared that if I stopped being the supportive little sister, you wouldn't need me anymore. And if you didn't need me, then who was I?"

I sink back onto the couch, suddenly exhausted.

"Remember when I got accepted to that summer internship at NBC when I was in college? The one in New York?"

"Of course. You were so excited."

"And do you remember what the first thing you said was when I told you?"

Jay thinks for a moment, then his face falls. "I asked if you knew anyone there. If you needed me to make some calls."

"Right. Because even when I accomplished something on my own, your first instinct was to take care of it for me. To fix it or improve it or make it better somehow."

"I was trying to help."

"I know you were. But Jay, do you have any idea how that made me feel? Like my own achievements weren't enough. Like I couldn't be trusted to handle things on my own."

"That's not what I meant..."

"I know that's not what you meant. But that's what happened. Over and over again, for years."

We sit in silence for a moment, both of us processing. I can see Jay trying to reconcile the version of our relationship that exists in his head with the reality I'm describing.

"I never wanted you to feel small," he says finally.

"I know. But I did. I felt like I only existed in your spotlight's shadow."

"You're not *just useful* to me at all. You're family. That's different."

"I know you love me. But love isn't enough if it comes with conditions."

"What conditions?"

"That I stay the same. That I don't grow or change or want things that make you uncomfortable. That I keep letting you make decisions for me because it makes you feel needed."

Jay is quiet for a long time. I can see him struggling with everything I've just said. Finally, he looks up at me with tears in his eyes.

"I don't know how to be your brother without taking care of you."

"Then we need to figure out a new way."

"You've always mattered," Jay says fiercely.

"I know that now. But for the longest time, I didn't. I can't keep living my life trying to be small enough to fit in the spaces other people leave for me."

We're both crying now. I hate that having this conversation hurts him, but I need him to understand.

"I'm not asking for your permission," I continue. "I'm not asking you to like my choices. I'm just telling you that I need space to figure out who I am when I'm not trying to be the perfect little sister."

Jay wipes his eyes with the back of his hand. "How much space?"

"I don't know yet. I just know that I can't keep calling you every time I have a decision to make. I can't keep looking to you for approval before I do anything. It's not fair to either of us."

He nods slowly. "You're right. I've been treating you like you're still fifteen."

"And I've been letting you."

"So what now?"

"Now I figure out who I am on my own. You figure out how to be my brother without trying to be my parent."

Jay is quiet for a long time, just looking at me. Finally, he smiles, sad but genuine.

"You know, I always thought I was protecting you. But

maybe I was just protecting myself. The idea of you not needing me anymore scared the hell out of me."

"I'll always need you, Jay. Just differently."

"Different how?"

"Like a sister needs a brother. Not like a child needs a parent."

He laughs, shaky and wet. "I don't know how to do that."

"We'll figure it out."

"Yeah?"

"Yeah."

He stands up and comes over to the couch, pulling me into a hug. I bury my face in his shoulder and let myself cry, really cry, for all the years I spent feeling invisible and all the conversations we should have had but didn't.

"I'm sorry," he whispers. "I'm sorry I made you feel like you had to be small."

"I'm sorry I never told you how I felt."

"You're telling me now."

"Yeah. I am."

We hold each other for a long time. When we finally pull apart, something feels different between us. Cleaner. More honest.

"So," Jay says, settling back in his chair. "It's serious with Ryan?"

"Yeah. It is."

"And the new job?"

"I love it. I'm good at it."

"I'm sure you are." He pauses. "Are you happy, Wren? Really happy?"

"Yeah. I really am."

He nods. "Then I'm happy for you. Even if I still think Ryan's an ass."

I laugh. "He can be an ass. But he's my ass."

"God, that's disgusting."

"You love it."

"I really don't."

But he's smiling when he says it. I know we're going to be okay. Different, but okay.

"You know," Jay says as I'm getting ready to leave, "if it had to be someone, I guess I'd rather it be someone who'd take a punch for you."

"You think Ryan would take a punch for me?"

"I think Ryan would throw himself in front of a bus for you. Which is the only reason I'm not throwing him out on his ass."

"Thanks for that ringing endorsement."

"Don't push it."

I hug him one more time at the door. "I love you, Jay."

"I love you too, little sister."

"Not so little anymore."

"No," he agrees. "Not so little anymore."

I walk out to where Ryan is waiting, leaning against the driver's side door of his car with his arms crossed. He straightens up when he sees me.

"How'd it go?"

"Good. Hard, but good."

I reach over and take his hand.

"Thank you for coming tonight."

"Always."

"I mean it. You didn't have to do that."

"Yeah, I did. We're a team now, Wren. Your battles are my battles."

I used to believe I had to stay quiet to be loved. That I had to make myself small to fit into the spaces other people left for me. But I was never small. I was just waiting for the world to listen.

I never needed to sparkle. I just needed someone who saw me in the dark.

I used to be the girl behind the camera. Now I'm not behind the camera anymore. I'm not the extra in someone else's show. I'm the whole damn storyline.

And I'm doing it all as myself. Not as Jay's sister or Ryan's girlfriend, but as Wren. Just Wren.

It's terrifying and exhilarating and absolutely perfect.

"You okay?" Ryan asks as we sit in the car.

"Yeah," I say, and I mean it. "I'm exactly where I'm supposed to be."

"Good," he says, bringing my hand up to kiss my knuckles. "Because I like you here."

"Just here?"

"Here, there, everywhere. As long as you're with me."

"You're a total sap."

"Yes, but I'm *your* sap."

"Yeah," I agree, leaning over to kiss him. "My sap."

He smiles against my lips. I sigh into his mouth, knowing that what we have is forever. He's a book with endless chapters and all I have to do is keep turning the pages.

RYAN

I WALK into the arena wearing a warm-up jersey that says "WREN'S #1 FAN" in bold letters across the back and immediately regret every life choice that led to this moment.

"Really?" Jay says, not even looking up from the clip-board he's studying. "That's what you went with?"

"Wren made it for me." I shrug. "What was I supposed to do, say no?"

"Yes. You were supposed to say no."

Calla appears next to him carrying what looks like a hundred gift bags stuffed with Hope Pantry merchandise. "I think it's sweet," she says, giving me an approving nod. "Very supportive-boyfriend energy."

"Don't encourage him," Jay mutters, but there's no real heat in it.

The arena is buzzing with activity. Crew members are setting up cameras and adjusting lights. Volunteers are arranging tables full of food donation boxes. In the middle of it all, Wren moves like she was born to do this. She's wearing her headset and carrying her clipboard, directing traffic with the kind of quiet confidence that still floors me every time I see it.

When I told her I wanted to do a charity hockey game for Hope Pantry, she didn't hesitate. Didn't ask why it mattered to me or whether it would be good for the show. She just said yes and then made it happen with the kind of efficiency that makes producers weep with joy.

She catches my eye from across the ice and grins, pointing at my jersey. I give her a thumbs-up, and she laughs before turning back to whatever crisis she's managing.

"You're so whipped," Ellie says, skating up to me while Jake trails behind, looking slightly terrified.

"I'm supportive," I correct.

"You're wearing a jersey with her name on it."

"And?"

"And she organized an entire charity event because you asked her to."

"Your point?"

Ellie just shakes her head and skates away, but she's smiling. Jake gives me a sympathetic look as he hands her a helmet.

"She's not wrong," he says quietly. "But for what it's worth, I think it's nice. Ellie talks about you and Wren all the time. Says you two are disgustingly happy."

"We are disgustingly happy. Just like you and my sister."

He cracks a smile. "Good for you, man."

Coach T and Mrs. T are looking on from their front-row seats. I skate over to them, tapping on the glass and then flashing them a heart made with my gloved fingers. Coach T smiles and puts his arm around his wife, who is beaming.

She cups her hands around her mouth. "We love you, Ryan!"

God, them being here is just the icing on the cake. My mom may have ditched Ellie and me, but the Thompsons were the best substitute that I could've ever dreamed of. I grin and point at them each again.

"You're the best!" I shout.

Coach T looks away, uncomfortable, and mumbles to himself. I imagine it's something like "Love you, too." Evelyn kisses his cheek and pats his hand. I skate backward, my heart racing.

All my favorite people are here right now.

I watch Ellie fire a puck into the goal with the focused intensity she brings to everything. She's wearing a Hope Pantry jersey too, but hers says "TEAM CAPTAIN" on the back. When I asked if she wanted to be part of this charity game, she said yes before I could even finish explaining what it was for.

That's my sister. Always ready to help, always ready to step up. Even when stepping up means playing hockey on live television with a bunch of reality show contestants who barely know how to stop without hitting the boards.

"You nervous?" I ask her.

"About playing hockey? Please. I could skate circles around half these people in my sleep."

"About the cameras."

She considers this. "A little. But Wren said they'd mostly focus on the game, not on individual people. And Jake will be taking photos for the behind-the-scenes stuff, so at least one camera guy won't be a stranger."

Her boyfriend Jake gives a little wave from where he's adjusting his camera settings. He's been documenting everything today, partly for the show and partly because

Ellie asked him to. I like that about him. He shows up when she needs him, no questions asked.

"Besides," Ellie continues, "this is for Hope Pantry. This matters to you, so it matters to me."

"I can't believe Wren put this together," I say, shaking my head. "It's way better than I could have done."

This whole event exists because Wren loves me enough to make my dreams happen. I mentioned to Wren that I wanted to do something for Hope Pantry. The next thing I know, here I am. That's *love*.

"Ryan." Wren appears beside me like she was summoned by my thoughts. "We're about to start. You ready?"

I kiss her on the lips simply because I can. "As ready as I'll ever be."

"Good. Because I have a surprise."

Before I can ask what she means, she skates out to center ice and taps the microphone that's been set up there. The crowd quiets down, and the cameras focus on her.

"Hi, everyone," she says, her voice carrying clearly through the arena. "Thank you all for being here today to support Hope Pantry. This organization does incredible work in our community, providing food and support to families who need it most."

She looks beautiful out there. Confident and poised in a way that makes it hard to believe this is the same woman who used to hide behind clipboards and production sched-ules. She's wearing a Hope Pantry jersey over leggings, and her hair is pulled back in a ponytail that swishes when she moves.

"I could stand here and tell you statistics about food insecurity," she continues. "I could talk about the impor-tance of community support. But there's someone else who should speak today. The person who made this event possible because this cause means everything to him."

My stomach drops.

"Ryan Haart," she says, turning to look directly at me. "Would you like to say a few words?"

The crowd starts applauding, and I realize I don't have a choice. Wren is holding out the microphone with a look that says she believes in me completely, and suddenly I'm skating toward her without really deciding to.

"I hate you," I whisper as I take the mic.

"No, you don't," she whispers back, squeezing my arm before skating away.

I look out at the crowd. Cameras, lights, and faces I recognize, and faces I don't. My mouth goes dry.

"Um," I start, and my voice cracks a little. "Hi."

Smooth, Haart. Real smooth.

I clear my throat and try again. "Most of you know me as a hockey player. Some of you know me from that reality show where I made a complete ass of myself on national television."

That gets a laugh, and I feel some of the tension leave my shoulders.

"But before I was any of those things, I was just a kid trying to figure out how to take care of his little sister." I find Ellie in the crowd, and she gives me an encouraging nod. "Not to get too deep here, but after my mom abandoned us, Hope Pantry saved us. Sometimes you can't afford groceries and rent and everything else life throws at you."

The arena has gone completely quiet.

"Hope Pantry was the place that made sure we didn't go hungry. Not just once or twice, but for months. I used to hide food in my backpack so Ellie wouldn't see how little we had at home. I was young and trying to be the man of the house and I was failing."

My voice catches and I have to pause for a second. Wren is watching me from the sidelines with tears in her eyes. Jay has stopped pretending to look at his clipboard and is staring at me with something that might be respect.

"The people at Hope Pantry didn't just give us food. They gave us dignity. They never made us feel ashamed for needing help. They treated us like neighbors, like family. And when we got adopted by the Thompsons, the staff at Hope Pantry celebrated with us."

I take a deep breath. "I never thought I'd be in a position to give back to them. Hell, five years ago I was still too proud to admit I'd ever needed help in the first place. But being here today, with all of you, supporting this organization that gave me and my sister a chance to survive and thrive... it means everything."

The crowd is silent, hanging on every word.

"This isn't about hockey," I say, my voice getting stronger. "This isn't about reality TV or celebrities or any of that. This is about making sure the next scared fifteen-year-old kid gets to eat dinner without feeling ashamed. This is about community. This is about taking care of each other."

I pause, looking around the arena at all the faces watching me.

"So let's play some hockey and raise some money and make sure Hope Pantry can keep doing what they do best. Taking care of people when they need it most."

The crowd erupts. People are on their feet, cheering and clapping. I hand the microphone back to Wren, who has to wipe her eyes before she can speak.

"Thank you, Ryan," she says into the mic. "Now let's play hockey."

The next hour is controlled chaos. The scrimmage is supposed to be a friendly game between reality show contestants, current and former players, and family members. What it actually turns into is a beautiful disaster.

Jake spends most of the game behind his camera, documenting everything from the sidelines. Calla cheers from what we've dubbed the penalty box, even though nobody's actually getting penalties. Ellie scores three goals and trash-talks everyone who gets in her way.

"Come on, Jake!" she yells at one point. "Put the camera down and get out here!"

"I'm documenting!" he calls back.

"Document from the ice!"

Jay "accidentally" bodychecks me twice, and I let him because I figure I probably deserve it for something. The second time, he grins and says, "Just making sure you're paying attention."

"Message received," I tell him, picking myself up off the ice.

Wren is everywhere at once, playing defense and directing cameras and making sure the donation boxes are visible in every shot. She organized all of this because I asked her to. Because Hope Pantry matters to me, which means it matters to her.

When she skates up to me during a break in play, I can't resist trying to trip her. She sees it coming and dodges, laughing.

"Really mature, Haart."

"You love it."

"I really don't."

But she's smiling when she says it, and when play resumes, she checks me into the boards.

"Penalty!" I call out dramatically. "Unnecessary roughness!"

"There are no penalties in charity hockey," she calls back, skating away.

"Then I surrender," I announce, lying flat on the ice with my arms spread wide. "I am defeated by the superior athletic prowess of Wren Rustin."

The cameras eat it up. The crowd loves it. But underneath all the performance, there's something real. Something that feels like family.

After the game, when the cameras have stopped rolling and the crowd has dispersed, the six of us end up at center ice. Ellie is flushed with excitement, her jersey damp with sweat. Jake is scrolling through the photos he took, showing Calla his favorites. Jay is talking to one of the Hope Pantry volunteers about setting up regular donations.

Wren wraps her arms around me from behind and presses her face into my back.

"Thank you," I whisper.

"For what?"

"For making this happen. For caring about something just because I care about it."

She turns me around in her arms so I'm facing her. "You don't need to thank me for loving you."

"Yeah, I do. You turned my crazy idea into something real. Something that's actually going to help people."

"You did the hard part. You got up there and told your story."

"Only because you believed I could."

She stands on her tiptoes to kiss me, and I can taste salt from the tears she cried during my speech.

"I'm proud of you," she says against my lips.

Before I can respond, Ellie crashes into both of us, wrapping us in a hug that nearly knocks us over.

"That was amazing," she says. "I'm so proud of both of you."

Jake appears next to us, camera in hand. "That speech was incredible, man. Really moving."

"Thanks. And thanks for documenting everything today. Ellie's right, you're good at this."

"It's easy when you've got good subjects."

Jay claps me on the shoulder, and when I look at him, his expression is different than it was this morning. Still gruff, still protective, but warmer, somehow.

"Good speech," he says simply.

"Thanks."

"I mean it. You did good today."

Calla appears beside Wren and pulls her into a hug. "Okay," she says, loud enough for all of us to hear, "he's growing on me."

"Just growing on you?" Wren asks.

"Fine. He's been around and I've liked him. Ryan's a likable guy. But now, I like him for *you*. He's good for you and he's good for causes that matter. It's a home run."

"That's high praise coming from Calla," Jay tells me. "She doesn't like anyone."

"That isn't true. I like plenty of people," Calla protests. "I just have standards."

We're all laughing when one of the photographers asks if we want a group photo at center ice. We arrange ourselves without really thinking about it. Wren in her Hope Pantry jersey, me next to her. Ellie and Jake on either side of us, bundled in their Hope Pantry gear. Jay and Calla standing behind us, his arm around her shoulders. I get Coach T and Evelyn out onto the ice.

It wouldn't be a family picture without them.

As the photographer counts down, I look around at these people who've somehow become my family. Ellie, who's been my constant since the day she was born. Jay, who's moved from tolerating me to actually approving of me. Calla, who's decided I'm worthy of her sister-in-law. Jake, who fits into our chaos like he was always meant to be here. Coach T and Evelyn, standing between me and Ellie.

And Wren. Wren, who made my dream happen just because she loves me. I put my arm around her waist and love the little shiver that I can feel running down her spine. My beautiful, smart, funny girlfriend.

This isn't some faux-reality show. This is my life.

I'm the luckiest man in the world. And I know without a shadow of a doubt that one day soon, I'm going to make this woman my wife.

forty-nine

WREN

A YEAR **Later**

I stand in Ryan's kitchen, barefoot on the cold hard-wood, sipping coffee that's too strong and scrolling through my phone. The morning light softens everything, even my hair, which looks better than it has any right to in the microwave's reflection.

This house feels like home now. It stopped feeling like Ryan's place and started feeling like ours somewhere around the second month after I moved in. When I reorganized his spice cabinet and he didn't complain. When he bought my favorite tea without me asking. When we had our first real fight about whose turn it was to do laundry and made up by having sex against the washing machine.

I pour a second mug full of coffee and carry it upstairs to the bedroom. Ryan has already been up to work out, although he doesn't have to anymore since he officially quit playing hockey a couple of months ago. The light is on in the en suite and steam escapes from the crack under the door.

Setting his coffee cup on his bedside table, I sit on the

bed and bide my time. Eventually, Ryan comes out of the bathroom with a towel slung around his hips, drying his hair with another towel.

I look at him, not even trying to disguise the fact that I'm checking him out. He's a marvel. Tan skin. Tall, muscular, and ripped. Abs like a fucking cheese grater.

How did I ever end up so lucky?

His sense of humor and personality are just bonuses on this mountain of a man.

Ryan groans and stretches in a way that makes my stomach flip even after a year. His chest hair is still damp from his shower. "You like what you see?"

I take in the sight of him. Hair sticking up in every direction, stubble covering his jaw, his smile still sleepy around the edges. He looks exactly like what he is. A man who's completely, ridiculously in love.

"You know I do, you deeply weird man."

He grabs a pillow and tosses it at my head. I duck, laughing. Coffee sloshes over the edge of my mug.

"Ryan! You made me spill."

"Come here and I'll make it up to you."

I set my coffee on the dresser and crawl onto the bed beside him, immediately sinking into the warmth he radiates. He wraps his arms around me and pulls me against his side. I fit there perfectly. Like I was made for this exact spot.

"We really did it, huh?" I murmur against his chest.

"Yeah. We did."

His voice is rough. I feel it rumble through his ribcage. We fall into comfortable silence. I listen to his heartbeat steady and strong under my ear. The weight of the world outside this room doesn't matter nearly as much as the fact that we're here. Together. For real.

The show made us celebrities for a while. Ryan already

was one, but now I am too, in a weird way. People recognize me at the grocery store. My Instagram followers went from two hundred to two hundred thousand overnight. The network offered me three different shows to executive produce after seeing how the finale played out.

The hockey season ended two months ago. They made it to the conference finals before getting knocked out, which was further than anyone expected. Ryan played some of the best hockey of his career. I got to watch most of it from the stands, wearing his jersey and feeling ridiculously proud every time the announcers mentioned his name.

"What are you thinking about?" Ryan asks, his fingers tracing lazy patterns on my back through my tank top.

"Everything. Work, hockey, the fact that people are writing conspiracy theories about us on Reddit."

"What kind of conspiracy theories?"

"That the whole thing was scripted. That the producers planned your finale meltdown from the beginning. That we're just really good actors who are committed to the bit."

Ryan's laugh is rough and low, sending a shiver up my spine. "If I was acting, I'd have an Oscar."

"You were pretty dramatic."

"I was in love. There's a difference."

"Are you still? In love, I mean."

He shifts so he can look down at me. His expression is so tender it makes my chest ache. "What do you think?"

"I think you're stuck with me."

"Good. Because I already bought groceries for two for the rest of the week."

I hit his chest playfully. "Romantic as always."

"I have my moments."

He does. Last week he surprised me with takeout from

my favorite Thai place because I'd had a rough day at work. The week before that, he drove an hour out of his way to get me a specific kind of donut that I mentioned liking once. Small things that show he pays attention, that he cares about the details that make me happy.

"Do you ever miss it?" I ask. "The show, I mean. The drama and the cameras and everyone watching your every move."

"Hell no. Do you?"

I consider this. "I miss some of the people. Jennifer still texts me pictures of whatever outrageous outfit she's putting together. Hana and I have lunch once a month. Even some of the other women and I keep in touch."

"That's not what I asked."

"No, I don't miss it. I liked parts of it, but I'm glad it's over. I'm glad we get to be normal now."

"Is this normal?" He gestures around the room, at us tangled up in bed.

"This is better than normal."

"Yeah. It is."

My phone buzzes on the dresser. I ignore it. It's probably another interview request or someone wanting to know if we're planning a TV wedding or some other ridiculous question about our relationship.

"Ellie called me yesterday," Ryan says.

"Oh yeah? How's the wedding planning going?"

"She's stress-eating cake samples and making Jake try on seventeen different tuxedos."

"Sounds about right."

"She wants you to be in the wedding."

I lift my head to look at him. "Really?"

"Really. She said you're basically her sister now anyway, so you might as well make it official."

The thought makes me unexpectedly emotional. I've never had a sister. Ellie has become one of my favorite people in the world. She's funny and smart and completely unimpressed by Ryan's fame, which I find endlessly entertaining.

"What did you tell her?"

"I told her to ask you herself, but that I thought you'd probably say yes."

"I would. I will. I love weddings."

"Good. Because we'll probably have our own to plan eventually."

The casual way he says it makes my heart skip. We've talked about the future in vague terms, but never anything this concrete. Never anything that sounds like a promise.

"Eventually?"

"Well, yeah. Unless you're planning to get bored with me and move on to the next hockey player who catches your eye."

"There are other hockey players?"

"Funny."

I settle back against his chest, my cheek finding the spot where his chest hair tickles. "I'm not going anywhere, Ryan."

"Good. Because I love you. And not just because the cameras are rolling."

"I love you, too."

It's the easiest thing in the world to say now. Easier than breathing. For months after the show, I kept waiting for the other shoe to drop. For him to realize that real life with me was boring compared to the heightened drama of television. For the honeymoon period to end and reality to set in.

But it never happened. Real life with Ryan is better than

anything the show could have manufactured. It's grocery shopping and Netflix marathons and him bringing me coffee in bed when I'm too lazy to get up. It's trash day arguments and ten-minute make ups. It's something solid. Something real.

"I have something to tell you," Ryan says. There's something in his tone that makes me nervous.

"Good something or bad something?"

"Good something. I think."

I prop myself up on my elbow to look at him. "Okay. What is it?"

"Coach T called yesterday. He wants to talk to me about coaching."

"Coaching what?"

"Ice hockey. Apparently there is a coach retiring for the Seattle Havoc. I'd have to work my way up. Assistant coach at first, maybe head coach eventually if I want it."

"Ryan, that's amazing." Her wide smile is radiant.

"Is it? I mean, I don't know anything about coaching."

"You know everything about hockey. You're good with people when you're not being a grumpy asshole."

"Thanks for that ringing endorsement. And that kind of behavior was saved especially for you."

She rolls her eyes and dodges that topic.

"I'm serious. You'd be a great coach. You understand the game. You know how to motivate people. Plus, you've been through everything these guys are going through. You could help them."

I shrug my shoulders. "It would mean moving to Seattle long-term."

"And?"

"And I wanted to make sure you're okay with that. I know your show films here, but after that, you might get offers from other places. I don't want to hold you back."

I stare at him. "Ryan Haart, are you asking me if I want to build a life with you in Seattle?"

"Maybe."

"The answer is yes, you idiot."

"Yeah?"

"Yeah. I've only been to Seattle once, but I loved it. I love the rain and the mountains and the coffee culture and the fact that people wear flannel unironically. And I love you. I want to go wherever you go. So yes, I want to be a hockey girlfriend and build something with you."

He grins and pulls me down for a kiss. "Good. Because I already told Coach T that I was interested."

"You were that sure I'd say yes?"

"I was hopeful."

"Just hopeful?"

"Okay, I was pretty sure. You're crazy about me."

"I am crazy about you."

"I know."

"So what happens now?" I ask.

"What do you mean?"

"I mean, we did the hard part. We fell in love, we survived reality television, we figured out how to be together in the real world. What's next?"

Ryan is quiet for a moment, thinking. "I don't know. More of this, I guess. Wake up together, go to work, and come home to each other. Fight about stupid things and make up. Build something that lasts."

"That sounds pretty good."

"It does, doesn't it?"

"Boring, but good."

"Boring is underrated."

"Says the man who proposed on live television."

"I didn't propose on live television. I declared my love on live television. There's a difference."

"Is there?"

"When I propose, it'll be private. Just us. No cameras, no audience, no producers trying to manipulate the moment."

"*When* you propose?"

"You heard me."

"Ryan," I admonish.

"What?"

"You just said *when*."

"Did I?"

"You did."

He's quiet for a moment. I can feel his heart beating faster under my palm.

"Hypothetically," he says finally, "if I were to propose, how do you think you'd respond?"

"Hypothetically?"

"Hypothetically."

I pretend to consider this. "I think I'd probably say yes."

"Probably?"

"Definitely. I'd definitely say yes."

"Good to know."

"For hypothetical future reference."

"Exactly."

We fall back into silence, but it's charged now. Expectant. Like we've just crossed some invisible line we can't uncross.

My phone buzzes again. This time, Ryan reaches over to grab it.

"It's Jay," he says, handing it to me.

I swipe to answer. "Hey, big brother."

"Hey, little sister."

"Hey, you."

There's a pause before Jay speaks, like the words are hard to say out loud. "I'm proud of you, Wren."

My throat tightens, and my vision blurs for a second. "For what?"

"For going after what you wanted. For not letting anyone tell you it was too risky or too crazy or too much. You always used to hide behind me. Not anymore."

"Thanks, Jay."

"I love you, kid."

"I love you, too."

"And tell Ryan I said congratulations on the coaching thing. He'll be good at it."

"How did you know about that?"

"Coach T called me, too. Wanted to know if you'd agree to let Ryan go to Seattle."

"And what did you tell him?"

"I told him you love Ryan and practically worship the very ground he walks on. So yes, I think you would say yes in a heartbeat."

"Well, he just asked. And I agreed."

I can hear Jay smiling through the phone line. "I bet."

After I hang up, Ryan looks at me with raised eyebrows. "He gave me a reference?"

"Apparently."

"Huh. Maybe he doesn't hate me after all."

"He never hated you. He was just protecting me."

"And now?"

"Now he knows I don't need protecting. I need supporting. There's a difference."

"Smart man."

"He has his moments."

Ryan pulls me closer. I curl into him, breathing in the scent of his skin and the faint smell of his soap. This is what home smells like now. This is what safety feels like.

"Wren?"

"Mmm?"

"I'm really glad you came on that stupid show."

"Even though it was a disaster?"

"Especially because it was a disaster. The best things in my life have come from disasters."

"Like what?"

"Like you. Like this. Like figuring out that sometimes the thing you think will ruin you is actually the thing that saves you."

I lift my head to look at him. His expression is so open and honest it takes my breath away.

"You saved me, too," I tell him.

"From what?"

"From thinking I wasn't worth choosing. From believing I had to stay small to be loved. From settling for less than everything."

"You were always worth choosing, Wren. You just needed someone to see it."

"And you saw it."

"From the first day. Even when you were hiding behind that clipboard like it was armor."

"I wasn't hiding."

"You were totally hiding."

"Okay, maybe I was hiding a little."

"A little?"

"Fine. I was hiding a lot. But I'm not hiding anymore."

"No. You're not."

He's right. I'm not hiding anymore. I'm not the girl who stands in the background waiting for someone to notice her. I'm the girl who speaks up in meetings and pitches crazy ideas and isn't afraid to take up space.

I'm the girl who fell in love with a hockey player on national television and didn't care what anyone thought about it.

I'm the girl who's running her own show and building her own life and choosing her own future.

"So," I say, settling back against his chest. "What do we do now?"

Ryan grins and pulls me closer, pressing a kiss to the top of my head. "Anything we want."

And for the first time in my life, I believe that's actually true.

I didn't win the show. But I won the life I wanted.

fifty

THANK you for reading Say Yes to the Nemesis. As a special token of my gratitude, I've written a bonus epilogue. It features your favorite characters – Ryan & Wren. Read it here.

Here's a list of all the couples in this series!

The Accidental Honeymoon - Jay & Calla - Woke up married
The Always Bridesmaid - Jake & Ellie - Fake dating (a FREE newsletter novella)
Say Yes to the Nemesis - Ryan & Wren - Enemies to lovers, brother's best friend

If you loved this book, please consider leaving a review. It's the best way to let me know that you want me to write more books like this one!

* * *

I'm so excited for what's next. I know that if you liked this, you'll love Dear #47, You're the Worst... It's Hunter and Juliet's story. Hunter was in this story and looking *fine*. Now it's time to head to Seattle to find out what he and the Seattle Havoc hockey team are up to! (Hint: it's dirty.)

Forbidden love is very close to my heart... and I am very excited to be able to present this combination of some my favorite tropes: enemies to lovers, sports romance, brother's best friend, forced proximity, spicy romance, hockey player hero, take-no-shit heroine, image rehab, opposites attract, forced proximity.

Here's the blurb:

Juliet Monroe would rather drill her own root canal than fake an engagement to Hunter Huxley.

But PR says it's the only way to salvage his image after a string of headline-grabbing disasters. Now she's stuck playing fiancée to the cockiest forward on the Seattle Havoc... and pretending not to fall for his smirky charm is getting harder by the second.

Hunter isn't used to hearing no. Especially not from the one woman who seems immune to him.

He's supposed to be a mess she cleans up.

But she might be the one in trouble.

Grab Dear #47, You're the Worst **right now!**

Vivian likes to write about troubled, deeply flawed alpha males and the fiery, kick-ass women who bring them to their knees.

Vivian's lasting motto in romance is a quote from a favorite song: "Soulmates never die."

Be sure to join her email list to keep up with all the awesome giveaways, author videos, ARC opportunities, and more!

Vivian's Works

Seattle Havoc
Hockey Romance
Dear #47, You're the Worst

Wildflower Lane

Small Town Rom Com
The Accidental Honeymoon
The Always Bridesmaid
Say Yes to the Nemesis

Cape Simon
Small Town Romance
The Grumpy Boss Agreement
The Fake Fiancée Proposition

Sinfully Rich
Steamy Billionaire Romance
Sinful Fling
Sinful Enemy
Sinful Boss
Sinful Chance
Sinful Teacher

Billionaires Ever After
Steamy Bad Boy Romance
His Best Friend's Little Sister
Claiming Her Innocence
His Fiancé To Keep
His Lovely Virgin

Hush Hush Club
Forbidden Billionaire Romantic Suspense
Such A Good Girl
Such A Spoiled Brat

Married At Midnight
Forbidden Billionaire Romance
Deal With The Devil

Wed to the Devil

Vow to the Devil

Ruined Castle Trilogy
Forbidden Billionaire Romance
The Single Dad
The Nanny
The Caress

Broken Slipper Trilogy
Forbidden Billionaire Romance
The Patron
The Dancer
The Embrace
Possessive

Fifth Avenue Villains
Fifth Avenue Devil

Royally Rich
Forbidden Royal Romance
Cruel Heir
Sinful Princess
Pretend Princess

King's Capture Duet
Dark Billionaire Romance
King's Capture
Queen's Sacrifice

Addiction Duet
Angsty Dark Romance
Addiction

Obsession

Other books
Wild Hearts

For more information....
vivian-wood.com
info@vivian-wood.com

* 9 7 8 1 9 5 9 8 3 0 8 4 9 *